Dedicated to grandsons Aaron and Eli
Whose ancestors pioneered in old California

ISBN: 1-4392-4303-4
ISBN-13: 9781439243039

Visit www.booksurge.com to order more copies.

DESTINY'S CHILDREN

A Saga of Early California

ROGER E. HERST

CHAPTER ONE

Uncle Wong Po-ching, who wasn't my real uncle, looked for two things in a burial site for his family: a location to convey a sense of eternity and a place where his kin might touch each other from beyond the grave. A grove of redwoods in California's Calaveras County, several over two thousand years old, met his criteria. It was there during the autumn of 1870 that my father, Theo Gallager, helped him lay to rest in the roots of an ancient sequoia Wong's wife, Mei Yok, who died giving birth to their son, Freeman.

Uncle Wong returned to his burial site again twelve years later when his son, with whom I had spent my earliest years as though a brother, died while studying Cantonese in China. Wong had Freedman's remains cremated and shipped back to California. I was eleven when my parents and I returned with him to Calaveras County to bury Freeman's ashes in the roots of a towering redwood next to the giant colossus that enshrined those of his mother. I recall standing beside his grave and peering upward along the trunk of a gargantuan redwood to the point where thick branches blotted out the morning sun. In the canopy above, the limbs of Freeman's tree merged into those from Mei Yok's. That was exactly what Uncle Wong wanted. The branches of two redwoods joined Mei Yok and Freeman together in death, as they had been joined so briefly in life.

In those days I never understood who owned these magnificent trees. It could be argued that no one other than God possessed such regal creatures. My father and Uncle Wong told me that in the early years when they were partners mining gold in nearby Mokelumne Hill this redwood forest was open land, accessible to anyone determined to hike into it. As an indentured worker new to California, Uncle Wong didn't speak much English and could think of no better way to identify this forest than "Big Trees," a name that somehow stuck throughout the years. When my father and Wong, then nearly bankrupt over the failure of an ill-fated mining enterprise, eventually left the Sierra foothills in the winter of 1871, they temporarily lost touch with these trees. During this interval, the Pickering Lumber Company acquired the property for logging. Only their sheer mass and remoteness saved these redwoods from the ax and saw blade.

When Congress passed the infamous Chinese Exclusion Act of May 1882, prohibiting more Chinese from coming to America, Uncle Wong felt as if everything he had worked for in his adopted country had been discredited. He could not accept that Caucasian Americans feared and hated his compatriots despite their achievements in the West. Wong's heart was broken but he soldiered on, stoically building a successful trading business in San Francisco with the hope that one day the contribution of the Chinese in America would be recognized and honored.

My father, mother, and I would accompany him to Big Trees each year on the anniversary of Mei Yok's death. Wong lit candles and burned incense. Mother read prayers. Dad was good at hiding his feelings, but in this place, which he regarded as a shrine holier than any cathedral on earth, he was often teary-eyed. While riding home to San Francisco after one such pilgrimage, he told my mother and Uncle Wong that upon his own death he too wanted to rest among these redwoods. When he died five years later fighting a forest fire in Humboldt County on California's northern coast, Uncle Wong, Mother, and I dutifully buried him at Big Trees.

Mom and I, two very strong-willed and independent women, possessed the strength to persevere even without the patriarch we both adored. Uncle Wong suffered even more. When Dad was alive hardly a day went by when the two of them didn't argue about every little thing, yet Uncle Wong had no desire to live in a world without my father. Mother and I insisted that he sell his house in San Francisco's Chinatown and live with us in our home on Laguna Street. He reluctantly obliged, but was never the same. After my father's death, his indefatigable energy just slipped away and his lungs, weakened from years of inhaling smoke and dust, became a home for tuberculosis. How fitting it was for Mom and me to bury him with his family among the redwoods he so loved.

In the early years, officers of the Pickering Lumber Company allowed visitors to wander through their forest and view the giant sequoia. But as more of these majestic trees were sent to the sawmills, company executives feared tree-hugging conservationists would crusade to protect those that were left. The forest was posted against trespassing, and guards patrolled the periphery. Mother and I considered asking for official permission to visit the graves of our loved ones, graves the Pickering folks didn't even know existed. But we decided that if company officials knew about the gravesites, they would prohibit us from entering the property and demand that we remove the remains of our people. We decided to make our biannual visits without alerting the guards.

Though by then we lived thoroughly urban lives, we became adept at moving through the forest clandestinely. Our footsteps were almost soundless and most of our communication was carried out by means of hand signals. In those years, I became aware that my mother was teaching me what she wanted me to know when the Angel of Death knocked at her own door. And when that time came, I knew exactly what to do and how to do it. So the forest at Big Trees became the cemetery of the Gallagers as well as the Wongs. It was our way of keeping our families together, even beyond the grave.

Now that my mother rests beside my father, and my father beside Uncle Wong, and Uncle Wong beside Mei Yok and Freeman, I am the last of a generation that lived during a pivotal moment in California history. Unwittingly I have become the memory of two families. In order not to forget their stories, I would constantly repeat them to myself. Memories took possession of me, anchoring my life in a previous generation. As I tramped through California's mountains and along her seashores, every sound, smell, and sight evoked a rush of remembrances. In my mind and heart the past eclipsed the present. As my years accumulated, I came to believe that as long as I remained in California I would find no refuge from these memories. It was either leave the blessed land or be thoroughly consumed by it. Eventually I moved to Baltimore and, after marriage, to Connecticut, putting three thousand miles between me and those haunting memories.

Still, every other year I made a pilgrimage to Big Trees and stood in the grove of redwoods, looking up into the interlocking branches where the souls of my mother and father, Uncle Wong, Freeman, and Mei Yok held each other tight. How prophetic Uncle Wong was to have seen the enchantment of this magic place.

After burying my mother, I had one last filial duty to perform. It was important to record the narrative of our families so that my son, who was then fighting in the trenches of France, might understand what happened. If he survived, I wanted my grandchildren to know at least as much about the Gallagers and Wongs as do the giant redwoods.

My witness is ephemeral, but theirs is eternal.
CORINNE HORN-GALLAGER
GROTON, CONNECTICUT, SEPTEMBER 1917

CHAPTER TWO

Gum San
January 1866

When the state uses a firing squad to intimidate its enemies, the executioners usually give the victim a brief moment of celebrity. But Private Wong Po-ching wasn't accorded even this small dignity. No riflemen were assigned the grizzly task of shooting him and none from the normally bloodthirsty cavalry were ordered to hack him to pieces with their sabers. Colonel Ning Xiao simply placed Wong on a bluff within easy range of enemy sharpshooters in the village below for them to do his dirty work. Wong's hands were unbound and his feet unfettered. He could have run away, but he didn't because peasant recruits in the Manchu artillery were not trained to think of self-preservation. Fellow cannoneers from Wong's brigade expected him to be cut down with the first volley of enemy fire, but, miraculously, that did not happen. A single, poorly aimed bullet dispatched from the hamlet below pounded the embankment several meters away, sending a cloud of dust into the afternoon breeze. Soldiers normally sighted in on their targets by first bracketing trial shots wide and low. Colonel Ning's officers assumed that the rebels would follow the same procedure. But after two shots the villagers fired no more.

Cannoneers whispered among themselves. Like Wong, they also hated Colonel Ning, who had deployed eleven cannon against a dozen or so peasant followers of Zeng Kuo-fan, the last Taiping Christian leader, holed up in the farming hamlet of Hsuan-tak and armed with no more than a few dozen rusty flintlocks. But when Ning's riflemen failed to dislodge them, the colonel trained his artillery on the village's flimsy huts.

No one was fooled by this. A few poorly armed peasant rebels presented little threat to the Manchu authorities or to Colonel Ning, who was less interested in them than in the hamlet's winter food stores. Warlord armies traveled on their stomachs, and as long as they had rice and their enemies did not, resistance remained minimal. Besides, everybody knew that Colonel Ning and his crony officers skimmed a large percentage from the expropriated peasant stores before what remained was shipped to Manchu supply centers.

At an early age Wong Po-ching had been orphaned by pirates who set fire to everything they couldn't haul from his native hamlet in their riverboats. His parents refused to disclose where their rice was hidden, not that their refusal made any difference. The pirates burned what they couldn't carry away and starving villagers died anyway. All but Wong. He managed to survive by working in a nearby factory mixing charcoal, saltpeter, and sulfur for firecrackers. A year later he learned that the Manchu artillery were seeking men with experience in handling gunpowder. At the time, it didn't matter to him whether he fought with or against one or another of the feuding warlords. The army provided rations, and everything was measured by the food needed to stay alive from one season to the next.

Wong was attached to Ning's foraging brigade, which was equipped with antique Japanese smooth-bore cannon, cumbersome to move in battle, but remarkably suited for static bombardment, particularly when aimed at unarmed hamlets along the Zenshui River tributaries. Wong's fearless abandonment when handling volatile black powder led to his promotion from a mere recruit to a full private, which in turn translated into better rations. The two cannon that Wong commanded acquired a reputation for consistent and accurate fire. Senior officers would often consult with him about the size of the powder charges and adjustments needed because of the winds. In camp there was talk of still higher promotions in Private Wong's future. But the destruction his cannon wrought on innocent villages had a cumulative effect on him. Each looted hamlet stirred memories of the village where he had been raised. After each salvo from his guns, the cries of distraught villagers reminded him of the suffering in his own hamlet. At night, when his cannon fell silent, the ghostly faces of the victims haunted his sleep.

In the pummeling of Hsuan-tak, Wong's ears rang from the constant discharge of cannon and his eyes burned from the black gunsmoke.

Hsuan-tak proved to be the turning point, though he wasn't sure why. It looked like other villages and its corpses would surely rot like all the others. During the break for lunch, rice stuck in his throat and his stomach revolted against food that cost so many lives to procure. He tried to force it down because he knew it would probably be the last nourishment he would see for some time. Once he had decided he would no longer be complicit in the destruction of Hsuan-tak, he could no longer depend on military rations.

When firing resumed after lunch, Wong packed his cannon charges with too much powder. In others, he stuffed sand. Consequently the cannonballs landed everywhere but on Hsuan-tak. When Colonel Ning witnessed the results, he jumped from his lunch table to reprimand his officers, who in turn blamed their lieutenants commanding the field pieces. Wong knew it was only a matter of time before they would discover his sabotage. When they did, Ning became furious and decreed that Private Wong should die by bullets from those he had tried to save. A squad of reluctant artillerymen prodded the saboteur onto a hillock in clear view of the village defenders, then immediately withdrew.

But the villagers of Hsuan-tak demonstrated an uncanny sense about the man they were supposed to execute and refused to cooperate. Wong's fellow cannoneers saw that Colonel Ning was determined to complete the job with his own revolver and began to jeer. Those with swords cracked them against the iron skins of their cannon, unnerving Ning, who wrestled to steady his firing arm. The officers yelled for quiet, but with little success. When Wong turned to face his executioner, the men fell silent. Visibly unnerved by insubordination in his ranks, Ning tried again to steady his shooting arm. A puff of smoke erupted from the pistol's muzzle, followed by a sharp crack. The bullet sailed past Wong and continued down into the village below. A second slug plowed into the dirt in front.

Ning grew angry. Determined to kill Wong on his third attempt, he took great care aiming and waited until the target was perfectly centered in his sights. The hammer on his revolver struck, but the powder charge misfired. A loud cheer of encouragement erupted from the cannoneers. The officers called out their commander's name to counter the troops' insubordination. Their chant spread unenthusiastically through the ranks until silenced by a single bullet from the hamlet. No ball whistled overhead. No dust erupted from the bluff. Did anyone see where it had gone? Was the enemy out of ammunition? The distraction gave Colonel Ning time to reload his pistol for a fourth shot.

Wong waited for more firing from below. Men from the regiment cried out for him to run before the officers took matters in their own hands and fired their carbines. Wong quickly calculated his chances. If he managed to survive a new salvo, he would have no more rations, no more clothing, and no more shelter. Without them, a deserter was certain to perish. But his cohorts had a different picture of their comrade's future. He had already been condemned and, sooner or later, Colonel Ning's bullets or those of his officers would cut him down. Either he ran now for his life or he was a dead man. It took several moments for him to reach the same conclusion. Flight was his only choice.

While sprinting as fast as his legs would take him, Wong heard Colonel Ning bellow at his officers to shoot, but none did. Then he heard the colonel order them to prevent his escape. Men started to pursue him but were met by a wave of recruits who instinctively dashed forward to block their path. In the brief scuffle that followed, the officers reckoned that it made no sense fomenting a mutiny to stop a lowly private destined to become prey for bounty hunters who made a lucrative living by capturing Manchu defectors.

At the edge of the camp, Wong could hear both Colonel Ning's shouts and the cheers of fellow cannoneers. During several days he spent wandering without food in the hills, he considered his options. After his own village had been burned to the ground and the villagers left homeless, Hakkas from the northeastern provinces moved in. Without family and without even a small patch of land to farm, starvation was inevitable. Every peasant knew what to expect. Illness set in first, followed by a loss of strength, then a dull, listless sleepiness until life slipped from the body. In the end, Wong believed his only hope rested in a mere rumor. At the moment, it was nothing more than unconfirmed rumor. Men in his regiment had spoken of *Gum San*, a land of golden mountains, far across the sea. There men could find work and food and, with some luck, enough money to set themselves up in business. Wong had no idea just how far away this Gum San was. He didn't even know in which direction it lay. No matter: a man with few alternatives can easily live with ambiguity.

In Amoy, Wong heard more rumors about Gum San. But ships to these golden mountains left from Canton. A ferryboat there was preferable, but he had forsaken his pay and had no money for passage. The journey by foot through the populous port cities would be long and dangerous. But having already prepared himself to join his ancestors on the bluff overlooking Hsuan-tak, the prospect of capture by bounty hunters no longer frightened him. To gather strength for the trek on foot, he had to steal food—an easy task for one already considered a criminal and sentenced to death.

In a steel shed east of the Port of Canton, a labor contractor from the Yung Wo Company sat behind a table pitted with black cigarette burns. He wore a blue suit with expensive brass buttons. A cigar smoldered but seldom moved in his lips. Two metal teeth, jutting from his front gum, were stained with tobacco. A quick look at Wong's tattered uniform, purposely stripped of its army buttons, failed to deceive him. "What have we here? Another deserter?" he said as his eyebrows rose sharply in a crude gesture of omniscience.

Wong canted his chin, allowing his eyes to drift downward, looking for the agent's sympathy but expecting little. He had previously concluded that he possessed definite advantages over other candidates: he was almost nine centimeters taller than the others and, because of his previous regimen of military rations and medical attention, was in better health. No eye disease. No cough. No addiction to opium. But was this enough for work in Gum San? He had no idea. If employers there paid more for strong workers than the Manchu government paid as bounty for returned deserters, he had a chance. If not, the contractor would probably pretend to accept him, then deliver him over to the authorities for a handsome bounty.

"Deserter," the agent repeated for emphasis, then lazily shifted his eyes to the smaller men in line.

"Send me to Gum San," Wong said, fearing that he was being shunted aside.

The agent's eyes drifted back in his direction. He tugged at a thin mustache rounding the corners of his lips. "We don't take deserters."

"No, you don't understand," Wong said, his exasperation apparent.

"A deserter will cause trouble in Gum San. We avoid trouble, scum. Sour fruit does not become sweet. Why shouldn't the Yung Wo Company collect your bounty here, without taking a chance on you across the ocean?" The agent signaled with a twirl of his forefinger in the direction of guards with heavy truncheons hovering nearby. They bullied their way through the throng of bodies crowding the agent's table.

Wong recognized the danger and, knowing he had but one last chance, struggled to control his anger. "I will work hard and not make trouble in Gum San."

Ashes from the agent's smoldering cigar fell to the table. A whisk of his hand sent them in Wong's direction.

"Take me," Wong pleaded.

The agent's palm opened flatly and he lifted his chin to communicate with the guards. A smirk curled his lips, the sole acknowledgment of a truth he dared not share with those around him: The Yung Wo Company actually preferred men with something to hide. In *Gum San Ta Foy*, San Francisco, the big city amid the golden mountains, desperate men feared being returned to China for punishment. If their past was clouded, they did not complain about additional fees charged for transport, food, and shelter. Few broke their employment contracts and disappeared into the vastness of California, particularly Celestials with dark skin. No, if the truth be known, desperate men were the best. But strong, healthy, desperate men like Wong Po-ching were the best of all.

"Nine months' labor for passage. Two months for food. One month for a commission to the Yung Wo Company," the agent barked, without lifting his eyes from the roster before him.

Wong glanced along the line of men in tattered blue cotton pajamas. Smaller than him, they had received only six-and-a-half months' servitude in Gum San. That was not fair. Why should he labor longer without pay? Some of them were undoubtedly deserters like him. "Six-and-a-half, like the others," Wong countered.

"Twelve months." The agent amplified the volume of his response. "The others are not deserters."

"Nine."

"Worthless scum. Twelve months. No bargaining."

Wong thought about the extra period of indentured service, then about the unknown conditions of labor in a strange country. The horror of running from bounty hunters hovered over him like a black thundercloud. What did it matter to the agent if another coolie were arrested, shot, or starved to death? What did it matter to him if Gum San was his only hope? "No. Nine months, tops."

"Next." With a flick of his fist, the agent's signaled for the guards to step forward and seize Wong.

Other recruits elbowed forward. Wong summoned strength to cuff a coolie on the shoulder and regain his place before the agent. "Twelve months," he said above the din of voices.

The labor contractor confirmed his instinct with satisfaction and, for the second time, waved off the guards with a back-swat of his hand. In the past his employer had rewarded his recruiting skill with a bonus and just now he had bagged the strongest, healthiest coolie for the longest term of servitude. The particulars of Wong's commitment were written into a ledger, along with information about his height and physique. In addition, there was a notation to the Yung Wo Company representatives in San Francisco. *Keep an eye on this man, Wong Po-ching. He looks to be a born troublemaker.*

Wong traveled to America aboard the steel-hulled Pacific Mail steamer *Japan,* on her second voyage from the Orient to California after being designed specifically for swift passages across the Pacific. She was a 360-foot-long side-wheeler, with 4,352 tons of displacement. The fifty-four other indentured workers in whose company Wong journeyed shared the forty-foot-wide hold with bales of cotton and hemp. Air below deck was putrid and the heat stultifying. The few coolies not suffering from lung infections were wretched with dysentery. The odor of vomit and excrement was ubiquitous.

Each morning the men chattered among themselves, trying to remain optimistic and cheerful, but by noon there was nothing left to talk about. Silence lay as thick as the stale air. During these long lulls, everybody wondered what he would find in Gum San. Had he made the right choice? Would the Land of the Golden Mountains offer more than they had left? Would there be opportunities to earn money? Would they ever return to their homeland to see their families? Now that they had left their hamlets and villages, who had moved into their hovels and was bedding down with their wives? If they returned, would their children still be there? And would their sons and daughters even remember them?

To make matters worse aboard the *Japan,* coolies were prohibited from going up onto the open deck except to dispose of their waste. So great was the urge to breathe fresh air that the travelers fought over the dubious honor of hauling buckets of human excrement topside. They wrestled over the buckets until several were overturned, dumping sewage onto the floorboards. There were no tools for cleaning up the vile-smelling mess, so it had to be done by hand. Battles ensued over who was responsible for the cleanup. Eventually they settled on competitive arm-wrestling to determine who would clean the floorboards and who would go topside with the refuse buckets. They agreed that each day there would be a new competition so that the privilege of going on deck might be shared.

At the time few realized that Wong—both stronger and larger than the others—possessed an innate advantage. Brawn won him the right to go topside, but wits were essential once he got there. After he had dumped his buckets overboard, the trick was to prolong precious time near the gunwales, staying hidden from the zealous deckhands who hated to see Chinamen anywhere on their ship. Several minutes of sea air in his lungs refreshed his spirits for the long hours of confinement and made him stronger than his opponents for the next day's arm wrestling. Every other day he wisely permitted an opponent to win the contest and enjoy the refreshing ocean air.

Hardly a week on the seas had passed before many coolies grumbled about returning to China. They repeated their belief that life in Gum San would only be temporary. Their pockets filled with gold coin, they would soon be united with their families in the Celestial Kingdom. Wong did not share such yearnings. He had no family left in China and no hamlet to return to. And, unlike his compatriots, he felt no compunction to be buried within the Great Wall of China, as had been the custom of the Han Chinese for as long as there had been memory. One generation passed away and was joined with previous generations, but only through the conduit of the sacred Chinese soil. Popular belief had it that the souls of those buried or cremated beyond its sacred walls were destined to wander for eternity without finding their ancestors. This, too, Wong was prepared to accept. If possible, his spirit would be joined with those of his ancestors from Gum San; if not, then his soul would remain in solitude forever.

During the third week of passage, *Japan's* starboard paddle wheel broke down, and during the repair the port wheel also had to be stopped. Once the ship ceased moving, the ocean swells felt much larger, frightening peasants who had lived their entire lives near tranquil rice paddies. The voices of the doomsayers drowned out those who counseled patience. Most cursed their misguided dream of seeking fortunes in Gum San. They lamented their fate, for even starvation at home was better than drowning at sea, where proper burial was impossible.

Communication with the ship's crew might have alleviated the distress, but there was none. The hatch above the hold remained locked except when Wong or a companion was permitted on deck and when rice soup, bread, and tea were passed through twice daily. Then late one night, vibrations in the vessel awakened the coolies. A rumble from the engine followed. The slurp of water against the ship's hull was unmistakable. When the paddle wheels began churning again, the sea swells diminished. At last the incessant rocking ceased. Still, the coolies remained frightened. Gum San was farther away than any had imagined. Each day of travel reduced the possibility of eventually returning home.

A week later, Fu Koung, the Yung Wo Company representative aboard, reported that the *Japan* was in sight of land. Nobody believed him. After all, hadn't the hiring already broken all its promises? But on Wong's next trip topside, he confirmed the report. Ahead there were hills, certainly not golden as expected, but a dull, uninviting brown, and partially covered with thick fog.

"No gold mountains! No gold mountains!" The coolies demonstrated their despair by shaking their fists. How was it possible that they had been duped into leaving the green fields of the Celestial Kingdom to find only dull brown mountains? Where was the sun shining on this enchanted land? More falsehoods. Lies, their trip on the sea had been nothing but monstrous lies. Their spirits fell like pebbles in a rice paddy.

That evening *Japan's* paddle wheels slowed and stopped altogether. The moment the engines ceased growling, the Chinese could hear voices of the sailors. The ship began to roll in the swells. What did it matter, for soon everybody would be on dry land! Crewmen clambered into a longboat to go ashore. But the hatch over the hold remained sealed. Something was wrong. Why weren't the coolies allowed to go on deck? No one came to explain this delay. Fu Koung had no answers.

Far from being the fulfillment of a dream, Gum San had become a living horror.

Cascade, California

The War of Secession between the States sent many of Pennsylvania's young men from farms and villages to far-off battlefields where the vastness of the nation stretched beyond their imaginations. Those who survived the bloody engagements in distant Southern states returned to their homes with a few dollars in their pockets and a new understanding of American geography.

My father, Theodore Drome Gallager, an only child of Irish immigrants who had settled in Philadelphia, had enlisted in the Army Corps of Engineers a year after Northern forces invaded Virginia during the internecine conflict between the states. Building light wooden bridges at the order of Generals McClellan and Burnside for the Army of the Potomac to ford Chickahominy Creek and the James River won Dad the coveted rank of major, then at the young age of twenty-eight. In the process, he learned that wood, which burned and rotted easily, was a poor material for bridges, leading him to believe that the future for heavy construction lay in steel. Those who recognized its building potential would eventually rule the nation.

To prepare himself for the post-war era, Father applied for transfer to General Grant's Army of the Cumberland, where he built rail lines to support military campaigns in the Tennessee Valley. Later he returned to Virginia to repair captured railroads for the federal assault on the Confederate capitol at Richmond. Soon after the surrender at Appomattox, my father was decommissioned and awarded a lucrative contract to repair the damaged wharves on the James River using the labor of freed slaves. While he was happy to provide these black folk with work, he found it difficult to supervise men who had only months before been slaves. In addition, the defeated rebels for whom he thought he was benefiting refused to accept Yankee authority on the docks. To make matters worse, construction materials were in short supply. Dad couldn't wait to free himself from the ravages of war. By the time his contract ended, he had little sympathy for the vanquished Southerners and, after witnessing the graft and hypocrisy of politics during postwar Reconstruction, had little more for the victorious Northerners. Like many disillusioned veterans, he succumbed to the allure of the West. With money earned in Virginia, he traveled by train to Kansas City, then joined wagons headed for California.

By the time my father was being considered for a job with the Central Pacific Railroad—known widely in California at the time as the CP—the company was on the verge of financial ruin. Construction of the first fifty-four miles of rail from Sacramento to Colfax in the Sierra Nevada foothills went without a hitch, but at the trestle over Long Ravine the CP's luck ran out. Irish and German laborers struck for higher wages. During their strike, the wood trestle at Long Ravine burned to the ground. Within a week, the CP's black-powder depot exploded, killing four and injuring twenty-two. The railroad owners, Charles Crocker, Leland Stanford, Mark Hopkins, and Collis Huntington, wanted blood. Someone's head had to roll for the unfortunate series of events, and who better than the superintendent of construction? Shortly after his dismissal, his replacement realized there was no way he could lay track over the Sierra summit without divine help and took to the bottle. A third superintendent got too close to a powder charge and lost an eye when a sandstone chip sliced through the left side of his face. The Central Pacific retired him before he lost his surviving eye.

When my father took charge in 1867, construction in California was a year behind schedule and the comfortable wartime subsidies Collis Huntington had inveigled from the Lincoln administration in Washington before the president's assassination had been wasted on a series of false-starts in construction and bad financial decisions. The prospects of bankruptcy put the Central Pacific owners at each other's throats. And this before their tracklayers had begun to cut through the most challenging terrain on the proposed line, the high Sierra over the summit at Donner, not far from where the Donner Party of settlers perished from starvation in snow and ice during the extremely bitter winter of 1846–'47. My father accepted his new job like a soldier receiving a field command while his troops, having been severely routed by the enemy, were fleeing the battlefield in wholesale retreat.

He was a tall, lean man, with fair, wrinkled skin dried from long hours of exposure to the elements and a thick, rust-colored mustache that completely covered his upper and lower lips when not talking, eating, or smiling. The brim of a sweat-stained Union officer's hat with the tarnished brass insignia of the Engineering Corps shielded nervous dark eyes that rarely stayed fixed on any object for long. A man not given to lengthy conversation, he spoke in crisp, short sentences. It took him only a few moments to discern whether a subject was worth talking about at all, and, when it wasn't, he would simply withdraw into a stony silence.

The map of the Western territories mounted inside his tent had originally been used in the Central Pacific's Sacramento headquarters when it was awarded a commission by Congress to build the western segment of what journalist referred to as "The Pacific Railroad." It illustrated the company's predicament better than the doleful speeches of owners Leland Stanford and Mark Hopkins. The transcontinental railroad, linking the Atlantic and the Pacific, was represented by two converging lines, the Central Pacific Railroad in the far West and the Union Pacific Railroad in the Midwest. When Dad accepted the Herculean task of finishing this massive project, less than sixty miles of revenue-producing track had been laid from Sacramento to the Sierra foothills. The rest amounted to broken rail lines, disconnected segments of unfinished roadbed, and unleveled terrain snaking eastward through gentle elevations. In his mind, this disarray was the result of the cumulative misdirection construction crews had received from the railroad's meddling owners in Sacramento. The miserable condition of the Central Pacific might have been understandable had the contrast with the Union Pacific's fortunes not been so glaring.

On Dad's map, a thick black line represented the Union Pacific's galloping progress from Omaha westward across the prairies. Admittedly the terrain in the Midwest presented fewer obstacles than the Central Pacific was encountering in the mountains of the Sierra Nevada. Still, Congress in Washington refused to pay for excuses. Track that wasn't laid was track that wasn't paid for. The ambition of my father's rivals was evident enough. Week by week, day by day, *the hungry bastards*, as Stanford referred to the Eastern railroad barons, gobbled up great tracts of land for the Union Pacific. Meanwhile Central Pacific construction teams were so bottled up in the mountains that gambling men offered heavy odds their competitor would be laying track on the eastern escarpment of the Sierra Nevada before the first Central Pacific locomotive chugged ninety miles up to the summit at Donner.

Despite the CP's dismal record, Leland Stanford publicly predicted that the Central Pacific would be in the Nevada Territory by late spring. In Washington Collis Huntington echoed this blustering battle cry in the rotunda of Congress. And if the owners' bravado wasn't placing enough pressure on my father, the railroad's impecunious treasurer, Mark

Hopkins, carped over every penny of expenditure. Of the Big Four—one grocer and three dry goods merchants—only Charles Crocker had a clue about road construction but, in my father's mind, that was the extent of his knowledge—a single clue and little more.

"One problem at a time," Father would tell himself as he battled simultaneously with his employers, the mountains, and his workmen. He thrived on overcoming engineering challenges, but people problems kept getting in the way. Keeping enough workmen employed on the line proved to be a greater hindrance than the formidable challenges of the massive Sierra peaks.

Reporters from San Francisco papers badgered him. "Listen, Gallager, we wanna know what's slowin' up the Central Pacific?" they'd ask, as if every journalist in the state didn't already know.

"Men," my father would reply with his characteristic terseness.

"You mean, Mr. Gallager, that if you had enough men you wouldn't be stalled in the mountains?"

"No, gentlemen, I'm not saying that. I'm saying if I had a steady workforce on the line, I'd have a good chance of beating these g'damn mountains. Who'll win in the struggle I won't say. But you can't fight without an army. So you're asking what's slowin' down the Central Pacific. And I'm answerin'. Men. Got it?"

"If you had the men, when would you have a locomotive on Donner Summit?"

"No comment."

"Come on, Gallager. Give us an estimate. All we want is your fair guess."

Theo hesitated before replying, "Soon."

"When's soon?"

"No comment."

From his army days, when Confederate raiders would attack Union campsites at night to kill sleeping Yankees, Dad was never a sound sleeper. While sleeping, he had trained himself to keep an ear peeled for sounds of danger, the hoot of an owl, the cocking of a firearm, rustling footsteps. He had gone to bed early on Saturday evening listening to the wind in the lodgepole pines outside his tent near Cascade. From time to time he could hear voices of drunken workmen carousing in tent brothels that had sprung up along the line. Women usually placated restless men who were eager to spend their wages after Saturday's payout. But this particular Saturday evening was different. My father expected that come sunrise many intended to break their employment contracts and sneak out of camp.

The Nevada Territory, just east of the mountains, was a lure that workers couldn't resist. Overnight the silver Washoe Diggings had become famous. Virginia City mushroomed into a boomtown of fortune seekers who had missed the California gold rush by a decade. Father didn't blame these men for using his railroad as the first leg of their journey to Virginia City. Had he been already in his early thirties he too might have succumbed to the lure of silver. But that didn't make his current job any easier. As long as there was nothing to prevent his workers from hightailing over the mountains to the Comstock Lode whenever they damn well pleased, he couldn't build track. If it was their inclination to flee, it was his responsibility to see that they didn't. Between midnight and dawn he mulled over a half-dozen plans to stop a flood of desertions by morning. No plan he could think of was without considerable drawbacks. The simplest proved to be the only one with even a dim chance of succeeding.

Before dawn he pulled on his britches and slipped into shin-high boots. The last item of his wardrobe was his signature wide-brim army hat. From beneath his mattress he took a military issue Colt .44 revolver and spun the chamber. Six cartridges. After inserting the weapon into his belt he repeated the process with a larger and older five-shot revolver manufactured at the Smith and Wesson Company in Connecticut. It occurred to him that more cartridges might be necessary. But for what he intended there wouldn't be time to reload, so why bother? If he couldn't get the job done with eleven bullets, a hundred wouldn't resolve the problem.

There was a strong element of desperation inherent in his plan, for even if successful it wouldn't solve the Central Pacific's long-term labor problem. At best it would only forestall it. Still, it was hard to take a long view when he expected to have only a handful of men on the line come Monday morning. A practical man who preferred action to abstract thinking, my father concentrated on his immediate goal. And to ensure he'd have a substantial workforce on Monday, he was prepared to use his pistols to dissuade the defectors.

One hundred and one miles from Sacramento, laborers' tents were pitched in a wide clearing of fir trees. As my father made his way between rows of canvas in the pre-dawn darkness, he listened to the snoring sleepers. On Sundays, to honor the Sabbath day, the daily routine changed. Instead of being up before first light, the men lounged in their bunks until the sun had risen. Only Miwok Indian cooks were active, preparing the men's breakfast of beef jerky, sourdough biscuits, and coffee. The food wasn't much different from workdays except that on Sundays it could be eaten at leisure. Dad was pleased to find his men still asleep. He had learned from General William Sherman in the Vicksburg campaign the value of surprise in molding men's reactions. And if nothing else, he intended to surprise his men.

He chose high ground on the camp's eastern perimeter and climbed onto a stone ledge for additional height. The Indians took little notice of him and continued to tend their fires. My father waited eleven minutes until he heard muted voices inside the tents. He then withdrew both revolvers from his belt and fired into the air one after another, each giving off a different report. Suddenly voices erupted throughout the camp. Fearing Yokut Indians, who were renowned for murdering sleeping miners in their bunks, they seized tools to defend themselves—axes, shovels, picks, and knives. Every tent had at least one rifle. Those who slept in their drawers scrambled for their britches. When they emerged from the tents they didn't find a gang of marauding Indians, but my father with two pistols aimed directly at them!

He peered along the blue steel of his Colt's rear sight and drew the muzzle into line with the chest of the lead workman. Then, as if he had changed his mind, he let the barrel drop. "You men just heard two shots," he bellowed in his officer's voice trained to command subordinates in the field. "Now those who can count should know there are still nine bullets left in my guns. In an hour or so, some of you plan to sneak out of camp and hightail it through the mountains to the Comstock. Those who make it are gonna have a good time in Virginia City. Fancy food. Comfortable lodgings. Pretty girls too. Maybe you'll even make a few extra bucks for yourselves. It sounds better than working in the mountains on this rail bed. Yes, it sounds damn good except for one thing: all you fellows have contracts with the Central Pacific, so those who intend to leave will be breaking the law. And if you break the law, up to nine of you fellows aren't gonna make it at all to the Nevada Territory. I got nine bullets here that say you're gonna stay with the CP and complete your contracts, to the last day and hour, yes, even to the last minute. What you do after that is up to you. But a contract is a contract, boys, and I expect you fellows to honor the one you signed with the CP."

The first round went to my father by default. Nearly four hundred men stood in silence, intimidated by their superintendent's threat or, more likely, still groggy with sleep. Until that moment, no one had entertained the possibility of getting shot for breaking a labor contract, which in reality amounted to nothing more than signing one's name at the bottom of an enlistment roster. Many who had signed with their initials couldn't even read the print above the signature spaces. One muleteer reminded his cohorts under his breath that on the eighty-four-mile train ride from Sacramento to Emigrant Gap, veterans told stories about Theo Gallager. They said he was half-Irish, half-mule, and a whole sonavabitch. Nobody challenged the truth of that accusation.

A burly German brandishing a repeating Winchester cried out in a thick middle European accent, "Arithmetic, *Herr* Gallager. Sheer arithmetic. Vee are hunderts. Nine bullets ain't gonna shtop us. A vise man vould let zose who vish just go. *Jah?*"

Dad glanced over the muzzles of his revolvers, knowing them to be inferior to the rifle now opposing him. Still, he pointed the Colt at the German, mocking his slurred Germanic syllables. 'Vise,' perhaps. *Jah?* But clearly none of you wish to be among the dead nine. By the time you complete your contracts you'll see locomotives pulling up these mountains."

Jeers of disbelief erupted from the crowd below. The roadbed was hardly fit for oxen, much less locomotives. Getting a train over Cape Horn was more formidable than herding Hannibal's elephants over the Alps. And as if the lower mountain elevations were not obstacles enough, there were still nine tunnels to be blasted from solid granite on the Sierra summit at Donner. It was likely that before locomotives could clear the pass at Donner, all those present in camp would be old men. None would be rich, and many would probably be dead.

"Better plan your futures in California and not the Nevada Territory," Father howled back, cutting through the laughter. "When we've beaten these mountains, you're welcome to go after silver. You all understand the power of these mountains. We've got hard work to do first."

"You may not zee zat time, *Herr* Gallager," the German shouted, gathering strength from those who encouraged him. "Zere are zo many of us. Zee odds are againz you."

"Right. But not one of you will risk getting killed before the rest of you boys get me."

"I vould not count on zat."

Father took his eyes from the German and surveyed the workers, some ready to tear him to bits with their calloused hands. If Dad had any sympathizers among this railroad crew, none voiced their support. He knew that the German wouldn't have difficulty hitting him with his Winchester. On the other hand, at the current distance, hitting the German with one of his two pistols would require an extraordinary shot. How many others were carrying firearms that he couldn't see? For a moment my father wondered whether he had gone too far. One thing was clear: however far he had gone, there was no retreat now.

The German stepped forward, indicating that he accepted the challenge. He didn't point his Winchester at Dad, but a single swift move of his right hand cocked the lever action, forcing a cartridge into the chamber and producing a sound even those who could not see through the bodies ahead recognized as a signal the German was now prepared to shoot. Lever actions on other repeating rifles clicked open and closed in at least five other locations. My father's revolvers were no match for a single Winchester alone, and now there were multiple muzzles pointed at him. The faint of heart were encouraged.

Father was in a jam of his own making, and to keep his adversaries off-balance, he needed to risk more than he had. He raised his voice. "To show you boys that I mean business, I'm going to reduce my odds and increase yours." Once again he did the unexpected and fired both revolvers twice into the air. When smoke from his weapons cleared, Dad bellowed, "Now the odds are even better for you. Only five of you fellows won't make it to Virginia City. So who volunteers to take the first steps from camp and meet his Maker?"

Men in the front ranks waited for the armed German to make his move. Six others with rifles began elbowing forward, their weapons high above their heads to show that support was on the way. My father sensed it would be even more dangerous once additional rifles arrived in the front ranks. He immediately fired another two rounds, this time into the ground not far from his boots. Gunsmoke again separated him from the men, but when it cleared he said, "Now I can only prevent three of you boys from sneaking out of camp. Show me who wants to die for Nevada silver?"

Four riflemen filled space made available beside the German, their weapons pointed skyward, waiting for a signal to lower them at my father. The German hesitated. Dad unexpectedly fired again, sending two additional slugs into the dirt. When the dust cleared, he lifted his Colt into aiming position and centered the German within his sights. "One shell left," he said. "This is your last chance, *Herr Deutschland*. Take one step toward Nevada and I'll bury you right here in California."

The riflemen waited but the German remained unwilling to lift his Winchester.

"So it seems that I know some arithmetic after all, doesn't it?" Father said, seizing the initiative. "Not one of you will take a chance. I don't need more ammunition. One bullet is enough, the one I won't have to fire." He paused to let his message sink in. When not a whimper rose from the crowd he resumed speaking, this time in a conciliatory tone, "All right now, boys. Eat your breakfasts. Have a good rest and a good Sunday. Wagons will be ready for those who want to attend church in town. For those of you with other ideas, I understand a new batch of ladies has just arrived in Hookertown from Oakland. Tomorrow morning at five o'clock, I expect to see each and every one of you on the line. Together we'll beat these mountains and someday you can brag to your children that not only were you part of the great Pacific railroad, you built the hardest portion."

The critical moment came when my father stuffed the Colt with a single bullet in the chamber back into his belt. He didn't think the German or any of the others would shoot an unarmed man, but you could never tell. These men were largely drifters and opportunists, capable of just about anything, including murder. Slowly he turned his back and jumped down from the boulder. At any moment a bullet might enter his back and puncture his lungs or heart. He walked away with deliberate slowness, giving any of the disgruntled men bent on shooting him an easy target.

Back in his tent, Dad wondered if the gamble had produced anything but temporary gain. At risk of his own life he had merely prevented a handful of men from leaving the line. Those determined to go might still steal away after dark, or on Monday walk into the forest to relieve themselves and simply keep going. He had succeeded in little more than briefly delaying the inevitable. A week at most. But come the next payday, he'd have to face the same desertions. Damn the Comstock Lode. Damn the Sierra granite. Damn the Irish, German, and Chilean workers. Father was angry enough to fire the final bullet in his Colt into the ground, just to let off steam. It occurred to him, however, that after what he had just done, it would be wise to remain armed at all times.

From his youth, the sole owner of the Crocker Construction Company that enjoyed an exclusive contract for laying Central Pacific Railroad track, the five-foot-seven-inch Charles Cornelius Crocker had never in his adult life been under two hundred pounds. This plump-cheeked, large-eared, and heavily whiskered man was bombastic and opinionated, given to dashing and sometimes injudicious decisions, a broad-brush approach to life rather than attention to fine detail. Whatever people thought of him, no one doubted his talent for making money, despite a score of financial setbacks. An unsuccessful miner in the early 1850s, he had later capitalized on his mercantile talents in the dry goods business. Miners needed picks and shovels, black powder, pumps, machinery, trousers, socks and boots, as well as grub for their bellies. *Big Charley*, as people referred to him behind his back but never to his face, possessed an uncanny sense about credit risks and lent lavishly, some said foolishly, to those he believed in. With few exceptions, those he underwrote repaid their debts and became loyal associates, more often than not steering new and more profitable business his way. In public addresses, he often attributed his commercial success to sheer luck—being at the right place at the right time. Privately he believed his success was well earned, a result of hard work and sound judgment. In the smoking room, armed with the pungent Mexican cigars he favored, he added an essential ingredient to his formula for achievement. Balls. "Without 'em," he liked to pontificate, "you might just as well be a steer in the pasture. Nobody's gonna hurt you there, but you're not gonna have any fun either."

A string of commercial successes brought Big Charley into partnership with the ex-governor of California, Leland Stanford, plus Mark Hopkins and Collis Huntington as an owner of the fledgling Central Pacific Railroad, serving small communities in California's Central Valley. In the early months of their partnership, none of these owners envisioned running track over the Sierra to anchor the western segment of a transcontinental line. That concept was the brainchild of Theodore Judah, the original surveyor and master planner of a railroad stretching from Nebraska to the Pacific. After years of promoting this venture to anyone who would hear him out, Judah traveled to Washington to encourage the federal government to provide financial incentives. Based on his survey, legislators eventually agreed to support a plan for one Eastern and one Western railroad company to begin construction, moving toward a central meeting point somewhere in the West. As an incentive, each company could keep for itself a healthy swath of land paralleling the rail bed, plus a lucrative bonus for every mile of track laid. A host of entrepreneurs proposed to build the eastern segment and few were surprised when Congress selected the Union Pacific, a railroad that lavishly rewarded its cronies in government. There was far less competition to build the more ambitious western segment. Collis Huntington successfully shepherded the cause of the Central Pacific in the capital and, for his lobbying expertise, became a twenty-five percent partner.

When the dreams of Crocker, Stanford, Hopkins, and Huntington finally came to fruition in 1866, Big Charley founded his construction company to lay the track. It was Charles Crocker's firm, rather than the Central Pacific Railroad, that later employed my father. Crocker, whose headquarters at the time was in Sacramento, demanded from Dad daily reports and replied by telegraph to almost every item with return directives. My father deeply resented his employer's interference with daily operations. After all, what did this dry goods merchant know about laying track? Once, in a furious mood, Dad quipped that were it not for his boss's interminable meddling, the Central Pacific would be laying track in the Wyoming Territory. The remark filtered back through the owner's network of spies and Crocker let Father know that he wasn't amused.

"You're wasting your time, Theo," he telegraphed back. "I'm running this railroad. Keep your nose to the track. That's what I pay you for. My ass is on the line here, not yours. If we fail, I'm going to be the brokest merchant in California while you'll just get another job. Maybe with the Union Pacific!"

After the confrontation with his workers at Cascade, Dad wasn't surprised to receive an order to come to Sacramento for a powwow with his chief. He had long expected the Central Pacific owners to fire him as they had previous superintendents. He told his associates before leaving Cascade that he was going to attend the Last Supper with the Crockers in their Sacramento mansion.

Charles and Mary Crocker greeted my father in the foyer, which was ornately decorated with furniture from Europe and the Orient. Mary wore a dress with far too many folds of silk encompassing a short, rotund body, and sported gold rings on eight of her ten fingers, including both thumbs. She struck Dad as a lady with pitifully poor taste in spending her husband's fortune. Crocker, on the other hand, gave the appearance of one for whom the same wealth meant little. Though he could have afforded the finest tailors, his jacket sagged from his shoulders in a downward tumble. His shoes disappeared below the ill-fitted cuffs of his trousers. Even his double chin seemed to have succumbed to gravity, disappearing beneath a loose collar.

Though the Crockers knew how to be cordial, conversation around their well-appointed dinner table was stiff. Mary talked about future trips she was planning to Europe. Crocker spoke of scoundrels and thieves in California politics seeking to separate him from his money. Their beef and potatoes were overcooked, but the local valley claret was the finest Father had ever tasted.

In the smoking parlor after dinner, Dad expected his employer to get down to business. Crocker offered him a Mexican cigar, which my father declined, then stroked his fantail beard and relaxed back into the cushions of a richly upholstered Chinese sofa. "The Union Pacific's got trouble with Injuns, Theo," he finally said, breaking the silence with a playful glimmer in his eyes, as if relishing how his competitors suffered. "Yes, they got Injuns and we got mountains. Their workers need meat for their bellies and buffalo are abundant. The Lakota and Creek warriors don't like white men taking what they consider *their* game. It's a big country, but the Injuns think they own most of it. Mind you, I don't begrudge them their huntin' grounds, but I don't appreciate their lack of hospitality, though I gotta say I'm not sorry they're making trouble for the UP boys. But you see, Theo, the UP's trying to bring civilization to these savages and they don't want to give up their old ways. I reckon a few thousand white men can't eat much buffalo. Besides, it don't taste good. Far too pungent for my taste. Give me a good old steer any day."

The after-dinner brandy, combined with the claret, had begun to make my father's head spin. Sooner or later his boss would rebuke him for the lack of progress in the mountains and get down to dismissing or demoting him. And when that time arrived, he'd need all his wits to defend himself. "It's not buffalo alone, Mr. Crocker," Dad said, fighting the effects of alcohol on his speech. "Seems killing Creek and Sioux tribesmen has become a white man's sport on the prairie. From what I hear, they're shooting three Indians for every buffalo."

Crocker wasn't accustomed to men expressing themselves so candidly. He looked leery. "Oh yes, it's no secret what the Union Pacific's up to. If Injuns don't want to get massacred they'd better move off the track."

"But that's where the buffalo are. And without buffalo these people will starve. Either they migrate and starve or they fight and get massacred. That's not much of a choice."

Crocker pondered that for a moment, then let out a loud "Huhmmmm. Well, it's a sorry business anyway. Still, if the Injuns were smart they wouldn't resist. It's a losing battle, you know." He paused to judge how far he should spell out his argument before coming to the point. "You see, Theo, in my view, progress is much like a railroad. If you're gonna sit on the tracks, you're gonna get run over."

Father recognized the honesty, but also knew that Crocker didn't give a hoot about Indians or about buffalo.

"Anyway, Theo," Crocker shifted his weight on the sofa cushion and grunted, "I'd personally rather be shooting Injuns than European laborers. Especially German and Irish workers."

A sense of relief pulsed through my father. So that was why Crocker had summoned him. Now he understood why he had alluded to Indian problems. Crocker had brought him to Sacramento for a reprimand over the incident at Cascade.

"My spies tell me you're going to shoot deserters. I don't like men breaking their contracts any more than you do, but you can't shoot men on my railroad. We're not running an army up there. If word of what you did gets back to Washington, Congress will cut off the gravy that makes my railroad run. Shooting Injuns Congress can overlook, but shooting white Christians is quite another thing."

"It was only a threat. I never intended to shoot anyone. I didn't have enough ammunition to do much damage anyway."

Crocker puckered his lips in a mischievous grimace. "Oh, I know that, Theo. You're not the kind of man who goes around shooting people for some silly scheme that wouldn't work anyway. But we can't let this kind of thing get into the papers. My partner, poor Leland, would have a heart attack. We've got enough enemies in Washington already."

"I need men. At the wages the company pays, I can't keep them working. Either we pay them more or I frighten them. Since you won't pay them better, I must resort to scare tactics. The dregs you send me understand nothing but violence."

"We've been through this wage business before. You know the CP hasn't got the cash. But just as important, it wouldn't work. Double the wages and Virginia City would still be attractive. You weren't in California during the Great Rush. I was. It didn't matter that men came out of the hills broken and busted. I was busted myself and I learned that it only took a few lucky ones to spread the fever. Nothing can stop such madness. Men fed on gold dust with the frenzy of seagulls over a school of herring. It only ceased when the gold ran out. And there are still hangers-on, hoping to find a few nuggets in the rivers. The Comstock Lode in Nevada Territory is just the same thing all over again."

Chiang Teh, Crocker's Chinese domestic servant, entered the sitting room. He bowed gently and shuffled forward, bringing a silver coffee urn and small cups and saucers on a tray. He wore no queue like many Chinese in San Francisco, but retained the traditional black skullcap. After he poured, Crocker restated his conviction that higher wages weren't the answer to the Central Pacific's woes.

Father cut him off. "If I can't use force, how can I stop the men from running off whenever they damn well please?"

"Even the formidable *Major Theodore Gallager* can't stop them," Crocker said with his usual ridicule for those who had taken commissions during the War Between the States. He never hid the fact that he had judiciously declined a Union commission in order to make his fortune in the West.

"With my guns I can at least slowed'em down," my father said.

"That isn't good enough. At the rate we're laying track, the Union Pacific will have their locomotives running down Market Street in San Francisco before we reach the summit at Donner."

He sighed to himself. So Crocker was warming up to firing him after all.

"Gotta change our strategy," Crocker said, "we gotta do something new. Something that hasn't been tried."

"How about raising wages? You haven't tried that yet."

"How about *not* raising wages? My partners will never agree to a cockamamie idea guaranteed to drive us into bankruptcy. I need a fresh labor force. Thousands of workers, at less, not more, than the current pay!"

"From the heavens," Dad said, his eyes darting upward toward the ceiling.

"Exactly, Theo. From the Celestial Kingdom of China. I need an army of Chinamen. Hard-working men like Chiang Teh here."

My father's snort revealed his contempt. Chinese coolies were cooks and laundrymen, extortionists and opium dealers. Most were barely five feet tall and without the physical stamina to blast and level roadbed in the mountains, much less lay track in the prairie. Occasionally you would come across a strong Chinaman among the miners, but that was the exception not the rule. Crocker was talking about several thousand, and from reports of travelers in China, almost everybody there was diseased and malnourished.

"They built the Great Wall and hauled stones from the Yangtze River gorges," Crocker said. "What's more, they work hard. Ask anybody who deals with them in San Francisco."

"I'd rather have a pack of Mexican banditos," Father growled. "Haven't we got enough trouble on the roadbeds? If you think my hard-drinking Irishmen are surly now, think what they'll be like when we order them to share their jobs with China John."

Crocker slapped both hands on his knees. "I already have. They'll be fightin' mad. Maybe you'll have to use those famous revolvers of yours to keep the peace. But when your Irish and Germans see what these Chinamen can do, they'll buckle under. My guess is they'll work harder to show that they're better than the Chinamen. If they don't, we'll fire 'em and put coolies in their places."

"Where the hell you gonna get regiments of coolies? They'd rather live in urban hovels than work in the mountains. You'll be lucky to get a dozen to stay on the line, especially in winter."

Crocker stood up, next marched across the sitting room to the window and gazed into the garden beyond, illuminated for the evening by a string of oil lanterns. "I've already thought of that. I've hired a labor contractor to bring fifty-five coolies from Canton." He pivoted around to assess my father's reaction and grinned with satisfaction. "They're already here, Theo. I mean in San Francisco right now. On the steamer *Japan*, docked at the Pacific Mail Wharf. And I want you to go down there tomorrow morning and fetch 'em. Take 'em up to the mountains. See what they can do."

My father followed Crocker to his feet and clapped his hands together loudly. "Jesus, that's all I need. Fifty Chinese runts wreaking havoc."

"It's only an experiment. If it fails, back to San Francisco they go. If it works, I'll get more. Lots more. I'm surprised a fine engineer like you wouldn't relish a chance to give it a try."

Dad drew alongside the railroad baron and gazed with him into a garden where the oil lanterns cast a patina of shadows on the surrounding shrubs. "It's not a question about giving it a try. Coolies wouldn't have to come to California if they could build their own railroad in China. History has already shown us what they have never done for themselves. Their experiment in their homeland has failed miserably."

"And so will we if I can't keep enough manpower in the mountains. I'll be honest with you. I've also got doubts about this, but I must give every possibility a try before I'm licked. Perhaps when you see my Chinese pets in San Francisco you'll change your mind. Until the first snows, that's all I ask. Give these little rascals a chance to prove themselves. Just till the winter."

My father pondered the prospects of absorbing fifty-five coolies in a camp always short of cooks and dishwashers, woodchoppers and errand boys. He had heard stories of how the Chinese worked well with mules and oxen. Rather than argue with Crocker and get himself fired, he thought of assigning the Celestials to tasks where their limited skills might prove useful. Three months wasn't a long time. Soon they'd be back in San Francisco. Or on a ship heading home to China, where they belonged.

CHAPTER THREE

San Francisco Bay

Two and a half days had elapsed since the *Japan* first dropped anchor and still the Chinese were imprisoned below deck. Summer fog cooled San Francisco Bay, but below the hatches, the temperatures rose into the high 90s. Coolies, who had endured ocean swells, seasickness, and fright with stoic fortitude, were now forced to confront the cruelty of life in Gum San. The company's spokesman, Fu Koung, appealed for patience. But the coolies' patience had worn thin and they were in no mood to wait any longer as prisoners in the ship's hold. Instead they divided into shifts and, hour after hour, day and night, banged tin teacups against the ship's stanchions. Vibrations traveled through the hull, rattling every nook and cranny as far away as the officers' quarters in the forecastle.

This unrelenting racket put the crew on edge, as well as my father, who had come aboard to relieve Captain Isaiah Steward of his Chinese passengers. As far as the Pacific Mail Steamship Company was concerned, that couldn't happen soon enough.

The *Japan* was neither equipped for nor licensed to carry more than a half-dozen passengers and it had no dedicated facilities for steerage. Getting caught by the Customs Service with a boatload of illegal passengers would mean a stiff fine or, as was the usual practice, a series of expensive payoffs. The ship's owners had sent Captain Steward instructions that, until disembarkation, no Chinese were to appear on deck. Unfortunately, because my father's ferryboat for Sacramento wasn't scheduled to leave until the following day, that meant the Chinese would have to suffer an additional day of hell in the ship's cargo hold. And to compound Steward's difficulties, a troop of women from the Chinese Protection League had arrived alongside in a steam launch and were demanding to come aboard, with or without the skipper's permission.

"Tell 'em they can't board," Captain Steward ordered his officer of the deck. "Say we're very sorry but this vessel is not equipped for women."

The launch was bobbing in choppy water about twenty yards off starboard. Four stern-faced women, cloaked in woolen overcoats against sea spray, glared upward, their eyes demanding permission to come aboard the more stable vessel.

"We've got a doctor with us," a heavyset woman bellowed to the deck officer, wrestling with a hood that shielded her head. "So don't try to put us off with excuses. We don't require special facilities."

"Impossible," Captain Steward said, interceding with a bellowing voice amplified by a megaphone. "My crew's been at sea for six weeks without setting eyes on a single woman. Language aboard ship isn't fit for female ears and in this state men cannot be controlled. You don't know what happens to sailors on the high seas. The animal comes out in them. I can't and will not vouch for their behavior."

Below deck, the Chinese continued to bang their cups on the stanchions, sounding a haunting percussion at water level and telegraphing bizarre happenings in the ship's hold.

The spokeswoman's dark eyes burned from below her hood, dripping with sea spray. "Not to worry, sir. We've been on whaling ships from the very depths of hell in the South Pacific. Far, far worse than yours."

"No, Ma'am, you haven't. I won't permit it. You understand? Absolutely not."

She shouted toward the skipper through cupped fingers, "We haven't seen a ship bearing Chinamen that hasn't got consumption. Maybe worse. You're aware that the Pacific Mail Steamship Company is fully responsible for importing diseased human beings into California. And if it can be shown there's an attempt to cover this up, the steamship line is subject to double or triple damages. To avoid such penalties, it's to your advantage that we make an inspection before you offload. Our surgeon, Dr. Horn, must come aboard immediately. If you won't work with us, we'll sail back to press our case with immigration authorities. We have good rapport with the newspapers. If you're not transporting Celestials, you have nothing to fear. If you are, all we want to know is the state of their health."

Steward frowned down at the huddled ladies, their backs to the blowing spray, then let his eyes drift up toward his officers. He didn't appreciate threats to his authority, especially from busybodies like these women from the Protection League. "There's no disease aboard my ship, Miss Whoever-You-Are. Of that you can be well assured. We take all precautions aboard the *Japan*. She's the healthiest ship on the Pacific. Absolutely no disease."

"Dickerson's the name, sir. Mabel Dickerson. And we're not assured by your declaration. Our doctor should make that determination, not the captain. So, if you please."

Steward glanced at the hatch over the ship's hold and, confident it was closed, said, "All right, Miss Dickerson. The doctor may come aboard. The rest of you ladies must be confined to the main deck where I'm now standing, or remain in your launch. I'm firm about this. Once aboard my ship you will not be permitted to move around or have any contact with my crew."

Officers of the Chinese Protection League broke into a discussion and quickly reached a decision. The entire delegation elected to leave the launch. Mabel Dickerson accepted Captain Steward's restrictions. Sailors began rigging lines to moor the launch alongside and lower a gangplank.

Meanwhile Second Mate Isaak Donahue had reached the limits of his tolerance for the noise emanating from below and presented the skipper with a plan to silence it. A good dousing with a fire hose under high pressure would shut the Chinks up and more than compensate for the trouble of pumping out the seawater afterward. As to the bales of cotton and hemp in the hold, only those near the floorboards should get damp, and they were scheduled to be offloaded and would dry on the docks. Under normal conditions, Captain Steward would have rejected a plan that might damage his cargo, but the persistent din from below had frazzled his nerves. Donahue's idea sounded pretty good to him. At the time, even my father concurred, believing it better to discipline the Chinese aboard ship than in the mountain camps. Under Donahue's direction, sailors readied the fire hose.

Just at this indelicate moment, Wong Po-ching emerged from the hatch hauling two buckets of human excrement. Caught in a gust of wind, the pungent odor of stale feces traveled along the deck. Sailors sneered and howled curses. Wong could not understand their language, but their scoffing carried a quality of contempt not lost on him. His reply in Cantonese encouraged others to add their curses. Weighing his inability to communicate with words, he was obliged to set the buckets on the after-deck and sign the predicament of his compatriots below with bold gestures. Swipes across his forehead indicated the intense heat below. By pounding his feet in place he imitated a man climbing the ladder to the main deck. He pretended to bathe by rubbing his hands along his chest and arms. The sailors took to mocking this charade. Hog grunts answered his Chinese responses. Crewmen from the forecastle clambered onto the main deck to enjoy the show.

"Visitors arriving on the main deck, sir," a mate called to Captain Steward, who had hoped to quiet down the Chinese before the meddlesome women came aboard. But that was suddenly not possible. Far sooner than he had anticipated, there were four visitors in black cloaks on the main deck, looking like a troop of nuns prepared for a squall. Donahue's hoses were not yet unspoiled.

"Miss Dickerson," the captain said, "where's your doctor? He's the only one I'll permit to move from this deck. Jacob," he waved at a deck hand, "bring these fine ladies hot tea from the galley."

The tallest of the women tossed back her hood to reveal a shock of red hair, tied into a bun behind her ears. Below it, strong features punctuated white skin mottled with an even sprinkling of freckles. Lifting a sculptured chin and presenting a broad Irish face, she announced, "I'm Dr. Horn. Dr. Harriet Horn."

The announcement caught the skipper off-guard. He had never considered that the physician he was allowing onboard would be a woman. Had he known that, he would never have permitted the party to board in the first place. But at this juncture how could he retract a pledge made within earshot of nearly everybody on deck?

"I'll need to examine your passengers," Dr. Horn declared. At that moment her eye caught Wong who had lifted his slop buckets again and was advancing in her direction. She stepped out to meet him, but he halted at a safe distance and set the heavy buckets on the deck in front of his feet. Simultaneously, my father moved forward to view the first of his new workers. The few Chinese he had seen in the Sierra camps were ugly pygmy-like creatures who, more often than not, bowed obsequiously, a practice he found thoroughly distasteful. But this Chinaman was different, relatively tall and rather handsome. What attracted Dad most was that, unlike his countrymen, Wong stood his ground before the hostile crew. At a distinct disadvantage with the English language, he nevertheless answered taunts from the crew with strong gestures of his fists.

Captain Steward ordered Second Mate Donahue to hurry along Wong with his duties and return him to the cargo hold as soon as possible. The officer, whose bronze skin and well-defined muscles exuded from his seaman's tunic, cried, "Pick up the buckets of shit," pointing with his finger, seemingly unconcerned that the Chinaman didn't understand English.

Wong stopped making sign language and gazed in wonderment. He had heard a single word repeated in English and tried to communicate by using it. "*Sheet, sheet, sheet,*" he said, unclear about its reference but proud to be speaking his first words in the language of Gum San.

"Shit," Donahue corrected, unabashed by his vulgar language in the presence of the ladies. "Now pick up those buckets and get moving."

The crewmen roared their approval. A deckhand ignored the females altogether and offered Wong another lesson in English. "Bucket of shit. You eat shit. China's a shithole."

Wong tried to repeat the strange phrases. The word *shit* he now got perfectly.

"That's right." Donahue felt encouragement from his crew. "Shit," and he pointed to the buckets at Wong's feet.

The Chinaman's cheeks rounded into a wide smile.

"What does a horse do when he lifts his tail?" Donahue was playing to the audience of his fellow seamen.

Wong wrestled with the long English sentence. The ship's mate repeated until others caught on and began to laugh. Wong laughed too, trying to be amiable.

"He shits, doesn't he?" Donahue provided the answer. He then did something that took Wong by surprise. His hand jutted forward and he snatched the Chinaman's black queue that hung from the crown of his head along his back. Up it went to imitate a horse lifting its tail. "Now shit!" Donahue commanded.

Wong swung around, ripping his queue from the second mate's hand. Lifting it was tantamount to squeezing his testicles, and to submit to such an indignity was a sign of abject submission. And no matter how these white men in Gum San treated him, Wong did not feel submissive. Without a common language to vent his rage, he shouted the only word he knew. "Shit. Shit."

The word and what it depicted coalesced into one. Wong grabbed a bucket of excrement and, in a single fluid motion, flung its contents in the direction of the second mate. A man of great physical agility, Donahue anticipated the Chinaman's motion and adroitly sidestepped the smelly slop, leaving an empty corridor through the crowd of spectators. Unfortunately my father stood foursquare at the end of this corridor while Dr. Horn was slightly behind and to his left. Neither was quick enough to avoid a broadside of brown and yellow feces. The bucketful caught them squarely on their faces and necks, splattering their torsos. My father released a howl of indignation then gagged on the glutinous mass that had entered his mouth and seemed to clog his windpipe. Dr. Horn was only slightly better protected. Two clumps of feces splattered her chest, with more clinging to her cheek.

Because the episode also caught the crew by surprise none of the sailors knew how to be helpful. In the absence of a plan to restore lost dignity, humor filled the void. Chuckles eventually erupted all around. But it was the reaction of a lady, a professional lady, at that, which cut the amusement short.

"Goddamn turds!" Dr. Horn exclaimed in a voice that seemed to get caught in dead space between the ship's riggings. Everyone heard this profanity as though amplified through a megaphone. She made no attempt to apologize or retract it. Instead, like a man picking leeches from his skin, she began to pluck at the fecal matter and wipe it off on a nearby ship's railing.

When they recovered, men around the Chinaman roared with laughter. Harriet Horn's uncensored reaction stirred them more than Wong's defiance. They saw no reason to defend a woman with such a foul mouth. Besides, Wong was the first coolie they had seen stand up to a ship's officer. The Chinaman had accomplished what many of them had secretly wished to do themselves, but lacked the courage. Their laughter sounded like a cheer, a fact that annoyed Donahue. Meanwhile, my father and Harriet Horn were wiping feces from their eyes and lips. But each swab of the hand seemed to smear the yellow-brown material even more. Father lifted his eyes to check out the plight of Dr. Horn who, despite her undignified condition, appeared inordinately attractive. She sensed him looking at her and returned his gaze, no less handsome and no less humbled. Their mutual predicament caused each to join in the laughter. They laughed so hard that neither managed to clean off the mess.

As he had done on the hillside above the village of Hsuan-tak in his native land, Wong stood waiting for punishment. There was no use trying to explain why he had fought back. Or why he had missed the target and inadvertently hit strangers with whom he had no quarrel. Besides, even if he managed to communicate with these strange people, why should they accept *his* explanation?

Women from the Chinese Protection League abandoned the restricted zone established by Captain Steward and clustered around Dr. Horn. The skipper attempted to herd them back but, unnerved by what had just occurred, ceded effective control.

Donahue could conceive of no appropriate punishment until the Chinaman uttered the one word they all understood. It suddenly became clear what he should do. The second bucket of excrement was on the deck before him. All he needed was some room to hurl it at the Chinaman. His crewmen agreed that this was, indeed, a fitting punishment, for it appealed to their seamen's sense of justice. In a bizarre moment of mutual understanding, Wong appeared not only to comprehend but to concur in this verdict.

He planted his feet apart so he could withstand the impact. Both hands were clasped behind his back, anticipating a broadside. It was a display of bravery that added to the crew's growing admiration for this Chinaman. Many would have broken out a huge hurrah had they not feared wrath from their officers.

The second mate knew he had but a single throw and took a half-dozen trial swings, careful not to spill the bucket's contents. One seaman led a rousing cheer for both Donahue and Wong. The last swing was for keeps. Contents of the bucket sailed over the deck at the Chinaman. But Donahue's aim was no better than that of Wong, who unlike him, made no effort to sidestep from its path. Half the excrement flew past the railing and overboard into the bay. The other half caught Wong's chest and arm. Cheering subsided. No one knew whether to consider Donahue's throw a hit or a miss.

"Get him below," Captain Steward howled. "Get this animal out of my sight and below deck."

The sailors stood in shock. The physician and Mr. Gallager would undoubtedly be afforded bathing facilities. But the Chinaman was obliged to go below without a bath. "Shame," someone cried out. Others repeated the chant. "Shame. Shame."

Captain Steward again ordered for Wong to be taken below.

"Clean him off first," my father interceded in a voice that assumed the authority of a commanding officer. "This man is on contract to the

Crocker Construction Company, so he's my property. I don't accept soiled coolies. If you want me to take him and his countrymen off your ship in the morning, you'd better see he doesn't smell like a shithouse."

"But he's on *our* ship," Donahue complained.

"Wrong, Mr. Donahue," Captain Steward said, quick to evaluate the implications of my father's threat and reverse a previous order. "Unfortunately, this Celestial is on *my* ship, and I'm determined to get him off. The sooner he and his stinking lot are disembarked, the happier I'll be. Let him clean himself off."

Two sailors guided Wong forward to barrels of seawater stored on deck. Before he descended to his countrymen below, many seamen gathered around him near the hatch, expressing a mixture of curiosity and admiration.

Wong stopped washing for a moment as he gazed at Captain Steward and my father. "Shit," he said with a good-natured laugh, then resumed his bathing.

A moment later Captain Steward was leading Father and Dr. Horn below deck to his private quarters and a shower compartment. "You'll have to take turns; I presume the lady will go first."

"Sounds good to me," Father said, introducing himself to Harriet Horn. "The name's Theodore Gallager. I'm superintendent of construction on the Central Pacific Railroad."

Horn thrust her hand out to shake his, but seeing that it was still covered in brown feces withdrew the gesture. She laughed mischievously. "Pleased to meet you, Mr. Gallager. My colleagues and I know the hold of this vessel is filled with Chinese. Now I have an idea what brings you aboard."

"You from these parts?" my father asked, avoiding the subject of using Chinamen on the rail bed in the mountains. "Not exactly. Amherst, Massachusetts, then Baltimore while attending medical school at the College of Johns Hopkins. But California's my home now, where the unimaginable seems to happen every day. Only in this state could a woman get hit with a bucketful of shit. Don't you agree, Mr. Gallager?"

"I witnessed far stranger things in Virginia, but that was during the war. You first to the shower, please."

"Now that doesn't seem fair to me. You received more of those feces than I."

"No, Ma'am, not all Californians have forgotten common courtesies. You first. While you're washing, it wouldn't be a bad idea for me to check on my coolies in the hold."

"You're a gentleman, Mr. Gallager, and I admire true gentlemen. But more, I admire men with humor. I trust this unfortunate affair could have ended much worse than it did."

Preliminary Report of Health Conditions Among Chinese Workers in California

FOR THE U.S. SENATE SUB-COMMITTEE ON IMMIGRATION
City of Washington

Submitted by Harriet C. Horn, M.D.
Adjunct Professor, Cooper School of Medicine
San Francisco, Calif.

Deplorable! Simply stated, the health of Chinese workers arriving in California is appalling. This observation is substantiated by members of the Chinese Protection League who, during the months of January and May 1866, visited six vessels transporting workers from China to San Francisco, California.

Celestials are brought to this country as steerage in the holds of cargo ships; no ships that we inspected were properly outfitted to transport human beings below their decks. They were not equipped with ventilation or sanitary facilities, sleeping bunks, tables or chairs, or supplied with recreational items to ease the boredom of long voyages. Of the 341 individuals we examined, 106 were seriously diseased. For example, 25 of the 55 Chinese laborers aboard the steamship *Japan* presented symptoms of lung consumption. 10 (not necessarily a different group) suffered from syphilis. 21 had diarrhea. 3 undiagnosed infections. Most Chinese males refused to submit to a genital examination by a woman physician, though 4 reluctantly agreed. 2 suffered from skin lesions on the penile shafts and testicles, both conditions consistent with the venereal disease described in several medical articles by Dr. Alfred Bateman II.

Long confinement below deck in a steamship's cargo hold is not much better than conditions under which slaves were brought to this country before Emancipation. The only difference is that the Chinese travelers are not chained together or to the ship. Yet they are nevertheless locked in the cargo hold and denied access to fresh air, toilet facilities, and exercise. The shipping companies claim that, while their passengers are transported in steerage, they enjoy daily exposure to fresh air and sunlight. Such assertions are laughable. All Chinese arrive in San Francisco pale, sickly, and underfed.

One cannot ascertain with any confidence the standard of food and water. The ship owners claim that they provide their Chinese passengers a healthy diet. The Chinese we interviewed reported differently. They stated that their daily soup consisted of scraps from the ship's galley mixed with worm-infested rice. Chinese travelers have apparently very low standards of dental care in their native land and their teeth appear quite filthy. Yet I observed that there must be something in their diet that benefits their teeth. They exhibit remarkably little decay. The light in these ships' holds is generally quite poor, so further examination of these Chinamen's mouths and throats is required.

I observed no signs of opium. All studies that I have reviewed indicate their addiction begins not in China (they are too impoverished to purchase opium in their native land) but in California joss houses and opium dens, after they have earned enough money to pay for the drug. If these Chinese workers enter the country without being addicted, it behooves us to keep them away from the evil influence once they are here.

Medical examination of Chinese laborers before they begin working is only the first step in evaluating their health. It is imperative to conduct follow-up examinations. I have decided to maintain contact with the 55 coolie workers aboard steamship *Japan* who were headed directly into the Sierra mountains to work on the railroad being built by the Charles Crocker Construction Company. Perhaps in clear Sierra air, they will avoid the unhealthy perils so prevalent in San Francisco's Chinatown. I'd like to determine whether the health of workers in the mountains is better or worse than that of those who remain in the cities. But this will require more study.

Harriet Horn, M.D.
Cooper School of Medicine

Dutch Flat
July 1866

Aboard the paddle-wheeler headed up the Sacramento River, Father instructed his Chinese laborers to separate into three groups and select a headman for each. Wong wanted to lead his group, but his cohorts chose Chan Yue because of his superiority in the American language. From Wong's point of view that was a bad choice. Chan Yue knew only a dozen more words than he, some fifty-six in all. The others could barely manage a single word of this strange language. Most refused to try the tongue-twisting syllables. Why should they? Soon their pockets would be filled with gold coin and they would be headed back to their native country.

Until the Chinese boarded a Central Pacific Railroad flatcar traveling through the Sierra foothills, they had no idea about the nature or location of their work in Gum San. As the train climbed from low-lying farmlands into the mountains, Douglas fir and tamarisk trees dominated the landscape. The mountains offered wide vistas where the eye could roam free of obstructions, a relief from the crowded quarters aboard the trans-Pacific steamer. Burly Irishmen and Welshmen worked beside the track, some as carpenters on wooden trestles, others as rock levelers in the cuts and fills. Beyond the thin roadbed there was nothing but forested mountains and, in the far distance, snowcapped peaks. Wong marveled at the uncultivated land that expanded as far as the eye could see. To his mind that was a good sign; every Chinese peasant knew that where there was land to clear and till there was no starvation.

When the locomotive slowed, Welshmen threw stones at the Asian newcomers. Two of Wong's cohorts were hit. The others looked for ammunition to hurl back in their own defense, but their possessions were too few and too valuable to toss at men beside the track. The land, Wong concluded, was friendlier than its inhabitants.

At Cape Horn where the track terminated, the Celestials had to climb down from the flatcar and continue another ten miles by open wagon along a dirt road to a place called Dutch Flat. A half-mile beyond a large camp of Welsh and Scandinavian laborers, Chan Yue ordered everyone to set up tents. The first meal in the new camp consisted of table scraps from the European workers: hunks of beef, fried quarters of potatoes, stale bread, and boiled coffee, nothing that Wong's countrymen could digest. A few, driven by hunger, gagged on the beef but did a little better with the potatoes. Within an hour, those willing to experiment with this new fare were suffering severe stomach pains. Eight vomited. Chan Yue ordered everyone to stop eating. Wong and several cohorts foraged in the nearby forest for edible roots or plants and returned with a bundle of greens and mushrooms. The cook boiled them until they were tender and added plenty of salt. Somebody produced tea from a neighboring camp galley.

The same day Wong and his compatriots arrived at Dutch Flat, Harriet Horn left her home on Laguna Street on San Francisco's western outskirts and sailed by paddle-wheeler to Sacramento with Sam Ting-nu, a Cantonese interpreter from Chinatown. From there they traveled by Central Pacific Pullman to the terminus of the passenger service at the Secretown Trestle. An ox-driven supply wagon transported them along a construction road hacked through thick forests of scrub pine.

The arrival of this pair in the Chinese camp caused considerable commotion. Railroad camps were the exclusive domain of men; even prostitutes were obliged to ply their trade in tent brothels erected at a specific distance from the workmen's quarters. The company had a rule that the presence of women near blasting and heavy machinery was absolutely prohibited. Nobody knew why Dr. Horn had come or what she planned to do. Sam Ting-nu requested an interview with Chan Yue, who was easy to find since the Central Pacific had yet to find jobs for its new arrivals. It took only a few questions for Harriet to assess the poor health of the newcomers. None of these fifty-five coolies had adapted to camp food and they remained too weak for meaningful work.

Word of Harriet's presence in the Chinese camp spread with telegraphic speed up and down the line and soon reached headquarters outside Alta. News of her unexpected arrival made my father's eyes narrow and his lips smack, as they did whenever he was annoyed. He entertained the idea of sending a deputy to determine the nature of her business, but buoyed by the prospect of seeing her again, delegated the supervision of arriving supply trains to a lieutenant and left immediately for the Chinese camp. Though he had quickly ascertained aboard *Japan* that she was not married, it was difficult for him to believe that a woman of her beauty and talent wouldn't have droves of suitors. And the more he thought about her the more certain he was that there was no place for a construction manager like himself in the life of this educated woman. He had made a mental note to visit her on his first trip to San Francisco, but didn't think it likely that she would see him.

Harriet's presence could not have come at a worse time. A host of engineering dilemmas were taxing my father, but none was as irritating as the problem of feeding his new Chinese workers. Irish and German laborers complained about everything from the hours of work to the wages they received. Food was never an issue because the Crocker Construction Company believed strongly that decent meals promoted high morale and work efficiency. Field galleys fed company workmen some of the best camp grub in California. The cooks were instructed to make whatever accommodations they could for the Chinese workers, but the coolies rejected just about everything they concocted.

When Dad arrived in the camp, all fifty-five coolies were squatting on their heels in a circle. Harriet Horn was in the middle engaged in a discussion through her interpreter. As Dad strode between the coolies, she turned and welcomed him with a disarming smile. "Why, hello, Theo Gallager. What a pleasure to see you under cleaner circumstances."

"It's a surprise to find you here, Dr. Horn," he replied, his eyes sweeping the squads of Chinese to calculate what had transpired before his arrival.

"Call me Harriet, please. After our experience together, we're entitled to a bit of informality, don't you think? I'm intrigued with Wong Po-ching. No doubt you recall he was responsible for painting both of us with shit."

"So, Harriet, what brings you here from Frisco?"

She ushered him into the middle of the group by offering a hand and holding on once he accepted hers. "By now you've probably figured out that I'm not one to stand on ceremony when it comes to language. I'm an only child, raised in a proper Massachusetts family. Back home no one ever says what he thinks until he's certain it will cause no offense. Most of what people in my home state say they don't really believe."

"Why are you here, Harriet?" he repeated, revealing his irritation.

"Two reasons. First, to see you again, Theo. I thought we might reminisce about our humbling moment on the bay."

"I never thought of it like that. I was just bloody angry; that is, until I realized this Chink never meant to hit us and never would have if that naval officer hadn't jumped out of the way. What's your second reason?"

"Second, to see the workers. I'm conducting health surveys for the United States Senate on Chinese entering California. Washington is concerned about the diseases they're bringing in. If you ask for my opinion, I think Congress is just hunting for an excuse to ban more Chinese from California. What I see here, I don't like at all."

"Do you think they're diseased?"

"I haven't examined them yet. That's a sensitive matter. They'll have to disrobe."

Theo laughed heartedly. "They've probably never seen a physician in their lives and I promise you they've never seen one who's female. And you want them to take off their pants? I'm no expert on Celestials, but that's asking an awful lot."

"We haven't gotten that far. Anyone can see they're underfed. I've been talking to them through Sam Ting-nu, my interpreter."

Father grimaced, unwilling to discuss an unpleasant matter that had already overtaxed his patience. "I'm not sure that's any of *your* business, Dr. Horn. If you've come here to make trouble, I can be inhospitable and run you out of camp. Responsibility for feeding my employees belongs to the Crocker Construction Company. And anywhere above Colfax my authority is synonymous with this company."

"How do you intend to put these men to work when they haven't eaten?"

"There's plenty of food. The company has an unblemished reputation for feeding its men. You're welcome to confirm this. These newcomers will eat when they get hungry. And they'll eat what we serv'em."

"That's just the point, Theo. Their digestive systems won't tolerate camp food. Do you know the diet in China?"

"No, and frankly I'm not interested. They could eat bird feathers and sheep hooves for all I care. But they're not in China. In California they'll eat California food."

"Beef, buffalo, or venison gives them diarrhea. How can men work when they're vomiting? Diarrhea steals their strength. Surely you must know what it feels like."

"That's irrelevant because I don't refuse to eat what's available. If they try, these men will get used to our food and, as you so delicately put it, they'll stop shitting."

"Diarrhea can lead to pneumonia. White men could get infected from the Chinese, then nobody will work on your line."

"Sounds as if you're threatening, Dr. Horn. And threats don't sit well with me. Kinda juices me up for a fight, and when my juices flow I get real nasty."

"That's apparent."

"And there's an opinionated, busybody streak in you, Harriet."

She laughed aloud, sharing her amusement with the Chinese who, in order to appear polite, mimicked laughter without the slightest idea of any humor. "I won't deny it. At least we know our failings. I only ask that you talk with these people. They're not asking for the world. They only want food they can eat."

"Negotiate? With my own employees? Who do you think is running this show? I don't mollycoddle my workers. If I start with these Chinamen there will be lines a mile long at my headquarters, men asking for everything from soap to tools."

"The way I see it, you don't have any alternative. Force-feed these Chinamen food they can't digest and you'll have some pretty sick men on your hands. Maybe some dead ones. Talk with them. Use Sam Ting-nu. Go ahead. I promise not to interfere." She placed her hand on the back of his and kept it there for a long moment.

"You don't understand what it takes to manage an army of workers."

"I won't dispute that. But *your* treatment of these men is little better than their mistreatment aboard the *Japan*. You saw how the Pacific Mail Company confined them. From what I hear about you, Theo, you fought in a war to prevent the mistreatment of black slaves. Nobody's watching out for these Asiatics. Nobody, Theo."

"That's just the point. You and a few churchwomen are the only people in California who care. Do-gooders just don't understand. Chinks are doomed in this state and probably every other state in the union. Nobody wants them, including me. But I'm responsible for their presence here on the construction line. As far as I'm concerned, the sooner they return to their own country the better."

"You know as well as I do that they're not going back."

"They're on contract. When the contract ends they won't have any way to support themselves."

"China's a wretched place. What man in his right mind would return to a nation that can't feed its own people? Think about that, Theo Gallager. But before you do, think about giving these people food they can digest. No venison and hardtack. You must have some pork around.

Some cabbage or mushrooms. There have to be trout in the river. And rice."

"I asked you to mind your own business, lady," he said. "I'm running this construction company. I'm not making special provision for Chinamen. Not today and not tomorrow."

"And I'm not leaving here until you stop starving them."

"Apparently you didn't understand me, Dr. Horn. You either shut up or get out of my camp."

"And if I don't?"

"I'll throw you out, and I mean that, Harriet." He did not wait for a response and waved for two assistants to usher her from the camp.

"You wouldn't dare," she said as the two approached. "I'll report this in Sacramento. And Washington. Your head will roll."

"It'll roll anyway if I let you run this place. Out you go until you learn not to poke your beautiful nose into things that don't concern you."

"But this *does* concern me."

"It's hunger and hunger alone that makes men eat," Dad said, determined to have the final word. A signal from his hand and his assistants manhandled her from the circle. She struggled enough to convince my father of her determination to get her way. None of the Chinese, including Sam Ting-nu, rose in her defense. The moment she was outside the circle she turned back toward my father and howled, "God knows what's running in your arteries, Theo, but it isn't human blood. You're a cold, mean-spirited sonavabitch!"

He bit his lip to prevent himself from replying in kind. Harriet Horn was clearly no lady and therefore deserved no civility traditionally accorded to members of her sex. Still, something inside harnessed his anger.

The moment she was out of sight, he marched to the periphery of the circle and grabbed a pick handle from a squatting coolie. He returned to the center with it raised in his hand, threatening with a hostile swing.

Sam Ting-nu, who had remained behind to observe the proceedings, noticed that his countrymen were unimpressed by Gallager's threats. They possessed an instinct about confrontation and sensed that the superintendent was posturing. Besides, beating unarmed men with an ax handle was inconsistent with what little they had noted about Americans. Sam Ting-nu stepped beside my father and offered his advice. "Mr. Gallager, word has it that you threatened Irishmen with your pistols. If you want these coolies to respond, you'll have to use pistols. Otherwise, they'll lose face. Get yourself a gun. Then they'll listen."

"I can do all the damage I need with this pick," he replied. "Maybe more."

"This isn't a matter of blood. We're talking pride here."

That thought caused my father to pause. It didn't make much sense to him, though he had to confess he couldn't think of a better idea. "Okay," Father said to Sam Ting-nu. "Call a recess. In an hour we'll talk more about food. In the meantime, I'll get a pair of pistols from guards up the line."

On the outskirts of the camp, Harriet Horn was waiting for her translator near a supply wagon, the wind gently lifting her red hair and returning it to her head. Father tried not to notice and marched by with his eyes turned away.

"Let's talk civilly, Theo," she said, immediately marching into step with him. Her voice had lost its earlier harshness.

He stopped and let his gaze slowly focus on her, reminding himself that she had gotten between him and his job, a bad omen between a man and a woman. "I've got no time for conversation, Harriet. You came here uninvited and got my men all riled up. If I don't get matters under control I'm likely to have a major insurrection. No more talk. I'm going to get some pistols. Your little friends will listen to the logic of bullets."

"You don't intend to shoot them, do you?" she said, mixing feminine horror with a tinge of incredulity.

"Of course not. I'm just gonna threaten. Despite what you said about me, I don't shoot men for disobedience. At least, I haven't till now."

"I don't get it, Theo. Why the guns?"

"To resolve this rebellion once and for all. We've got more important things to do on this construction line than quibble over food."

"And you need guns for that?"

"According to your man, Sam, or whatever his name is, yes."

"Then take mine," she said, unhitching from her shoulder a traveling satchel and sitting it on the ground to open. Next, she leaned forward to fetch from it a large revolver with an exceptionally long twelve-inch barrel. In bending over, her blouse fell open, exposing a seductive cleavage. She appeared to take note of the exposure and did something that surprised my father. Instead of bolting up and closing her blouse, she leaned still farther forward, inviting his eyes into the deep shadows.

When she straightened up, her eyes gathered him in with a hint of conspiracy. "Return the pistol to me in San Francisco, but for heaven's sake don't shoot anybody. Incidentally, you might want to read my report to the Department of State in Washington. I brought a copy for you." She removed from her satchel an envelope and handed it to him.

"You ever shoot this revolver?" my father asked while weighing the unwieldy Emerson .44 in his hand. "Kinda big for a woman like you."

"If I can't outshoot bandits, I'd better be able to outgun them. If you were traveling alone, what weapon would you carry, Theo?"

"One like this, I suppose. But if I take this Emerson, what will you use to defend yourself on the way home?"

"My big mouth. Some say that's my wickedest weapon. I reckon all the gunfire is going to be around here. I'll slip out of camp and down to Secretown without a hitch."

A half-hour later, Dad was pointing Harriet's .44 at the Chinese laborers while they were explaining their grievances. Within the following hour, both parties had reached a preliminary compromise. The cost of food purchased from Chinese merchants in San Francisco: dried oysters and cuttlefish, bean sprouts, rice, dried shrimp, and salt pork would be subtracted from the coolies' pay. Drayage fees for hauling it up to the mountain camps remained a matter of contention until my father reluctantly conceded that the Crocker Construction Company would absorb the freight costs as far as the railhead, but wagon drayage beyond that remained the responsibility of the coolies. Chan Yue huddled with his advisors and rejected the offer.

Father lost his temper and in a moment of passion fired Harriet's revolver into the air. Little did he know that was exactly what the Chinese were expecting. They quickly added a few new foods to the existing shopping list, then agreed to have the wagon drayage docked from their weekly wages. A deal had been struck.

En route back to his headquarters at Alta, Father kept shaking his head in disbelief. He simply didn't understand these strange people. While working on the James River in Virginia, his workers had come from different parts of the country, homeless stragglers left in the ravages of the war. And there were plenty of newly freed slaves who had no concept of working for wages. The defeated Rebels, a defiant lot contemptuous of those who had whipped them on the battlefield, were the worst. But these Chinese were so utterly inscrutable as to make them wholly unfit for American life. To my father, the gulf separating Chinese and Western cultures was unbridgeable. The sooner he returned them to a ship heading for China the better it would be for everyone.

Once the Chinese were healthy enough to work, Wong's team was assigned to loading rock onto two-wheel tip carts operated by Hibernians who made it clear from the outset that they resented working with Orientals and refused to coordinate their movements with those assigned to work alongside lifting heavy rock into the carts. On the mountainsides there was little room to maneuver and when the drivers made errors they blamed the Celestials for knocking the carts off-balance. A friend of Wong's, Hoo Shuk-lin, was working near a ledge when a driver deliberately backed his cart into him. He let out a howl and struggled to keep a foothold on the narrow ledge of the embankment, beyond which was a sheer drop of over a thousand feet. Witnesses claimed the driver could have pulled his cart away to help Hoo Shuk-lin regain his balance but that he purposely stalled. Unable to scratch a toehold in the crumbling stones, Hoo tumbled over the ledge and rolled into the gorge below, kicking and thrashing to break the fall. But the angle of his descent proved too steep to prevent him from tumbling faster and faster. Somewhere along his fall Hoo's neck broke.

The driver asserted at a debriefing conducted at the headquarters camp in Alta that the dead Chinaman was hidden in a blind spot below the bed of his cart when the accident occurred. Three Chinese witnesses testified to the contrary. They claimed several white men observed what had happened but refused to tell what they clearly saw. A formal protest lodged by Wong Po-ching and Chan Yue confirmed Father's premonition about putting Chinamen on the line with Irishmen. Hoping to end the matter once and for all, he transferred the Irish driver to another position higher on the summit and issued a strong directive about safety.

Wong expected more violence against his people and organized a guard around the Chinese camp. That night, three Hibernians under the influence of whiskey smuggled from Sacramento entered the Celestials' camp to teach them who ruled the roadbed. Wong's forward lookouts caught the intruders by surprise, defending their camp with a shower of rocks. When a half-dozen more Irishmen arrived to reinforce their beleaguered countrymen, the Chinese turned a high-pressure water monitor on them. In the ensuing battle, Wong's followers struck steel rails together to produce an ear-shattering sound. The darkness conspired to confuse the marauders, who judiciously withdrew to fight their enemies under more favorable conditions. But that night a Hibernian failed to return to his camp. In the morning, his compatriots saw turkey vultures circling the American River canyon and sent out a search party. Though no body was ever discovered, the Irishmen concluded that the Chinese had resorted to murder. What began as a mere skirmish ended in a declaration of war.

Wong doubled his guard. A day later, five Irish and Scandinavian blasters stole into the Chinese camp and buried a fifty-pound keg of black powder under a tent. After midnight, they returned to ignite the fuse. Explosions were common in the mountains, but not in the wee hours of the morning. The blast annihilated the tent and killed four sleeping coolies. The remainder fled to the forest in terror.

By dawn Dad was at the Chinese camp, alarmed but not surprised by what had transpired. He had repeatedly warned Charley Crocker that something like this would happen. If the coolies were not removed from the line immediately, escalating violence was inevitable. That morning he gave a speech before the Irish laborers near the reconstructed trestle at Long Barn, which sounded to them like old-fashioned blarney, because they reasoned that Dad shared their Caucasian hearts and could not possibly side with the Celestials. Surely he must regard the counterattack on the coolies as justified. After all, was it not the Chinese who had started this fight? They just got what they deserved.

A wiry, muscular man with heavy muttonchops on his jowls spoke for the Caucasians in a County Cork brogue, stating they did not want to work beside Celestials. If the Crocker Construction Company insisted on forcing them to work together, his cohorts would go on strike. My father loathed being threatened, but he had to acknowledge the leverage his white workers possessed. A labor strike would defeat his plan to lay twenty-one miles of track before the first snowfall and force a complete shutdown of operations at higher altitudes. To make it to the summit before winter without a Caucasian workforce seemed impossible. Still, he had to admire how his little Asians had stood up to the larger and more numerous Europeans. If nothing else, they had debunked the myth about Chinese obsequiousness. Yet laying track was paramount; mediating between hostile nationalities had to be a secondary concern.

Dad intended to put these facts directly to Crocker, Stanford, and Hopkins when they made their monthly inspection of the track the following Saturday. He knew them to be pragmatic businessmen. In the face of this labor turmoil, Crocker would have to admit that his plan to use Chinese on the rail line was a failure. There was simply no other way of looking at it.

Wong was among the Chinese delegated to make another appeal for justice. Knowing only a few phrases in the white man's tongue, he listened to Chan Yue speak pidgin English. "China man not safe. Ireland man usee powder again. China man stopee him quick."

My father hated how these Celestials butchered his language. Distracted by all the discord, he failed to grasp the implications of Chan Yue's words. If he had, he would have heard not just the fractured grammar but a wail of desperation. At the very moment when he should have been responding to the agony of these foreigners, he was thinking about what he would tell Crocker, Stanford, and Hopkins. From the moment they had arrived in the mountains the Chinese had upset his construction schedule. If it wasn't one thing, it was another. Their problems had begun to consume not only his workday, but those of his operational foremen. Instead of building a railroad, his senior engineers found themselves playing nursemaid to a bunch of unappreciative and intractable Asian children.

That very evening, the entire Chinese camp pulled up stakes and silently marched through the forest to a higher elevation, only a half-mile above the campsite where the Irishmen were settling in for the night. Sixteen Celestials marched confidently toward the Irish tents and, on a bluff beyond the camp, lit small fires, which brought the Irishmen out to have a look. Damned if there wasn't a troop of little Chinks in their blue tunics and baggy pantaloons, speaking tones the Hibernians couldn't pronounce, squatting on the ground and boiling water for tea! What was this? Bravado? Or just peasant stupidity? More Irish arrived to observe their uninvited guests with considerable wonderment, thinking that the little runts had wandered into the lion's den like a flock of unwary sheep. The Europeans rapidly came to a consensus about how to exploit this windfall. The time had come to rid the Crocker Construction Company of these Celestials once and for all.

The Chinese continued to squat, chattering among themselves in Cantonese and leisurely sipping from small crockery cups while their enemies formed a vanguard armed with picks and shovels. And, of course, a few Winchesters. The smallest Irishman, a man the others called O'Shannery, brandished a pickax over his head and invited the little imps from Asia to fight out their differences like self-respecting men. When the Chinese paid no attention, O'Shannery taunted them with a combination of catcalls and lewd gestures. Still the coolies appeared unflappable in their slow enjoyment of the tea. Occasionally one would angle his head politely toward a tormentor and smile. Even crude insults about their mothers' vaginas failed to stir a response. Cowards! Sneaks! Vermin! Why wouldn't they come forward to defend their honor and that of their parents?

Then suddenly all hell broke loose. The tent for storing the Hibernians' food exploded with a deafening blast. Flames shot skyward, illuminating the camp. Men in the front ranks, imagining long days without meals, dashed back for sand and water to quell the flames. But as they organized their response, the scope of the disaster spread. A sleeping tent nearest the storage facility also exploded, with bedding and personal effects flying into the air. A series of agonized groans punctuated the pandemonium. Someone near the fires cried out that there was a trail of black powder burning toward still another tent, sending firefighters into the blackness to stomp on this fuse with their boots. But just as the trail appeared to be smothered out, another secondary fuse glowed in the dark, this one simultaneously forking in several directions. Buckets of sand arrived too late. Those trying to stop the proliferating number of sizzling fuses abandoned the second sleeping tent only moments before the explosive detonated. More bedding rained down on men working to put out the flames.

The camp was suddenly aglow with a network of fuses. The more the Irishmen tried to prevent additional explosions, the more they found themselves misled by a cunning arsonist. Trails of powder crisscrossed each other, some fizzling out harmlessly and others igniting new fuses. In the dark there was no way of telling which were duds and which were real. A tent near the remains of the first explosion remained intact, but the third, fourth, and fifth succumbed to flames. The sixth tent set off fuses that ultimately blew up the ninth and tenth.

As the volatile web of explosions expanded, the entire camp came under fire. Tent by tent men trying to put out the fires were forced to retreat or risk personal injury. Just when they thought they might have succeeded in saving a tent it was detonated from a fuse they hadn't figured on. In the end, the Irishmen managed to save only three of twenty-six tents.

When the attack had run its course, the Irishmen focused their attention on the origin of the conflagration. No one doubted who was responsible, or why the troop of Celestials had planted themselves on the bluff overlooking their camp. O'Shannery led an assault on the position where the Chinese had been squatting. But by the time he and his men arrived, they found only the small fires the Celestials had used to boil water for their tea.

Within minutes, hordes of hysterical workmen were running down the track toward the Chinese camp, excited by the thought of exacting revenge. All they needed to turn a flogging into a bloodbath was what the Chinks had just done. But somehow in their anger the Europeans had missed the Chinamen's camp. Or gotten lost in the dark. Had they overrun it? Or lost their directions? Arguments broke out. A group headed farther down the track where they were sure the Chinese had encamped. Another gang hunted for their prey in the nearby forest, groping and stumbling in the tangles of dead-fall pines. Slowly, their leaders came to realize that for the time being their Chinese enemies had gotten the better of them. Not only had they decamped, but they had run off and were hiding somewhere in the darkness. The moment of reckoning would have to wait until sunrise.

Back in the demolished camp, cries for revenge rose throughout the night. Of the three tents that survived, one housed the store of whiskey, allowing the victims to drink away their humiliation. In various states of inebriation, no one wondered if the survival of the whiskey tent was coincidental or part of the Chinese plan. The vows of the drunkards proved to be even bloodier than those of the few still sober. Sierra streams would run with blood. Not one Chink would return to Frisco, much less his homeland.

Meanwhile the troop of Chinese had reassembled within earshot of the ravaged camp. Chan Yue translated any words he could make out. This time they avoided lighting fires that might reveal their position. Though their tea was cold, they were warmed by the elation of victory.

On Saturday morning Father found his European laborers sleeping off the effects of the night's drinking. Those he awoke were in no condition for work. This situation couldn't have come at a worse time since Charles Crocker, Leland Stanford, and Mark Hopkins were scheduled to arrive at the railhead before noon and proceed immediately by wagon to the construction zone. There was no way Dad could hide the obvious, nor did he wish to. The full responsibility for this fiasco lay with Crocker and his fantasy about a Chinese labor force. In my father's mind, Charles Crocker was on the hot seat, not him.

Still, sinister thoughts crept into his mind. Whenever and for whatever reason construction slowed, the Central Pacific moguls had a habit of drawing blood from the reigning superintendent. Though this mess was Big Charley's fault, my father believed that his tenure as construction super had most certainly come to an end.

The coolies alone showed up for work. They loaded the tipcarts with blasted rock, but there were no drivers. In frustration, Father allowed some to mount the wagons and drive the mules. To his surprise, the new drivers handled the animals and machinery with admirable skill. By midmorning, the workflow began to pick up. Rumor spread through the Irish camp that the sonavabitch Gallager was firing all white men and assigning Chinks to do their jobs. A few Irish, their heads aching with hangover, reported for work, too weary and too sick to protest their predicament. When the Central Pacific owners and their accompanying wives arrived at Cape Horn shortly after lunch, work had almost been restored to normal.

Leland Stanford was shocked at the sight of Chinese driving the tipcarts and wagons because his partner had never gotten around to telling him about the experiment with Chinese labor. Given Ex-Governor Stanford's outspoken political tirades against the Chinese presence in California, it was clear why. Not that Crocker ever took a politician's public bluster seriously. In his view the governor didn't give a hoot about the Chinese, but fashioned his public speeches to curry favor with voters. That meant that if using Asian labor expedited the building of his railroad, he'd be the first to press for importing more coolies.

A meeting in Theo's headquarters tent was tense and acrimonious. Stanford accused Crocker of making major decisions behind his and Hopkins's back. Crocker absorbed the governor's accusations with the self-assurance of a man who had bet heavily at the racetrack and won.

The deception meant little as long as his experiment succeeded and, from Dad's preliminary report, the coolies appeared to work quite well.

Even the stolid, usually poker-faced Hopkins joined in the laughter when he learned how the Chinese had taken revenge on their enemies. Father had apparently underestimated their ingenuity, for whoever had laid out the grid of fuses knew a helluva lot about black powder, to say nothing about the mentality of the white workmen. The penny-wise Hopkins insisted that the coolies be docked for damages to the company's property. A new debate erupted in which Crocker argued so forcefully for his Chinese pets that Dad suspected his motives.

Out of earshot of the others, Crocker told my father that before sharing important new plans with his partners, he had wanted to make a thorough inspection of the construction sites. No, it wasn't a lack of trust in his superintendent, but, yes, he did want to see for himself how things were working out. Crocker gave my father one of his patronizing pats on the shoulder, signaling that in good time he'd know what new plans he had in mind.

Wong first set eyes on the three railroad owners when they arrived by carriage on Saturday to inspect the roadbed, four miles east of the railhead. He maneuvered his tipcart as close as he dared without drawing their attention and watched the legendary tycoons with no little wonderment, asking himself what kind of men wielded power in Gum San. In the Celestial Kingdom, emperors and warlords governed, but here in the mountains he failed to see any uniforms or government officials. Decisions seemed to be left to distant, powerful businessmen. Based on his limited experience in China, Wong was puzzled about how a man like *Meester Crocker* had become so powerful. In his homeland a man followed in the footsteps of his father. Farmers of the land raised their sons to be farmers, and shopkeepers made their sons shopkeepers in turn.

The largest of the three tycoons, the one the Irish called *Stan...ford* possessed an imposing physical stature. To Wong this was what a powerful railroad mogul should look like. He traveled with a sizable retinue of advisors, engineers, and personal secretaries. Rumor circulated in camp that he didn't trust his business partners and brought experts along to verify everything that was reported to him. As Wong approached, he found the railroad tycoons less regal than he had expected. Their dress was uniformly black and undistinguished, no gold buttons, medals, emblems, or gilded swords, though their heavily powdered women were expensively attired in colorful silks and with sparkling jewelry. Stanford and Crocker were heavyset; Hopkins lean. Though Wong accepted them as men of enormous power and wealth, he sensed in their cautious footsteps a certain vulnerability. From a distance, they seemed dependent on others to explain the construction process.

Crocker kept tugging at his fantail whiskers and gesticulating. His partners were talking all at once and nobody appeared to be listening. My father pointed repeatedly at the mountainside while speaking with great force. Wong guessed that the superintendent was describing the difficult terrain where, 1,400 feet above the American River, there was little or no room to maneuver machinery. In order to level a roadbed you had to blast away a platform. But the siding was solid granite and only triple charges of black powder were powerful enough to dislodge it. Each time the blasters exploded their charges; fresh rubble tumbled down onto the newly cleared roadbed, doubling the work. Levelers found themselves repeatedly clearing the same site. Progress was measured in feet rather than miles.

At sundown, Wong was among the last to unhitch his mule so it could feed on thin grass beside the roadbed. It was half past eight and the summer sun hung on the cusp of the horizon, leaving residual warmth from the day's heat in its descent. His attention was distracted by the figure of a tall man marching purposefully past him toward the mountainside where the blasters had stopped for the night. By this hour, other workmen were settling into their camps in anticipation of dinner. Their supervisors had left on horseback seeking relaxation in one of Dutch Flat's three saloons and four brothels. Wong asked himself why anyone would return to the mountain at that hour. To satisfy his curiosity, he followed, keeping out of sight. The man appeared to be gazing out over the valley, lost in thought.

At first Wong didn't recognize my father. In the past, Dad's head had always been covered by an army hat. But now that the sun had gone down, he was bareheaded. As Wong drew nearer, he spied my father standing as though conversing with the mountain. To Wong, who grew up in a world where animate and inanimate things commingled, this did not seem strange. In China, men talked incessantly to gods that presented themselves in tangible forms. As Dad's English syllables collided into one another, it sounded as if he were voicing anger with the mountain. That did not seem unreasonable to Wong because the granite was impeding the railroad's progress.

Wong suddenly sensed that this was a private matter between the superintendent and the mountain god. Good manners required him to retreat immediately, but in making his escape his lead foot sent a rock careening against another with a sharp crack.

My father whirled around and caught him in the act of back-stepping. "Who's there?" he barked with a mixture of alarm and consternation.

"Wong. Mee, Wong," Wong said, even his own name sticking to his tongue.

Dad stepped quickly in the Chinaman's direction. To him all Chinese workmen looked pretty much alike. But the man who had caused trouble aboard the *Japan* he knew by sight. "You overheard me?" he asked with a tinge of shame.

"Coolie Wong."

"I don't care if you did, Wong. Everybody knows these goddamn mountains. Just wait till the Union Pacific comes barreling up the eastern escarpment. Its progress will stop here too. You remember this, Wong. If I can't get through these mountains, the Union Pacific won't either. So right here's where the great Pacific Railroad dies. There isn't going to be a transcontinental railroad. Neither the Central Pacific nor the Union Pacific's gonna meet up, at least not in these parts. Maybe south in Mexico, but not in the Sierra." My father paused to consider Wong's hand gesture. "You understand what I'm telling you? *Tu sabes? Comprendes, si?* No? Yes?"

Wong shook his head. "Noee. Noee."

"But you do understand these mountains, don't you? I think you understand a helluva lot more than you let on. God made these mountains strong so we couldn't blast through them. You understand that, don't you?" Wong didn't try to answer. Rather, he studied the image of my father. In the fading light his stature appeared diminished. His commanding voice had given way to defeat. Wong understood enough to know that in winter work on the roadbed would cease altogether. He also knew that the Irishmen talked about blizzards as early as the end of summer. Early snows this year would further delay progress.

"So you've come to California for nothing," Dad bellowed, aware that the Chinaman was unable to understand. "Nothing. Nothing. None of you runts will see this railroad completed. We'll ship you back to China. And you can tell your grandchildren how you once worked on a roadbed that was never finished. The company went broke. Its superintendent went off to build lumber roads. And you can tell them that you worked for a dumb engineer who couldn't beat these goddamn mountains."

"Gold Mountain," Wong ventured to repeat the English phrase. "*Gum san,* old gold mountain." He bowed his head. More English phrases came to mind but none held coherently together. In the Celestial Kingdom mountains were barriers against foreign invasion, walls behind which peasants could work in safety. But in Gum San they were obstacles to be scaled, conquered, and traversed.

Wong bowed again and inched backward. He left my father standing in the darkness and returned to his tipcart. After stabling his mule in a makeshift corral, he walked back to the Chinese camp. By now the twilight had given way to darkness, the time when other workers ate, rested, and washed or repaired their clothing. Some coolies conversed about walking along the roadbed to Dutch Flat where, rumor had it, a brothel had been built for Celestials.

"How could that be?" Ying San-li asked. "As far as we know, we're the only Chinamen working on this railroad. Who would bring girls for so few customers, unless the white men like them too?"

"Oh, no, no," Hui Chow responded. Everybody knew he was a man with more imagination than wits. "In Dutch Flat are Chinese girls from Formosa. Singsong women from Frisco. Let's sneak out of camp to see."

"And what will you pay with?" Wong said, expressing his irritation with the naiveté of his compatriots. "Nobody here has received a single dollar for months. Our wages go to the Yung Wo Company in Frisco. Do you think these dream girls will let you poke them for nothing?"

Ying San-li laughed, saying, "If they don't exist, what's the difference how much they cost?"

The entire band enjoyed the humor. Wong was right. It didn't make any sense that there were Chinese girls in Dutch Flat. But someday they would come and someday his fellow workmen would have money to pay them. In their loins, they all felt the urge for women. When they had signed up to come to Gum San nobody had given much thought to such yearnings. But now that they were far from the Celestial Kingdom and there were no native girls, they knew how to handle themselves. There was no privacy in the tents, so masturbating occurred in front of coolie brethren. Everyone did it, just as everyone peed and everybody shit. Only they took special care not to do it where white men could see and make fun of them.

While his comrades drew out their evening meal chattering about their impressions of America, Wong tramped back along the rails to see the private sleeping cars that had brought the company owners and their wives to Long Ravine Bridge. His fellow Chinese often accused Wong of having cat's eyes to see in the dark. It wasn't quite like that, but there was something in his eyesight that magnified light, and following the rails, even without moonlight, proved easy for him. At Long Ravine, he found two Pullman cars parked on a spur.

The railroad owner called Hopkins, Wong later learned, seldom traveled far from his home in Sacramento and therefore did not possess his own railcar. This evening he and his wife slept in a Central Pacific car attached to Stanford's. There were lights in all of them, but shades were drawn over the windows. Wong strained to hear voices inside but without success. The smell of broiled beef escaped from the galley vents, and occasionally servants would appear on the platforms scraping dinner scraps onto the shoulder. Wong wondered what food was being discarded and regretted having missed dinner in the Chinese camp. There would be nothing until breakfast.

An hour later, when the servants retired to another car farther down the track, Wong saw a huge man appear on the platform of the largest Pullman, the man they called Stanford. Smoke from his cigar passed over the clearing toward Wong. After pacing back and forth on the tiny platform, the ex-governor descended the stairs and marched alongside the railroad cars. He stopped, faced the wheels of the Pullman assigned to carry Hopkins and his wife, and unhitched his trousers to relieve himself.

Wong listened to a light stream ricochet off the steel. "Big man, weak pee," Wong thought to himself. Stanford's heavy steps on the crushed rock siding punctuated the night's silence. Near his own car he halted, squinting in the darkness to make out the dim silhouette of a man. Wong inched forward into full view, unable to manage simple English words of greeting. A long moment of silence became uncomfortable.

Stanford cleared his throat. "Hello," he said, his voice uncertain.

"Her-oo," Wong repeated, and quickly rehearsed a supplementary English phrase, but Stanford was too swift. The railroad owner spun around and retreated toward the Pullman steps. At the last moment he dropped his smoldering cigar and ground it into the gravel beneath his feet.

A moment later a lock clicked shut on the Pullman door. The final sound was that of a security chain thrown over the latch.

Sunday morning Wong was up at dawn while his compatriots were still lying on their cots, enjoying Sabbath rest. He felt that he had spent the evening profitably but he wasn't sure why. Meeting my father and Leland Stanford had inspired him. While it was still dark, he moved forward along the line to Cape Horn. The Hibernians had left their tipcarts and machinery where they were last used. Piles of shovels and barrels of black powder were stacked nearby. Only the mules and oxen had been moved to the rear. Monday would arrive soon enough and men would return to their toil.

At first light, Wong climbed forward over granite slabs that blocked the line. Below, a thin thread of blue-green and white water snaked through the gorge cut by the American River. Above, individual digger and sugar pines clung to the stone face of the mountain. In the distance there was a solid forest of tamaracks and maples, interspersed by thickets of manzanita and chaparral. His eyes scanned the terrain surveyors had marked with whitewash for the future roadbed. When it became impossible to move forward, he climbed some three hundred feet higher and peered down on the end of the construction site. From this bird's-eye view, it was possible to calculate the enormous tonnage of rock that needed to be removed. Everyone agreed on the use of black powder, but the current method of setting charges ahead of the levelers failed to take advantage of gravity to get rid of the rubble. The terrain brought to Wong's mind stories he had heard around his family's hearth before his hamlet was ransacked and destroyed.

Though he had never personally seen the Yangtze gorges in Szechwan Province, in the army he had spoken with Hakkas who had. They told stories about how engineers had cut roads through the granite by staging a novel attack on the hard rock. To maximize the power of their explosives, blasters were lowered over the cliffs in wicker baskets. From these gondolas, blasters then drilled powder holes at the weakest points in the mountainside with steel mauls, eventually packing them with charges. Once the charges were set, the gondolas were winched back up the mountainside and the long fuses ignited. Debris from the explosions tumbled down the mountainsides instead of remaining on the roadbed to be cleared by levelers.

It occurred to Wong that if such stories were true, there was no reason why the same method wouldn't work on the mountainside below. And if such tales were not true, what difference did it make? The concept still had merit. And the more he thought about it, the better he liked the idea. He felt confident it would work but didn't know how to communicate that to the men who supervised the construction. For help he planned to consult his comrades.

What Wong didn't know was that the opportunity would present itself far sooner than he expected. He never intended to speak directly with the railroad owners and he certainly didn't believe he commanded sufficient vocabulary. But as he was descending from the ridge, Crocker, Hopkins, and Stanford, along with their wives, architects, surveyors, and a coterie of advisors and secretaries, were standing at the end of the level roadbed, not far from where my father had lashed out against the mountain the previous evening. To the rear, a gaggle of personal valets and servants waited to tend to their patrons' needs for water, tobacco, or spirits. Someone in the forward group saw Wong descending toward them and drew the attention of the others. All were curious who was climbing on the face of the gorge like a mountain goat. As it turned out, there was no place for Wong to jump down onto the roadbed except directly in view of everyone.

"Mee, Shit. Mee, Shit," he announced to refresh my father's memory, bowing so that his pigtail flopped over his head and swung like a pendulum. Standing tall, he pointed to his chest. "Mee, Shit."

Dad's face was flushed with anger and embarrassment. This Chinaman possessed a talent for appearing at the most inconvenient times. And who did he think he was by stealing the attention of such important dignitaries?

Jane Stanford, who was always playing the role of the governor's wife even when her husband was no longer an active governor, cocked her head to one side and let her eyes rest on her husband for an appropriate response. But the governor, who was never known for quick repartee, deferred to my father.

Mary Crocker, who never took herself for anything loftier than an astute shopkeeper's wife, was the first to recover from shock and laughed aloud, which had a contagious effect on the others. Her gesture encouraged Wong to bow again, saying, "Mee, Shit."

Hopkins turned on Father, demanding to know how this Chinaman carried such an unmentionable name. That put Dad in an awkward position because he was certain Charley Crocker had failed to inform his partners about how Chinese laborers were hired by the Crocker Construction Company. A furtive glance at Crocker confirmed this suspicion. Misrepresenting the truth was not Dad's first choice, yet he quickly realized that Hopkin's question was prompted more by a quest for entertainment than for information. Instead of being dragged into revealing the details of his visit to the *Japan* in San Francisco Bay, Dad replied, "I have no idea what this chap is talking about. I assume he's just picked up camp lingo."

Stanford's and Crocker's staffs, which had remained behind on the roadbed, were not privy to the short exchange with Wong Po-ching. While the CP owners were consulting about the progress or lack of it, their staffs argued over the unfortunate selection of routes for the Pacific Railroad six years before by Theodore Judah. Not that anyone had an alternative through the Sierra or that the Central Pacific Railroad could afford to make a change. It had already committed the lion's share of its financial resources to the Donner Pass and, as Comptroller Mark Hopkins kept insisting, the larder was absolutely empty. Some creative accounting had kept the railroad's creditors from learning the full truth, and additional subsidies that Collis Huntington had promised to extract from the federal treasury had failed to materialize. It was only a question of time before their enterprise would have to cease operations altogether.

Wong interrupted just as bickering among the staffs filtered forward to the owners. He pointed to the granite above the roadbed. "Meester Gallag'r, blassee there. Vary, vary hard."

That much everybody already knew. Jane Stanford huffed impatiently. What could one expect from a Chinaman with such a disgusting name?

Wong was undeterred. He spoke with a combination of gesture and mispronounced words. Stanford wanted him sent back to camp, but Crocker wouldn't hear of it. Instead he stepped forward and made sweeping gestures with his arms, a signal to his personal servant, Chiang Teh, who was smoking in the rear with other valets. When Chiang drew near, Crocker ordered him to translate Wong's words. The two Asians immediately established that they spoke different Chinese dialects. Nevertheless, Chiang, who conversed with Chinese from different parts of China in San Francisco, managed to translate a fair share of Wong's meaning.

Wong's plan was not complex. Along the Yangtze gorges in China, men were lowered over similar inclines in wicker baskets to plant black powder in the granite. They were then hauled back to the top and the fuses lit. It had been accomplished in China, why not in Gum San?

The idea was novel yet ingenious. No CP planners or engineers had ever suggested lowering blasters over the ridges, probably because they judged such an operation implausible. Or too dangerous? Who the hell was foolish enough to try? The thought of putting a hundred and fifty to two hundred-pound man over the side in a basket then hauling him back up hadn't been thought of. But a hundred-pound coolie, why that was another story!

Stanford, who always entertained the possibility of riding his railroad into the U.S. Senate and possibly the White House, ridiculed Wong's proposal. He had long identified Crocker as a Sinophile. Putting a troop of coolies on the construction line was just the beginning. No doubt he had plans to import more. Early in his campaign for governor, he had eschewed allowing members of that "degenerate nation" to enter California and compete in the white labor market. That position won the workers' vote. Stanford considered himself an astute judge of men, and there was no doubt in his mind that the California electorate would not tolerate a wave of Chinese workers in the state. Using Chinamen to plant powder charges was not only patently impractical but offensive to the sensibilities of fellow Californians.

Crocker had long since learned not to debate openly with his pompous partner who, he believed, possessed a visceral dislike for facts and an incorrigible appetite for political power.

Wong punctuated his show-and-tell narrative with staccato phrases, disconnected and studded with linguistic and technical errors, yet surprisingly clear.

It was Crocker who finally indicated that he was taking this Chinaman for more than Sunday morning entertainment. Through Chiang Teh, he posed several questions. Could coolies who had been trained for nothing but leveling rock handle explosives? Would any of them volunteer to go over the side in baskets? What type of fuses did he have in mind?

"Mee cannon man. Wong cannon man. Usee much powder. Makee boom, boom," Wong repeated, painfully aware that his English sounded different from the others. Too many *ees*. Not enough full phrases. Still, he made his point through Chiang Teh that his countrymen could handle powder and, under the right conditions, do it well.

What kind of baskets would be needed?

Made from wicker reeds.

How would they select the blasters? Wong smiled. "More dollar. Chinaman workee good more dollar."

Hopkins frowned at the thought of someone, least of all a Chinaman, extorting his company for higher wages. He was prepared to resist setting that precedent at all costs.

"How many men would we need?" Crocker began calculating the actual cost aloud.

Stanford protested the loss of time. Since he categorically ruled out hiring more Chinese, there was no point continuing this train of thought. The Central Pacific Railroad would not employ a single new Chinaman, not as a leveler and not as a tipcart driver, not as a blaster in wicker baskets or any other conveyance!

"Of course not," Crocker said quickly switching from Wong to address my father, "at least not without a thorough study by the superintendent's staff. My construction company can't risk endangering the lives of its employees. What this man has just proposed is no more than an idea. It could be based on a fairy tale his parents heard in China. But since none of us purports to be an expert in such matters, it's prudent to let our engineers resolve the subject. No doubt we'll find our initial judgments vindicated. If this man's plan, yes, a man with the name of *Shit*, were practicable, we most certainly would have done it long ago. Now, isn't that so, Leland?"

Stanford knew he was being patronized. He grunted his concurrence under duress.

My father was gratified that his employers were deferring to him. He dismissed Wong and, as soon as the Chinaman was out of sight, he steered the conversation back to where it had been before being interrupted. They were talking about the need for more mules and oxen. Crocker deflected the question and reintroduced Wong's proposal. Stanford refused even to consider the broad outline of the plan. Hopkins reminded everyone that it really didn't matter one way or the other.

As soon as their creditors learned the truth about the CP's finances, they'd shut down the operation. Whether blasters went over the side in baskets or jumped into the American River buck naked was immaterial.

After the group dispersed, Crocker invited Father to his Pullman. There he asked him in confidence whether the Chinaman's scheme had even a remote chance of success. *Remote* was as far as my father would commit himself. Without more men, the Crocker Construction Company didn't have the manpower to make it to high altitudes that season.

Crocker took a shot of brandy from his pocket flask and passed it on to Father for a snort. "Let's drink to the Chinamen on Cape Horn," he toasted.

"What Chinamen?" Dad asked.

"Those on the high seas right now. I've ordered the Yung Wo Company to procure a thousand more of these boys from Canton. They'll start arriving in San Francisco in about two weeks."

Dad shot a suspicious glance at his employer. So that was his secret! All along he planned to import more Celestials. "Do your partners agree?"

"Agree? You've got to be kidding, Theo! They can't agree on what to eat for breakfast. I never took the idea to Leland or Mark. Collis is in the East and therefore out of the picture. It's one of those issues, Theo, that if you have to ask, the answer is always no. So why ask?"

"You know these new Chinamen will work up here?"

"No, I don't. But so far I've been right. Why doubt my intuition now?"

"You're not taking this fellow Wong seriously, are you?" Crocker beamed while stroking his fantail whiskers. "Very seriously."

"Well, I'm telling you it won't work. Sounds reasonable, but it won't pan out in practice. There're just too many imponderables."

"Make them ponderables, Theo. I'm ordering you to give it a try."

"Your partners won't approve."

"I'm not asking them. By the time they get word about what we're doing up here we'll have the grade along Cape Horn leveled. They never argue with success. Leland will eat his words about the Chinese. The only thing he wants more than support of his precious voters is profit from his railroad. As far as I can see, this is the only chance he's got."

Father handed the brandy flask back. "What if I won't do it and quit?" Crocker took a long swig and let the flask linger on his lips. "Quit? Not you, Theo. My guess is that this railroad means as much to you as it does to Leland. It's your chance to be somebody. I don't believe Theo Gallager would throw that opportunity away. Our Chinaman has just shown us how to do it. And deep down you know he's right."

"You're sure I won't pack it in?"

"Absolutely."

"Think you know a lot about me, don't you?"

"No, Theo. Truth is you're a mystery and that's why I like you. I don't respect men I understand."

My father took that as the concluding remark. He didn't quit on the spot. But he also didn't accept Wong's plan. He left both options open for further consideration. If he wasn't on the job in the morning, Big Charley would know he was a bad judge of character.

CHAPTER FOUR

Cape Horn

W ong's cunning infuriated my father. In addition to the normal characteristics generally ascribed to Celestials, Dad felt he was devious, inscrutable, mysterious, and untrustworthy. But worst of all, Wong was cunning. First he had tempted Charley Crocker with his idea of sending Chinese blasters over the mountainside in baskets and then, when the railroad owner had committed himself to the project, led his countrymen on a labor strike. Such demands particularly infuriated the CP owners because eighty percent of the Chinese working in the Sierra foothills, including Wong Po-ching, were on indentured contracts and their wages were sent directly to the Yung Wo Company in San Francisco, which in addition to organizing the workers' transportation to California also functioned as a fraternal organization overseeing their general welfare once settled into new jobs. Technically, whatever wages they earned didn't belong to them anyway. So the strike wasn't really about these contract workers, but about the veteran twenty percent who had already worked off the cost of their indenture.

Mark Hopkins got on the telegraph wire. How dare Wong lead men into refusing work at the prevailing wage! And who the hell did this runt think he was? Dad received a confidential message from the Central Pacific treasurer.

TAKE CARE OF THE PUNK STOP MH

It wasn't like the impecunious treasurer of the Central Pacific to venture far from his account books, yet the striking Chinese seriously imperiled the already precarious financial condition of his company and he wasn't beyond taking serious measures to save it. How carefully he had chosen his words; the message gave my father a wide range of options, without actually ordering the use of violence. Still, railroad officers appreciated that accidents often happened during the operation of heavy construction equipment. Yet assassination was not Dad's way of handling his problem. To his mind, Hopkins didn't appreciate how things worked in the field. Wong had become a clan leader, and making him into a martyr wasn't the way to break a strike.

The Chinaman's terms for ending the dispute were quite simple. Nothing short of equity with Caucasian laborers. His countrymen who did the same tasks as the Caucasians should be equally compensated at twelve dollars a month. Those who exposed themselves to the additional dangers and volunteered to become sappers working out of wicker gondolas were entitled to an extra eight dollars per month hazard pay. Father had earlier extracted a significant concession from the Chinese regarding the cost of bringing special food to the work camp. The company paid the full cost of hauling white workmen's food to the roadbed while the Chinese had to pay a portion of the drayage for their food. That relatively small concession gave Charles Crocker leverage in arguing with Stanford and Hopkins. As long as the Chinese didn't press for *absolute* parity with the white laborers, Crocker was prepared to bring Chinese wages up to match those of the white workers. It was his considered opinion that the company ought to settle quickly before Wong and his cohorts realized they had been taken.

Stanford was adamant about not knuckling under. In the company boardroom he played the pope preaching a repetitive sermon. In California, anti-Chinese sentiment was a disease on the verge of becoming an epidemic. True, Crocker's construction company had kept the price of labor down by importing cheaper Chinese contract workers, but that was bound to backfire. Once nosey newspapermen spread the story of negotiations between the CP and their Chinese employees, all hell would break out. The brief honeymoon enjoyed by the CP up until now was nearing an end. Soon it would become impossible to recruit new white laborers to work on the roadbed. Europeans would never accept the same pay as their Chinese competitors. No one with an eye on the presidency of the United States could afford to overlook this elementary fact.

In a moment when he was overwrought with bleak premonitions about his railroad's future, Mark Hopkins inadvertently leaked the Central Pacific's dilemma to the press. To a reporter's question about

Chinese demands for higher wages, he snapped in resentment, "You gotta understand that it's not the policy of my company to respond to demands from foreigners. That's usually done with labor contractors. But in this case, the Chinks up there in the mountains got me by the balls and are squeezing the living juices out of 'em."

Aggressive newsmen cross-examined Crocker on statements made by Hopkins. Crocker replied, "What your papers have said about Mr. Hopkins is both wrongly attributed and false in fact. The quote from Mark is absolutely spurious."

"How can you be so certain, Mr. Crocker?" a young reporter from St. Louis dogged the railroad owner.

Crocker guffawed raucously, until his laugh turned into a hacking cough that wouldn't stop. When he finally recovered, he said in between deep breaths, "Because, because Mark's balls haven't functioned for years."

Hoopla in the press forced the three recalcitrant partners to grudgingly give in to the striking Chinamen. Hopkins had, after all, captured the truth with his indelicate imagery. The Central Pacific was in no position to quibble with a relatively small number of Chinese laborers over extra pay. What none of the partners realized at the time was that the agreement elevated Wong in his compatriots' eyes to equal authority with Chan Yue as clan leader. If Stanford, who considered himself a practical businessman, had to eat crow in order to get what he wanted, he would. But not without thoughts of extracting vengeance. From the very beginning, he had believed that Crocker was wrong by importing Chinamen and allowing construction to become dependent on them. As a California politician, he believed his partner had underestimated the hatred toward these Celestials and the power of public opinion. It was only a matter of time before aggrieved Caucasian workers would vent their hostility on the Asiatics, and he didn't want his railroad in the middle of that fight.

As Wong's project at Cape Horn took shape, my father's doubts increased. Chinese laborers in navy-blue dungarees and black leather boots had hacked a narrow path along the high ridge above the roadbed, several hundred feet higher than where Wong had stood before descending upon the railroad owners and their wives during their tour of the construction site. Over this new path they hauled all the necessary equipment: wicker gondolas, wooden hoists, spools upon spools of hemp rope, barrels of black powder, and a vast assortment of chisels, hammers, and picks. Lastly they brought water, food, and tarps for shade. Compared to the heavy construction equipment on the roadbed below, the jerrybuilt machinery on the high ridge looked like children's toys.

From the beginning there were problems with supplies gathered in local markets. Halyards woven from hemp were certain to fray and possibly break when they rubbed against sharp rock on the mountainside. Wicker from the Sacramento Valley was strong enough for weaving birdcages, but proved to be too weak for weaving gondolas to hold men, even the light bodies of Chinese workmen. And to make matters worse, feuding broke out among the Chinese themselves. Those on the ridge looked up to Wong as their leader, while those working the grade below remained loyal to Chan Yue. Rumor had it that rival tongs were preparing to battle for supremacy. Dad had learned the power of bribes in Chinese culture, but this time they didn't work. He was unable to learn where and when this confrontation would occur.

Not surprisingly, a series of mysterious accidents impeded progress on the ridge. Fire burned a hoist that fell onto a store of black powder. This, in turn, exploded in a dazzling display of nighttime pyrotechnics. Batches of hand tools rolled off the precipice and tumbled into the ravine below. Feed for the mules was spiked with poison; fifteen died and over a hundred were so sick they were unable to work. Oxen could be substituted for mules in open areas, but in a confined space along the mountainside they couldn't be turned as easily as the mules. Wong conceded that Chan Yue's followers were jealous of the extra pay his men were getting but he ruled out the possibility that his rivals would sabotage Central Pacific property. In China rivalries were common, but in their feuding it was not the custom to destroy the possessions of an uninvolved party. Somebody outside the Chinese camp, he reasoned, must have caused the damages. Who exactly was behind these "accidents" he didn't know, but he promised my father he would find out.

Four nights later, Dad was awakened from a restless sleep by a human wail coming from the Chinese camp. He quickly dressed and ran along the track to a spot where Asians had already gathered in a clearing, illuminated by torches. Mounted on a wooden scaffold, his arms and legs bound with rope, a naked Chinaman was issuing a continuous stream of dreadful howls. To Dad's horror, the man's wrists were nothing but bloody stumps, left after his hands had been cut off. Far worse, if anything more brutal could be imagined, his penis and testicles dangled from a rawhide string around his neck. A dull ache spread between my father's legs and his mouth went dry. Never in the war fighting Southern rebels had he witnessed such shocking barbarity. Even Rebel soldiers, who harbored boundless hatred for Northerners they felt had invaded and violated their farms and homes, showed more respect for a prisoner's genitals.

Chinese workmen were jeering in their own language. To Father's surprise, Wong and Chan Yue, competitors for leadership of the Celestials working for the CP, stood side by side, hatchets in their hands.

Dad regretted that he hadn't brought his revolvers. "Jesus!" he cried out, surprised to see the two rivals conspiring in this act of torture. The man on the scaffold shrieked but no one came to his rescue.

Wong was the first to address the superintendent. "Meester Gallag'r, lookee here. Ngok Gingshee workee Union Paseefik. Ngok makee boom, boom." He then cast his arms away, imitating a man under orders from Union Pacific officers throwing tools over the ridge of Cape Horn.

My father didn't believe the charges of Union Pacific sabotage until Chan Yue produced evidence taken from the castrated saboteur: Seven five-dollar gold pieces, a map printed in Omaha, Nebraska Territory, and a small ax with the unmistakable brand of the Union Pacific Railroad burned into its handle. In a fair trial such evidence would have been introduced against the accused. Everyone knew possession didn't necessarily prove guilt. Still, that was California not Chinese law. None of the spectators spoke out against this summary punishment. Wong later explained to my father that Ngok Gingshee's sabotage of the Central Pacific had dishonored his countrymen. To redeem themselves the entire Chinese workforce had taken justice into their own hands and spared the company the burden and embarrassment.

Father marshaled his firmest military voice and thundered, "Cut that poor sonavabitch down immediately!"

Wong issued a spate of orders. Coolies moved slowly to untie Ngok.

To an aide who had come up alongside, my father ordered, "Get the company surgeon up here quick and, for God's sake, bury this man's balls someplace. Far away."

Wong nodded his willingness to comply.

My father surveyed the coolies, most shrouded in darkness. They acknowledged no wrongdoing in this cruelty. Quite the contrary: they had acted according to a code of honor sacred in their homeland. In China, their employers would have taken notice of this loyalty and rewarded them. But Dad felt no such gratitude. He knew he would have to find a way to demonstrate his displeasure over what they had done, but at the same time he needed to ensure their cooperation blasting through the mountainside at Cape Horn. What had happened reinforced his doubts about the propriety of hiring Chinese. The cultural gap between China and America seemed unbridgeable. Yet despite his lingering qualms about these Chinese workers, he had to acknowledge that the Central Pacific was now wholly dependent on them.

En route back to his tent, Dad heard a single scream, then nothing. He guessed that before the surgeon arrived, the coolies had put Ngok Gingshee out of his misery. Or more likely, held a blade onto which the traitor fell or was pushed. Dad really didn't want to know the details. Nor did he wish to launch an investigation that would inevitably trigger an inquiry by California state officials. He wondered what, if anything, he should report to the CP owners.

Later that night while resting on his cot, he had difficulty blotting out the image of the Chinaman's severed genitals. One thing was certain: He had misjudged these men from across the sea. In the end, he could not avoid an unpleasant truth: that Wong and Chan Yue had done the railroad a service. Everybody had underestimated the determination of the Union Pacific to slow down the CP in any way possible. More sabotage, he concluded, was likely. He was inclined to think in military terms, viewing Ngok Gingshee's act of sabotage as a preliminary skirmish, a mere prelude to much greater battles in the future. As rival railroads narrowed the distance between them, increased competition was inevitable. Two railroad armies had yet to commit their cavalry or infantry to combat.

Charles Crocker traveled to Cape Horn to observe the first Chinese blasters, equipped with drills, steel mauls, wooden tapping rods, and black powder, drop over the ridge in their flimsy gondolas. Governor Stanford took a different course, for there wasn't the slightest doubt in his mind that Crocker's scheme would end in disaster. He had deliberately scheduled speeches in Monterey so he would be unavailable at Cape Horn when this catastrophe occurred. He said publicly that he was sending his personal photographer to capture for posterity the Central Pacific's engineering ingenuity. Crocker wasn't fooled. His partner was less concerned about an historic record than having evidence of culpability should something go wrong.

Behind a parade of Chinese supplying Wong's blasting team, Crocker marched with my father. His breath was short and sweat streamed along his brow. Dust on the trail choked the marchers' throats. Between puffing, the railroad magnate hacked a raspy cough. He complained about how the four thousand-foot altitude gave him a headache and marveled at the Chinese who seemed unaffected by the reduced oxygen at that height. When they reached the summit, Crocker cautiously inched toward the ridge, one hand holding fast to my father's arm. Below on the floor of the gorge, the American River thinned into a tin thread of blue, dotted with streaks of white rapids. Feeder streams, which earlier in the year had brought melted snow to the river, were now dry.

Because the blasting operation was largely considered a Chinese affair, my father had left to Wong details of an opening ceremony. The coolies had boiled tea on an open fire while Sing Huang and Yee Jin-lee distributed round rice cakes baked in a reflector oven beside the fire, then fried and salted in lard. Crocker had been invited to inaugurate the enterprise with a speech, but after a few meandering sentences, he cut his address short. When he raised his cup in a gesture of salutation, Wong stepped forward to answer. In English!

The Chinaman had rehearsed his words, though the syllables grated on his ears. How much he wanted to speak this new language without an accent. But his first phrases were still framed in a Cantonese cadence. He needed to flatten down the tone, only he couldn't manage to do that while concentrating upon his pronunciation. "Ancestor spirit no failee Chinaman. Big train come through mountain. Wong makee boom, boom. Train come through mountain. You see. Wong makee boom, boom."

"The bloody fool's gonna tumble into the canyon and kill himself," my father said to Crocker. "Life doesn't mean much to these poor bastards."

Crocker was watching the Chinese winchmen tinker with their claptrap machines and paid only limited attention to his superintendent. Without looking at him, he responded, "Oh, stop worrying, Theo. I've got a feeling he'll make it okay. And if he doesn't...well, then."

"Then no other Chinaman will follow him over the side," my father completed his thought, though he was certain that was not what his boss wanted to hear.

Crocker looked at my father and grimaced playfully. "Why of course they will," he said, jingling his pocket filled with small gold pieces. He had a habit of rattling coins in his pockets, perhaps to impress on others that he was, indeed, a man of material substance. "I never met a Chinaman who wouldn't work for cash."

My father said, "Warm air from below rises along the gorge so Wong's got to contend with a swift updraft. He's never done anything like this before and he has no idea how strong that can be."

"He'll find out, won't he, now? You're always expecting the worst, Theo. Must be something in your upbringing. Everybody always tells me why something can't be done. I prefer men who tell me what they can do, like this fella, Wong."

"My job is to avoid trouble," Dad said, offended by his boss's cavalier attitude toward employee safety. It was easy for rich men to send their workers on dangerous missions that they themselves would never dream of attempting. Father's eyes ranged out over the gorge before returning to Crocker. "One thing I learned in the war: Men can build bridges and aqueducts, dams and roads, but Nature will confound us whenever she can. Let's both remember that God didn't put these mountains here for nothing. These days I'm inclined to think that perhaps the good Lord doesn't want our railroad coming through these passes. I'm no churchgoing man, you understand, Mr. Crocker, but I have a sense that our Maker's got some kind of plan for us. Perhaps the Almighty's thinkin' you fellas can go along the prairie and the seashore, but not through My mountains."

Crocker cleared his throat by sipping from the clay cup one of the Chinese had handed him, then spat the bitter contents onto the ground. "That sounds like heresy to me, Mr. Superintendent. I wouldn't want you talkin' like that to the men. I reckon a few of our boys are religious, in one manner or 'nother. I don't want them thinkin' thoughts like that. We'll get through, all right. Wong's got the right idea." He laughed, imitating the Chinaman's pidgin English. "Lookee see, Meester Gallag'r. Makee boom, boom. And he will. I have every assurance that he will."

When they turned from the ridge, they found Wong inside the gondola rehearsing signals with his winchmen. Once the basket dropped over the side, there would be no visual contact between those on the ridge and the blaster in the gondola. And swirling wind, coupled with the contour of the mountain, made it unlikely that they would be able to communicate verbally. That left the hemp rope attached to the gondola as the sole medium for transmitting signals. On the spot they established a simple signal code. One tug on the lanyard meant to stop either lowering or raising the gondola. Two tugs signaled a reverse in the last direction, at five-foot intervals. Three pulls signaled the winchmen to haul in the hemp slowly until another single tug told them to stop. Four tugs from the gondola indicated that fuses attached to the charges had been lit and to haul in rapidly. Wong believed that more signals would just create confusion.

For added safety, an observer had been stationed on the roadbed below to provide semaphore signals to those on the ridge. He was spotted near a stand of lodgepole pines, but the trees blocked his left side, making some of his semaphore unreadable. When he failed to find a more visible position there was general agreement among those on the ridge that they could not rely on him. The operation would have to proceed without the benefit of his observations.

Dad was correct about the wind. Standing on the ridge, one could feel no more than a gentle morning breeze. But conditions along the mountainside were altogether different. There, warm air rising from the gorge in uneven gusts swirled around the rocks where Wong intended to plant his blasting charges. From the moment the gondola went over the side, it was buffeted by squalling updrafts. The frail craft swung and dipped, making it impossible to bore holes into the granite for powder charges. On the ridge, everybody gathered to consider postponing the work until conditions became more favorable. But this notion was abandoned when my father pointed out that as long as warm air rose from the gorge, strong air currents were inevitable. Even on a windless day, air was in motion along the perpendicular wall. When Wong was unable to set any of the charges, it became necessary to haul in the gondola and devise a means to stabilize it. Here, Dad came up with a solution. Additional hemp lines were thrown over the side for the gondola's pilot to seize.

On his second journey below the ridge, Wong secured the ends of these new guidelines to the granite with metal spikes. Once that task was accomplished, he would attempt to attach his gondola to one or both to minimize the effect of the swirling air. That was the theory. The practice proved to be something else entirely. The lines minimized but did not eliminate the infernal swaying. Wong found that embedding a battery of ten charges into ten holes took nearly two hours longer than originally planned. Nevertheless, by early afternoon the boreholes were finished. The next step was to attach fuses that had been manufactured a week before in the Chinese camp.

It was Wong's plan to ignite the lowest tier of four fuses first then have himself hoisted to a medial tier where another three were waiting. Once that was accomplished he had four fuses to light above them. Then, four sharp tugs on the line would bring him rapidly to the top. In the Manchu artillery they used an oil-soaked rope to ignite powder charges. But since it was too dangerous to keep anything burning near the black powder stored in the gondola, Wong was compelled to rely on ordinary matches. Here again, the wind confounded his plan by making it difficult to keep a flame burning long enough to light the charges. Igniting the lowest four changes took longer than he anticipated. Once the fuses sputtered alive, the margin for error narrowed. Two tugs on the line signaled the winchmen to pull Wong to the middle three charges. Valuable seconds were lost when the guideline on his left unexpectedly got tangled. It couldn't have happened at a more dangerous moment because below Wong's fuses were burning close to their charges. He had no alternative but to cut free from the stabilizing line and accept being bobbed around by the air currents. The moment he managed to ignite the second set of fuses he gave his line two tugs and was hoisted up to the final bank of charges. As soon as they were hissing, he took a final look over the side at his handiwork. Despite all the difficulties, his plan had worked. Chooley Crocker and Meester Gallag'r would see!

But things were not going precisely as he had foreseen. Smoke sputtered from only two and not three positions on the middle tier. Perhaps he had rushed during the lighting, or just had been careless. It was clear that one fuse had stopped burning altogether. Damn the wind. Or was it a faulty fuse manufactured by his associates?

Wong calculated the time necessary to drop down one tier and relight the dead fuse. If he moved without delay it was possible, but only with seconds to spare. He tugged twice, notifying the winchmen to lower his gondola the five-foot interval. But the foreman at the crane was confused by a double tug when he expected a signal that it was time to be hauled quickly to the safety of the ridge. Instead of letting out the line, he looked to my father for instructions. Before Dad could process the possibilities, Wong repeated his double tug, assuming that his countrymen understood his intentions. My father's eyes searched for the observer on the roadbed below, but could not find him among the trees.

Finally the foreman ordered his winchmen to let out their line. But valuable seconds had been lost. The lower tier of charges exploded just below Wong, blowing massive chucks of granite from the mountainside and cascading rock into the gorge below. The middle three detonated an instant later, destroying the gondola's wicker floor. To avoid falling through it, Wong clung to the halyard. Still, that was only temporary because the fuses above him were burning perilously close to their powder. Recognizing that there was more explosive danger above him than below, he tugged twice to lower the gondola. But the sound of discharging powder confused those working the winch lines. Their instinct was to haul Wong up rather than lower him.

Too late. Up came the gondola, almost horizontal with the yet unexploded charges. And there wasn't time to clear them. As they ignited, the gondola's remaining guideline snapped. Hunks of rock blew from the mountain, shredding what was left of the flimsy basket. A rock the size of a double fist pounded into Wong's ribs. The halyard alone kept him from tumbling into the gorge. The coarse rope burned his palms. How long could he count on his fingers to hold on?

Just when the halyard began to slip, his feet touched the surface of the mountain and found a thin foothold. How secure this was, he couldn't tell. Certain the halyard was insufficient to prevent his fall into the canyon, he made a desperate decision in favor of the ledge. A combination of debris and dust clogged his vision. To hold onto the ledge required both hands, leaving neither free to wipe blinding dirt from his eyes.

Men at the hoists felt the halyard go slack. When they hauled it in they found only shredded line. The explosion had brought the observer into a clearing from where he dispatched a series of wild signals. It was Crocker who first deciphered the message. To everybody's surprise, Wong was still alive, clinging for his life on the jagged mountainside! "That little billy goat is still with us," he exclaimed, raising his fist in a gesture of victory. "It's a miracle, but he's there."

Just then, a late charge exploded. No one knew where it originated or whether it had blown Wong from his tenuous refuge. Once the sound stopped echoing, the foreman, Chang Lan, suggested sending a second blaster over the side in a backup gondola to evaluate the situation. Crocker cautioned against it. His experience in commerce had taught him an inviolable rule of thumb: Never throw good money after bad. This accident had brought him to his senses. As much as he hated to concede defeat, he had to admit that Dad had a better sense of what to expect then he. While hypothetically feasible, the scheme posed many practical problems, among them the inability to communicate amid unpredictable winds and unreliable blasting fuses. Wong would probably pay for this foolishness with his life, but there was no sense sacrificing another man to rescue one already doomed.

A stern, contemplative expression came over my father's face. "Okay," he said, "I'll go after Wong."

When he was annoyed, Crocker had a way of wagging his head so that his heavy jowls seemed to vibrate. He replied, "There are still undetonated charges down there, Theo. You don't know exactly where Wong planted them. And what's more, you're half again as big as that Chinaman and far too heavy for one of our gondolas. They weren't designed for a man of your size."

Dad squinted at his employer, evaluating not only his words but the motivation behind them. Was he genuinely concerned for his welfare? Or just being assertive in light of the current situation? My father wanted to demand that he not meddle in operational decisions. Let Crocker reign in Sacramento, but not on Cape Horn. What Dad actually said was far less confrontational. "If the coolies don't see us making an attempt at rescue, none will ever go over the side again. It's taken me months to understand them. They must see us trying to save their compatriot."

"Aahhh," Crocker expelled his breath in a victorious blast. "You were against this enterprise from the beginning, Theo, but now you've changed your tune. I was the optimist, not you."

"I've still got reservations, Mr. Crocker," my father said, "but this is about rescue. Soldiers never leave their wounded on the battlefield. That's the only pledge an officer makes to his troops. Never, never abandon a man, even a Chinaman."

"There must be somebody else," Crocker snarled.

"And by the time I find him it'll be too late."

Chang Lan helped my father attach the second gondola to the rig. Both agreed it would have been better to move this apparatus to the south and a bit closer to the overhanging rim, yet time was of the essence. In addition, Father had the benefit of the snarled guidelines they had jerrybuilt to assist Wong, though there was some question about how useful they would prove to be. Any rescuer would need to swing from side to side, depending on Wong's exact location.

The minute the gondola disappeared over the ridge it became painfully clear that it had been designed for a hundred-pound man, not someone seventy-five pounds heavier. How my father intended to add Wong's weight to the frail contraption baffled everybody. The halyard looked thin enough for a man to unravel with his hands, and that was *before* the abrasive granite began shredding its external fibers. To make matters worse, a swirling wind proved to be no more merciful to my father than it had been to Wong.

The Chinaman's ledge in what remained of a glacial crevice was hidden from view. That Wong was nowhere in sight confirmed Dad's suspicion that perhaps the observer below had over compensated for his earlier failure. Or perhaps the Celestial had managed to scratch a temporary toehold for himself but was unable to hold on. But if that were so, why wouldn't the observer have seen him fall and semaphored the news?

Father was about to give up his search when the wind lifted the gondola away from the mountain and, for an instant, revealed Wong who produced a series of howls, telling my father where to maneuver his unwieldy craft. Each attempt to stabilize his fragile gondola was confounded by the wind. In the end there was no way to move laterally except by pulling the gondola over the granite facing by hand.

My father's fingers began to bleed. As he inched closer, his words of comfort went unanswered; perhaps, he thought, because the deafening explosives had damaged Wong's hearing. Yet with a series of hand signals Wong communicated that he couldn't grab onto the gondola without losing his balance on the ledge. Given this unhappy situation, he had no alternative but to abandon the ledge and leap free from the mountain. A miscalculation guaranteed him a gravesite in the gorge below.

Father kept glancing around for the telltale smoke of undetonated fuses, though dust from the shattered rock probably camouflaged it. In every series of charges there was bound to be one or two late detonators.

In the excitement nobody had bothered to tally the exact number. Meanwhile the wind caused a steady stream of pebbles from the blast area to rain down on him, and the halyard kept fraying with a hissing sound as it wore against the rough granite. Blood on my father's fingers prevented him from establishing firm holds on the surface of the rocks.

His commands to Wong were in English; Wong responded in Cantonese. Twice it became necessary for my father to abandon his hard-won position and repeat the tedious horizontal movement. Below, the observer sent continuous semaphore to those on the ridge. What he transmitted was a desperate scene of failure. Each time Dad worked his gondola near Wong, gusting air currents drove the basket in a counter swing. The gap appeared impossible to close.

Wong eventually came to the same conclusion and decided to gamble with his life. When Father's gondola moved to the closest position, the observer witnessed the Chinaman jump, his knees bent and his arms extending forward like an acrobat sailing toward a trapeze bar in midair. Disaster appeared certain, for just as he propelled himself out over the canyon the gondola swung in the opposite direction. My father had never agreed to Wong's desperate leap, but what could he do? To compensate for this rash maneuver, he leaned far out over the basket rim, stretching to snatch Wong's wrists. Drawn down by gravity, the Chinaman seemed to drop below the gondola, his hands flailing for a hold on the bobbing basket that was fast moving in the opposite direction. My father's feet left their anchorage as he extended his reach both out and down. At the last moment, the wind shifted favorably. His left hand adroitly clamped over the Chinaman's right wrist and held long enough for his right hand to grab Wong's tunic.

The Chinaman kicked his feet, churning air. Dad's grip tightened. Next, Wong swung a hand over the wicker rim while my father adjusted his hold by snatching the waistband of the Chinaman's pantaloons. Both men continued calling commands in their respective tongues. They wrestled until Wong maneuvered his center of gravity higher toward the rim. There wasn't enough room in the gondola for two men, but no matter. As unstable as the craft was, if the halyard held without snapping, the winchers might be able to haul them up to the ridge.

My father signaled with a double tug. Moments later the winch turned. Additional weight required additional muscle, which the few white men attached to the Chinese team on the ridge immediately provided.

Sharp edges of granite ripped into the thin lifeline. Though Wong and my father had come from different cultures, their minds worked in similar ways, both asking how long this cord would support more than twice the weight for which it had been designed. Within seconds both men recognized the problem, yet only Wong perceived a solution based on an assumption that the halyard would snap before they reached the ridge. To lighten the gondola became imperative. He had only an instant to save the life of the man who had risked his own life for him.

When he made a move, Dad was taken by surprise. In a single leap Wong scrambled from the gondola rim onto the first ledge that looked promising. His fingers scratched the rock surface for a hold as he exclaimed his first English declaration. "Upee, Meester Gallag'r. Go, quick!"

My father tried to pull him back but the gondola was already several feet higher than his reach. The halyard above him looked more like a thread than a line. Even without Wong's weight Father needed considerable luck to survive. Thirty more feet before he heard voices from the ridge. He howled back at Wong. "You goddamn bloody fool!" He was still chiding the coolie from afar when friendly hands seized the gondola and hauled it over the crest of the ridge. Cheers rose from the winchmen. White men working with the Chinese clustered around their superintendent with congratulations.

Dad shouted, flailing his elbows to make room amid the crowd of well-wishers. In seconds he was issuing orders to rig a new basket for Wong. This time he knew exactly where to position it. And by now the observer below was signaling as he should have all along. If Wong could hold on, there was a good chance they might still pluck him from the mountainside.

It took another twelve minutes to complete the rigging, and when they dropped it over the side the wind bounced it around like a hollow log in white water. Several attempts to lower it within Wong's reach failed. Winchmen let it out then hauled it in. Up and down, over and over, until their exhausted muscles ached. To keep them cool, a white man doused water over their shoulders. Then, to everybody's surprise, the gondola swung near Wong, who seized an opportunity he knew might never come again. He quickly abandoned his rock ledge and jumped toward the moving basket. The halyard tightened. His hands caught and held. A minute later he managed to crawl over the rim. The winchmen felt tension on their gears. They had hooked their fish, but would the line hold long enough to haul it in?

The moment Wong reached safety his arms were waving. He berated his countrymen in English. "Two tug, down. Why you wait?" he howled, pointing to the sky. "Why you wait?"

Coolies responsible for the original confusion hung their heads in shame. Not one offered an excuse. Crocker approached the Chinaman and added his congratulations.

"He didn't have a chance," he said to my father, unconcerned that other coolies might understand his English.

"Not a goddamn Chinaman's chance," my father said. He had heard the expression used in reference to the haplessness of the Irish but not the Chinese. Their misfortune seemed more fitting.

"How much work time does this fellow Wong owe the Yung Wo Company?" Crocker asked, stroking his whiskers in a customary manner.

Dad had other matters on his mind and was insulted that his boss was thinking of money at such a time. He shrugged his shoulders in annoyance. How should he know without referring to the company's books?

"Whatever it is," Crocker said, "pay off his bond, Theo. Make our Mr. Wong a free man."

The order took my father by surprise because generosity was not a trait he had observed in Crocker. To the owner's mind, an employee owed his maximum to the company at all times, even if that meant sacrificing his life. He asked Crocker, "Are you aware of the precedent this sets?"

"No. Frankly I haven't given it any thought. But now that I do, this strikes me as a pretty good idea. We owe this chap something. Let's make an example of him to his countrymen. My guess is that with some refinement and practice we can improve on his method. Wong showed us that the idea of embedding explosives is feasible, now didn't he?"

My father didn't like where Crocker's remarks were headed. After the near-disastrous episode, he expected his boss to terminate the experiment and order him to return to established blasting methods. "You're not suggesting that we continue this ludicrous idea after what's happened, are you?"

"You wanted to rescue Wong," Crocker shot back. "You said yourself that if you didn't go after him no other coolies would follow him over the side. If you didn't want to continue, why'd you do it?"

Crocker's ability to twist ideas annoyed my father, especially since he couldn't come up with a better response than this: "I didn't want to leave Wong on the cliff to die."

"Major Gallager's getting soft and, I sense, a bit sentimental. But the way I see it, one setback doesn't spell defeat. Wong had the right idea. Only we gotta refine our machines and practice our signals. My bet is that our little Chinaman won't be beaten either. Ask him, because if he's still game, I'd hate to say I'm finished."

Father made it a personal policy to call an adversary's bluff. But before he put the question to Wong, he paused to ask Crocker, "And what if Wong won't return? Then what?"

The railroad baron screwed up his eyebrows nearly to the hairline. "Why, then, Theo, I'll find other coolies who will. If the price is right they'll do whatever I ask."

Crocker's low opinion of men irritated my father. Not everybody could be bought and sold, as this mogul believed. Not Wong Po-ching. And certainly not himself.

Porters were transporting Wong to base camp on a stretcher when my father caught up with him. The wounds he'd sustained on the mountainside had been temporarily bandaged until a surgeon could be brought to the railhead. There were many things he wanted to tell the Chinaman, but there was virtually no trail and it was difficult to keep pace. Though Wong had been hopping around just after they'd lifted him onto the ridge, his strength had definitely waned. On the stretcher, he looked like one of the many war casualties Father had seen in the bloody Wilderness Campaign northeast of Richmond. Tired, bewildered, beaten. His eyes were closed until Dad started to talk.

"I want to thank you, Wong." Father's expression of gratitude was interrupted as the stretcher-bearers lunged ahead. He was forced to wait until there was space to return alongside. "You saved us both out there on the cliff. You understand what I'm saying?"

Wong tried to smile but gave no indication that he understood. His ears were still ringing from the explosions. His teeth, which always hurt when he was under tension, now ached.

"You understand, Wong?" Dad raised his voice. "English? Yes? No? *Sabes, si?* You understand my English?"

Wong shook his head and with one finger pointed to his ear. He was deaf.

"You're a free man, Wong," my father yelled. "Mr. Crocker instructed me to pay off your indenture. You understand that? *You're a free man*! Now all your wages belong to you and nobody else."

"Noee. Noee," Wong said, cuffing his ears to indicate that he couldn't hear a thing.

"Thanks, Wong," Father repeated and gave up trying to communicate. But he marched alongside the stretcher anyway. It was the least he could do for the injured Chinaman. And then when they neared the original roadbed, Wong tried to talk more. "Thankee, Meester Gallag'r," he said. With his hands he pointed over his head to the high ridge where the two of them had momentarily teetered together.

Dad didn't need a full explanation. If Wong had saved him, it was also true that he had saved Wong. The reciprocity appealed to him. "It's okay, Wong," he replied, then turned to climb back to the ridge and make sure no further accidents would occur. The hike provided a few moments for him to dwell on his thoughts. Until Wong and he were dangling in the gondola he hadn't thought much of these Celestials. But now he had to respect Wong's bravery. Twice he had risked his life and jumped from a ledge. Most men would have been too frightened to take the gamble. Was Wong different from the others? Or was he a fair representative of his compatriots? Perhaps, my father thought, he had misjudged their capabilities. But how would he learn more about these little fellows when the barrier to communication was so great?

Donner Pass
November 1867

Wong Po-ching, who had unexpectedly found himself no longer an indentured worker in Gum San, didn't know his age. If his parents had ever mentioned the date during his childhood, he had never bothered to remember it. In China, this was of little consequence, for one measured age not by the passage of years but by the seasons and, when food was short, by the month. Besides, he had never developed memory for past events, and in his native land people spent little time reflecting on what had gone before. In America, men asked him about his age so often that he was inspired to come up with an estimate. After a while he couldn't remember what ages he had supplied. In order to be consistent, he invented a birth date for himself. In August of 1867 he declared himself to be twenty-five years old.

At twenty-five, another clock was measuring time within his body. The infrequent sight of a woman near the construction area would cause his sex organ to swell and his scrotum to contract. It didn't matter whether she was attractive or ugly, white or Oriental, married or single. In earlier days he had learned how to relieve himself. But this method no longer seemed to work. No matter how much semen he flushed, he produced more at a ferocious rate. He knew his body was talking to him. Other coolies frequented the singsong women in tent brothels that, of late, had sprung up behind whorehouses for white laborers. Wong visited these singsong girls too, but resented the cost of their services. As he pondered the reproductive cycle, sex puzzled him. Gum San was unlike the Celestial Kingdom where children were everywhere. But in the Sierra, children were rarely seen. Wives and families remained in the shadows of most white workers, if they existed at all. Sometimes these fathers talked about their spouses with great affection, but more often they cursed and ridiculed them. But their children were different. Of them, they spoke with a mixture of fondness and sorrow.

Wong came to the conclusion that he wanted a wife and a family. But for a Chinese laborer in Gum San, even a free laborer as he was now, acquiring a spouse presented insurmountable difficulties. As far as he could determine, only wealthy Chinese merchants in San Francisco imported women from the Celestial Kingdom and he had not heard of a single marriage. To obtain a bride would require an enormous sum of money, money to bribe immigration officials, money for the broker's commission, and much more to lure a woman from her native village, pay for her passage over the ocean, and reward her family with a dowry.

Each way of making money in Gum San Wong found to be blocked by his inability to speak English. The pidgin dialect he was picking up in camp might work for basic communication, but it wasn't the language white men spoke among themselves. Without being able to communicate fluently in their tongue, acquiring a substantial sum of money would be impossible.

Fluency became a high priority, and in a few weeks Wong's vocabulary exceeded that of his fellow workers (even Chang Lan), though it must be said that verbs and prepositions continued to confound him. His sentences remained broken and his singsong cadence a telltale sign of his foreign origin. To correct these deficiencies he vowed to seize every opportunity to speak with white men. Never mind his errors. Never mind his lack of vocabulary. And never mind the ridicule he was bound to incur.

To implement his plan, he sought out white men. While his ribs were healing from his injuries at Cape Horn, he washed laundry and mended clothing. No task proved too menial for an excuse to enter the white men's camps and talk with them. From each conversation he planned to glean a new word or turn of phrase, for Wong was convinced that if he could speak English well, he would make money. And with money he would purchase a wife. And with a wife he would have children in Gum San.

One by one the Chinese corrected the snags in Wong's original blasting scheme and succeeded in leveling a roadbed along the mountainside above the American River. By September, there were tracks along the gorge at Cape Horn. By October, this track was linked with forward sections from Dutch Flat, the first tunnel at Grizzly Hill and the second at Emigrant Gap. Each link allowed supply trains to transport rails, ties, powder, and heavy machinery closer to the construction sites where mules and oxen moved these materials still farther forward. Everybody's spirits were buoyed by notable progress as autumn arrived, but a series of early blizzards presaged a severe winter. Old-timers swore that this year snow would be thick by December. They based their predictions on instinct rather than science, yet it was their past record that caused worry among Central Pacific management.

Fortunes were not as gloomy for the Union Pacific; by that time, forward UP construction crews had entered the Wyoming Territory, hell bent to acquire every foot of real estate the federal government offered and prosper with the rewards paid for completed track. The treatment of the coolie saboteur discouraged other Chinese traitors from vandalism and sabotage against the CP, but by this time white men in the Union Pacific employ were causing trouble at CP construction sites. They proved to be more of a nuisance than a real impediment and, from my father's point of view, demonstrated how little the Union Pacific owners, Thomas Durant and General Grenville Dodge, really knew about the Central Pacific's construction problems in the mountains. Despite the remarkable conquest of Cape Horn, a far more formidable impediment awaited ahead, the hard, unchallenged granite of the summit at Donner where the CP needed to bore tunnels wide enough for passage of the new, larger locomotives now being manufactured in the East.

Theodore Judah's original survey for the Pacific Railroad in 1854 had called for nine tunnels up to Donner Pass and another five on the Sierra's eastern escarpment. In Judah's day no one thought about testing the granite for hardness. That oversight proved to be the Central Pacific's nemesis. So tough was this regional rock that black powder would scarcely crack it.

When newspaper stories about Cape Horn failed to captivate readers as they once had, California journalists started probing my father's problems higher on the summit. Papers dependent on advertising from the Union Pacific no longer had to manipulate facts to slant public opinion against the Central Pacific. When powder suppliers in China learned how much was needed to blast the Sierra tunnels, the price soared to sixty dollars a barrel, five times what it had cost only two years before when the first track was laid at Colfax. After its success at Cape Horn Hopkins circulated an internal memorandum to the CP's management how the railroad that had been given a short reprieve by the injection of new money from San Francisco. That capital, unfortunately, only covered past debts and there was little left for day-to-day operations. Better, admonished Hopkins, to cut their losses now and not wait until construction was bottled up in the High Sierra. They still had a chance to sell off some of the company's assets *before* creditors started picking at the carcass. This was the moment to find dreamers who still wanted to get in on the Pacific Railroad. Once financial experts truly understood what the CP was up against, the current owners would be lucky to get more than pennies on the dollar for their original investment. Huntington, Stanford and Crocker appreciated their partner's view, but had come to enjoy the celebrity of being owners. Except for Hopkins, each one, for his own reasons, was determined to hold on as long as possible, hoping for a miracle.

And that miracle arrived in the form of a new explosive—nitroglycerin, a chemical compound that promised ten times the destructive power of black powder, though experts cautioned that it was also a hundred times more volatile. Crocker withheld information about this wonder explosive from his partners because he considered them to be naysayers rather than gamblers like himself. He wanted to experiment with nitroglycerin blasting oil on the softer granite in tunnels at Cisco and Red Spur, but my father objected on the grounds that it was both dangerous and outlawed by the California Legislature. An iron-hulled schooner carrying this nitro had blown up while moored at the Market Street Wharf in San Francisco. Half of the commercial area near the wharf disappeared into the water, along with sixty-three men and four women. An investigation uncovered similar disasters at quarries and mining operations. Legislators banned the manufacture and use of nitroglycerin anywhere in California until safety procedures for handling it could be devised. If it were used by the Crocker Construction Company, my father pointed out, the entire CP management would be subject to arrest and imprisonment.

Unaware of Crocker's plan, Stanford, ever with an eye upon reclaiming the Governor's Mansion as a steppingstone to the White House, publicly denounced this new explosive and, in a series of emotional speeches, pledged that his railroad would never willingly endanger the lives of its cherished workers, whether they were white men or Celestials. By the time Big Charley got around to talking with his partner about using nitroglycerin at Donner, Stanford was inexorably on record as opposing it.

From the Central Pacific's new office in San Francisco, where he had moved to be closer to the sources of money, Mark Hopkins calculated the cost of introducing nitroglycerin and deemed it too expensive. "Too damn dangerous," wrote Collis Huntington from New York.

With his partners allied solidly against him, Crocker confirmed his original conviction that his railroad would never be built with the consensus of its owners. To disguise his intention and proceed with the illegal explosive, he placed orders for massive supplies of black powder from Asian manufacturers at the then greatly inflated price.

Father tendered his resignation.

"Suppose you won't endanger anyone?" Crocker asked in the innocent manner he often used while cajoling others to adopt his unpopular views. "I mean, Theo, that all the accidents you've heard about have occurred while *handling* the stuff, haven't they?" My father was wary. Too many times he had been beguiled by this wily dry goods dealer, whom he believed could sell umbrellas to Arabs in the desert. On the matter of nitro blasting oil he was determined not to let Crocker bamboozle him.

"Come on now, Theo," Crocker said, refusing to relent. "You've read the reports I sent you. Nitroglycerin is dangerous when you move it from place to place. Once you put it where you want to do the damage, it works wonders. You just have to handle it with respect, that's all."

"It's illegal," my father countered, his patience wearing thin. "We could both end up in the state prison at Point San Quentin."

"Declared illegal by the same legislators who are against nitro because they haven't yet figured out who's gonna pay them for promoting it. What the hell do political hacks know about building a railroad?"

"They know that nitro's dangerous and that we could hurt many of our workers by using it."

"It's dangerous to those who don't know how to move it safely."

"Which is most everybody with his head screwed on right."

"And those without imagination, I might add."

Dad gnashed his teeth absorbing Crocker's cockiness. When he recovered, he said, "Now that I'm no longer officially an employee of the Crocker Construction Company, I can be impertinent and ask my ex-boss if he's planning to roll up his own sleeves and work with the blasting oil himself. Or will he enlist his Chinese pets to blow themselves to smithereens in the name of the Pacific Railroad?"

Crocker patted his paunch and let a sneer cross his face, then said, "No, Theo. I have no intention of rolling up my sleeves. Nor do I have any desire to send others to meet their Maker. Not even coolies, who don't seem to recognize a Maker anyway. I intend to manufacture nitroglycerin near the tunnels and reduce the risk of premature explosion in transit."

"But that's still illegal and you know it."

"Illegal only if we get caught."

"There's an army of newspaper men snooping around the mountains at all times. If they're in the vicinity, they'll discover your factory."

Crocker raised his eyebrows and jerked his head so the fantail beard appeared to expand. "Well, Theo, not too near. We'll have to hide it somewhere these busybodies won't think of looking. The most unlikely place. Maybe down near Donner Lake. Surrounded by thick forest."

"But that will mean transporting it up to the tunnels. You won't get many volunteers for that job."

"Don't need many. Just one, someone who can handle a good mule team. Can you crack these tunnels with black powder, Theo? Forget the amount of powder. Can you do it?"

My father shook his head. "Not this winter. Maybe next, provided I have enough explosives."

"We've only got this winter. By next year, the Central Pacific will be sold at ten cents on the dollar. It's nitroglycerin now or never. The question is whether Theo Gallager wants to take the gamble and make something of himself. Or if he's inclined to mosey off to a quiet and undistinguished life building lumber roads."

"Got anybody special in mind to transport the stuff?"

"How about Wong Po-ching?"

"He's too smart for a suicide mission."

"I'll make it worth his while. I've been watching that little devil. He likes money and will do whatever it takes to get it. I can make it very sweet for him. Look what he was prepared to risk at Cape Horn."

"You got someone who knows how to make this glycerin oil?"

Crocker had to think for a long moment before revealing a secret. "Yes, I have, Theo. A Scotsman by the name of MacGreggor, James C. MacGreggor. As a matter of fact, he's in Sacramento as we speak, buying supplies and chemicals. Secretly, of course."

"A good man?"

"We'll see, won't we?"

"Not we, Mr. Crocker. If something goes wrong, your Mr. MacGreggor will wind up in jail. It won't take long before they'll throw you in the pokey too. And maybe your partners. I wouldn't be surprised to see Governor Stanford behind bars."

"That's one way of looking at it. But I prefer to take a more optimistic view. If it goes right, we'll all be rich. But it sounds as though you're not interested in sharing these riches."

"You've already got enough money."

"Maybe I do. But you, Theo, don't. And that's why I'm counting on you and Wong to help."

"There're things men won't do for money."

"But building a railroad isn't one of them. Just listen to the sound of the words," and here he drew out the pronunciation of each word, "*The. Pacific. Railroad.* What kind of a man wouldn't want his name associated with building something great? What man wouldn't want to be known as the builder of the transcontinental track? Taking a risk for something as grand as this shouldn't be illegal. And the way I figure it, nobody should get hurt. Especially not Wong or you."

Father refused to give Crocker an answer on the spot. He had always considered himself a deliberative man, one willing to weigh the evidence before making a decision. But all the evidence required an understanding of nitroglycerin, and all he knew about the volatile substance was what he read in the papers, not through personal experience. Before being sucked into another one of Crocker's schemes, he needed to know more about this explosive. And he would have to know something about this fellow, James MacGreggor, in whose hands Crocker had just committed the future of the entire venture in the Sierra passes. Did this Scotsman know what he was doing? Or was he just another pie-in-the-sky dreamer hoping to get rich quick in California?

CHAPTER FIVE

Calaveras

Against his better judgment, my father capitulated. He viewed his work building the transcontinental railroad as an enormous personal challenge; the thought of being beaten by snowcapped mountains was humiliating. He hadn't passed up an engineering career in the East to end up cutting timber roads and constructing railroad trestles in the West. Crocker, always a shrewd observer of men's motivations, read his desires like a biblical verse. The CP owner knew he wouldn't resign as superintendent of construction when there was still a chance of cutting through the Sierra granite, even if that chance required breaking the law, not for a selfish, but for a worthy cause. Crocker gave Father time to ponder his dilemma, then sweetened the deal by promising a significant financial bonus—if and when there was a locomotive over the Donner Pass and headed down the eastern escarpment into the Nevada desert.

The deal was even more lucrative for Wong Po-ching. One hundred dollars a month, four times what a coolie could earn with a hammer and pick! And with his shelter and board fully paid. Enough for Wong to send a deposit to the Yung Wo Company in San Francisco for purchasing his wife in China. Dad told him the project involved working with very volatile explosives, but failed to disclose their exact nature, or that the California Legislature had banned its use. Not that it would have frightened Wong. In China, peasants grew up with little respect for their provincial governments or the laws that kept ruling officials wealthy. For the underprivileged, defying the authorities was a way of life. How different, he asked himself, were matters in California where laws were written and enforced by wealthy white men to protect their property?

My father recognized that Wong's experience handling black powder under combat conditions in China qualified him to work with nitroglycerin. Controlled blasting in a tunnel, even with the volatile new explosive, had to be less hazardous than setting cannon charges during the chaos of battle. And unlike most sappers who became superstitious and consequently overly cautious about their craft, Wong appeared fearless. Dad wondered if he knew enough about nitroglycerin to be afraid.

Crocker was a master at managing information. Yes, he had told Dad about the Scotsman, MacGreggor, who purportedly knew how to manufacture the blasting oil, but misrepresented the status of his new project. MacGreggor wasn't in Sacramento gathering supplies, but past that phase and had secretly built and equipped a small factory in the forest near the outlet of Donner Lake. My father wasn't pleased to learn he had been by-passed, but by now he was already implemented in Crocker's scheme. Rather than complain he vowed to take control by personally introducing Wong Po-ching to MacGreggor at the new factory.

The day before the trip, thirty-two workmen failed to show up for work. Eleven were AOW, the rest were in their bunks, sick with food poisoning. Armed with his now famous revolvers, one on loan from Harriet Horn, my father showed up in camp to intimidate those who might wish to follow the deserters. Simultaneously, he sent Wong on his own to meet MacGreggor.

Not more than five years older than Wong, the Scotsman was a wiry, nervous man who possessed a mop of ruddy hair that completely covered his ears and neck. A childhood pox had left his exposed skin mottled and pitted. At some point in his career he had sustained an injury to his left hip, yet he moved about with remarkable agility and when he walked, it was faster than most men, as if to purposely demonstrate how this injury would not slow him down.

When a Chinaman showed up to transport the nitro from the factory to the tunnels, a distance of over six miles, he was alarmed. A solitary man who had become accustomed to conversing with himself, he had little patience for Wong's Pidgin English and Asiatic habits. From the outset they started on the wrong foot. Two days later, he showed up at the headquarters tent to express his reservations about being alone with a Chinaman in the mountains. While he slept Wong could slit his throat. Or steal his equipment.

Though my father assured MacGreggor of Wong's character and extended the company's guarantee of his safety and possessions, he feared what might occur at the mountain factory. And images of the tortured and emasculated saboteur from the Union Pacific returned to memory. Wong had already shown to what lengths he would go to protect his fellow compatriots and himself. It was not inconceivable that if MacGreggor offended him he just might get his throat slit. At the same time, he wouldn't put it past the Scotsman to take matters in his own hands and find an excuse to eliminate Wong first.

When the time came for Wong to move a team of mules from the Chinese camp at Dutch Flat to Donner Lake, it was my father who told him, "Be careful, won't you?"

"Of blasting oil? Or of Mister MacGreggor?"

Father made an odd noise with his lips. "Both. MacGreggor is Mr. Crocker's man, not mine. Frankly, I don't trust him. If you have trouble, don't handle matters by yourself. Come to me first. You understand me, Wong?"

Wong squinted as if concentrating upon my father's words. Dad, who had come to take nothing for granted, repeated his instructions, using as simple vocabulary as he could. In the end, he believed he had conveyed himself adequately, particularly stressing the importance of avoiding confrontation with MacGreggor.

As Father expected, tension between the two men at the Donner Lake factory grew. Wong thought that MacGreggor was disrespectful because he had not taken time to learn his name and constantly referred to him as *boy*. "My name, Wong," he kept reminding the Scotsman. "Wong. You call me Wong, Meester MacGreggor."

"I'll call you exactly what I damn well please," MacGreggor replied. "If I want to call you *boy* then that's what I'll call you. Understand that, *boy*? And don't keep staring at me with those slant eyes of yours. Train them elsewhere."

Wong bore the insult. Though he didn't like his new boss, isolation in the forest provided an opportunity to practice English, including a healthy dose of Scottish swear words. If nothing else, he intended to improve his speech while at the Donner factory. Additionally, he studied Scotsman's chemistry, noting how he carefully mixed sulfuric and nitric acids to extract a pure glycerin compound. To this soapy compound sawdust was added for stability.

Crocker and my father arrived secretly at the Donner factory to witness MacGreggor's first test. He had estimated the blast comparable to seventy pounds of black powder, the quantity needed to crack the granite at the summit. But when smoke cleared over a pyramid of target stones Wong had gathered in a forest clearing, the result was disappointing. Contrary to expectations, the glycerin oil produced an explosion comparable to only a quarter-keg, not enough to be effective in the mountain tunnels. Little did my father and Crocker realize that MacGreggor was pleasantly surprised that his compound detonated at all. He had represented to Crocker in Sacramento that he possessed first-hand experience in producing nitroglycerin in Germany. But, as both Crocker and my father expected, that was an exaggeration. He had once watched a skilled Swiss chemist produce the explosive but had never duplicated this feat—that is, until the actual test, which proved, if nothing else, that he was on the right track. He was certain that by tinkering with sequences of the mixing acids a more powerful explosive was certain to follow.

Crocker was crestfallen. His lips smacked audibly and occasionally an anemic looking tongue would sweep the corners of his mouth. The tips of his shoes kicked into the duff of pine needles and sent clumps into the air. With his penchant for vast mood swings, the failure of MacGreggor's experiment was tantamount to the demise of his railroad. In defeat, he chastened himself for becoming intoxicated with foolish schemes. In this blue mood, he mumbled that sheer obstinacy had led him to believe that nitro would save his investment.

"Meester Gallag'r," Wong interrupted. "Wong think Mister MacGreggor not pack charge right. Maybe too tight. Charge need more air."

Dad turned toward Wong, taking note of the improvement in his English. He respected his expertise with black powder, but nitro was a different animal. With nitro, Wong was a neophyte.

MacGreggor insisted on a second test and only reluctantly agreed to pack the charge according to Wong's suggestion. This was an improvement, though the second charge still lacked the firepower required. Crocker's face remained screwed into a scowl. For one who had clung so adamantly to a dream, the fall was particularly hard. My father persuaded him to give MacGreggor another chance. If it failed he would withdraw the labor force from the Sierra tunnels before the first snowfall and close down construction for the winter. That would give the CP time to seek a new infusion of cash to resume construction come spring.

When their meeting ended, my father and Crocker returned by the same means they had taken earlier that day. Father rowed Crocker across Donner Lake in a rowboat and gathered their horses on the northern shore. During the ride, Crocker mused about the future. Of course, the railroad's ruin would damage his fortune, but he had made sure he and Mary would not be destitute. He was thinking about returning to his original love, gold mining. Precious placer metals had already been swept from California streams, but rich underground veins still ran the length and breadth of the Mother Lode. Plenty of men invested in mining but were usually under-capitalized and eventually went bankrupt. They left behind opportunities for smart buyers, and Crocker believed he knew a promising deal when he saw one. He made a practice of purchasing only *borasca* mines in which extensive structural investment had previously been made, and he never paid more than five cents for each dollar of value. He calculated that sooner or later he was bound to hit a worthy vein in one of the mines he had purchased. Though most financiers of his stature no longer looked to precious metal as a source of wealth, Charles Crocker never lost the lust for gold that had brought him to California in the mid-1850s.

Ironically, it was Crocker's old love of mining gold that determined the location for MacGreggor's third and final test. Though he had agreed to return to the Donner factory as soon as MacGreggor was ready, Crocker invented excuses as to why that was inconvenient. Telegraph messages bristled from his Sacramento office to the railhead and then were conveyed by Wong to MacGreggor. The deadline Crocker had originally set for a new test returned to haunt him and, rather than face it squarely, he traveled to Calaveras County to inspect an abandoned gold mine that he could purchase for a pittance of its ground value. If the mountain wouldn't go to Mohammed, the maxim went, then Mohammed would have to go to the mountain.

My father arranged for MacGreggor to demonstrate his explosive in a secluded forest of giant sequoia, twenty miles east of Mokelumne Hill and approximately forty miles from the nitroglycerin factory at Donner

Lake. Crocker wasn't worried by the added danger of transporting the explosive so far. If Wong couldn't move it over relatively smooth, well-traveled roads, he certainly couldn't transport it up rugged elk trails from Donner Lake to the tunnels on the summit.

For Wong, seeing the giant sequoia trees that my father had once spoken of with such reverence was well worth the peril of transporting nitroglycerin. Had his eyes not witnessed these marvels of nature he would never have believed trees could grow as tall as these Sierra sequoia. While waiting for Crocker and my father at the rendezvous site, he explored a grove of the giants, whose fibrous bark surrounded trunks measuring twenty to thirty feet in diameter! Nearly two hundred feet above his head, sunlight trickled down through a bushy canopy shading the forest floor where pine needles and fallen cones formed a thick carpet. He noted how few birds chanced soaring through the entangling branches of these conifers. The sheer mass of these monsters implied longevity, but how many years it had taken from them to grow so large puzzled him. Perhaps hundreds? Or more? When he measured his own stature against one colossus, he felt small and insignificant. The giant redwoods placed him properly in Nature.

To MacGreggor, he relayed his feelings. "Vary old. Vary old."

MacGreggor had no time for sentimentalities. His mind was focused on preparing his experiment. It was his last chance to show what nitroglycerin could do and he had no intention of losing the income he intent to gain from it. Despite his pledge of secrecy with Crocker, he nourished hopes that other construction companies in California would purchase what he manufactured. Perhaps other railroads too, and that didn't exclude the Union Pacific; that is, if the price was right. But before he could peddle anything, he first had to manufacture a compound that approximated the explosive power people had come to expect. Wong's praise for the sequoias inspired him to change his plan. Rather than test his concoction on a cairn of rocks that Wong had painstakingly constructed, why not topple a far more massive redwood?

Crocker and Father were late in arriving. During their journey, Dad had attempted to remain optimistic, while Crocker was mentally preparing himself for failure. MacGreggor could read his skepticism on his dour face. Still, he was not one to abandon an idea that had once caught his fancy.

Normally a Chinaman was expected to refrain from speaking with white men until specifically addressed. But the moguls of California did not frighten him. Quite aware that he had provided the CP with the means of breaking through the mountains near Cape Horn, he lacked no confidence in approaching the railroad owner and took his protest about destroying a redwood tree directly to him.

"Vary old," he said. "Not good to hurt vary old tree. Tree have ancestor. Tree live long time, Meester Crocker."

Crocker, who regarded nature as a field of conquest, especially when it came to making money, didn't see the issue from the Chinaman's perspective. Farmers in the Sacramento Valley vilified him for strip mining in the Sierra foothills with high-pressure water hoses, polluting the water they needed for agriculture. At Bloomfield, near Nevada City, a battery of his hydraulic monitors relentlessly carved away the hillsides, leaving behind wastelands unsuited for either agriculture or herding. Nature could regenerate just about any countryside except those that had been systematically denuded by high-pressure monitors.

"There're plenty more trees where this one comes from," Crocker engaged Wong. "Look around. What do you see? There's forest for miles and miles. Do ya see any lack of new trees? Even if MacGreggor's successful, which remains to be seen, it won't matter in the larger scheme of things. The forests are vast and their age is irrelevant. Hell, there are saplings everywhere you look. Some grow up to become old granddaddies, some don't."

"Spirit live in tree. Live long time in tree."

"Nonsense, Wong. But if you're right about spirits living in these trees, then let them find a new home. This is California, not China. We do things differently in this country. Besides, I don't believe these redwoods are any older than neighboring oaks and cedars. Bigger, yes, but older, no. They're big because they grow fast. If MacGreggor knocks one of these monsters down, a new tree will grow back mighty quick. You can see for yourself that they're cannibals. They grow out of each other and compete for light and water. That's why some are bigger than others. The law of the jungle operates in a forest just as it does on the savannah. The strong grow stronger and the weak perish."

Wong tried to comprehend Crocker's logic. He didn't understand words he had never heard before. He looked to my father for further enlightenment. "You think that true, Meester Gallag'r?" A cough sounded from deep in my father's throat while he wrestled with a diplomatic way of disagreeing with his employer. "Well now, that *could* be true. I'm not convinced these trees are as old as people say. And even if they are, Mr. Crocker has a point. There are plenty more of them. More than any forest needs."

MacGreggor called for Wong from the base of the target sequoia where he was making a final adjustment to the detonator. Crocker nodded for him to end their conversation and help the Scotsman. Wong looked to my father for a final verdict, but receiving nothing marched toward the redwood, where MacGreggor was unhappy with what he saw. In a rare moment of agreement, Wong noted a kink in the detonator fuse that might suffocate the required oxygen and extinguish the fuse prematurely. MacGreggor felt the kink could be straightened by hand and ordered Wong to see it done.

"No, Meester MacGregg'r," Wong said. "Fuse no work."

MacGreggor was impatient, arguing that if the fuse failed they could devise another way of detonating the nitro. But there was no purpose to this invention until it failed. He stepped back to the clearing to apprise Crocker and my father of the potential problem and from there call to Wong to light the fuse.

Wong remained near the target, pondering various alternatives. The tree was supposed to fall to the south, but the way the charge was set you couldn't be certain. If the sequoia toppled to the west or east, the trail to the north might be blocked. Moving along the forest floor cluttered with downed branches could be dangerous. Judging by foliage surrounding the upper reaches, the sequoia might get tangled for several minutes before its weight overcame temporary opposition and tumbled to the ground.

When everybody was in position, MacGreggor called for Wong to light the fuse. He got it sputtering and moved rapidly in the opposite direction of the proposed fall. In places you could see the fuse burning and in others it fell below his line of sight, only to become visible again several yards away. Everyone waited impatiently for it to pass the kink and continue on toward the nitroglycerin. From their viewing position, Crocker, Father, and MacGreggor could only estimate where that was. When the fuse stopped hissing, they looked ahead in anticipation. Tense moments passed while all waited for it to come alive as dormant fuses often did.

After an exasperating wait, MacGreggor ordered Wong to find out what was wrong. My father understood the danger and asked for patience. They waited another few minutes before MacGreggor waved his arms. Wong crept forward cautiously, his attention focused on the kink. Suddenly he burst into a run following the trail of the faulty fuse. Approximately a yard from the trunk of the redwood, he seized it to sever it with his knife, eliminating the danger of an unwanted explosion. When the deed was complete, he turned to the observers and gestured with his hands.

MacGreggor cursed, knowing there wasn't sufficient fuse material in his saddlebag to improvise an alternative. "Re-light what you've got," he cried out, cupping his mouth for amplification.

My father howled, "He'll do nothing of the kind. That's suicide."

Wong didn't seem to hear. He had already approached the charge and appeared to be hopping between the trees. Occasionally he would stoop to pick up something. MacGreggor started to move in his direction but was restrained by Dad's hand. A moment later it became clear why. Wong had taken a position beside a young sequoia and was throwing rocks at the charge from about twenty-five feet. The first missile hit the tree and bounced into thick duff. A second landed in a clump of coniferous cones nearby. Two more misses, one short, one long. The fifth flew along a perfect trajectory. Wong dove for cover an instant before it struck the explosive. There was a flash, followed closely by a flat thud that rocked the forest floor. Overhead the sequoia's branches scraped their neighbors, opening a sliver of light in the dense green canopy. Shafts of brilliant sunlight suddenly pierced the normally shaded forest as a shrill crack reverberated through the wall of neighboring sequoias. As if these giants were determined not to lose a member of their family, their branches tethered the weakened trunk in an upright position. Crocker scowled at MacGreggor, certain that once again he had been misled about the power of this new explosive.

My father was thinking that he would sent Wong back to help MacGreggor dismantle the Donner factory, then have him return to Cape Horn and evacuate with other Chinese workers to San Francisco. If the Crocker Construction Company was going to close operations through the winter, there was no point to maintain an idle workforce. And as for the Chinese who at that moment were traveling to California in the hold of several Pacific schooners, that was Crocker's problem.

His reverie was broken by thunderous shrieks echoing from the forest surrounding the target redwood. It was so sharp and commanding that he immediately identified it as the death moan of a dying colossus. So nitroglycerin had done the job after all!

The sequoia's mammoth trunk, once balanced vertically upon its roots and held in place by its neighbors, leaned forward to upset the delicate forest equilibrium. Surrounding trees that had contributed to the delayed destabilization, now with collapse pending released their patient and stood firm to protect themselves. All sixty tons of this massive creature began to slip through the outstretched jungle of branches, viciously tearing the forest in its descent. At each interval there was less opposition, for once uprooted, no invention of nature was capable of stopping the downward plunge. Limbs ripped and slashed through the forest, cutting a wide swath from the canopy while emitting a thunderous wail. As this falling mammoth hit the ground, an enormous thud echoed through the remaining forest. The ground trembled. The sounds of lament continued as the grove adjusted to the death of a family member, then suddenly all voices fell silent.

MacGreggor released a shriek of victory. Crocker pounded him on the back in hearty congratulations. Once again the fortunes of this railroad mogul seemed to turn from ruination to success.

My father called for Wong to join the others for a shot of whiskey. But Wong good-naturedly waved him off. Instead he returned to inspect the torn stump of the fallen giant. Nitroglycerin had lifted the roots from their moorings in the earth, exposing fibrous heartwood. One particular area caught his eye. Rather than shredding in a tangle of ripped fiber, the tree's core broke cleanly, exposing a relatively flat surface where it was possible to observe many concentric rings. Chinese folklore taught that each year a tree enlarged itself by adding a new ring and growing from the inside out. If that were true, this provided Wong a clue to the sequoia's age. With his knife he cleaned the surface to observe more circles. In the small area flat enough to expose these annual growth lines, there were more than a hundred rings! Wong mentally multiplied his sample tenfold. At least a thousand additional rings were hidden in the gnarled core! Perhaps even two thousand!

His estimate, rough as it was, presented an astounding conclusion that caused him to question his assumptions. Was it really possible that the tree was more than a thousand years old? He knew of no living creature to boast that. Of course, there were stories about the longevity of forest spirits in the Celestial Kingdom, but he had never given much credence to such myths. He concluded there was something wrong with his sample and returned to make a second tally. If anything, he had underestimated. That caused him to consider how MacGreggor's charge had destroyed a tree at least a *thousand* years old.

When Wong eventually joined the celebrating party, they offered him whiskey from a flask Crocker had produced. He accepted, took a few swallows, and coughed at the fiery sensation in his throat. The others laughed. When he cleared his windpipe he spoke directly to Crocker, voicing his opinion about the age of the fallen redwood.

MacGreggor glowered at him with disapproval. Crocker was less judgmental. "What makes you think that, Wong?"

"Meester Crocker, each year tree get new ring."

"And you counted over a thousand rings?"

"No. Too many. Wong make guess."

"And what's your final estimate?"

"One, maybe two thousand ring. One, maybe two thousand year."

"Hogwash," MacGreggor interjected. "There's no tree in God's universe anywhere near that age." He looked to the blank expression on Crocker's face then to Father for support.

"If you're right, Wong," my father said, "and I'm not saying you are, that makes this tree here as old as Jesus Christ."

"Not right kill old tree," Wong said, avoiding a reference he didn't understand.

MacGreggor exhaled a healthy gust of expletives, wondering how long his employer would entertain a Chinaman's moralizing. Why they wasted time listening to him was a mystery. He told himself it didn't matter because soon he'd be a rich man, with or without Crocker and his construction company. If they didn't want to use his explosive, there were many others in California who would.

"No kill more tree," Wong repeated. "Vary old."

Crocker cleared his throat and studied the fallen sequoia from afar. Yes, he had read how trees tended to add rings with successive years. But were these sequoia like oaks and poplars? And how good was Wong's sample? With that in mind he marched over to the fallen trunk to check for himself. While he had no intention of actually counting rings, he could see that Wong had not exaggerated. The rings were numerous, perhaps more numerous than the Chinaman believed.

Crocker called for my father to share what he observed. It didn't take long to reach an agreement. There was a damn good chance that this very tree was alive when Jesus of Nazareth walked upon the earth! Once Crocker and my father realized they had erred, they became military commanders whose glory was besmirched by the memory of dead soldiers left on the battlefield. Both men had the decency to suspend their celebration, but that didn't stop them from planning for the future. Using nitroglycerin to fell giant redwoods was one thing, but to cleave through inanimate granite on the Sierra summit quite another. MacGreggor was rewarded on the spot with a bonus of gold and encouraged to produce as much of his explosive as he could. Wong was ordered to accompany them back to base camp and take charge of additional mules for transporting nitroglycerin to the mountain tunnels. Weekly shipments would begin with the first snow.

Crocker's departure from Calaveras was considerably happier than his departure from Donner Lake three weeks before. He was buoyed by new optimism. If they could deliver nitroglycerin to the tunnels, the Central Pacific might be out of the mountain by spring. And by summer they might be racing over the Nevada desert to snatch up land from the Union Pacific that would someday translate into extremely lucrative revenue.

Summit

A bitter wind forced icy air through the lapels of Father's sheepskin parka as he hiked three miles down track to meet a delegation of newspaper reporters arriving on the Monday supply train from Sacramento. Just as the old-timers in these parts had predicted, snow began falling in early November, a month earlier than normal. Since the warm days of October, the temperature had dropped more than thirty degrees. Crocker had done his best to prevent journalists from reaching the tunnels, but, seasoned professionals that they were, they anticipated his tricks. The more he tried delaying tactics the more determined they were to investigate rumors that the Central Pacific was using illegal explosives inside the Sierra tunnels.

It was impossible to stop workmen from talking, especially when they drank in local saloons or stole away from the rail bed to seek their fortunes elsewhere. And for a few dollars the journalists were willing to advance, they unburdened themselves. Under heavy pressure, Crocker uncharacteristically buckled under their demands and authorized a tour of the construction. But at the same time he ordered my father to hide the railroad's full progress. Tunnel 4 was scarred with the carbon markings of black powder and emptied kegs were strewn near the entrance. Crocker offered to transport the pressmen via a CP train, obligating them to the Central Pacific's hospitality…and its control.

I CAN'T STOP THEM, THEO Crocker telegraphed his apologies.

PRAY FOR A STORM

My father crumpled the telegram in his fist and scribbled out a reply for the operator.

MAKE THEM RIDE THE MONDAY SUPPLY TRAIN TO SODA SPRINGS, STOP USE AN OPEN FLAT CAR STOP SHIP 500 KEGS OF POWDER ON FORWARD AND AFT FLATCARS STOP INSIST CROCKER CONST COMPANY NOT RESPONSIBLE FOR ACCIDENTS STOP PRAY FOR A BLIZZARD NOT A STORM STOP THEO

The reporters arrived at Soda Springs after a five-hour delay while an engine fitted with a snowplow cleared track near Cisco. Crocker followed instructions and failed to add a passenger car for their comfort. Like a bunch of coolies the reporters were forced to huddle together on a flat car confronted by freezing winds. With full knowledge of the black powder being transported on flatcars ahead and behind them, no one even suggested lighting a fire for warmth. When a correspondent from Philadelphia jammed a cigar between his chops, his colleagues threatened to push him overboard if a match got near it. At one point when the locomotive had to contend with ice on the track powder kegs creaked and threatened to break loose from their moorings.

An officer from Central Pacific Headquarters in Sacramento shepherding the newsmen to the construction camp at Soda Springs was effusive with apologies. Early winter weather had forced the Crocker Construction Company to cut back equipment and personnel to a point where operations were virtually at a standstill. The comforts and hospitality normally extended to visitors by the CP during the summer and fall were simply unavailable in winter. Had reporters elected to visit in spring they would be receiving the hospitality for which the Crocker Construction Company was renowned.

When the train finally halted at the end of the line, reporters hobbled off the flatcar, blue from cold and pale from fear that at any moment one or more of the powder kegs would break loose and blow them to smithereens. My father greeted them on the platform where he launched into an unusually wordy welcoming speech while they faced even colder temperatures than at lower elevations. Several left the assembly and without an invitation headed for the warmth of a storage shack, and hopefully a cup of anything hot to drink. When the rest looked as though they would stampede after the defectors, Father invited everyone into a heated mess tent.

Whiskey flowed freely. But there was no hot tea or coffee or anything to eat. The newsmen were wary of drinking on the job but they were cold, hungry, and without alternatives. As alcohol fogged the heads of men with empty stomachs, their laughter interrupted the railroad superintendent.

A reporter from the *Examiner* in San Francisco asked my father over the din of voices, "How much blasting powder is the Central Pacific using in those tunnels?"

Dad gave a slight jerk of his head and smiled. "Military secret, sir. I don't have to remind you men how the Union Pacific, would love to read a figure like that in your fine newspapers. You know, of course, that during the war, old Bobby Lee gleaned much of his military intelligence from newspapers printed in Baltimore and Philadelphia. I was an engineering officer on the receiving end of General Burnside's failure to censor the press at Fredericksburg and I'm damned determined not to duplicate his mistake. No soldier reveals his weapons to the enemies, now does he?"

"You can't hide it all, Gallager. We saw plenty of powder on the train coming up here."

"Did ya, now?" he said in his best Irish brogue. "Well, how many kegs? If you counted you've got your answer. Weather permitting we have three supply trains coming up each week. Multiply it out, Gentlemen. And there's your answer."

"That's a helluva lot of powder."

"In all deference, my friends, I'm not sure you comprehend how big and how strong these mountains are. You can't blast'm with firecrackers."

"You must be damn well through these mountains by now."

"Wish that were true. The granite's real hard and takes four times as much powder than rock at lower elevations."

"Using anything stronger than black powder, Major Gallager?"

"Yep," Dad emitted an artificial cackle. "Dr. Jenkin's Cure All."

A moment of laughter, then a seasoned old-timer with flowing silver hair snatched a corncob pipe from the corner of his mouth and pointed the stem at my father, demanding, "No, Mr. Gallager. You know damn well what he meant. Are you using nitroglycerin up there? Glycerin oil, Gallager, that's the stuff we're interested in. A Chinaman in Secretown said that men were using blasting oil up on the summit. You know, the yellow stuff."

"Baah!" My father almost expectorated. "What do ya want from a Chinaman? Probably a drunken one at that. Besides, nitro's illegal. We'd love to use it if we could without blowing up half the mountain and all our crew with it. But we can't. We're good engineers, not murderers. So we've got to chisel away with powder. Slow and costly, but it works."

"Will the Central Pacific make it over the pass by spring?"

Father thought about the ramification of answering the question, then offered, "Military secret. An officer doesn't disclose his time schedule either."

A third journalist waved a whiskey bottle to signal he wanted the floor. His words were a bit wobbly. "We wanna go inside the tunnels to see for ourselves."

"Nothing doing," my father shot back. "Company rule. Only workmen enter the tunnels. It's just too bloody dangerous. Cave-ins are more frequent than we'd like and there's no predictin'm. The workspace is packed with machinery and carts—all dangerous. We haven't broken the rule yet and we don't intend to start now. But if you want, you're welcome to come to the tunnel entrances. I'll answer any questions you've got there. But understand this before we move out of here. Nobody goes inside. This is for *your* safety, not mine."

"Let just one or two representatives inside," the bottle swinger said.

"Maybe at Tunnel 4, but we'll have to check once we get there."

Grumbling broke out. Some hooting. The alcohol raised the level of noise several decibels. The delegation had weathered the cold and risked travel with kegs of black powder for an opportunity to see the tunnels for themselves. Then, in an arbitrary ruling by the superintendent, they were denied the very thing they wanted most. One newsman from Denver declared his intention to stick around until the construction company changed its mind.

"Sorry, Gentlemen," Dad said. "The railroad can't accommodate you in camp. It's a free country and you're free to go wherever you wish. But if you decide to stay in the neighborhood the Central Pacific hasn't got any lodging. Food stores for the winter are at bare minimum. That means no bedding and no meals. Only a skeleton crew of blasters and muckers work for the next few months. No conveniences. No comforts. So if you fellows want to catch the supply train when it returns to Colfax this afternoon, you'll have to get cracking. Otherwise it could be a cold, hungry week. Anybody willing to march to the tunnel entrances with me is welcome. And keep your eyes open. At this season the bears are hibernating, but we got some pretty wild mountain men around. They're nasty fellas left over from the gold days, who wouldn't mind steal'n a winter jacket or two that caught their fancy. There's a rumor circulating that when they're real hungry they don't mind some roasted human flesh. I don't give this much credence, but when somebody disappears in the mountains, people in these parts begin speculating. They get folks kinda nervous. Hell, you might see something worth writing about. But you'll have to keep your eyes peeled, cause from what I hear you don't get much of a chance to defend yourself. By the time these mountain men pounce on you from a rock ledge like a mountain cougar, it's too late."

My father's comments produced the intended effect and unnerved the press corps. His announcement about lack of facilities in the camp engendered a wave of disappointed grumbling Without room and board there was no choice but to return with the afternoon supply train. To salvage the trip from complete disaster, most reporters followed Dad outside, prepared to march with him to the tunnels, though they had little expectation of discovering more than the Central Pacific wanted them to see. The last to leave the mess hall snatched up several bottles of whiskey—compliments of the Crocker Construction Company.

My father set the pace with long, deliberate strides, designed to tire the city slickers, several of whom were double-stepping to keep up. Stragglers thinned out along the icy roadbed fearful of getting lost and constantly looking over their shoulders for signs of mountain men. A few cried out for their leader to slow down but Dad maintained his pace. As the grade increased he gradually accelerated, leading the reporters a mile and a half along the level track from Tunnel 4 to Tunnel 7, and finally circling back to Tunnel 4. At each location, the men were permitted to look into the darkened entrances but not to enter. Guards posted outside ensured that no stragglers at the end of the line might steal back and venture inside. Kegs of powder were piled everywhere, some empty but more filled. And just to authenticate the impression my father had masterfully cultivated, two detonations occurred deep inside Tunnel 7, transmitting an echoing blast to those standing at the entrance.

At Tunnel 4, Father invited his guests to venture with him some 1,600 feet into a short tunnel already completed and cleared of all digging machines. The odor of black powder lingered in the confined space. Throughout the tour, he talked freely about persistent supply problems that slowed rail-building. So difficult was the task in the mountains that it became necessary for the Central Pacific to revise its estimate of where it might hope to join the galloping Union Pacific. Instead of meeting somewhere in Utah, a more realistic target would be in the Nevada desert. Eastern pundits were betting the Union Pacific would lay track clear up to the California state line. Some went farther than that and bet the eastern escarpment of the Sierra.

The journalists could feel their story slipping away. Theodore Gallager had provided them little or nothing startling. Some concluded that their editors had erred in believing a story existed. Once convinced that their suspicions were unfounded, they lost their enthusiasm. The weather and the lack of food became an obsession. The tour ended with the prospect of having to spend the night shivering under the stars.

Once back at the Soda Springs railhead, Dad felt in the mood for a little compassion. Hot tea and biscuits appeared while the reporters waited for the supply train to depart. After going so long without refreshment even this token hospitality brought cheers of gratitude. No more whiskey appeared. Two hours later, a locomotive puffed a ghostlike steam into the chilling air as it approached Soda. Behind it traveled an empty saloon car, a significant improvement over flatcars provided earlier that day.

My father contained his delight until the reporters boarded and the train was chugging along the track in the direction of Colfax. He danced a short jig beside the railroad ties. An entire troop of reporters had come and gone without gathering a single shred of evidence against the Crocker Construction Company. For all their meddling, they got stories barely worth the paper they were printed on—absolutely nothing to titillate their readers from St. Louis to New York.

Dad wrote the real scoop in his imagination.

CENTRAL PACIFIC ACCOMPLISHES ENGINEERING FEAT OF THE CENTURY

Donner, California. Daring, but true nevertheless. To blast through granite on Sierra peaks, the Central Pacific Rail Road Company has been manufacturing the new explosive called nitroglycerin at a factory near Donner Lake, California. Each night a Chinaman has transported this extremely volatile explosive on a caravan of 8 mules up to Donner Summit where remarkable progress had been made in cleaving tunnels through what was hitherto believed to be impenetrable granite. Each mule carried more explosive power than 60 kegs of black powder. And all over icy trails in the dead of winter! The plan was the brainchild of Wong Po-ching, Superintendent Theodore Gallager and Central Pacific owner Charles Crocker. Because of this startling progress, nine tunnels are expected to be completed by early spring. The race with the Union Pacific

Rail Road through the Nevada and Utah Territories will soon begin in earnest. Gamblers who put their money on the Union Pacific's fortunes will soon have a rude awakening. Those who were bold enough to buy Central Pacific stock are destined to reap justified rewards.

Father filed the story in his memory for future publication. He wanted it told. The world should know what marvels had been accomplished at Donner. But not until he had actually punched his track through the granite and over the eastern escarpment. He had vowed to conquer or be conquered and now he was beginning to taste the sweetness of victory. The mountains would be his after all.

By mid-January Wong's deliveries of nitroglycerin absorbed the full production of the Donner Lake factory. Each night his mules climbed to one of five tunnels on the western escarpment and four smaller ones the eastern slopes. Chinese blasters and muckers worked three shifts around the clock in the dank, smoke-filled air. The good Lord had answered Crocker's prayers for foul weather. Inordinately heavy blizzards isolated his construction workers from civilization in the Sacramento Valley. Two supply trains per week were the only links between people in the valley and those in the mountains.

Crocker had no intention of allowing his secret to leak. Armed guards ensured that no one ventured beyond the railhead at Soda Springs. While not inside the tunnels, Chinese laborers were quarantined to their camps where the use of English was discouraged. Even if one or two coolies deserted and made their way back to civilization, few might communicate what was seen. Crocker had ruminated over the treatment of his "little pets," for come spring they would be handsomely paid and put on ships back to Canton where they could live in relative wealth for many years.

Progress on the summit was ahead of schedule until unseasonably warm weather in early February threatened to wreck Crocker's plans. Snows, which once camouflaged the tunnel operations, began to melt. Stanford reported that in the state capital rumors about nitroglycerin refused to die. Hound dogs in the Legislature were on scent, yelping for blood. The ex-governor, who had been kept in as much dark as the press, became indignant and accused lawmakers of libel, threatening legal action. Crocker took perverse pleasure in watching his partner make a fool of himself.

My father knew that the deception was bound to backfire and had constantly warned Crocker against keeping his partner in the dark. But nothing could persuade the headstrong Crocker to include the ex-governor in his secret. In Crocker's mind he was not responsible for informing Stanford. If the ex-governor insisted on gallivanting around the state without taking time to educate himself about his railroad investment, that was *his* problem, not Crocker's. Any day of the week the president of the Central Pacific could have made a personal inspection of the tunnels to see for himself. But the fact was he hated the cold and wasn't going to inconvenience himself until the weather turned.

In early March, my father's worst fears came to fruition. Stanford took accusations against his railroad as a personal insult and threatened to confront his accusers in a series of old-fashioned duels—with pistols, would you believe it? Reports circulated from Sacramento that every morning the governor was seen outside his mansion improving his marksmanship, which was never much good and didn't seem to improve with practice. Those close to Stanford knew he was purposely creating the image of someone who was prepared to back up his threats. Few believed the overweight, physically clumsy governor, would actually face those who libeled his company. His advisors pointed out that even if he subdued one or two, his chance of surviving a series of duels was statistically very poor.

Reason eventually won out. Rather than confront enemies of the Central Pacific one at a time, Stanford reasoned it was better to silence all rumors once and for all. As an ex-governor he exercised his right to address a joint session of the State Assembly and Senate. And there, with voice choked in righteous indignation and arms flailing like an evangelist on the verge of a revival, he answered charges about nitroglycerin in the Sierra tunnels. His speech climaxed with a demand, not a request, but a demand that the Legislature send a delegation to see for itself. What's more, he pledged to put the full resources of the Central Pacific Rail Road Company and his private Pullman cars at the delegates' disposal.

Crocker telegraphed my father in desperation. Unless this inspection was canceled, the Central Pacific was about to get caught red-handed. Dad wired back that they wouldn't get away with the same trick they had played so successfully in November. Nor could they hide the enormous progress and convince savvy politicians that it had been accomplished with black powder alone. More damning were vast stockpiles of powder that had accumulated unused near the tunnel entrances.

It was Wong who provided a solution for disposing of the unwanted powder. He added pack animals to his caravans from Donner Lake and on return journeys hauled away the unopened kegs. After transporting nitroglycerin, moving black powder proved quite easy. My father was so upset over the legislators' visit that he left the final disposal of the powder to Wong's judgment. Dumping it into streams was the easiest and safest means. But at the time such tributaries were still frozen over.

To break the monotony, Wong had been returning his unloaded mule team to MacGreggor's factory over deer trails, and on one such exploration had discovered a cave near Mirror Lake. Unlike most in the region that were damp and in the spring flooded, this was inordinately dry. At the time he did not carry enough oil to explore the dark caverns beyond the cave entrance, but he had made a mental note to return with torches. Dad's instructions to dispose of he black powder stirred memories of this place. The dry cave would serve as a temporary warehouse until spring when streams, swollen with melting snows, would carry the powder away with little or no trace.

On his first transport he carried a dozen kegs, bringing torches to explore beyond the cave entrance. It took only a few minutes to confirm his initial impression that no moisture seeped inside. Some fifty feet into the cave he discovered the charred remains of an open fire and a steel sewing needle. So other travelers had also used it—Nomlaki Indians, perhaps, or maybe descendents from the Donner Party that had perished in these mountains twenty years before and about whom Caucasians often spoke with such deep reverence.

PRIVATE AND CONFIDENTIAL
6 March 1868

Dear Theo,

To bring you up to date with the unpleasant situation here, or should I say the catastrophe, there was no other way but for me to come clean with Leland who, as you can imagine, was less than a gentleman. He became a snarling bobcat. I won't repeat his threats, but they were hotter than one might expect to discover in Hell. Needless to say, he refused to retract a word of what he had said before the State Legislature. No doubt, in his brain, he's contemplating criminal action against me—his partner!

My guess is that despite Leland's bluster he will do nothing, unless we get caught, which is now quite probable. If we could only postpone the politicians for a month. But how? I implore your suggestions.

CC

7 March 1868
Dear Mr. Crocker,
Have your Padre pray for foul weather!

Theo

March 8th
Dear Theo
I'm doing better than that. I'm praying myself.

CC

March 9th
Dear Mr. Crocker,
I fear that that in the Divine Court the prayers of sinners like us will be rejected. If the Almighty Judge knows what's been going on here, he's not likely to be our strongest advocate. I recommend more earthly endeavors. Send all supplies for a full month immediately. We'll store our food, tools, and equipment in the completed tunnels until spring. Absolutely no supply trains after that. Give us total and absolute isolation until the spring thaw. Without supply trains Governor Stanford's cohorts will have to arrange their own transport, which is not impossible but inconvenient. We'll batten down the hatches and hope to wait out the next winter blizzard—if we're lucky enough to have it.

Send my regards to Governor Stanford.

Theo

The last supply trains arrived at Soda Springs as my father had requested. Food and fuel were taken directly to the Chinese camps. Equipment was moved into the tunnel entrances. Fresh mules were integrated into Wong's teams carting nitro up and powder down the mountainsides. Dad prepared for a blizzard, only it didn't come. Quite the contrary, the weather remained unseasonably warm. Snow banks began to thaw with a sludgy runoff, turning the ground outside the tunnels into mud so thick that wagon wheels could not operate.

Crocker utilized every wile he possessed to postpone the legislators' visit. In private communications with my father he wrote how Stanford was working against him. Bullheaded and illogical as Crocker considered his partner to be, the ex-governor was not acting in his own interest by encouraging an inspection. Crocker suspected that Stanford intended to sue him for enough to pay for his entire investment loss in the railroad venture.

When a date was settled for the visit, Crocker could have owned up to his company's use of nitroglycerin and accepted the consequences. But that was not his way. He had a blind faith in luck, though this time he confessed that perhaps he had pushed it too far. Dad urged him to convert his partners into co-conspirators by being ruthlessly frank with them, but he learned there were deeper grievances between the partners than the glycerin oil.

On the day scheduled for the Assembly's visit, weather favored the delegation with bright, warm temperatures. The Central Pacific's propaganda bulletins declaring operations in the mountains nearly at a standstill haunted the company that issued them. One look at the spectacular progress made on the toughest portion of the track was bound to reveal this deceit. Moreover, the investigators were certain to bring along Chinese interpreters to interview blasters and muckers. For a modest fee Chinese workmen would blab all they knew, including how their compatriot Wong Po-ching had secretly delivered the forbidden explosives.

My father racked his brain to avert disaster. Crocker came to the camp headquarters to parley and, in a rare moment of depression, admitted defeat. The thought of going to prison obsessed him. Ambition, he was willing to admit, had driven him beyond reason. His Day of Reckoning was near.

That night Crocker stayed up late in order to see the final shipment of nitroglycerin enter Tunnel 7. After blasting on the following day, Dad planned to re-introduce black powder and lie to the inspectors.

"What do ya think, Theo?" Crocker asked him, probing for a favorable response.

"Not a chance in hell they'll believe that," my father replied. "Particularly since the company's gone out of its way to hide our progress."

They argued amongst themselves until Wong found Charles Crocker conversing with my father in the headquarters tent. Most Chinese workmen would have shied away from the bossman, but not Wong, a co-conspirator with Crocker. By then, he felt completely comfortable in my father's and Mr. Crocker's presence.

Dad saw in him an opportunity to break off his argument with Crocker and turned to provide instructions. "When you return to the factory," he said, "don't bring any more of the nitro up here. Just wait in camp until I tell you what's next. You understand that, Wong?"

"Why stop now?" Wong questioned the Central Pacific owner directly. "Two week more. Tunnels almost finished."

Crocker noted the Chinaman's new facility with English and attributed the fact to daily conversations with MacGreggor. He decided on the spot to take Wong into his confidence. "You see," he explained, "the authorities will soon take legal action against me and the company. You know what that means?"

"Yes, sir. But why let government men see?" he responded with boyish innocence in his tone.

"They're arriving on a train at noon tomorrow. Governor Stanford invited them. If they get near the tunnels, they'll know exactly what we've been up to."

Wong considered that for several seconds. "Then stop train," he said without a hint that this might not be possible.

"Not that easy. If an engine breaks down, Wong," Crocker sounded didactic, "they'll call for a replacement locomotive. If we blow up the tracks? They'll smell a rat."

"No," Wong interrupted. "Make big snow on tracks. From mountains. You know," and here he struggled to pronounce a new word in his vocabulary, "Ablache...Abalanche."

"An avalanche?" my father corrected.

"Yes, avalanche. At Cisco, mountains hold much snow. Make it fall down on track. Train no travel to Soda."

The idea momentarily intrigued my father who said, "I've read how people produce artificial avalanches in the Alps by firing cannons into alpine snow packs. But we haven't got any cannons. Certainly we couldn't get any here by tomorrow."

"Wong climb on ice. Put explosive into ice and make boom, boom on snow pack. Big snow fall on track."

Dad watched Crocker curl his lip as though taking Wong's idea seriously. To the Chinaman he said, "You can't carry enough powder on the side of the mountain to make enough snow fall."

"Yes, Mr. Gallager," he said, careful to pronounce Gallager instead of Gallag'r. "Wong carry nitro on back. Nitro make plenty big boom. Frighten men on train. They go back quick to Sacramento."

Crocker understood well that desperation led men to injudicious decisions. Still, Wong's plan was the only one that had even the slightest chance for success. Daring alone had advanced him to his elevated position in life and he saw no reason why it wouldn't favor him again. Particularly when he had run out of viable alternatives.

My father voiced his objections in rapid succession. Crocker had come to expect that he would. And when the superintendent stopped telling him why it wouldn't work, he turned to Wong and asked, "You really *want* to do this? Packing nitroglycerin on your back over an ice field has got to be dangerous."

"Suicide," Father interjected. "You're about to murder this fellow."

Wong opened his palms in supplication. "That depend on what Mr. Crocker pay Wong."

Crocker smirked. "How much? You're going to be the richest Chinaman in California."

"Five hundred dollar, Mr. Crocker."

Crocker lifted his jaw to flare his fantail beard like a porcupine and purse his lips. "Extortion. Bloody extortion." He said it more for my father's benefit than from a genuine disagreement over the sum. Wong could have asked for twice that amount and gotten it immediately. "What the hell you gonna do with all that money, Wong?"

"Wong be rich man."

"Money's only good if you invest it in something," Crocker said. "Where you gonna put your money?"

A twinkle glowed in the Chinaman's eyes. "Wong send money to Yung Wo Company in San Francisco. Buy wife in China. Bring wife to California."

"Jesus, Wong," Dad interrupted, feeling the need to protect him against Crocker's incessant exploitation. "That's no way to get a wife. You goddamn little fool. If they don't steal your money outright in Frisco, they're gonna send you the ugliest woman in the whole Orient. She's gonna be so diseased they won't even take her back. And you're gonna be out all your cash."

"No, Mr. Gallager. Wong get good wife, you see. Wong need more money. Lots more money."

"Don't count it until you get down safely from the mountain," my father replied. "My bet is that you'll never make it."

Crocker looked elated. The Central Pacific finally had a plan, a long shot admittedly, but at least it had a plan, and his construction company had a few more days of life before being sacked. Maybe prison wasn't as close as he had thought. "Theo, tell you what I'm gonna do. You put your money on failure, and I'll bet on Wong' s success. If he succeeds, we'll each give him five hundred, so he gets a thousand dollars. If not, then I'll pay *you* five hundred. Want to take that bet?"

Dad knew to be wary of betting against one of California's cleverest businessmen, a man he knew to be rash and irresponsible. In the back of his mind he was thinking that if he won, he would donate his winnings to a charitable cause that helped Chinese workmen, most probably Harriet Horn's Protection League. In any case, he had no intention of personally profiting from Wong's misfortune. "You got it, boss," he said.

"Good." Crocker patted the Chinaman on the shoulder. "You understand that wager, don't you, Wong?"

"Yes, Mr. Crocker."

"Then listen to this. If you make a good job of the avalanche you'll get not only five hundred from me but five hundred more from Mr. Gallager. That should give you something to think about when you're packing nitro up the mountain. A thousand bucks, Wong. You'll have that wife of yours sooner than you think."

Wong smiled. "I make good avalanche."

"But be careful, you hear. I'd rather have a rich Chinaman than a dead one."

My father wanted to say something as noble as his employer but nothing came to mind. Though his money was riding against Wong, he was nevertheless pulling for him to win. Looked at from a different point of view, his contribution would encourage Wong. And if they could make it one more month without the government meddling in Central Pacific construction, Crocker would return to him the five hundred dollars, in addition to a handsome bonus. This might be the best money he had ever wagered.

After Crocker left, Father gave final instructions to Wong, then planted his hand on the Chinaman's arm and added, "I know I'm betting against myself here, but you be very careful, Wong. I want you to make the biggest goddamn avalanche this state has ever seen."

CHAPTER SIX

Cisco

That Wong lived to see his avalanche was partly due to his physical stamina and partly to a miracle. Oddly, the most dangerous portion of cascading snow proved to be the easiest to avoid. He had become adroit at handling nitroglycerin, and the process of transporting it on his back to the snowdrifts went without a hitch. But his fuses were characteristically unreliable and threatened disaster, as they had in the redwood forest of Calaveras. Experience had taught him to respect the fickle nature of these devices because no matter how well measured and packed, they nevertheless burned at different rates, depending on temperature, mixture of the powder, and dozens of less quantifiable conditions. Superstitious sappers imbued them with mysterious powers and made a habit of reciting incantations before igniting them with the embers of a cigar well-chewed as a result of worn nerves.

In the case of Wong's avalanche, the fuses burned inordinately slowly. Normally that would have worked to a sapper's benefit. But not in this situation. By the time Wong had climbed into position and planted his charges, he estimated that Governor Stanford's train was approaching Upper Cascade trestle, only a half-mile from the spot where he intended the snowpack to fall. Since he had no desire to endanger the lives of those traveling in the train, his avalanche needed to bury the tracks, not the passenger cars. And just as importantly, there was no benefit to the CP if snow blanketed the tracks *after* the train had passed. It was essential for Wong's plan that the avalanche occur *before* the locomotive reached Cisco.

The thousand-dollar reward, lost if he botched the job, drove Wong to gamble. When the fuse sputtered too slowly, instead of seeking shelter and waiting for the inevitable, he scampered back up the mountainside to make an adjustment. But by the time he discovered that he had underestimated the burn point, it was only ten inches from the charge. Quick reflexes sent him flying helter-skelter down the incline again only a minute before the detonator discharged, and an instant later a tremendous secondary explosion rocked the mountain.

The thrust caught him from behind and propelled him in the air along his original trajectory, away from the blast. He landed in a snowdrift. Instinct told him to extricate himself immediately, before more snow buried him deeper. The possibility of suffocating frightened him even more than being crushed or frozen. With all his strength, he struggled to his knees then scrambled as hard as he could toward the protection of nearby pine trees. A moment later, more falling snow rolled him head over heels. His legs jackknifed inward and his shoulders crumpled while his hands attempted to both stop his fall and shield his head from impact with tree trunks and boulders. During these tumultuous moments, he maintained his consciousness by jabbering to himself in Cantonese. This stopped only when he realized that his tumble had ended. Earlier injuries sustained during the risky detonations from a gondola at Cape Horn swirled in his mind. This time there were no burns or hearing loss. It was too soon to tell whether he had any broken bones or injured vital organs. Weight of snow about him pressed his elbows and arms tightly against his body, making it difficult to claw for a few inches of maneuvering room.

By the time he managed to crawl into the daylight, a steam engine named *Jupiter*, which later represented the CP Railroad at the Golden Spike ceremony outside Ogden, Utah, had braked to a stop where the tracks beneath it disappeared under snow that had plunged from a higher altitude. A stiff wind across the American River ravine carried traces of smoke spewing from the locomotive's funnel-shaped stack. From Wong's perch above the train, he saw the figure of a man stumbling through the snowpack, presumably trying to grasp the dimensions of the slide. Wong could have told him it was hopeless. The avalanche covered more than a half-mile of track and no plow of the Central Pacific was strong enough to punch through a barrier of that magnitude. For the time being, Governor Stanford's train wasn't going anywhere but in reverse. A thousand dollars, please, Meester Crocker and Meester Gallager!

The gabardine suits Leland Stanford wore never seemed to fit. A robust man with a heavy frame, he could gain or lose twenty pounds in a few months, leaving his vest either popping at the buttons or sagging over his suspenders. On this morning, he was accompanying twenty-four members of the California state Senate and Assembly to inspect the tunnels at Donner Summit. A man who worried about everything, he was nervous at the prospect of these lawmakers uncovering his company's perfidy in the tunnels. As he sashayed through the Pullman cars he had put into service for these legislators, a twitch around the lips betrayed his discomfort. Of course, as soon as Big Charley had told him about what was going on, he immediately consulted several eminent attorneys who advised him that not only was the railroad in legal trouble, but its officers were personally liable for fines and risking possible imprisonment. In Stanford's mind, because the Central Pacific owners had never issued a directive about the use of nitroglycerin on their railroad, they bore no responsibility for any legal violations. The decision to employ glycerin oil had been made unilaterally by Charles Crocker in his capacity as president of the Crocker Construction Company. It was merely a coincidence that Crocker was also a co-owner of the Central Pacific Railroad; his ownership signified absolutely nothing. The Crocker Construction Company and its principals had committed crimes, not the Central Pacific Railroad and its officers.

Ironically, Stanford was not unhappy with this new turn of events. He had long recognized that it was time to depose Crocker as czar of the railroad's construction operations. A couple of years in the state penitentiary at Point San Quentin would keep him out of the business long enough to teach him that the railroad's president, not the VP for construction, was the proper senior executive to oversee controversial operations. Crocker's days of toying with the fortunes of the Central Pacific were nearly over.

The visit of California legislators to the Donner tunnels had an unlikely champion in Llewellyn Hubbel, speaker of the Assembly from the county of San Leandro. Often criticized for his lethargy in ferreting out corruption in the state capital, Hubbel, nevertheless, knew how to turn a scandal to his own advantage. It didn't matter to people in Iowa, Ohio, or New York that California politicians were up for sale to the state's agricultural and shipping magnates. He liked to say in public that reconstruction in the old Confederate states defeated by war had dulled the public's appetite for clamping down on political corruption elsewhere. Americans had seen so much malfeasance since then that the electorate had come to think of corruption as being synonymous with political power; even an honest politician, if he managed to stay in Congress long enough, the thinking went, would succumb to temptation.

These days the press's ravenous hunger to report on scandal seemed to have waned. But the mendacity of a company Congress had selected to build the western segment of the Pacific Railroad had rekindled fire among journalists. Suddenly they had something big with which to stir their readers. Hubbel had cultivated a talent for knowing which headlines would titillate the public. Ambitious to become a U.S. senator from California, he could hardly afford to avoid the publicity when it came his way.

Small coal furnaces heated the CP railcars against the frigid March air. From Blue Canyon around to Sailor's Spur *Jupiter* had chugged through lush pine forests, then crept at a slower speed past Putnam's to Emigrant Gap and from there to Miller's Bluff. East of Blue Canyon Bridge, the train climbed slowly up the eighteen-degree incline. A screech of metal brakes signaled that the locomotive was stopping unexpectedly as she outran the steam spewing from her bulbous smokestack. Passengers looked out through the windows unable to figure out why they were no longer moving. Reports circulated through the Pullmans that the engine had come to a halt because of snow on the tracks. A lot of snow.

Stanford collared a steward, demanding an explanation. The man shrugged his shoulders in ignorance then followed the ex-governor to the platform and quickly down to the roadbed. That proved excellent timing because they were met by the locomotive's senior engineer who dragged a bad leg as he half-marched and half-hopped beside the track. "Avalanche," the engineer announced and pointed over his shoulder a hundred yards beyond the locomotive. "Musta happened just before we arrived. The snow came down from the slope up there." A finger at the end of an outstretched arm signaled the direction.

"How much?" Stanford asked, acknowledging with a nod of his head Llewellyn Hubbel's presence behind him.

"Can't tell from here," said the engineer, rotating on his good leg for better footing on the snow and then replanting his bad one. "I've sent my stoker forward to evaluate the situation. A good plow will do the trick. There's one at Emigrant Gap. But it's gonna take a few hours to get it up here."

"Nobody said anything about this avalanche," Hubbel interrupted in the accusatory tone he often used to put others on the defensive.

"I didn't know about it, sir," the engineer replied, as if the accusation had been directed against him. "Nobody notified me. The snow must have come down early this morning. Damn good thing it didn't hit us. I heard stories of these things rollin' down from the mountains. Can't stop'em, ya know. They can roll a hundred-ton locomotive right off the tracks. It's no easy task to dig out of one of these things, I can tell ya."

"Well, Leland, how the hell we going to get up to the tunnels?" Hubbel snapped. "We're busy men and we didn't come all this way not to inspect your tunnels. We couldn't be more than a few miles from the first one right now."

"Six miles," the engineer said, then accompanied Stanford and Hubbel who had set out to inspect the snowpack for themselves. They were arguing in frustrated voices when the stoker who had been sent forward returned with news. The track, he reported, was buried under tons of snow for at least an eighth of a mile or more. Forcing *Jupiter* through without a snowplow, he said, was out of the question.

The significance of this phenomenon occurred to Stanford in stages. He feared that his political colleagues would blame him and his company for a delay, but a moment later decided that there was no way they could hold the CP responsible for an act of God. It dawned on him that the legislators might now abandon their plans and return to Sacramento. If so, the CP would just back *Jupiter* up until they found a spur to reverse directions and continue down the mountains. It was suddenly conceivable that the Central Pacific might be spared a nasty lawsuit after all. Yet the thought of Charley Crocker getting off the hook spoiled his relief at the fortuitous turn of events. Crocker, he knew from past experience, enjoyed at least seven lives. Still, on balance, it was far better to see him go free than to risk discovery of his company's skullduggery in the tunnels. "Well? What do ya think?" Stanford asked Hubbel.

The speaker growled in indignation as though he held Stanford personally responsible for the impasse. Then he marched over to confer with his colleagues, who had lined up in front of the glacier-like snow bank. Though bundled in a heavy parka, a junior assemblyman from San

Diego was shivering so severely that his teeth chattered like a baby's. He asked Stanford in broken speech if it were possible for the Central Pacific to provide horse-drawn wagons on the other side of the avalanche. Using the telegraph running parallel to the track, they could order the wagons in advance, then tramp around the snowpack and move up to the tunnels in wagons.

The engineer warned them that it was very likely the avalanche had also knocked down the telegraph lines paralleling the track. A journeyman engineer volunteered to climb a pole nearby and try his hand at raising someone on the other end. A few minutes later he called down from his perch. No luck. He was able to communicate with an operator back at Cascade, behind the train, but could raise no one farther up the line.

Hubbel rejoined Stanford, this time with an expression of suspicion. "I'd say this is a damn curious act of nature, Leland. I'm not a mountain man myself, but we got a few in our delegation who are. And they say it's plenty peculiar how this avalanche fell right on the tracks." He glanced over his shoulder and squinted at the distant peaks. "This kind of obstruction makes a man think mighty hard. I read somewhere that avalanches can be induced, you know."

tanford knew how to look offended, throwing his shoulders back and lifting his beard to look down at the shorter state senator. "Now, Llewellyn, are you insinuating foul play here? If so, then state it clearly so my railroad can defend its honor. And while you're at it, tell me how someone could make an avalanche occur."

"With cannon fire. I've read that they do it all the time in Switzerland. They make the snow fall in places where it won't do any damage."

Stanford released a synthetic laugh from deep in the abdomen. "Do you see any cannon around, Llewellyn? If you haven't noticed, the Central Pacific's a railroad, not an artillery battalion. We don't own cannon and if we did, we wouldn't deploy them here. They'd be better served defending the capitol in Sacramento against politicians who oppose legitimate business development in this state."

The remark got Hubbel's dander up. If the other legislators didn't understand the drama unfolding before them, he most certainly did. To them, the avalanche was no more than a natural impediment. But to him it constituted evidence of Governor Stanford's duplicity, and here he recognized a political advantage.

With one foot on the snow bank, the speaker addressed his cohorts in a voice usually reserved for speeches before joint assemblies. "Is six miles so far to walk, gentlemen?"

"That's six miles in one direction and another six back," a state senator from Santa Barbara reminded him.

"Should we let a little snow stand between us and those who depend on our judgment to defend the state's interests? If you're timid, I say stay inside the train. But I'm ready to walk from here to Virginia City if I have to. Anybody else wants to is welcome to join me."

The wind muffled much of what Hubbel had to say and his normal evangelical voice failed to convince more than a half-dozen of his fellow legislators to follow his lead. The majority elected to retire to the train's saloon car, where Stanford gave stewards orders to see they were generously taken care of.

After donning winter clothing they had brought along, Hubbel led six legislators over the snow, the majority on the youthful side. Ex-Governor Stanford loathed walking almost as much as he detested the cold, but he feared letting the ambitious Hubbel head for the tunnels unchaperoned. Having pledged his full cooperation to the Assembly and Senate, how could he do any less?

From a promontory high above the stalled train, Wong gazed down on his handiwork. At first he believed that the train had no alternative but to back down the mountain toward Colfax. What he observed changed his mind. Seven men left the train and were heading through the snow bank. As he watched, they appeared to detour from the thick snow for easier footing in the adjacent forest. He feared that if they reached the tunnels, Mr. Crocker wouldn't pay him the thousand dollars. Somehow, he'd have to devise a way of seeing that the seven men didn't reach the first tunnel. He started walking toward them, but had to stop abruptly. His swollen ankles made walking extremely painful.

As the ranking assemblyman, Llewellyn Hubbel assumed leadership of the delegation, though his sense of direction was far inferior to his skill as a political dealmaker. A mat of heavy cumulous clouds precluded him from navigating by the sun, and thick stands of ponderosa pines, heavy with snow, obstructed the surrounding terrain. Mistrust of Leland Stanford complicated his path finding. When Stanford declared the proper direction to be eastward, the suspicious Hubbel led his party to the northeast. And when others suggested alternate routes, he pressed forward, thoroughly convinced of the reliability of his internal compass. When the troop eventually circled back to discover its own footprints, the speaker's navigational skills came under attack. Two young assemblymen proposed that they return to the train immediately in time for a late lunch, that is, if they could still find the track, then resume their march after they had some sustenance.

The legislators were caucusing when Wong caught up with them. The Chinaman's outer garments were ripped and caked with dirt. His black queue had become unbraided and his hair hung in cascades over his shoulders. Blood from three gashes had frozen on his face.

"Well, well," Hubbel announced. "Here he is, gentlemen. We have not made it to the infamous tunnels, but we most certainly have encountered the abominable snowman."

"Men are going in a circle," Wong announced, taking note of the lawmaker's insult, though he might have revised his opinion had he looked at himself in a mirror. "I will show the way to the train. No problem. It isn't far. No problem."

Hubbel examined the coolie with a skeptic's eye. From his appearance he seemed to be in greater need of help than his fellow legislators. "Is this one of the rascals you got working on your railroad, Leland?" he growled. The ex-governor shivered beneath his sea otter coat and studied Wong, but more out of curiosity than contempt. He had never paid much attention to the Asians who worked at the construction sites. Still, this one looked vaguely familiar. Ignoring Hubbel's question he addressed Wong directly: "Do I know you?"

"Mister Stan-ford. I met you near Cape Horn."

"You know me? Then we've met before, haven't we?" Wong nodded. "Outside the train near Cape Horn. Mister Stan-ford came out of train at night and said hello. You smoked a cigar, then made a big piss on wheels and when back into your car. I heard you attach the chain lock."

Wong's revelation about the ex-governor relieving himself outside his Pullman produced gentle laughter among the lawmakers.

The governor, never one to be embarrassed by being the brunt of humor, cleared his throat, a sign of his discomfort. Even less did he enjoy the thought that others might interpret what this Chinaman said to indicate that he was a Sinophile like Charley Crocker. Nothing could be further from the truth. Unable to think of a clever rebuttal, he merely asked simply, "Well, what the hell are you doing out here?"

Wong sensed that Crocker had not told his partner about the avalanche and decided to lie about his injuries. "I come down from Soda Spring. I fell in the rocks and need help." He pointed to his bruised ankles. "Foot's no good."

There was a gasp of disdain from Hubbel. "You trust that cock-and-bull story? Why should we believe a degenerate like this? He looks like a wild beast. I tell ya, this man's obviously been up to no good. My guess is he snuck up to see what he could steal."

Stanford kept looking at Wong to confirm an intuition that his association with the Chinaman went deeper than a greeting outside his railroad car. He snapped, "Were you up on Cape Horn with the basket men?"

"Yes, sir, Mister Stanford. I Wong Po-ching. I went down the mountain in the first basket. You ask Mister Gallag'r. He'll tell you."

The mention of my father's name jogged Stanford's memory. He had never paid much attention to Chinese names because they all sounded like mumbo-jumbo to him. Still, the name Wong Po-ching was somewhat familiar. Hopkins had often spoken of a man with a name like that. "How far's Soda Springs from here?" he asked.

Wong thought quickly and decided to tell what he knew. "Five, maybe six miles."

That corroborated what the train's engineer had told them. "Is there much snow on the tracks?" Stanford asked.

Here Wong was on firmer ground. Since he had seen the extent of the snowpack from a high altitude, he could answer with authority. "Very much snow, Mister Stan-ford. Much snow fell on the track."

"A half-mile, maybe a mile?"

"No more. Maybe two. Maybe three." Wong now exaggerated.

"Can you lead us to Soda Springs?"

The Chinaman looked at the dejected politicians. "Yes. But we must make a big circle around the snow. It will take much time. I can show the way. We will come to Soda sometime tomorrow. I got a bad foot and must walk slow."

Stanford didn't think the legislators were up to an overnight trek in the cold, but played along with Wong's game. "Are there horses at Soda Springs?"

"No, sir. Horses can't walk in thick snow. In Soda there are mules. We can ride on mules."

Hubbel grunted his displeasure. "No. Absolutely not. I will not permit these distinguished gentlemen to ride common pack beasts. No, I will not permit such indignity. We're not riding them."

"So we must continue on by foot," Stanford said, sensing a new advantage over the speaker.

One by one, Hubbel's delegates began to change their minds about pushing on to inspect the tunnels. One assemblyman talked about his busy schedule in Sacramento. Another reminded them that they had brought no provisions for dinner. A third worried about the Chinaman's integrity. The speaker, always sensitive to subtle changes of mood, shifted his strategy. He too was cold and tired. The victory he could almost touch was now slipping through his fingers. Perhaps it was time to cut his losses and approach the summit tunnels from a fresh perspective. In the end, he pronounced a verdict rather than permit others to present him with a *fait accompli*. He marshaled his most convincing voice to proclaim that, due to uncertainties ahead, a return to the train was the only prudent course of action. He carefully avoided the word *retreat*. Anyone who wished to persevere was certainly entitled to. Those who wished could accompany him back to the train. Each of the six legislators voiced his disappointment but, with nothing to show for hours in the cold, agreed with the speaker and elected to forgo inspecting the tunnels for warmth and refreshment.

Wong limped ahead, unraveling the circuitous trail. There were cheers when the politicians emerged from the woods and could see the funnel-shaped stack of engine *Jupiter* silhouetted against the snowpack. During the walk back, Hubbel kept his thoughts to himself. His years in Sacramento had taught him to recognize the delicate line separating victory from defeat. The avalanche had prevented him from making political capital from the Central Pacific's operations in the Donner tunnels, yet it also convinced him beyond any doubt that Ex-Governor Stanford had something important to hide. Bankers had already written off his railroad as a financial cripple. CP stock was grossly depressed; friends of the railroad in Congress had largely abandoned ship to champion more lucrative causes. But the single-minded determination of the Central Pacific to prevent an investigation showed that perhaps the pundits had been too hasty. True, nitroglycerin in the tunnels might spell scandal, but it might also spell opportunity. The question that kept gnawing at him was this: how could he profit from the wealth these tunnels would one day bring the Central Pacific?

Before re-boarding the train, the speaker drew close to Stanford and said in a low voice, "Sorry we didn't get to the tunnels, Leland. I know you would have liked a chance to defend your company's honor. But everything has its time and its place, now doesn't it? Don't forget to invite me to the ribbon-cutting ceremony when these tunnels are finished. I expect to be on the first train over the summit." Hubbel paused to see if Stanford was picking up the signal he was sending, and when he caught a slight rise in the governor's eyebrows, he added, "Count on me to help make that possible, Leland."

The remark took Stanford by utter surprise. It took him a long moment to think before finally saying, "Well, we'll see now, Llewellyn."

"You can always use a well-positioned friend in Sacramento. And I'm not talking just influence, you understand. I know the CP has a ravenous appetite for cash. Nothing like cold cash, you know. With pressure on your reserves, only well-heeled shareholders can hold onto this railroad until you break out of these mountains. I'm talking about investors who appreciate a daring enterprise when they see it. Resources are available, my friend. When you're ready, Leland, look to me."

Stanford was dubious. He had been at the vortex of politics in Sacramento and understood how money motivated individuals. He whispered, "Well, of course, we can always use investors, Llewellyn. A company like the Central Pacific never has enough cash and, let me say, I like what I'm hearing. I like it a lot. If I catch your drift I'd say this might be a good way to end a cold, unhappy excursion."

Promontory Summit, near Ogden, Utah
10 May 1869

Llewellyn Hubbel possessed a reputation for getting what he wanted and, with respect to the Central Pacific, this reputation was well-earned. He carefully nurtured a friendship begun that winter day between himself and Ex-Governor Stanford, lunching with him often either in a private dining room located in the basement of the state capitol, or in one of Stanford's favorite local restaurants. Hubbel produced a string of wealthy investors who, when secretly apprised of the railroad's genuine progress digging tunnels at Donner summit, generously opened their pocketbooks but never mentioned to each other the word *nitroglycerin*. Neither Hubbel nor his friends had any need to know details of how this explosive was manufactured, transported, or employed in the summit tunnels.

While others in Sacramento predicted the demise of the Central Pacific, Hubbel foresaw the railroad's breakthrough in the Sierra, followed by a dash across the Nevada and Utah deserts. It proved to be the sweetest financial coup he had consummated as speaker of the State Assembly. At no point had it been necessary to conspire with the railroad's management, or to accept fees for political courtesies in the capital. All that was required was for him to borrow money from friends to purchase stock in a nearly bankrupt railroad, then to champion this enterprise before audiences naturally inclined to favor local companies offering jobs to California's growing army of unemployed.

News that Theo Gallager had finally punched through the impregnable granite and was now laying track on the Sierra's eastern escarpment sent Central Pacific stock soaring. Hubbel was careful never to purchase so many shares that his stake drew unwanted attention. Still, his relatively modest investment made him rich, an unattainable dream for a politician intent on not becoming beholden to bankers and industrialists. But just as importantly, his strong support of the CP identified him with a homebred enterprise that would help ensure his future election as a U.S. senator from California. His most coveted reward was neither fame nor fortune, but a chance to ride on the first ceremonial train through the tunnels over Donner Pass to participate in driving the final spike linking the CP and the Union Pacific railroads just outside Ogden, Utah.

Once the Central Pacific laid track beyond the original California-Nevada line, fourteen miles east of Reno, Crocker retired Wong from manual labor working on the track. Or, as he put it, "I'm domesticating that boy." From then on, no more workmen clothes, only the white jackets and aprons of a steward in Crocker's private dining car. Wong did not enjoy domestic work nearly as much as toil on the line, but by then the writing was already on the wall. Rumors spread like consumption through the Chinese work camps. Congress had decreed that the Central and Union Pacific railroads would meet near Ogden, at a place called Promontory.

The Central Pacific was laying track at the rate of six miles a day in its race eastward through the desert. Once out of the mountains, Crocker's construction company could find all the skilled German, Irish, and Welsh laborers it needed. They were big, brawny men whose size and weight gave them an advantage over the smaller Chinese. Many of Wong's compatriots had already been sent back to San Francisco for passage home to China. Others, who could still find work in camps along the newly laid track, were saving cash for uncertain futures elsewhere in Gum San. Still others found temporary jobs building levees in the Sacramento Delta. But as everywhere in California where competition for scarce jobs intensified between Chinese and Europeans workers, so did hostility between the races.

Wong found serving rich men in Crocker's saloon car demeaning, but at least he had a job, which was a lot better than most of his countrymen.

Locomotive *Jupiter*, the pride of the CP that had once taken lawmakers as far as Wong's avalanche, hauled Crocker's private train through the Sierra to rendezvous at Promontory, Utah, with Engine 119 of the Union Pacific for what the papers dubbed the *Golden Spike Ceremony*. The saloon and dining cars in which Wong worked were filled with dignitaries from early morning to late at night. For three days, Stanford, Hopkins, Huntington, and Crocker entertained officials and their wives, lavishing upon them the best California clarets and the finest cuts of beef. Crab from one coast, lobster from the other symbolized the uniting of the continent. Journalists, who joined the celebrants at various stations, ate in a car farther back but occasionally made forays forward to interview the railroad magnates and their distinguished guests.

The train had already passed through the Sierra and was rolling along at the maximum speed of thirty-one miles per hour over the flat Nevada desert. Wong waited for an opportunity to speak privately with Crocker, but folks kept milling around the millionaire, who appeared to relish every moment of his glory. Time was racing for Wong, almost as fast as engine *Jupiter*, because he believed that once they reached Ogden, Big Charley would be lionized by well-wishers and unavailable for private conversation.

In the saloon car, Crocker was dressed in a fresh black mohair suit with a white boutonnière in his lapel, and he was beaming with a smile of victory so effusive that it made his face look like a round ball. People had once called him a fool, a dreamer, even a madman. Far from being a vindictive man, Crocker could have used his money and influence to punish his critics. Instead he summoned his detractors to his table one by one and treated each to the railroad's finest cuisine and spirits. He was satisfied when, by the end of each meal, he had extracted apologies for derogatory remarks once made against him.

After one such guest was dismissed, Wong refilled Crocker's coffee cup and announced in a rather loud voice that he wished to speak with the railroad owner. Jane Stanford, who neither forgot nor forgave Wong's impertinence at Cape Horn two years before, broadcast his request for the amusement of her guests. To her delight, Crocker squirmed. Everybody knew he was a Sinophile, perhaps the most notorious in all California. But no one believed he would abandon his distinguished guests to talk in private with a heathen Chinaman, a mere steward at that! Nearby tables hushed to hear his response.

Big Charley rotated his torso to view just about everybody in the car and gently shaped his beard into a thin cylinder. He understood far better than these voyeurs that bold thoughts and even bolder actions had brought him success. Those who feared challenging the status quo would forever wallow in mediocrity. And when it came to acknowledging the request of another human being, whether an Asian or Caucasian, he would not be constrained by custom. "Yes, of course, Wong," he said in a voice loud enough for all to hear. "Yes, indeed. Sit right down together at my table and have a good talk."

Crocker appeared to enjoy every moment of this spectacle. He knew his guests would censor their responses, at least in his presence. But behind his back, he expected them to gossip in malicious tones.

"You want something to drink, my friend?" he asked the moment they were seated at his private table, forward in the car.

"No," Wong answered.

"This is a red-letter day. You've earned something to lift your spirits. If I say it's okay to drink on the job, then it's okay. How about some whiskey or wine?"

Wong smiled but did not accept the offer. His eyes remained fixed on his employer until Crocker showed that he was now ready to stop playing to the audience and focus his attention. "Many newspaper men on the train," Wong said by way of getting to what was on his mind. "They will write many words about your railroad, yes?"

Crocker nodded. "I should certainly hope so. This is a historic moment, you know. We're going to be a great country someday, Wong. Maybe more powerful than Britain or France or Russia. And when men ask what made these United States of America so great, they'll have to acknowledge the nation's debt to the Pacific Railroad. The CP is half that picture, the better half, I like to think. You can't have a modern country if people and commodities can't move from place to place. That's Europe's secret, of course. Without the Central Pacific it would never happen."

"Many Chinamen help, Mr. Crocker. Two hundred twelve Chinamen died in the mountains near track."

Crocker pouted in disbelief. "Oh, no, Wong. That's much too high. Maybe fifty or less. But two hundred, never. No, that's way, way too high."

"We keep count. Every name written down by a Chinese scribe. Each month we put the names and dates in book. Two hundred and twelve died. The book is in San Francisco. You can read it in Chinatown there."

Crocker cleared his throat and glanced at the eyes trained on him. In the newspapers that statistic wouldn't do the Central Pacific any good. He made a mental note to see that journalists never learned about this book in San Francisco. The thought that Wong might be setting him up for blackmail crossed his mind, but he dismissed it as being inconsistent with the Celestial's character.

"When Chinamen leave the railroad," Wong continued, "they have much trouble. White men don't think Chinamen work hard. White men don't trust Chinamen. They think we smoke opium. They think we're weak. But you know different, Mr. Crocker, don't you?"

Crocker fanned his whiskers, somewhat relieved that Wong was no longer talking about how many Chinese had died laying track for his railroad. "Yes, Wong, I do. Frankly, I don't understand why there's so much hatred for your race. We wouldn't be here today without your countrymen. They've made a significant contribution. And you personally, well, that goes without saying."

Wong leaned forward over the white tablecloth, soiled by previous diners. He lowered his voice but spoke with determination. "Then, Mr. Crocker, tell the newsmen what Chinamen did for the CP. Tell the newsmen so they can write about Chinamen in their papers. White men must know what Chinamen did for CP. They must know what Chinamen can do in future."

Crocker started to turn away, but, aware of the many eyes trained on him, checked himself. His lips tightened and his eyes narrowed. He was prepared to accept almost any wish of Wong's but this. It was not the truth that was in dispute. Far from it. He agreed with Wong's view of the Chinese sacrifice for the railroad. Still, there was a wide chasm between the truth and the facts the American public was ready to accept. The presence of Chinese on the construction line had been well-publicized; it could not be hidden. But the Central Pacific's official position had always been that these Celestials had done nothing more than menial work, and then only for brief periods of contract labor before returning to China. He had made sure that as the track neared completion, Chinese workers were dismissed. Crocker's partners agreed to little among themselves, yet they concurred entirely on withholding from the public the full extent of the Chinese contribution. None wanted to endanger the company's future revenues by force-feeding Americans facts they didn't want to hear.

"I agree," Crocker sighed, "there are hard times ahead for your people. If they're smart, they'll catch the first boat back to their homeland. There's no place for them in America, you know. Of course, a few will find work as domestics. A few in business in San Francisco, Stockton, maybe Sacramento. You, Wong, you can stay with me as long as you like. I promise you'll always have a job. As long as you want to work, I'll employ you. But the others? They should return to their own people as soon as possible. It's better for them and better for us."

"Americans must know what they did for the railroad," Wong insisted.

"Tell the newsmen, Mr. Crocker. They must write about Chinamen in their papers."

Crocker avoided the Chinaman's eyes. Normally he would trade on the ambiguity of words to disguise his intentions. Men in government were without scruples and deserved to be lied to. Men in commerce knew one's word was only as good as one's bank account. But Wong Po-ching was different. Crocker could have made a dozen promises to Wong. But he didn't want that. Wong deserved better. "You're asking a lot," he finally said, his voice revealing his discomfort. "I think you understand conditions in California as well as I do. Maybe better."

"Help us Chinamen, Mr. Crocker. They helped you."

"I already have, friend. I gave them work when nobody else would. I paid them fair wages. How much more can you ask?"

Wong was taken back. He had recently learned a new English word but wasn't sure he could use it correctly. Now there was nothing to lose. "Truth," he said in a sharp tone. "Mr. Crocker, tell the truth to newsmen."

A sigh escaped from deep inside Crocker's chest. He glanced over Wong's shoulder to evaluate the onlookers, most of whom had lost interest in the conversation and were now talking among themselves. "We'll see. I'll do what I can," Crocker answered.

"Then you will tell newsmen?"

"I said that I'd do what I can. Now how about you? Will you stay with the CP? With me?"

Wong shook his head. "No. I will send for wife from China. She will come next winter. Maybe the following spring. I want to live in a house. Have children."

"And be the richest goddamn Chinaman in California," Crocker said, completing the prophecy.

Wong worked a smile to his lips but without enthusiasm. "Maybe, Mr. Crocker. And maybe not."

"What will you do?"

"Dig for gold. There must be much gold in California. Only it is very deep in the ground."

After merchandising food, dry goods, and mining machinery, gold was Crocker's original love, his lifelong hobby, his undying passion and the only success that kept eluding him. "Wherever you want to work, Wong. You know I own several mines. Most are dry, but there are at least nine still in operation. I'll see you have a good job in any one you want."

"No, Mr. Crocker. I work a long time for you. I don't want to work for Charley Crocker no more. Time to work for Wong Po-ching."

"Haven't I treated you right?" Crocker sounded offended and simultaneously surprised. "Damn, you've made more money from me than half your countrymen."

"You treat me good. Now I want to work for myself. For my family. Dig my own mine."

"Where?"

"Near the big trees."

Crocker was puzzled. "You mean in Calaveras County? Where MacGreggor blew up that sequoia?"

"Big trees very old. Very wise. I have money to buy a mine. Maybe I can find gold. But it is deep in the ground."

Crocker laughed aloud. "Not there, my boy. I've got an old mine near those parts. Bought it cheap and never gotten a single dollar out of it. Veins are everywhere but near those giant redwoods. Altitude's too high. Go somewhere else. Otherwise you'll die a poor man."

Wong bowed his head. He rose suddenly from the table. "No, Mr. Crocker. There's gold near the big trees. I know it. You will see. I will find gold there."

The railroad owner pounded his fist on the table, drawing the attention of his guests. He laughed from his belly and cocked his head high so the fantail beard was parallel with the table.

"What's so funny?" Jane Stanford called from across the car.

Crocker scowled, scrutinizing his partner's wife with her wing-like ears and drooping eyes. She never missed an opportunity to disparage him, and he, consequently, made a point of blunting her attacks. "Oh nothing you'd understand, Jane," he roared. "It's funny, something that would appeal only to one with a sense of humor. This Chinaman makes me laugh and that's why I like him."

Though nobody knew exactly why, Crocker's laughter spread from table to table until almost everyone was chuckling. Even Jane Stanford had to join in. Wong slipped from their sight onto the platform and a moment later disappeared into the adjoining galley car.

At the Central Pacific campsite beside the track at Promontory, everyone was joking about the Union Pacific's incompetence. Though their portion of the track was completed, it seemed that they were unable to run the first train over it on time. UP owners and staff had been obliged to travel to the railhead by wagon the day before to participate in the festivities. The truth was that the train had stopped in Wyoming to take on fresh provisions and resupply its diminished stock of whiskey. Still, that didn't stop an old rivalry.

A little after three p.m., Eastern Time, soldiers bivouacked to the east of Promontory fired several volleys from their carbines. Shortly thereafter, Engine 119 tooted her whistle, announcing her late arrival. Engine *Jupiter* responded with her own welcoming blasts. Telegraph operators from both railroads relayed the news east and west. The Central Pacific's ceremonial train emptied as everyone raced forward to witness the historic moment of contact. Two giant locomotives crept slowly toward each other with their engineers hanging on all sides. Some had bottles of whiskey in their hands. A few had champagne. Dozens of arms reached out to form a symbolic bridge.

Wong had not had a chance to leave the train since its arrival at Promontory. Then suddenly all the guests abandoned the dining and saloon cars for the open mesa, leaving him with nobody to serve. Curious to see for himself what was happening, he dropped from the platform to the roadbed and entered a crowd of bystanders. His white apron and steward's pants contrasted with the formal black of the dignitaries and the navy blue of the U.S. Army. For the first time since his arrival in Gum San, Wong felt conspicuous, and not just because of his white jacket. There were no other Asians in the crowd, though black-skinned Negroes were performing menial tasks for Union Pacific officials and groups of Comanche and Sioux Indian prostitutes milled around the edges of the crowd, enticing workmen looking for a good time. But not a single Chinaman. Even more disconcerting, no one seemed to notice the absence of Wong's countrymen.

Hundreds of simple wooden headpieces over Chinese graves along the roadbed in California marked their ultimate sacrifice for the Pacific Railroad. No doubt after several seasons, weather would erode even these modest traces of coolie labor. Who would know then the contribution and sacrifice of these Chinese workers?

As the only Chinaman present at Promontory, Wong felt compelled to represent his countrymen. He ripped off his steward's cap and allowed his black queue to drop over his shoulders.

Many of the dignitaries from the East had never seen anyone from China. As Wong walked through the celebrants, women looked at him disdainfully and expressed surprise at his self-assurance, with little concern that he might understand their disrespectful remarks. The men were more aggressively vocal in their ridicule. Wong tried not to take offense. What did they know about China, a nation with historic roots older than the giant sequoia of Calaveras County? It wasn't their animosity that annoyed him. Rather, what stirred his anger was that his countrymen had already proven themselves in Gum San to be worthy of praise not scorn. They had struggled to come here from afar; they had toiled, succeeded, and died, almost entirely in anonymity. It never occurred to any of those toasting the achievement of the Pacific Railroad that if his countrymen had not blasted a roadbed through the Sierra Nevada, none of them would be standing where they were that day. The record of the Chinese immigrants' vital work was being obliterated before his eyes.

Engines *Jupiter* and 119 blew their steam whistles and puffed thick black smoke into the air. Slowly they chugged in reverse to make room for a ceremonial final spike linking the Pacific Railroad from ocean to ocean. Wong was determined to move as close to the speaker's dais as possible. Workmen, who had been warned in advance to stand some distance away, saw him among the VIPs and started shouting obscenities. To them, not only was it unfair for a coolie to enjoy a privileged view of the proceedings, but it was an outright insult to white men, particularly those in the company of women.

Wong ignored the jeers. His attention was riveted on photographers arranging groups of people in front of the two locomotives. If his purpose was to represent his race, what better way than to be immortalized in photographs? People would later look at these pictures and see at least one Chinaman at Promontory. Somebody would have to ask why more were not present.

But carrying out his plan proved more difficult than he thought. Many others also coveted a place in photographic history. They scrambled and elbowed for positions before the lens. Wong received jabs in the ribs from both men and women. Hands clawed at his arms to drag him away. A photographer yelled to his assistant: "Get that goddamn Chink out of my picture. Put a collar on the rascal and keep him out of sight."

Union Pacific stokers volunteered to help the assistant photographer. Three of them closed in on Wong from different directions. Two grabbed his arms and lifted him off the ground. Others helped drag him in the direction of Locomotive 119, hostile territory of the Union Pacific. Wong struggled to free himself, throwing elbows and kicking with his feet. His hijackers accused him of ruining countless photographic plates. He became the target of blows to his stomach and head. The assistant cameraman viciously whipped his ears with the back of his hand. Someone else locked Wong's arms behind his back, giving his associates an unobstructed target. A knee rose into his groin, jamming his testicles into his pelvis. Wong groaned and wrenched free to land a few of his own counter-punches. That only encouraged others to join in the beating.

The assistant photographer yelped as Wong's teeth pierced the skin of his forearm.

His shriek drew spectators from the track. Men from the Union Pacific clustered around. They had heard about Celestials working for the Central Pacific. In each work camp stories proliferated about these aliens, raising the level of myth. According to these oft-told tales, Asians, who multiplied like jackrabbits in their homeland, were as numerous as the legendary Mongolian hordes. Christian folks who had come into contact with them testified that they were as inscrutable as wolves, as unpredictable as Mexican banditos and as promiscuous as Indian whores. For many at Promontory, this was their first opportunity to demonstrate how unwelcome these coolies were in America.

Wong's knees finally gave way under repeated blows to his ankles. Each time he tried to gasp for air, a new punch in his ribs seemed to collapse his lungs. His breaths were short, sapping his strength to resist. At some point, air became more precious than balance. It felt as though more fists had joined those already beating him, making it impossible to distinguish one blow from another. The taste of blood was in his mouth and swelling had blinded one eye. His testicles ached. The sky above him began to blur into a blanket of gray.

Suddenly the beating stopped. Feet that had been clustered tightly around him shuffled back and a patch of daylight opened in the canopy of bodies overhead. He peered up through his only functioning eye and tried to distinguish the figure of a large man hovering above. A hand shot forward but did not strike. Rather, it came to rest in the crook of his arm and gently tugged upward. Before he could focus on the man's features, he recognized my father's voice.

Dad ducked under Wong's arm and stiffened, supporting almost all his weight. Once Wong was standing, Dad turned his attention to the attackers, who couldn't understand why anyone would want to help a Celestial and why they weren't being rewarded for doing everyone a favor. He threatened to avenge their crime with his own fists if they threw another blow at Wong. The assistant photographer sized up the physical prowess of the Chinaman's rescuer and announced that he was needed elsewhere. When his associates failed to follow, Father started to remove Wong from his shoulder to implement his threat. The crowd moved back to provide enough room for a real fight. After so many dull speeches, an old-fashioned brawl would certainly liven up the day. Everyone seemed disappointed when mounted soldiers arrived to break it up.

Wong insisted on walking unassisted between groups of hostile spectators back to the Central Pacific saloon car. He wobbled but never stumbled. Once they got there, my father sat him at a table in the vacant car and fetched a wet cloth to clean his bruises. The ache between Wong's legs began to subside and his breathing became more regular. His attackers had cracked an incisor tooth that would probably have to be removed. My father had already witnessed Wong's remarkable powers of recovery at Cape Horn.

"They said you're a troublemaker and ruined photographic plates," Father commented while cleaning blood from Wong's face. "Is that true?"
"If a picture is trouble, then, yes, Mr. Gallag'r."
"Why the hell'd you do that?"
"If you don't understand, there's no purpose to tell you. Thank you, anyway. Many times Mr. Gallag'r has helped me."
"I'm afraid this will be the last time, Wong. My work for the CP is finished. I'm headed back to California. I have a horse and on the way back want to visit my track one last time."
Wong pointed in the direction of the ceremonies. "I think you are missing the speeches. Mr. Gallag'r is a big man now. They're saying many good things about you. Go and listen."
Dad used table salt to cleanse Wong's wounds. Painful as it was, salt prevented the onset of infection. "I know what they're saying and don't give a goddamn for their tributes. As soon as they pound down that last

spike, it's all over for me. The track's down. I did what I set out to do and built the CP line from Secretown to Ogden. Time for me to be moving on. In a couple of days there won't be anybody here but a telegraph operator. They won't even remember my name."

"But the track won't disappear. The track will be here for many, many years."

My father smiled appreciatively. At least Wong understood his passion to build something lasting. Endurance is what he wanted, not praise.

"Why did you help me, Mr. Gallag'r?" Wong asked.

"Why?" The question caught him off-guard. Crocker had asked him a similar question at Cape Horn. It was hard to answer then, but not now. "Well, Wong, you could say because we're now partners. Not employer and employee. I was looking to talk with you when I found those bullies from the UP. I had no idea you were under the pile until I stepped in to find out what was going on. So you could say I didn't set out to help you this time. It just happened."FCisco

The Chinaman's expression went blank until my father started to explain his remark about the two of them being partners. "Theodore Gallager and Wong Po-ching as partners! Imagine that! I went to say good-bye to Mr. Crocker. He told me he wanted to reward your service to his company. He said you want to mine for gold and he's decided to give you an old mine in Calaveras, near those big trees. But the law in California makes it illegal for Chinamen to own land, so he's made me your partner. The mine's going to be deeded in my name with an understanding that half of it belongs to you and you can work there as long as you want. Half the profits, if there are any, go to you or your family. The other half belongs to me and my heirs."

"Mr. Crocker has already paid me." Wong looked puzzled.

"He wants to show special appreciation. Only don't get excited. The mine is absolutely worthless. Barren. Dry. Not a goddamn ounce of gold in her. The truth is that Big Charley would never give us a mine that had a chance of making him money. In my judgment you deserve a helluva lot more and I told Crocker that."

Wong savored the idea of living near the giant sequoia. That in itself was a reward that he didn't expect my father to understand. "Maybe we will find gold, Mr. Gallag'r. We must go deep, much deeper than the first miners. Gold is deep."

Dad chuckled. "Not me, partner. I've already frittered away a good part of my life and can't afford to waste the other scratching for gold that isn't there. If you want, you go and dig. But you're digging for yourself. There hasn't been any gold taken out of the area for a dozen years, so you can dig and dig and the deeper you go the poorer you'll be. Work Crocker's mine and you'll always remain a coolie. Invest your wages in a business in Francisco. Don't waste it on that worthless property."

"Go deep, Mr. Gallag'r."

"You don't have the capital to dig deep. To go deep requires expensive machinery. You'll just claw away with your bare knuckles."

Wong shifted his weight and for a long moment listened to the sound of applause outside on the tracks. A volley of carbines firing in the distance sounded like firecrackers on Chinese New Year. "No," he asserted. "I must dig very deep."

"Powder's expensive. Where the hell you going to get the money or the credit for it?"

"We have more powder than we need, Mr. Gallag'r. And we don't have to pay for it either."

My father's eyes narrowed.

"We have the black powder I took from the tunnels at Donner," Wong said matter-of-factly. "Seven hundred and twenty-one kegs. I took them from the tunnels on the summit and hid them in dry cave near Mirror Lake."

My father had always assumed that Wong had scattered it in some ravine or dumped it into a spring stream to decompose. True, the Chinaman once mentioned a cave near Mirror Lake. But most caves were so damp any powder stored in them was bound to be ruined. In the excitement of building track in Nevada, the matter had slipped his mind.

"Jesus, Wong. You never cease to surprise me. That powder technically belongs to the Central Pacific, you know, but then I don't suppose it will ever make a claim. Hopkins has never mentioned a thing about it. My guess is that he doctored his account books and wrote it off as if it had been used in the tunnels. So if nobody makes a claim, why shouldn't you put it to use? Good luck."

"Mr. Gallag'r come work with Wong. We go deep together. Plenty powder to go very deep. We will be good partners."

Dad toyed with the idea for a luxurious moment before rejecting it.

"Come to big trees, Mr. Gallag'r."

"No, Wong. I'm headed north. To Humboldt County, along California's north coast. I bought some timberland there. Now that we've got a transcontinental railroad more people will be coming to California. They'll be needing houses and wagons and boats. I reckon the country will have a big appetite for lumber and I intend to satisfy it. I'm looking for big bucks now. More than I can make as a construction superintendent. A helluva lot more than in a failed mine."

"Why do you want so much money, Mr. Gallag'r?"

"Why does any man want money? Power, I suppose. Freedom. And, of course, for a family."

"But you don't have a family."

"Not now, but someday maybe I will. Got to find the proper woman first. I'm not a gambler like you, Wong. I'm not marrying any woman I don't see first."

"Then Mr. Gallag'r never marry. Never have children."

"Maybe."

"Did you see your trees in Humboldt County?"

Father grunted his embarrassment. He had hoped to avoid the subject. When the timberland had come up for sale, he had studied a map for hours. The timber was eighty percent coastal redwood, *sequoia semprivera*. Better than most men, he understood the quality of redwood for construction, its resistance to termites and wood rot. Crocker had just paid him a large bonus and there was no time to make an inspection. True, the purchase was on impulse, but then if he had waited, the opportunity would have slipped away. Risk taking was in his blood.

"I've seen letters from reputable lawyers," my father answered. "And I know exactly where the timber is located. The challenge is not the timber, but to devise a way to get it out by coastal barges. That's my work, Wong. I know how to build roads. Only this time it won't be railroads but timber roads."

Wong smiled for the first time since the beating. To extend his lips was painful, but a humorous thought tickled him. "Mr. Gallag'r think I loco to send money to Yung Wo Company for a wife. 'Sight unseen' you say. Maybe it the same for trees you've never seen. I think you're loco too, Mr. Gallag'r! Wong and Gallag'r both loco like drunken Injuns."

Dad bellylaughed and looked to the barman for a parting drink. But the barman, like everybody else, was outside at the ceremonies. His eyes switched back to Wong. "There's a difference, friend. I don't have to sleep with my trees if I don't like them. You'll have to sleep with your wife. Mine's strictly a commercial deal. If it pays, fine. If not, then maybe we'll be partners in a gold mine after all."

There was a long pause as each man pondered the uncertainty of the future. My father chewed a bit from his fingernail. He would have liked to stay with Wong longer, but wanted to saddle his new horse and ride a few miles before dark. The sooner he said good-bye to this phase of his life, the better. He was about to stand up when a conductor entered the saloon car. He stepped inside and addressed my father. "Mr. Gallager. They want you out on the speaker's platform; they expect you to make a speech."

Father looked uneasy. "Tell 'em I got nothing to say. They can see my work. Nine hundred and two miles of it, from Miller's Tavern to Promontory. That's the only statement I have to make."

"Mr. Crocker told me to fetch you, sir."

"Well, you tell Mr. Crocker that I'm staying right here. By the time they've put down the final spike, I'll be on my way to California. Tell that to Big Charley."

Wong interrupted. "Not right, Mr. Gallag'r. You've come far to Ut-ah. You should leave with good thoughts. Say some words to the people."

My father signaled for the conductor to wait outside for his decision. "What should I say? They've said everything a thousand times. Always it's the same praises. Patting each other on the backs. Giving each other awards."

Wong closed his one good eye and bowed his head. Stray hairs from his queue fell over his shoulder. His voice was low, almost a whisper. "No, Mr. Gallag'r. They're not saying everything. Nobody talks about Chinamen. Nobody says what Chinamen did for Central Pacific. Americans not know that Chinamen work hard. They think we are animals. They don't know that we are good working men."

Outside on the track, whistles were blowing again, followed by applause. There were also cheers. The conductor stuck his head back into the saloon car. "They're calling 'Gallager, Gallager,'" he reported. "You'd better come out and say something, otherwise, they'll likely come and drag you there. Mr. Crocker will be furious."

Dad shot a glance at Wong and then eyed the conductor. He inched forward and balanced himself. Expletives escaped from his lips and an angry, determined scowl settled on his face. "You coming with me, Wong?"

Wong relaxed back into his chair and swung his head from side to side. "No, Mr. Gallag'r. There's no place for a Chinaman here. I learned that. They'll beat me again if I go out. You go quick. I'll see you before you leave for California."

"Stay here, partner. I want you here when I come back. This won't take long."

The audience had been waiting several minutes for my father's arrival. Grenville Dodge, Thomas Durant, Crocker, and Stanford were on the podium, filling the hiatus by making jokes with those in the front rows. Stanford had introduced most of the Central Pacific dignitaries, including the speaker of the State Assembly, Llewellyn Hubbel, who incidentally had enjoyed every moment of the historic ride from Sacramento in Crocker's private car. Crocker's words exaggerated the mystique surrounding his superintendent, but then everybody was in a festive mood and some under the influence of alcohol and the beating sun, so exaggerations were to be expected. He spoke of Father's tenacity and engineering skill, painting him into railroad history as a single-minded man with an obsessive passion to lay track. Crocker would have expanded these praises had my father not shown impatience by wedging himself toward the lectern. The railroad owner paused awkwardly in mid-sentence to acknowledge my father's presence. Laughter from the audience eased the transition. Crocker joined in the good humor and sidestepped to let my father speak.

Dad had reluctantly agreed to say a few words, but once given the opportunity, was at a loss for a theme. What? How? Why? He cleared his throat twice without finding the right beginning thought. Until he started speaking, he didn't know what he was going to say. "Many. Many. Many."

A whistle from below filled the silence. Several people coughed in their impatience.

"Many things will be written about the Pacific Railroad, Ladies and Gentlemen. Most are untrue."

The crowd nodded approval that history was part memory and part myth.

"When Theodore Donahoe Judah surveyed the route for the western track fifteen years ago, he was mad, absolutely mad."

This time there was laughter.

"Choosing Donner Pass in the Sierra Nevada was sheer lunacy. Frankly, had the survey been given to me, I would have recommended a southern route through Mexico and then north through Texas, along the Rio Grande. That would have made the overland journey a little longer, but it would have spared this superintendent many sleepless nights."

The crowd clapped and cheered at my father's honesty. "I think we'd have had a better chance fighting the Mexicans for the right of way than Mother Nature in the mountains. We came damn near getting our asses licked back there in the Sierra."

A mumbling arose over Father's vulgarity before an audience that included quite a few women. Some pretended not to hear; others whispered that they expected a tough construction boss to use profanities. And Gallager had a reputation for speaking his mind.

Father raised his voice to reclaim attention. "By now, most of the stories about the Central Pacific have been told and retold. But there's one story that hasn't, and I don't suspect any of you here really want to hear it, or that you reporters standing out there will write it in your papers if you do."

My father paused to allow a sudden surge of whispered speculation to quiet down. "Look around, friends. What do you folks see? City people. Railroad workers. Soldiers. Government officials. Two locomotives. Reporters. Photographers. But look again and tell me who's missing. Tell me who should be here, but isn't." Dad ceased speaking and surveyed the audience from one end to the other, as if he expected someone to come up with the correct answer. Crocker blanched. Stanford nervously chewed on his upper lip.

"You don't even know who's missing, do you? And that's what's wrong with this whole goddamn affair. You don't even *know*!"

People shuffled their feet looking away from the speaker. Murmuring rippled through the ranks of self-important dignitaries. They didn't travel all the way to Utah to have a construction superintendent belittle them, or to imply that they were bigots.

My father's voice rose to drown out the whispering. "So I'll tell you who isn't here. Thousands of laborers from a land far across the Pacific

Ocean. Today some of these hardworking men are toiling in the marshes of California. Most have been shipped home to China. Some are fishing for salmon on the northern coast. About two hundred died along the track, yes, track that was under my supervision. Two hundred of these faceless men perished building the Central Pacific roadway. I know many of you here don't think of Chinamen as human, or fully humans. I heard folks call them little runts. Weird little pagans. But take it from Theodore Gallager, for what his word is worth, and go write it in your newspapers. The Central Pacific wouldn't be here today without them. Without Chinamen, there wouldn't be any track to the Pacific Ocean."

The audience was dumbstruck. Not a word. Not a peep. If surprise was my father's intent, he had certainly achieved it.

"So that's my story, Ladies and Gentlemen. Now go cuss and swear against Theo Gallager. Say he's mad. Say he's mistaken. Say he's a damn fool. Or go back along these tracks and find the graves of those dead Chinese. Stop in the Sierra tunnels and say a prayer for those who gave their lives so this country would be joined coast to coast by this track. See for yourselves. And if anybody asks you if what you just heard is true, say you heard it from Theodore Gallager."

Reporters lining the north side of the track scribbled furiously into their notebooks. Other spectators expressed curiosity about what would happen next. Leland Stanford hacked a cough from behind Father's right shoulder. Dad just stared out from the lectern, devouring those in the audience with fiery eyes. Somebody inched behind him and he could hear heavy nasal breathing. A hand touched his waist. It was gentle and friendly.

"I wish to thank Theodore Gallager for his personal statement here today," Crocker said while closing in on the lectern to gaze out at the expectant faces. "Yes, Theo. Of course, not everybody agrees with you."

Hoots interrupted Crocker's remarks.

"Coolies go home," a workman shouted. "We don't want this country swarming with yellow vermin. Chinaman John, get out of America."

Crocker threw up his arms for silence. "Ladies and Gentlemen ..."

More anti-Chinese slogans filled the air. Father gnashed his teeth but held his temper. Crocker kept whispering to him not to overreact. Finally he placed a hand on my father's ribs and ushered him aside. No resistance. Why should Dad resist? He had said everything he wanted to and had no illusions about persuading anyone. A path opened for him to retreat along the Central Pacific track.

Crocker waited until my father was out of sight, allowing time for many to vent their hatred. When the vitriol petered out, he signaled for the band to start playing a peppy march.

Dad collected his travel bags and saddled his horse, then sought out Wong in the saloon car. The Chinaman had washed himself and put on a fresh apron. "Don't go back into that mob," my father warned. "Next time I won't be around to rescue you, my friend."

Wong stepped down from the saloon car and limped with my father, who led his horse on foot. They walked westward, in the opposite direction from the ceremonies. As long as they stayed close to the Central Pacific train, nothing would happen.

"I'll be in touch with Crocker in Sacramento," Dad said. "As far as I know, you can start working our mine whenever you wish. That is, if you're stupid enough to try. I wouldn't."

"Then when Mr. Gallag'r make much money, he will give Wong a job, yes?" Father smiled. "Sure, friend. But next time you don't work for me. We work together as partners. When's your new wife arriving from China?"

"Not for a long time. Maybe the end of the winter or early spring."

"You gave all your money to the Yung Wo Company? They'll cheat you for sure."

"The Yung Wo Bank works for family association. It won't cheat me. I'm a member of the family now."

"If you're headed back to Sacramento on this train, you'll be passing me on the track in a couple of days." My father turned to look back at the Central Pacific cars. A band was playing and intermittently they could hear the bang of a heavy hammer striking steel. Both Dad and Wong acknowledged without speaking that dignitaries were nailing down the final spikes. It was all over. Really over.

"When I'm near Mokelumne Hill, I'll come see you at our mine," Father said as he started to mount his horse. "Gotta check my property from time to time." He pulled himself into the saddle and leaned over to take Wong's hand in his and said, "Bye, partner."

Wong took my father's hand and shook it, holding firm for an extra few seconds. As Dad straightened up in the saddle, the Chinaman bowed his head and mocked his earlier pidgin English. "You come see Wong, Meester Gallag'r. Wong makee boom, boom."

Dad spurred his horse into a trot. The Chinaman watched until he had gone a quarter-mile. Behind them, the whistles from *Jupiter* and the 119 sounded in unison. The brass band started up again. A few soldiers galloped alongside the track. A volley of shots rang into the air. Telegraph lines now paralleling this fresh track of steel transmitted instantaneously the final blows as the golden spike sank into the ground, binding together the vast continent of America.

In San Francisco's Fort Point at the base of the Golden Gate, a battery of 220 cannon discharged a festive volley into the bay. Two thousand six hundred and twelve miles away as the crow flies, fire sirens wailed aloud on Fifth Avenue in New York City. The Liberty Bell in Philadelphia sounded in recognition of America's indomitable spirit. Ship horns bayed in Boston Harbor while paddle-wheel steamers on the Mississippi at St. Louis answered antiphonally. A symphony of bells tolled merrily from the decks of ships anchored along the quay in New Orleans. North and south, east and west, locomotives hauling cargo and passengers blasted their steam whistles. From the Atlantic to the Pacific, the nation marked this historic moment with sound.

It had been accomplished. A mere century before, few dared dream that such an engineering miracle would come to pass. Thirteen American colonies between the Atlantic and the Allegheny Mountains had expanded west across the vast prairies, then over the Rocky Mountains and Sierra Nevada—as far as the Pacific Ocean.

Suddenly the entire continent this young nation had embraced was joined together by a ribbon of steel.

CHAPTER SEVEN

Village of Sei Ho, Canton, China
August 1869

Mayor Ng Fook believed that wealth and power entitled him to do whatever he pleased, no matter how repulsive. His legs were too short for his heavy torso, topped as it was by a giant head anchored directly to his shoulders with virtually no neck. Particles of pork fat and kernels of rice were often entangled in his bushy whiskers. People refrained from shaking his hand because it was usually coated in oil, or sometimes moisture from between the legs of the village maidens he would penetrate as a show of his authority. He made a practice of urinating in public wherever and whenever he pleased, making his mark on walls, fences, and stairs with curlicue designs. Village loafers and sycophants would gather to watch his yellow streamers with a mix of awe and reverence. If they ventured too close, he trained his stream on their legs and feet for sport. Nothing gave him greater pleasure than when children traced his urine trails with whitewash to endow the village with an indelible record of his excretions.

If anyone had been guilty of opposing the Punti landlords in the Hakka Rebellion, it had been Mayor Fook, yet he was also the first to recognize the imminent collapse of this insurrection and, as a matter of survival, had shifted his loyalty to the victors. As a result, he avoided the fate of his former comrades in arms, who one by one had been dragged before Punti tribunals for ransom. Rumor had it that the mayor had paid dearly for his freedom, but the actual sum remained a matter of speculation. He quickly learned to demonstrate public respect for his new Punti masters and made a point of waiting outside their headquarters during political tribunals. What the new rulers called *trials* fooled nobody. Nothing occurred in their courts that bore even a remote resemblance of justice.

While a series of Punti trials ensued, sisters Mei Yok and Mei Ling waited with other villagers of Sei Ho to learn their father's fate. Not that they held much hope for justice being served in their father's case. After an extremely brief hearing, the court would take its time before arriving at a verdict to encourage the family of the accused to raise a blood ransom that, more often than not, far exceeded its resources. Punti judges pretended not to notice as impoverished loved ones borrowed, extorted, or stole to meet the required ransom. The Mei sisters had raised every possible yen and could tap no new sources. Without additional money, it was certain their father would be beheaded.

Mei Ling was the village beauty, with smooth, clear skin, strong, even teeth, and symmetrical cheeks, eyes, and lips. Her black hair was long and shiny. Only a slight squint to compensate for her acute nearsightedness marred her features. Many Hakka warriors had approached her father with offers of marriage, but he was not deaf to her wishes. None of these suitors appealed to her. Unfortunately the man she ultimately selected was mortally wounded in a senseless provincial battle against Punti regiments. Mei Ling's father was duty bound to return what was left of her dowry already taxed at sixty-five percent by the Punti government. The rebellion left Mei Ling with neither a husband nor a dowry, and her father with a debt he had no prospects of repaying.

It went without saying that her far less attractive younger sister, Mei Yok, had no dowry at all. Several inches shorter than Mei Ling and many pounds lighter, she had thin, stringy hair that required constant attention to keep it from falling into her eyes. Due to a large gap between her front teeth, her speech was punctuated by a swishing sibilance. Even worse, none of her features seemed in balance. Where paired, such as ears and cheeks, each side seemed at war with the other. For more than an hour, she had stood in silence with her sister outside Punti headquarters waiting for grim news about their father.

"The Punti lords must think we're holding out," Mei Yok whispered in her squeaky voice. "Why else delay their decision?"

"I've been thinking, sister, that Mayor Ng Fook has influence with them," said Mei Ling. "We have nothing left to offer him but our bodies."

Mei Yok interrupted with a dismissing snicker. "May the Punti bastards chop off the tip of his pecker so his piss runs down his leg and not on others."

"But the mayor could intercede if he wanted. Only he can stop the inevitable. I'm going to offer myself to him. I could give him much pleasure, enough to bring Father home again."

"I am not as desirable for marriage as you, Mei Ling. Let me do it," Mei Yok countered.

The idea did not sit well with Mei Ling. For as long as she could remember, she had avoided comparing her physical attributes with those of her sister. It was not Mei Yok's fault that she was small and unsightly. But by the same token it was obvious that any offer of sex she extended to Ng Fook would be rejected. The time had come to talk openly about what had so long been taboo. "You think he's blind, sister? You think that when he looks at you he sees a princess? You're too narrow at the hips. Your eyes don't focus. Your chest is flat. Ng Fook will not want you, sister. Face facts; has he ever tried putting his fingers between your legs as he does to the other village virgins? He has often pursued me."

Mei Yok remained silent, her eyes dropping and her lips pursing.

"Ahaah, there you are, sister. Anyway it's *my* duty to Father. But I will not stoop to Ng Fook. I don't trust anything he says. I'm going to the Punti officers. I know how to make men wild with desire." The volume of their arguing rose to a point where other bystanders could hear. Punti rulers demanded absolute silence from those waiting to hear sentences. No mumbling, no whispering. Spectators feared that such disobedience might draw collective punishment on the innocent. They tried to silence further discussion.

Mei Yok didn't care and said to her sister, "Why should the officers want *you*? You're blind as a bat. You bump into everything. Every month you have terrible cramps and bleed for days. Half the month you'll be out of commission. How can a bleeding woman satisfy officers?"

The argument was interrupted when the courthouse door opened. The hamlet's deputy mayor and district tax collector appeared. Several of those waiting swooned, for it appeared as if they had been successful in redeeming loved ones. But as the prisoners inched forward, chains clanked around their ankles, a sign that insufficient ransom had been raised. Cheers changed to groans. Guards armed with giant, flat swords they used to club as well as stab, barred family members from embracing their menfolk. The condemned were paraded forward as though contaminated with disease. When a scuffle ensued, the guards started beating the bystanders.

For the sake of the family, Mei Yok knew she had to talk with Mayor Ng Fook *before* the officers laid eyes on Mei Ling and accepted her offer. She took advantage of the distraction to leave her sister and thread her way forward through the crowd in the direction of Ng Fook who was chatting with a contingent of Punti collaborators in the first row of spectators. Once nearby, the mayor's entourage tried to stop her from addressing him.

"Be respectful," a henchman warned. "Woman, be silent and calm."

"Ng Fook," Mei Yok shouted while pointing to the Punti headquarters, "I am Mei Yok; my father is being tried inside. I need your help to save his life."

The mayor belched aloud and shifted his weight on fat toes that curled over the soles of his sandals.

"Tell the officers to release my father. In return, I'll give you anything you want."

The mayor mopped his bewhiskered chin, savoring an invitation from a rival's daughter. "And how, Mei Yok, do you propose that I accomplish this?"

"Barter with the rulers. You know how to trade. You do business with them all the time. Okay, so do business on my father's behalf. Trade whatever is necessary for his life."

The mayor gurgled deep in his throat, the prelude to a laugh. He made no secret of his business with the authorities; indeed, he enjoyed knowing that others viewed him as a man with friends in high places. "Yes, business. But that presumes you have something to trade. What can you offer?"

"Myself. I have only myself. My body."

The mayor's cohorts *aha'd*, but said nothing to reveal an inner delight.

"Have *you* something to give the officers?" she asked.

His expression was flat. "Why should I trade anything of mine for you?"

"Because after my father goes free, I will be yours. Do with me as you please."

The crowd emitted a sequence of exclamations. Mei Yok was the daughter of a respected family. Civil war had evidently brought a new level of degradation to the village.

Ng Fook studied the young woman's body to determine if she appealed to him or might be more suitable for one of his sons. How he wished her delicious sister, Mei Ling, were making the same offer. Now that was a body worth coveting! But Mei Yok was another story. He briefly thought about selling her to a brothel. Unfortunately, civil war had filled the local whorehouses with orphan women at a time when many young men had been killed in the fighting. Those who managed to survive in combat couldn't afford these women or, if they could, could pay only pennies. One last possibility came to mind, but an intriguing one at that. To work out all the details would require some private negotiations.

He signaled to Mei Yok and waddled through the open space in front of Punti headquarters. She trailed behind, her chin high and her eyes defiant as she glanced at the courthouse, fearful that her father would appear any moment in chains marked for execution.

The mayor, on the other hand, was in no hurry to negotiate with the authorities. He had business to perform first and unfastened his britches, then worked the shaft of his penis through the opening. When the stubby member was fully exposed, he proceeded to rain a circle on the dusty ground. His stream thinned into a drooping arch and trickled urine close to Mei Yok's feet. The final drops splattered his britches.

He closed his flap and smiled at Mei Yok with an air of superiority. "It may already be too late to save your father. The court never reverses a decision."

"Why wait? Talk to them immediately."

"If I do, are you willing to leave the province?"

"For how long?"

"As long as necessary. Maybe forever."

"You'd sell me to another province? Which one? How far away?" Her shoulders quivered in shock. She had previously thought only of physical submission and had not considered leaving the village. This was a new twist and required time to think through.

"That depends, but if you want to save your father you must tell me now, otherwise it will be too late."

One quick glance at the courthouse and she knew he was right about that. "Accepted. I'll go."

Ng Fook's cheeks expanded into a victorious smile. So it was done. He had just consummated a deal that promised substantial rewards. Half of the substantial fee he would earn from her sale to a labor contractor in Canton he would pledge to the Punti officers for her father's life. The other half he would pocket for himself.

The bargain with Mei Yok required consummation. Since she was now his chattel, he could do with her what he wanted. His hands sorted through the folds of her tunic and felt for her buttocks, then pulled her toward him roughly. His middle finger scratched for an opening. She fought back an instinct to smack the repulsive man.

"Hurry," she said, trying to make his entry easier by squatting forward. "You promised to stop the Punti verdict. If my father does not go free, you have no claim."

That prospect sobered him and he removed his hand. He wiped his finger on his tunic and scurried forward to the Punti offices. There were many witnesses. A deal had been struck.

Mei Yok returned to the place where she had left her sister, but could not find her. Fellow Han peasants refused to say where she had gone. They showed little sympathy for Mei Yok's degradation, nor would they condemn the mayor's collusion with the authorities.

Negotiations inside headquarters dragged on. This was a bad omen. But toward evening Mei Yok's father emerged from the courthouse to a rousing cheer from those who waited tirelessly with diminished hopes. No manacles. A sign that he had been pardoned. Mei Yok rushed forward to escort him from his captors.

"Ng Fook, bless him, negotiated my freedom," he whispered to her. "Why a man who has opposed me all these years should intervene on my behalf is a mystery. But Punti rulers respect his judgment or his money or his business. I suppose he will now demand payment from me. But that will wait. Hopefully, you and Mei Ling will be married before that."

Mei Yok bit her tongue and said nothing. Together they talked about her father's arrest and imprisonment, waiting for Mei Ling to return and celebrate. But she did not return. Later Mei Yok searched the village for clues to her sister's whereabouts until a beggar told her that he had seen her slip into Punti headquarters through a back door. The perpetually drunken Shish Tao-ting also testified that he had seen Mei Ling disrobed with officers near the river. People warned Mei Yok not to believe anything a lout like that would say.

Mayor Ng Fook was not one to dally when it came to making money. Mei Yok remained in the village of Sei Ho only one night before he shipped her to Canton attached to a caravan transporting rice. She left without saying good-bye to her father or her sister, who returned to the family hamlet much abused in body and reputation. There was no fanfare and no tears. When friends and family inquired about her, all that anybody knew was that she had left the village. The wise elders, who knew everything that happened for miles around, suspected that she would be shipped out of China, though the mayor refused to confirm this. About Mei Ling they were more philosophical, noting that now the beautiful one had lost her value as a virtuous wife. She, too, was destined to leave the village.

The cost of sparing his life weighed heavily on their father. His suffering was particularly acute when he would chance upon the figure eight patterns of Mayor Ng Fook's urine splayed on the walls of village buildings.

Heckendom Mine

When Charles Crocker had deeded his Heckendom Mine in the hills east of Mokelumne Hill to my father, it never occurred to him to have his secretary notify the mine's caretaker, Joseph Kearny, who had immigrated along with his brother from County Cork, Ireland, when thirty-four years old and never known another home in the United States. An introvert loner, Kearny had settled into a quiet life overseeing the mine property, with few responsibilities except to prevent thieves from stealing mine machinery and squatters from establishing a claim to the rights of abandonment.

Since everybody in Calaveras County believed Heckendom's gold had been depleted years before, title to the mine meant nothing to him. On his occasional forays into Mokelumne Hill to purchase supplies, he made a habit of visiting Digger's Saloon for a few drinks. There he regularly ridiculed his employer, Charles Crocker, for neglecting the mine. When Crocker's secretary eventually sent a letter introducing my father as the mine's new owner, he was pleased to hear about a change of ownership. Dad's larger-than-life reputation lingered in California well after he had pushed tracks into the Utah Territory, and Kearny sensed this was the kind of man to recognize the Heckendom's potential. But to his disappointment Theodore Gallager never showed up to take possession. In his place came Wong Po-ching in blue pantaloons and a silk skullcap above a long braid of hair hanging down back, accompanied by a dozen of the dirtiest, scrawniest coolies ever seen in Calaveras County. Kearny sent an urgent telegram to Central Pacific headquarters in Sacramento demanding clarification. Crocker's secretary wired back.

NO ERROR STOP CHINAMAN WONG PO-CHING IS GALLAGER'S PARTNER STOP WONG TO TAKE PHYSICAL BUT NOT LEGAL POSSESSION OF PROPERTY STOP MORGAN R GROELICK, FOR CHARLES C CROCKER

Wong acknowledged Kearny's position at the Heckendom and immediately offered him a job. No wages, but, like the coolies, he would be paid a percentage of the mine's earnings—provided there were any. Food? Vegetables, rice, and whatever else the Chinese miners might scavenge from the countryside. If Kearny wanted to get his own grub, that was no problem, but the business could not afford to provide him with a separate allowance. Shelter? Kearny could continue to occupy the mine cabin. The Chinese would live in surplus Central Pacific tents Wong had purchased from his previous employer at a deep discount. Wong intended to live with his men as he had always done while employed by the Crocker Construction Company.

Arrival of the Chinese dashed Kearny's private dream of striking a vein near the surface of the Heckendom. Until Wong arrived at the Heckendom, he had given little thought to the presence of Chinese in California. After it, Kearney's indifference turned sour. To his knowledge, no white man in all of California worked for a Chinese employer. And none on equal partnership terms. To accept Wong's invitation reversed a natural order built into society. The more Kearny thought about it, the more strongly he believed that a Chinaman, irrespective of what legal papers he might possess, had no business running the Heckendom. If nothing else, Kearny believed he had established squatter's rights, which meant that not only couldn't Wong legally offer him a position at the mine, he and his countrymen had no authority to trespass on the Heckendom property. The more he stewed over this upsetting turn of events, the more he resented the very presence of Chinese in the Christian state of California.

Kearny sulked off to the county seat at San Andreas for legal counsel. En route, trappers, timber men, and miners in the wayside saloons shared his indignation. Kearny's story confirmed their own feelings about how badly out of hand matters with the Chinese had gotten. One after another grumbled about being overrun by hordes of heathen Celestials. Politicians in Sacramento claimed that the Chinese had never been more than contract laborers, mandated by law to return to their homeland as soon as the term of their service ended. The reality was altogether different. While a few Chinamen boarded steamers for the trans-Pacific journey back to their homeland, too many remained in California. Wasn't Wong Po-ching a perfect example? The Lings, Chings, Wahs, and Lees were now to be found in all the mining towns, taking white men's jobs, sleeping with their women and stealing everything that wasn't tied down or locked up.

In the saloons, men talked about a series of articles in the *Sacramento Union*, written by an eminent veterinarian, Professor Horace Rutherford from the University of California at Berkeley. In his articles, Professor Rutherford attempted to solve a mystery concerning the Chinese in California, one that had long perplexed Christian folk. While there were plenty of male Celestials around, there were few Chinese females in the state. Common knowledge had it that these male Celestials had a voracious sexual appetite. The professor wondered how so many males satisfied their sexual urges with so few females. An extensive study on three generations of California sheep suggested an answer.

It seemed that during the past decade, the eye formation of the sheep had been drifting closer to the snout and toward the center of their heads. To explain this phenomenon, the distinguished scientist produced impressive-looking drawings and diagrams. On one side of the page he sketched dozens of Chinese faces, parallel to sheep heads. Triangles overlapping the faces and annotated with scientific measurements showed a definite congruence between the position of Chinese and sheep eyes. The professor next discoursed on bestiality found among miners and hermits who spent months, sometimes years, without the company of women. He avoided committing himself to a firm hypothesis, leaving his readers to draw their own conclusions.

Few of Kearny's saloon mates followed the scientific peregrinations of Dr. Rutherford, yet fear of an onslaught of Chinese was growing rampant, so the article comparing Chinese men to sheep had a strong resonance, particularly to those who had never bothered to read it. Moreover, there was universal consensus that profit-motivated industrialists were responsible for importing cheap labor to the United States. Collusion between the railroads, the steamship companies, and the banks was an open secret. Of course, California's representatives paid lip service to the workingman, but nothing was done to end the practice of indentured labor. They talked fiery words, but did nothing to stop the flow of Chinamen arriving in California, men unchecked, uncounted, and desperately hungry for work. No white man could live, let alone raise a family, on the meager wages paid to these Chinese.

Word of Joseph Kearny's crusade preceded him along the network of roadside taverns. Until then, everybody had heard stories about white men being displaced from their jobs. But Kearny was the first to lose his land to a Chinaman. His barroom speeches echoed a resentful sentiment that was surging through the populace and spawned a host of anti-Chinese slogans: *Chinks Go Home. California for White Men. End Chink Sodomy.*

Joseph's younger brother, Dennis, had immigrated to America on the same ship with him. Of medium build, with a slight bow in his spine that caused him to drag his left leg when walking, Dennis made a habit of peering through round spectacles with intimidating intensity. His silky tenor voice, put to an Irish ballad, could move folks to tears, but when used to deliver political speeches from a soapbox, could arouse the passions of those who followed his brother. This weapon he used sparingly, both as first mate on a coastal lumber skiff and later as the director of a cooperative drayage business at the San Francisco docks. As tensions grew between management and labor, he was elected chairman of the Workingman's Party of California.

Word of his brother's campaign to throw the Chinese out of California alarmed Dennis. He had done business with many Chinese in San Francisco and had difficulty understanding the depth of his brother's contempt. As far as he could tell, the number of Chinese in the state was small and, at worst, presented little danger of displacing more than a handful of white workingmen.

Fear that Joseph's crusade might land his brother in jail prompted Dennis to travel to Mokelumne Hill. To recover the mine was one thing, but cleansing California of its Chinese population quite another. It took all his powers of persuasion to convince Joseph to opt for legal action rather than vigilante violence. A local lawyer they had retained informed them that the state allowed each county to levy a miner's tax on foreign nationals. But because few foreign miners remained in the depressed industry, several counties concluded that the cost of collecting this tax was greater than the potential revenue. While enforcement became lax, state law was clear that Wong Po-ching owed Calaveras County six dollars per month for each foreign worker he employed at the Heckendom. That kind of cash was certain to put him out of business.

Joseph Kearny's story convinced retired Captain Wade Sickle III, decommissioned from the Twenty-Second Ohio Cavalry and currently Calaveras County tax collector, that Californians were likely to sympathize with collecting a tax on Asian miners. Wong Po-ching and his troop of Chinamen at the Heckendom presented a test case. So appealing was this cause that seven county employees agreed to help Captain Sickle in the collection.

The idea of reenacting his war days and galloping onto the mine property tickled Sickle's fancy. With that in mind, he led nine men, including Joseph and Dennis Kearny, in a race along the last quarter-mile from a grove of lodgepole pine down a dusty road toward the Heckendom. This dramatic entry failed to impress the Chinese crew because, at the time, Wong and his men were working inside the mineshaft and could neither hear nor see what was going on outside. A laborer operating near the mule-driven hoist called though the shaft to Wong, announcing the visitors. By the time Wong scrambled into the sunlight, Sickle's men were already engaged in vandalism.

Wong ran toward the cabin and, recognizing Joseph Kearny, addressed him directly. "You got no right to do this," said Wong, flailing his arms and pointing to the vandals cutting ropes and overturning water barrels.

Sickle dismounted and, surprised that the Chinaman could speak English, responded with affected authority. "We got every right so long as you haven't paid your miner's tax."

Wong's coolies emerged from the mine and moved into a protective semicircle near their leader.

Sickle pulled out a wad of papers and waved them in front of Wong's face. "I'm the elected tax collector in this county. Name's Captain Wade Sickle the Third. Says in these papers here that any claims to work this mine are invalid so long as your miner's tax isn't paid."

Wong evaluated the seriousness of the white man's assertion and eventually reached forward to inspect the tax warrants. Though he could read neither English nor Cantonese, instinct told him he would be at a disadvantage if the white men sensed this illiteracy. It took all his wits to pretend he was reading. How long would it take to read through such documents? Should he move his lips, as he had observed others doing? Or his eyes? How fast should they move over the writing? Would his coolies give him away?

"Nobody pays a miner's tax in this county," he said, lifting his eyes with deliberate slowness.

"That's because they're white men. This tax is on foreigners like you. Not native folks," Joseph Kearny interjected.

"Many white men are foreigners in California, Mr. Kearny," Wong said. "When did you come here?"

"Four years ago. Well before you."

"Are you a citizen?"

Sickle's cohorts murmured their surprise at the Chinaman's boldness.

"Makes no difference," Kearny said.

"It's still unfair. It's a bad law," Wong replied.

Sickle signaled for Kearny to quiet down and allow him to perform his duty. "That's a matter of opinion. Anyway, it don't matter what you think 'cause the law says that you gotta pay before you do any digging."

"We're not mining, Mr. Sickle. Not yet. We're just repairing shafts and cuts. Look around. No tailings up here. We haven't lifted a single cart of ore. There's no tax on repairing things, is there?" Sickle looked around at his associates for a response. Clearly he was unprepared for the question but eventually rallied. "Makes no difference, Wong. Same thing whether you're digging or fixing. The *intent of* this miner's tax is directed at people working on mine property."

Wong was aware that his coolies were becoming impatient and were eyeing weapons they had left at strategic places for just such a confrontation. He had been warned that white men might try to prevent them from working the Heckendom and drilled his men on the use of picks and shovels for weapons. All he had to do was issue an order in Cantonese. But the white men had access to guns and his coolies didn't.

"How much tax?" he asked.

"Six dollars per man."

"Nobody pays that much," Wong objected.

"In Calaveras County, it's six. Maybe cheaper elsewhere, but here it's six."

Wong flung his arms in an angry gesture and pivoted forty-five degrees on his toes, enough to observe a couple of his workmen. One had followed foreman Ho Lung-chi's example and crept close to his pick. The other froze, looking fearful. Wong wanted to box his ears for letting white men intimidate him.

"It's the middle of the month," he said to the tax collector. "You can't charge us six dollar for the whole month. Half maybe. But not six dollar."

Dennis Kearny noted hesitation on the part of Captain Sickle. He and his brother wanted to force the Chinese from the property and had little interest in replenishing county coffers with miner's taxes.

"Middle of the month or not," he said to Wong, "it's still the same six dollars a head. Nobody works this property till it's paid." After counting the Celestials and doing some multiplication in his head, he continued, "Seventy-eight dollars, I reckon. Seventy-eight dollars must be paid in full. No, correction. Eighty-four," he added, spotting an additional Celestial partially hidden by a wagon.

A deputy took an aggressive step forward, demonstrating his determination to collect every last cent of the tax and triggered a chain reaction. A Chinese worker whirled a steel pick above his head to threaten the deputy, stopping him dead in his tracks. That movement momentarily distracted the other deputies, who had taken their eyes from Wong's defenders. When their attention returned, they found themselves surrounded by Chinese, each brandishing sharp picks. Because they didn't know how to read the expressions on Asian faces, there was confusion about the intent. Were they bluffing?

Sickle cursed his foolish oversight for not having thought to bring a pistol and teach these little bastards that he meant business. "Call these pygmies off me," he cried to Wong.

Dennis Kearny thought about the saddle rifle he carried. Unfortunately it was still tucked into a holster on his horse and not the easiest weapon to extract on a moment's notice. "Tell your Chinks to drop those picks," he bellowed.

Wong tilted his head but remained silent.

"Or we'll come back with guns and blast you off the place."

"You're not invited," Wong replied, his voice fearless.

"We don't need an invitation," Kearny replied. "My brother's been on this property for three years and will exercise his squatter's rights. The previous owner never bothered to establish his possession; therefore, the property belongs to the one who has worked it for the past three years. You certainly can't make that claim, now can you?"

Wong had no understanding of the legal technicalities mentioned by Kearny but after glancing at the damage the white men had already caused, he said, "You'll need an invitation now."

"Hell we do," Joseph yelled and lunged toward Wong. His movement was so fast he caught the Chinaman off-guard. A second later he grabbed Wong by the arm and spun him around. Next came an act that sent the other coolies shrieking with indignation. Joseph had Wong's black queue in his hand and, in a fluid movement, whipped it around his hostage's neck into a noose, putting pressure on his windpipe. The attempted suffocation of their leader by means of his queue made the offense particularly outrageous.

A deputy seized the moment to lunge for Kearny's saddle rifle, but was intercepted by two of Wong's guards. To race through the gauntlet they had established was to risk being impaled by several steel picks. Joseph Kearny tugged on Wong's queue, showing that unless the coolies backed off he intended to cut off their leader's air altogether. Wong gagged and couldn't manage a response. That prompted his men to do the unexpected. Rather than withdraw, they went on the attack. With a series of intimidating movements, they forced the troop of white men back from the mine cabin toward their horses. Humiliation at the hands of much smaller Chinamen inspired one deputy to escape through the cordon of bodies around him. He nearly broke free when a pick caught him in the seat of his pants, knifing through his trousers and ripping into his buttocks. The blow staggered him. As soon as the Chinaman withdrew the pick the victim stumbled and collapsed onto the ground. A series of coolie war cries punctuated his wail. On his knees, the injured man tried to stand on wobbly legs but was unable to maintain his balance and sank to the ground.

The confrontation distracted Kearny, who carelessly eased tension on Wong's queue. The slack provided Wong with room to throw a heel into his captor's shin. Kearny stumbled and in that instant, Wong ducked from beneath his own hair and wrenched the queue from his captor's fingers. Once their leader was free, the coolies were ready to take revenge on the white men.

While the moment belonged to his men, Wong understood that their advantage was only temporary. They might defeat the white men for now, but more white were certain to return. And when they came back they would be armed with six-guns, Winchesters, and law books. Gum San had taught him a lesson not to be forgotten. The Land of the Golden Mountains was white man's country. Chinamen shared in its bounty by sufferance, not right.

The injured deputy called for his comrades to take revenge on the insolent Chinks. Joseph Kearny shouted obscenities and demanded that Wong's men drop their weapons and fight with their fists like true men. To prevent a bloodbath, Sickle fumbled through his papers as if they might contain a new law to use against the Celestials.

"Stop," Wong commanded his men in Cantonese. "No more fighting."

The coolies were slow to lower their weapons. They grumbled and made hostile gestures in Wong's direction, but they appreciated that without their leader's blessing there was no point in resisting.

"I'll pay," Wong said, first in Cantonese and next in English.

Sickle felt a sense of relief as the Chinese lowered but did not drop their picks. It was a good sign, though he never believed for a moment that Wong would capitulate or that the coolies could actually raise the tax money.

"The little runt hasn't got a nickel," one of the deputies declared. "That's why he's up here scratching the old quartz vein for a strike."

"I said I'd pay," Wong absorbed the derision and repeated in a louder voice.

"Seventy-eight dollars," Sickle said.

"Eighty-two," Dennis Kearny corrected.

"Seventy-eight," the tax collector said, leering at Kearny. He wasn't prepared to resume battle for his personal commission on the additional four dollars.

Wong nodded his acceptance and detached himself from the others, marching to the mine cabin. He clambered onto the wood platform and, a moment later, disappeared inside. Parties of Chinese and white men stared at each other angrily while they waited in silence for Wong to reappear. When he did not, mumbling broke out among the white men.

Someone said that he had probably snuck out the back and hightailed it into the forest. Such speculation ended when Wong pushed the door open. In his hand was a leather pouch.

"How much you got there?" Joseph Kearny asked.

"Sixty-six dollar. Count the men. Mr. Kearny counted wrong. We have eleven not thirteen men here."

Sickle threw a glare of annoyance at Joseph Kearny, for if this were true it was an embarrassing concession to the law that he intended to honor. Rather than entrust to one of his men the task, he began recounting the Chinese himself.

"Some of these little bastards snuck off," Dennis Kearny said, glowering at the band of workmen to indicate that he knew exactly who had escaped into the trees. "There were more here a moment ago. I'm tellin'ya, there were more."

"Eleven." Sickle finished his tally and called out. "Anybody see anybody run off? In what direction?"

Nobody had actually witnessed any coolies dashing away.

"Where did you get that kind of money, Wong?" Dennis Kearny asked. "Stolen, I'll wager. That's how most of ya live in the Mother Lode. Steal a little here, snitch a little there. And, 'course, sneakin' into miners' camps and pinching gold from their sluice boxes and rockers."

"Maybe from the mine itself," Kearny's brother added. That was both good news and bad news. Good, because maybe the Heckendom wasn't dry after all; bad, because for the moment the Chinks still had control over it.

Sickle recognized how Dennis's remark was likely to incite additional violence. He said, "Don't make no difference how a man pays his taxes. The county don't inquire into the source of his money, so long as he pays. If you think these coolies have been stealing, then take it up with the sheriff. But I got the tax money I came to get. My job's finished, at least until next month."

"Give me a paper, please," Wong said. "You can't take gold without a paper."

The tax collector hadn't thought to bring his receipt book because he never imagined that he would actually collect any money. "Sorry, I didn't bring my book. You can trust me. I been the tax collector in this county for two years. The citizens wouldn't keep me if I wasn't honest."

Wong scuttled down the four stairs to the clearing beside the Kearny brothers and declared for their benefit, "You saw that I gave Mr. Sickle the tax money, didn't you?"

There was a tacit admission of fact so neither brother spoke up.

"Then I don't need a paper. I got witnesses." To Sickle, Wong said, "I think you won't cheat me more than you already have."

"You don't seem to understand the law in these parts," Dennis Kearny said. "Nobody's cheatin' you. And I don't appreciate the insinuation that we are. Chinamen don't talk to white folk like that. We're gonna teach you foreigners some manners."

"Not now, you're not," Sickle interjected. "Not while there's a county official here collectin' taxes for the citizenry."

The wounded man called for others to help him stand up. No one went to his aid until a nearby coolie offered a hand. Then two white men stepped alongside to support their cohort's weight. The rest of the coolies opened a path for them to hobble away.

"We'll be back," Joseph Kearny pledged.

Wong kept his mouth shut. When he worked for the Central Pacific there had always been white men like my father to protect him. But all that had changed. Now that there were more Chinese in California, conditions were different. There was far more hatred and far fewer white folk to provide protection. Wong had little doubt that the Kearnys would be back. And next time they'd come with more than Wade Sickle the Third.

Wong's men were exuberant. Their leader had been right all along about white men. Powerful though they were, they were not invincible. The time had come for Chinamen to stand up and defend themselves. No more "Yessee, Meester Whiteman; noeee, Meester Whiteman." That hadn't built respect. On the contrary, it had only encouraged white men to abuse Chinamen more. And for their subservience, they earned only low wages and the white man's contempt.

Wong permitted his workers to vent their feelings before commenting on what had happened. In contrast to their high spirits, his were gloomy. It was gratifying to him that his countrymen had finally perceived the truth about their white neighbors, but they had failed to draw the proper conclusions. Exhilaration blinded them to the fact that nothing substantial had changed. They had just won a small skirmish, but not a major battle. A war was coming and they possessed neither guns, lawyers nor popular sympathy to fight it.

The eyes of Wong Po-ching were on fire as he gazed over his cohorts. A ruddy glow burned his cheeks. He was talking rapidly, emptying the venom in his gut. The encounter with Sickle, his men, and the Kearny brothers had taught him a lesson. His words, usually sober and measured, were suddenly heavy with emotion. Yes, he had battled the white man and, yes, he had won a small victory. What had just happened convinced him beyond a doubt that white men hated the Chinese. They hated China. They hated the language of Chinamen, his customs and his very presence in California. You didn't have to look far to figure out how things had come to such a pass. Wong's countrymen were imported for no other reason than their willingness to work cheap. Other than that, white men had absolutely no respect for anything Chinese. Wong's bitterness rose to the surface until he said something he never intended to say in public; just as white men hated the Chinese, so he had begun to hate white men.

In a moment of unbridled passion, he snatched his braided queue and flung it about, not as a symbol of pride, but as a symbol of subjugation. The Chinese had clung to it as if it were an umbilical cord, binding them to their sacred homeland. But the reality was different. The queue was nothing but a symbol of contempt. With his camp knife, he threatened to cut off this queue. It was, to his mind, a symbol of the difference between Chinamen and white men. As long as a Chinaman wore it, he was calling attention to this difference. That observation made him consider what had hitherto gone unquestioned. In objective terms, there was not a shred of evidence that the queue tied a Chinaman to his ancestral land. Chinese adoration of the queue was nothing more than mere superstition. The queue might be significant in China, but in Gum San it meant only degradation.

The coolies shouted en masse. "No, honorable Wong Po-ching! Do not disgrace us by removing the sacred queue."

Pak Nan-chi, a portly deputy foreman, whose age and experience the younger men respected, waved his gnarled hands to attract Wong's attention. "Think of reunion with your ancestors. Think of the bond that ties us with all Chinamen. Do not break that bond. Do not disown us, Wong Po-ching. Do not dishonor our fathers."

Wong threatened with the knife, flashing it high above his head, then beneath his queue. "I'm not returning to China. Never. Not now and not in a year. Never. Never. Gum San is my home now. Clearly we can't live in Gum San with dignity and still wear the queue. Wear it and you'll be slaves forever." He grabbed at his blue tunic originally sewn in China. "This too must go. And the slippers. And the pantaloons. Everything from the Celestial Kingdom. And good riddance too."

Pak addressed the younger coolies clustered around him. "He's gone mad! Our leader is crazy like a frightened mule. Yes, he's been a good leader. But troubles have overcome him. He's lost his balance and is failing. White men have injured him."

"I command you to cut off your queues," Wong howled at his men.

His workmen fell silent. Eyes that shortly before were gleaming with excitement were suddenly downcast. No one wanted to look at their leader.

"Honorable Wong Po-ching," Pak said, "if we cannot do what you say, it's our duty to leave immediately."

Wong studied his deputy foreman's expression for some willingness to back down, but found none. One by one he examined his men, who appeared still bound to a failed mythology from the Celestial Kingdom. None knew as much as he about the ways of America.

Pak also counted his men with his eyes. Not one, even among the three who had slipped into the forest out of fear and had inadvertently lowered the head count and reduced Wong's taxes and had now returned, indicated that he was willing to follow Wong's example. If it became necessary to leave the Heckendom and face unemployment in Gum San, then so be it. At least they would face an uncertain future with their queues intact.

"Listen, Pak Nan-chi," Wong said, "I won't demand that all these men cut off their queues. Not all. Only those who see things as I do. The rest may keep them until they understand Gum San. Then they will willingly change their beliefs."

Pak clapped his hands in glee. Good: Wong was no longer forcing his men to face an unwelcome ultimatum.

"But you must all witness this," Wong cried out and scrambled onto the cabin porch and whirled around. He was standing foursquare before his men as he brought his camp knife close to the long, braided hair on his shoulder. In an instant they saw the blade slash into the braid in a swift sawing movement. It moved at a ferocious speed, biting deeply

into the tress of hair. There was no sign of pain on Wong's face. Once
the blade had passed cleanly through the hair, he displayed the severed
queue in his left hand for all to see.

Several coolies wailed. Others clawed at their skin until blood began
to ooze forth.

What terrified them was not Wong's act, but his own response. Rather
than cry out as they wanted to do, he danced an Asian jig, displaying the
queue above his head as a sign of victory. Next he thrashed it through the
air like a whip, producing a swishing noise.

"You see," he said, "no harm comes to me. I'm American now."

"No. No. Wong Po-ching is not like Americans."

"He's mad," another called out above the din of voices.

Wong laughed aloud. "Not mad. Absolutely sane." And with that
statement he threw the queue as far away as possible. It sailed through
the air and finally landed in a clump of chaparral as though it were
nothing but refuse.

A coolie turned to retrieve it.

"Don't put a hand there," Wong shouted, his voice firm and
unwavering. "It's gone now. My queue's gone. I don't want it any longer."
A second later he disappeared into the mine cabin.

The following morning the coolies waited for Wong to issue
instructions for the day. Not one had followed his example and cut his
own queue. When their leader finally came out on the porch, there
was additional alarm. His head was neatly cropped close to the scalp.
Gone too were his faded blue coolie pantaloons and tunic. In their place
he wore a tattered red flannel shirt and trousers left behind by Joseph
Kearny or perhaps by Jeremy Heckendom, the original owner who had
sold the mine to Charles Crocker.

Wong paced before his men who held back their laughter. Their
ridicule didn't bother him, for he had already consigned the events of
the previous day to the past and was now thinking only of the future.

"What happened here yesterday," he announced, "was just the
beginning. Expect vandalism. Expect harassment. Expect bloodshed.
The Kearny brothers came unprepared. They were kicking themselves for not bringing more guns. They will return with many rifles to
shoot us."

The coolies swooned and started to jabber among themselves.

Wong's voice rose above their caterwauling. "How do we fight against guns?"

Silence. Not one dared speak, even if he had an answer.

"Tell me, how do we fight their guns? With our own guns, of course."

"White men won't sell Chinamen guns," someone said.

"Maybe we'll steal them," another said.

The workmen huddled in heated discussions. What their leader had said made sense. Everybody agreed that their picks and shovels were useless against firearms. Some said it was better to leave the Heckendom before blood flowed. Better to be poor and out of work than dead at the mine.

Wong listened as these fears were voiced. Then he said, "We don't have guns. And we can't buy them. We don't have enough money and white men won't sell them to us anyway. But we have another weapon if we're not afraid to use it." The coolies glanced around in wonderment. Did Wong Po-ching know something they didn't? Or was this just more of his madness?

"Powder. Black powder," Wong said. "I know where a large cache is stored. Not too far away. Maybe twenty miles. We must bring it here to fight against the white men."

Black powder!

In their minds, this remark confirmed Wong's mental affliction.

Everybody knew that shortages of black powder in California had sent the price skyrocketing. White men were stealing it from each other. There had been many shootings over this precious explosive. And if white men were willing to kill each other for the scarce powder, what would stop them from murdering coolies who possessed it?

"I hid the powder when I worked on the railroad. Nobody knows about this except me and my partner," Wong continued, oblivious to the skepticism of his men. "Someone will have to go fetch it."

"Wagons with gunpowder will never make it back here," a mine mucker said. "There are too many bad white men on the roads. They'll think we stole the stuff from them so they'll just steal it back from us."

"Last night I was so angry I couldn't sleep. All I could think about was the future. Now I've got a plan," Wong said. "I'm going to send Ho Lung-chi and Lee Shi-tong with two wagons. They will leave tomorrow morning to bring the powder here from Mirror Lake."

"Highwaymen will take it from them," somebody cried out.

"Not if Ho Lung-chi and Lee Shi-tong wear white men's clothes. They'll put on white men's hats. No queues showing."

"White man will still accuse us of stealing."

"If they try, we'll blow the wagons up. We'll rig detonators. Put powder under the seats. If trouble comes, we'll light the fuses, then jump off and run. No white man would think we're capable of that. It will take them completely by surprise."

"You should go with Ho Lung-chi and Lee Shi-tong," someone called out.

Wong smiled for the first time since the visit from Wade Sickle. "I would like to. But I must go to Frisco to meet my bride. The Yung Wo Company sent a telegram. My bride is there now, waiting for me in Chinatown. If I postpone, I might lose her."

The coolies became animated. With the visit of the tax collector and his henchmen, they had forgotten that their bossman was scheduled to collect his bride. No singsong girl. No whore. A real virgin. From the hamlet of Sei Ho, Kwangtung, in the Celestial Kingdom.

That evening when the coolies gathered on their bunks they talked among themselves. Wong's plan to fetch a bride from San Francisco was proof he was absolutely insane. To their knowledge, no Chinaman in all of California had succeeded in bringing a wife from the Celestial Kingdom. What made Wong believe he would succeed where others had failed, or never tried? Yet, in a strange way, his madness appealed to them. First, it gave him strength to stand up to the white men. But even more important, it compelled him to purchase a wife from China. Didn't every coolie in California want a woman, a real wife to bear him sons?

In the end, they admired their bossman. True, he was completely loco, but wasn't everybody else in Gum San?

CHAPTER EIGHT

San Francisco

Mr. Daniel Gutherie, Editor   2 April 1870
Territorial Enterpriser
Virginia City, Nevada

Reference: Your letter of 29 March 1870

Dear Dan:

The public underestimates these Celestials. If you want my opinion, there's been a conspiracy in the capital to befuddle everybody. Hack politicians in the pockets of industry have led us to believe that the Chinese were imported to perform jobs unfit for Christians and then will soon return to their homeland. Some may. But the truth is that once in California, most will stay in this country. They may have funny eyes and eat disgusting things, but these Chinamen aren't stupid.

My spies tell me that Celestials are now bringing women from China to marry! Does that sound like a people who expect to return home? From what I hear of their impoverished nation, who in his right mind would want to?

I know the thought of Chinese settling in California curdles the red blood of white Christians, who appear to be appalled in public that the Celestials patronize a string of brothels that have sprung up. Why such pious souls don't feel a similar revulsion for white men who frequent their own palaces of ill-repute baffles me. I suspect these upstanding Christians want to deny them the natural exercise of their loins. For them no brothels and no marriages.

There's a juicy story here, Dan. If it's true that these coolies are starting to import wives, the public will soon be outraged. It's the duty of a good newspaper to follow a lead as it unfolds. I know you think this is a wild goose chase, but I want to track down the truth, wherever it might lead. I'm off to Chinatown in Frisco to search for a Chinese bride—not mine, of course. As you know, my sins lean in the direction of sigars, whiskey and tobacka, not women.Sam

Daniel Gutherie, Editor
Territorial Enterpriser
Virginia City, Nevada
Mr. Samuel Clemens   7 April 1870
239 Montgomery Street at Bush
San Francisco, Calif.

Dear Sam:
Mind on whose toes you tread! When you expose the hypocrisies of your fellow men don't expect them to enjoy your wit. I believe you have more critics than faithful readers. How do I know? Because they complain bitterly to me. Take my word for it—this Chinese matter is hotter than you think. Anything you write is certain to rebound against my paper. We're not dealing with facts here, but hot, boiling emotions. I needn't tell you how unpopular the Chinese are these days.
If I refuse your expedition outright, you'll write terrible things about me in a rival paper. So I've judiciously decided to do no more than clip your wings. $25.00 is all you get for expenses. I don't want you to enjoy yourself while on this ludicrous expedition. And if I don't like what you've written, I won't pay for it and, for sure, I'm not going to print it. Be forewarned.
                                                    Dan

   Wong had been to Gum San Ta Foy, San Francisco, the Big City of the Golden Mountains, on three separate occasions to buy supplies and negotiate with the Yung Wo Company for new mine workers. Each time, the overcrowded, malodorous streets of Chinatown made him long for open spaces in the mountains. Sacramento Street, on the border of this Chinese quarter, was lined with claptrap wooden structures ready to collapse with the first autumn storm. Clotheslines, heavy with tattered blue and black pantaloons and tunics, partially obscured Wong's view of the sky. Narrow alleys were congested with merchants hawking dried cuttlefish, salted cod, noodles, and unroasted green tea in bright red and chartreuse cartons. Slatted crates of live coastal crabs and abalone were stacked on the pavement. Bamboo cages filled with ducks and chickens waiting for slaughter leaned against the brick walls of ramshackle buildings.

Everywhere Chinese denizens of this quarter stared at Wong, asking themselves if this was a Chinaman dressed in white man's clothes? Or an apparition? Where did this bumpkin from the mountains find the temerity to cut his queue? Beyond being disrespectful, his deportment amounted to betrayal of Chinese tradition. Sophisticated people in Gum San Ta Foy understood how isolation in the mountains could do strange things to a man. They had seen many white miners from the Mother Lode lose their mental faculties and wondered if a Chinaman was susceptible to the same mysterious forces.

Wong chose not to return glares or respond to whispers. What did his countrymen really know about life outside the city? They made a practice of staying within the security of Chinatown. Each day they talked Chinese, ate Chinese, and dressed Chinese. Of what value was Gum San to them?

Officials at the Yung Wo Company headquarters on Portsmouth Square were equally displeased with Wong. They argued that a dress code identified members of their society wherever they might live and work. And not only was the queue a symbol of unity with their homeland, but a sign of fealty to its Manchu rulers. Woe to the man who defied Chinese custom and abandoned these cherished symbols.

Mention of the Manchus gave Wong reason to spit on the floor. He knew most Chinese in America hated their corruption, arrogance, and cruelty, though none would say so in public. He spit a second time to emphasize his utter contempt.

The official in charge of liaison with the homeland left Wong standing in his office while he conferred with an associate in a nearby room. Minutes later a mousy-looking man dressed in a silk tunic with crimson-colored buttons returned to say they were unhappy with Wong's insolence. By flaunting Chinese customs, he was being fined. Even worse, an offender like him might be dishonored in a public ceremony.

"I didn't come to argue with the honorable officers of the association," Wong said, interrupting the official who hadn't finished his diatribe. "All I want is my bride. I paid for her. In fact, I paid for her two or three times over. I've come to fetch her then I'm gone. I'll be far away from here and won't cause officials of the association more trouble."

Another official mopped his slick hair back behind the ears and flicked orange peels from his desktop to the floor. "Your future wife is in Chinatown, only there are still outstanding charges."

The announcement was a rapier in Wong's gut. Throughout negotiations with officials of the Yung Wo Bank, there had been an endless series of incidental charges. There were additional fees for unexpected bribes. It turned out that food cost more than anticipated, or so they told him. And, at the last moment, passage for steerage class across the Pacific had doubled. Everybody who had anything to do with his future wife, no matter how trivial or tangential, demanded a supplementary fee, which had to be shared with other handlers. Such charges had already exhausted the bonus Wong had earned from Charles Crocker. Since the mine was producing only a trickle of gold dust, it was a mystery where Wong would find the money to pay for the added extortion.

"How much?" Wong asked.

The official leaned forward over a filthy desk, squinting at Wong. Thick glasses distorted his eyes into grotesque forms. "One hundred thirty six dollars."

"For what?"

"Extra costs. Incidentals. Bribes to state officials at the dock."

"That's extortion," Wong bellowed.

The official lifted his chin and narrowed his eyelids so that now the irises of his eyes disappeared. "You're addressing the Yung Wo Association, young man. It is not your place to question us. The fees are set. Either you pay or ..."

"Or what?" He denied them the satisfaction of completing the threat.

The official relaxed back into his chair and rubbed the armrests. "Virgin women are in demand here. Your woman will fetch a good price on Dupont Street. Or in one of the singsong houses. Surely she's worth far more than a hundred thirty-six dollars."

How many times had the association threatened to sell his bride to someone else? Wong was about to explode but something inside cautioned him against it. The extortion was bigger than a single official. Many corrupt men were waiting to take his place. If he refused to pay, these men would confiscate the deposit he'd already paid. His only chance was to shell out the additional sum and take possession of his bride as soon as possible, thereby ending the cycle of charges.

"I haven't brought that much money," Wong told them.

"Too bad," said the man, failing to provide any sympathy.

"How much time do I have to get it?"

"Twenty-four hours."

"I need more. I've come from Mokelumne Hill in the mountains. That's a two-day journey home."

"Twenty-four hours. We have several bids for Mei Yok, if you don't pay."

Wong's brain was suddenly flooded with thoughts, most conflicting. Where could he raise one hundred and thirty-six dollars on such short notice? Would another association lend it to him? At what interest rate? My father would have given it to him in an instant, but Dad was then in Humboldt County, or at least that's where Wong thought he was. Then Wong remembered hearing that Charles Crocker had moved from Sacramento to San Francisco and now lived in a mansion on a big hill. If he could find him, Crocker was certain to extend a loan.

"I'll be back tomorrow," Wong stated.

The official bowed his head and watched Wong back step to the door. What he didn't see occurred the moment Wong was in the street. He turned to the association building and made a series of lewd gestures with his hand. My father had been right from the beginning. The Yung Wo Company had cheated him all along. And the bloodsuckers weren't finished yet. One hundred thirty-six dollars wouldn't be the last of it. Before he concluded his business, they'd surely trump up additional charges.

En route from the new headquarters of the Central Pacific Railroad on Third and Townsend streets a new idea struck Wong. The Yung Wo Company had temporarily lodged the coolies he had brought to the Heckendom at the Globe Hotel on Becket Street. He had always assumed the hotel kicked back part of the rent to the association. If that were true, the association stood to make a profit from lodging his bride there too. Why not just go there and steal her away? To hell with the extra one hundred thirty-six dollars!

Wong calculated the risk. He had sworn loyalty to the Yung Wo, one among five major tongs in Chinatown. Failing to pay a fee might lead to serious consequences. He had heard that those who crossed their tong ended up slashed to death and their extremities scattered in the Pacific as food for crabs. With many fellow Chinamen prepared to sell information about a fugitive, where would he hide? Association officials knew about the Heckendom Mine, but he was sure that none of them would bother to take revenge on him there. Still, it was possible they might hire an unemployed worker to slit his throat.

For years Wong had saved for his bride and enriched the Yung Wo. He asked himself why it was improper for him to take from the association what was already rightfully his. As for potential enemies, he had already fought off white men with their guns. Hired killers from the association didn't frighten him.

Mr. Daniel Gutherie, Editor   2 May 1870
Territorial Enterpriser

Dear Dan:
Enclosed are the results of my investigation in San Francisco. My expenses far exceeded your niggardly allowance. Perhaps acknowledgment that this story was not a wild goose chase will thaw a frozen heart that denies me my legitimate expenses.
I know that upon first reading you'll say that what I have written is offensive and unsuitable for your readers' eyes. Dan, less daring editors would expunge such offensive language. Don't do it. This is the language of Chinatown and anyone who purports to recount life in this Asian compound must use the lingua vulgarus common there. So to speak.
A word about our readers who I have reason to believe are at least 50% female. They strike me as a truth-seeking bunch with good sense and a yen for good humor. The question is at what point will their sensibilities become offended? That, Mr. Editor, I leave to your judgment. I believe our readers will enjoy learning about the bizarre nuptials of these Celestials without the benefit of censorship.
If you feel squeamish, I suggest you read with only one eye open. Or, better yet, squint.

                        Sam

Chinese Nuptials in Chinatown
By
Mark Twain

For those unable to travel across the Pacific and see ancient Cathay, I recommend a visit to San Francisco's Chinatown, sixteen square blocks of masonry and wood buildings, housing perhaps 7,000 to 12,000 Chinese. The colony is composed almost entirely of men, rarely standing over five feet tall, dressed in their native blue and black trousers, jackets and skullcaps. Long pigtail queues of braided black hair hang from the back of their necks, often reaching to the waist. They brought with them the filth of the Orient or have masterfully re-created it in California. The eye cannot help being offended by the dark, crowded hovels in which these people live, nor can the nose avoid the ubiquitous odor of human sewage. The point of visiting Chinatown is not to seek pleasure, but to satisfy curiosity.

I arrived at the Globe Hotel which is, in reality, a combination shirt factory, opium den and sleeping quarters piled several stories on top of each other. On the ground floor Chinese tailors sew shirt collars and sleep in unventilated chambers. One floor above is a large, dark room carpeted with thin mattresses upon which Asian men recline, smoking opium in waist-high water pipes. It is commonly believed that opium stimulates the sexual appetite but I saw nothing to confirm this. Rather than sexually aroused, the impoverished Chinamen who ingest this drug appear to be in a lackadaisical stupor. The odor of their narcotic permeates the factory and wafts upward into the sleeping quarters. Anyone visiting the Globe is bound to breathe the fumes, though no medical authorities claim this endangers one's health.

It was in these quarters that I sought to verify a rumor that coolies are importing wives from China. I had heard that a particular fellow who had previously worked on the railroad in the Sierra purchased a wife through the good offices of his fraternal association and intended to take her with him to a mining camp in the mountains. The thought of one purchasing a wife like chattel may be offensive to stouthearted Christians; still, one can conjure a practical advantage over the normal courtship in California. One might argue that a marriage arranged by an intermediary removes from the courtship equation both passion and the foolishness that inevitably follows. I leave to my readers to judge for themselves the advantages and disadvantages of this nuptial system.

At the Globe, I reasoned it would be easier to find the prospective bride amid a sea of single men than the prospective groom, so I began my search in the living quarters on the hotel's third floor. To my surprise, I found the groom already there.

The coolie to whom I refer stood out from the others. Taller than his compatriots by a foot and handsomer by a league, he was not dressed like his brethren, but in white men's clothing. Brown cotton trousers bagged around his seat and the sleeves of a faded red-checkered workshirt was rolled many times at the elbows. What was particularly striking was that he wore no queue of braided hair. The other Celestials also noticed these differences and seemed upset with him. Some laughed and clapped their hands; others made assorted noises by blowing air through their nostrils in the manner of baboons. It occurred to me that this fellow, dressed like a miner, might speak English, so I asked if the others were making fun of him.

He took a long moment to size me up, then said with a measure of skepticism in his voice, "Yes, sir. It does look like it, now doesn't it?"

I followed up, "May I ask you why, sir?"

"They say I'm a fool. They say I paid for a virgin wife but will receive a woman poked a thousand times on the ship to America. They say it's cheaper to fuck a whore." [Dan, I can see your eyebrows colliding with the crown of your head. You're saying to yourself, your friend Sam Clemens has lost his senses if he believes I'd print such foul language. Note please, the quotation marks. I'm only reporting exactly what the Chinaman said to me in English.]

The lecherous expressions of the young Chinese bucks clustering about telegraphed their willingness to violate another man's bride. Some massaged their crotches. These, you will note, were not the same men smoking opium on the hotel's second floor.

"Is it true?" I asked the tall Chinaman.

His attention was momentarily distracted but eventually returned to me. "I don't know. I haven't found my woman yet. She's supposed to be in one of these chambers. Nobody will tell me which one."

"Do you mind if I tail along? I won't intrude. Your name, sir?"

As soon as the words passed my lips I realized how strange they must have sounded. It's a safe bet that nobody had ever called this Celestial "sir."

"Wong Po-ching," he answered. "From Moke Hill, I mean Mokelumne Hill in Calaveras County."

My invitation to help look for his bride was received with little enthusiasm. I tagged along anyway.

We moved through various public rooms where men shook their fingers at Mr. Wong and made rude gestures. On one occasion he stopped to answer his revilers with what sounded like abrasive language. He eventually learned that several women were on the floor above, girls in their middle teens imported to whore in mobile brothels that traveled with migrants working at farm settlements in California valleys. When he reached the room where these women were supposed to be, we were confronted by a corpulent guard with a revolver who made it clear that no man could enter without paying him personally a fee. Wong seemed to be a seasoned bargainer for he ended up paying the guard about half of what I had to pay to follow him into the women's quarters.

What I soon found were hapless, diseased and emaciated girls, the hideous result of poverty and ignorance. Though Celestials are not U.S. citizens, the state permits them to practice prostitution without interference. Men, both white and Asian, pay handsomely to abuse their young bodies. Such girls are imported as a commercial commodity, like grain or timber. Their condition once arriving in California is nothing short of appalling.

Mr. Wong noticed a female crouching in the rear, outside a circle of prostitutes. Something must have told him she was different from the others. The guard forbade him from approaching her, but Mr. Wong knew how to change the guard's mind by offering several coins. He immediately threaded a path between the other girls and stood beside the woman in question. When he asked if she might be Mei Yok, she looked surprised but nodded her head affirmatively. A cautious smile puffed her sallow cheeks. Wong broke out into a jig, his feet stamping on the floor in what I later learned was a sort of mating ritual. Of the conversation that followed, he was good enough to translate a few words for me.

"I was promised to a man named Wong Po-ching," she said in a low voice, almost a whisper. "I think that's his name. But during the journey here, I began to think it was a joke. I came to believe they were taking me to serve as a singsong girl. Like the others."

Wong dropped to his knees beside her. Mei Yok's eyes, which appeared to focus at different points, were embedded beside a flat but symmetrical nose. Large ears poked through straight black hair like shark fins in the ocean. The fact that she was plain and skinny didn't seem to discourage Mr. Wong. He appeared oblivious to spectators, who had burst into the women's quarters without paying any fee, and gathered around. Wong Po-ching and Mei Yok chattered in Cantonese as if they were cousins reunited after a long separation.

Much has been said about the difference between Chinaman and white men, and far less about their similarities. My visit to the Globe Hotel convinced me that white Christians have no monopoly on cruelty. The Chinese who encircled Wong Po-ching and Mei Yok were mostly young men who had been on the high seas for months without contact with women. A fellow coolie who had succeeded in acquiring a wife apparently drove them mad with jealousy. One after another declared that he had personally copulated with Mei Yok aboard the vessel on the high seas. Not once but many, many times. As did all the other passengers. If this was correct, Miss Mei Yok had been a very busy woman.

Being several inches taller than the others, Wong Po-ching might have selected one or two rogues and with his fists taught them a lesson in courtesy. But he was remarkably restrained. The hot bucks needed some taming, but he must have realized how they outnumbered him.

"Mei Yok's perfect for singsong house," a rascal from Fukien Province declared. "No man can satisfy her lust. This whore's been punched by a thousand peckers."

Wong exposed his teeth and snarled, "You lie."

The audience broke out in laughter. Wong's gaze slipped from the accusers to Mei Yok, who appeared wilted in disgrace. The little slivers of her eyes closed down and her head slumped into her chest. A slight shiver rocked her torso.

"The Yung Wo Company guaranteed she's a virgin," Wong said.

"Of course," the fellow from Fukien howled, "every official in the association's poked her. Now they want to pawn off this worn-out cunt on the first fool who'll take her. And for a fat fee to boot!"

"Horny bastards. You lie because you're frustrated. Once I was on a ship for many months with no women. We all went mad with desire. There were no singsong girls for us then. If you know what's good for you, you'll close your mouths." He looked to Mei Yok for a defense, but found her eyes still downcast.

"You see," said the man from Fukien, "this whore doesn't deny it. She can't. Too many men have screwed her. Both on the ship and here in Gum San Ta Foy."

"Tell them it isn't true, Mei Yok," Wong said. "You tell them outright. I'll believe you."

Her head swayed from side to side, denying the accusations. But no words came from her lips.

The spectators chanted their amusement. Mei Yok's silence said everything.

"You lie," Wong growled. "You bastard liars ..." his complexion became flushed and his eyes burned with fury. For an instant his hand dropped to the trail knife in a sheath on his belt but he did not yank it out. His fist rose in a signal of combat. "I'll prove that Mei Yok's a virgin. I'll show all of you. She'll be my wife and I'll show you her virgin's blood. Right here. Right now. Then you'll choke on your foul lies."

A swoon of disbelief emanated from those surrounding the betrothed couple. Idle men from dormitories on adjacent floors arrived to observe the altercation and, perhaps, the pending brawl. Fights were always good entertainment, particularly if waged over a woman, never mind if she were desirable or not. And Mei Yok was definitely not in the former category.

Mei Yok came to life with a sense of alarm. "Not here. Not now, Wong Po-ching. No *sese-sese* here. Not before all these eyes."

"Why not? I'm not ashamed and you shouldn't be either. A good woman has nothing to fear but the loss of her honor."

"Please. Not here. No *sese-sese* in front of these people."

"It must be. This is a matter of honor for you and me. For your father. And for the Yung Wo Company."

A newcomer elbowed his way to the front ranks and pointed at Wong. "So now he'll rape her, then throw her out on her ear like other sluts. She'll be in the singsong house tomorrow morning." Wong had had enough. His knife suddenly flashed in the air, defying the mocker to continue. Its slashing blade quieted those in front. Mei Yok rose from her knees and, with tears in her eyes, placed a hand on Wong's arm. "Don't fight over me."

The knife cut another circle in the air with a swishing noise. "I'll cut out their tongues. Then I'll cut off their balls."

"No, Wong Po-ching. I don't want a dead husband. Don't fight these evil men. They only want to hurt me because I say no when they expose themselves."

"Hahaah," the man from Fukien cried, "it's Mei Yok who opens her cunt to all takers."

Wong lowered his knife and studied his bride, searching her for the truth.

"Wong Po-ching should not believe these men," Mei Yok said. "They lie so you will leave me. Once you're gone, they'll do what they want." Her voice dropped to a mere whisper. "My husband, come inside me but don't fight. They'll hurt you and then I'll have no one in Gum San to protect me. Come inside me."

The hostile hoots changed into expressions of disbelief. Would this couple really consummate their union in public? Before everyone's eyes?

He took her hands in his and drew her to the floor before him on their knees. This act convinced the others that he rejected their accusations and accepted her purity, enough for marriage. The insults suddenly stopped. The murmuring tailed off into a respectful silence. Spectators in the front row pushed back to enlarge a space for the couple. Two elderly men prepared a mattress while Mei Yok unfastened her slippers and carefully set them at the foot of the makeshift bed. Wong followed. Tea arrived from somewhere in the hotel in a dented pot. I learned later that the drinking of tea was a ritual for Chinese couples before the wedding bed. The couple kneeled in front of each other and, in a Chinese custom, touched teacups together, sipped once, then twice and then three additional times. Each sip symbolized a state of marital harmony that would probably be the envy of white families.

[A note to my readers: Christians of good morals and common decency would certainly vacate a room where a couple are engaging in conjugal relations. But these Celestials have different customs. To them, sex, while personal, is not private. The production of children is, after all, a public event, for these offspring will be part of a community larger than the family. Since many men stood at respectful distances to witness Wong and Mei Yok consummate their marriage, I saw no reason to leave. One might think these Celestials are less modest than we. Yet after seeing their crowded quarters, I wonder where they might normally find privacy for conjugal

unions. For Christians, privacy in the practice of sex is a matter of decency; for Orientals, a luxury.]

There wasn't a peep from the audience until Wong and Mei Yok had crawled under a woolen blanket. The viewers began a nuptial chant and closed their circle within a hair's breadth of the couple. Wong's head alone was visible but there was much movement beneath the blanket. It is noteworthy that throughout this ritual, there was no nudity. Physical contact occurred while dressed, or nearly so. On the other hand, Mei Yok showed little inhibition about expressing her pleasure. Both she and her husband emitted a steady flow of swoons and coos. Their breathing became rapid as movement beneath the blanket increased.

Males circling the wedding bed seemed to enjoy what they imagined to be happening. A few massaged their legs. There appeared to be no shame in this and no debauchery either.

Wong's gasps were brutish and lusty; Mei Yok's shrill and explosive. Their hips poked mounds in the blanket. The young men began echoing the couple's pleasure with animal yelps. Then suddenly, as if all knew the exact instant, the crowd quieted down. The blanket stopped undulating and sounds beneath it ceased.

The couple emerged not to cheers or congratulations but to stark silence. Wong had demonstrated that he believed Mei Yok a virgin. Her blood would prove it. All eyes were riveted on the mattress.

An elderly man, grizzled and gray, was appointed to inspect. He stooped down beside the marriage bed. Whispers rippled through the ranks, and it seemed as though the revilers would start their ugly taunts again. With his fingers the appointed judge smoothed the cloth surface. That triggered hoots from rogues who believed all along that Mei Yok was no virgin.

The judge leaned over the bedding for closer inspection. Back on his heels he emitted a single guttural sound. Yes. Yes, indeed, a broken hymen had left its telltale spot.

The revilers pressed forward to confirm this but were stopped by a stern warning. The old man raised his hand with authority. The verdict was final. Further confirmation was unnecessary.

From the rear some men demanded to see for themselves.

"The blood's there," the judge barked. "My word is final. Mei Yok was a virgin."

Discontent rippled forward but was overwhelmed by a groundswell of congratulations. The majority began clapping their hands in approval. Mei Yok was in her husband's arms, a wide smile expanding over her thin, emaciated lips.

When the crowd moved away from the mattress, I cautiously approached to see for myself. The sun glowed through a distant window with extraordinary light. If the bloodstains were there, I would have seen them, but they were not. I crouched lower to be absolutely sure. No blood. Absolutely none. You could draw many conclusions from that, but only one is valid.

I am now forced to revise my judgment about the cruelty of these Celestials. The young bucks are, indeed, ill-mannered and craven. But they accepted the old man's wisdom. Once Wong had demonstrated how much he wanted Mei Yok for his wife, there was no point in further resistance. Their envy spent, they could only hope for wives themselves. In the end, Mei Yok did not need to prove her virginity. She had been declared a wife by fiat. You could say that Wong Po-ching married her by public acclamation.

This was the first Chinese marriage in California, perhaps in the United States.

I count myself fortunate to have witnessed it.

The Barnston Road

Joseph Kearny sent Oliver Plumb and Michael Tobias to monitor movement in and out of the Heckendom Mine while he and his brother retreated to the Hotel Leger to plan their next move against the Chinese usurpers. A day later, Plumb and Tobias reported that Wong Po-ching had left the mine in a mule-driven wagon, traveling alone toward Stockton. Two of Wong's coolies had also left the mine in two additional wagons, headed in the opposite direction.

In their hotel room, Joseph and Dennis Kearny considered what this could mean. The foreign miner's tax had apparently failed to break Wong's spirit or determination to keep working the mine. Quite the contrary: It now appeared as though he were trying to resupply operations, perhaps with heavy machinery and provisions, perhaps with more coolies, or both. They also speculated that wagons traveling in different directions were meant to be a diversion. The Kearny brothers concluded that under no circumstances would they permit Wong to resupply. One way or another, the wagons had to be stopped.

Dennis recited a litany of criminal acts associated with highway robbery. Isolated communities in California had little patience with highwaymen who threatened their commerce. Hangtown got its name from stringing up those who offended the county's sensibilities against robbery on the open roads. But as they searched their memories about previous hangings, they could not remember a single incident in which a Chinaman had been the victim of such a robbery. In Hangtown they hanged white men for stealing from other white men. But stealing from a Chinaman was different. Dennis commented that it was a sad day when the Kearny family was reduced to committing crime. But how else could they protect the Heckendom?

"It don't matter anyway," Joseph reminded his brother. "Chinamen can't testify against us in court. Even if we're charged there's no chance of conviction, that is, as long as everybody keeps quiet. If we pick the right men to help, there's nothing to worry about. No court in this county will listen to Chinese testimony."

"I won't be party to stealing," Dennis said. "No matter what's in those wagons. Our mother and father didn't raise us to be highwaymen. I say we stop those wagons and find out what's inside. Maybe we'll smash the axles. Or burn the cargo and drive off the mules, but take nothing for ourselves. It's no crime to scare off the drivers. But I don't want any stealing, you understand?"Joseph remained pensive. He disagreed with his older brother but, as always in the family hierarchy, he deferred to Dennis's judgment. The lookouts saw only that three wagons had left the Heckendom. To catch up with them was nearly impossible. But sooner or later, the drivers would be headed back, easy targets for an ambush.

Ho Lung-chi and Lee Shi-tong were exhilarated but cautious about the plan to collect gunpowder from the cave at Mirror Lake. They knew the outgoing journey would be less dangerous than the return trip. From the moment they loaded forty eighty-pound kegs of powder onto their wagons, they became agitated. Not only was there an inherent danger in transporting black powder, but the slow moving wagons were bound to attract highwaymen. No Chinaman in California believed that local sheriffs would lift a hand to protect them or their property, if in fact the powder even belonged to Wong, something they had their doubts about anyway. Along the route, Ho Lung-chi imagined white men behind every bolder, ready to pounce on them and steal their cargo. Against firearms, the small axes they had placed below the buckboards were worthless.

Lee Shi-tong held the opposite view. The strongest advocate of Chinese self-defense among Wong's coolies, he welcomed a chance to confront his tormentors in hand-to-hand combat. They had beaten the Kearny brothers and their henchmen once before and, if necessary, could do it again. With that in mind, he had taken responsibility for installing a fuse attached to a keg of powder under the buckboard. A slow-burning fuse ran through a hole under the driver's feet and was connected by another fuse to a detonating keg buried at the bottom of the load. He hooked up a similar device in Ho Lung-chi's wagon and taught him how to ignite it with Chinese cigars they planned to smoke in areas where ambush was likely.

On the home stretch, Lee Shi-tong let his mules saunter back along a familiar road. So far, Wong's instruction to tuck their queues under large leather hats and to dress like white men had worked remarkably well. Along the circuitous roads of El Dorado and Amador counties, no one had accosted or threatened them. Matters might have been different had the white men on the road seen Chinese coolies driving heavily loaded wagons. That was a temptation difficult to resist.

Lee Shi-tong, feeling a sense of relief, let his reins go slack and his mules set a lethargic pace while both men admired the shale gulches of the Mokelumne River's North Fork. Their eyes were constantly searching for alabaster outcroppings of quartz, the telltale signature of gold beneath the earth's crust. From Wong they had learned that quartz often signaled the presence of gold. Sooner or later they were bound to come across such an outcropping. If they happened to discover such a vein exposed near the surface of the mountain, quarrying deep into the Heckendom mine might not be necessary.

The moment the Kearny hijackers spurred their horses from behind a granite hillock, Lee Shi-tong regretted his momentary distraction. It took him only a few seconds to figure out what was happening. There were two horsemen obstructing his path in front and two closing in behind to block an escape. Both wagons were suddenly engulfed in a swirl of dust. He cried out in Cantonese to Ho Lung-chi. They had lost valuable time by riding into the ambush. But if they moved fast they could still execute their contingency plan.

Lee Shi-tong stopped daydreaming and hauled in on the reins.

Joseph Kearny spurred his horse, creating a fresh cloud of dust and coming alongside the lead mule to grab its bridle. His brother fell behind him to get control of the second beast. From the rear, their cohorts closed in on the trailing wagon, moving to stop Ho Lung-chi's mules. Intimidating pistols whirled in the air, but there was no shooting.

Lee Shi-tong aimed his whip a half-dozen feet over the heads of his animals and hauled it in fast enough to make a loud cracking sound. That diverted his adversaries long enough for him to aim his whip at Dennis's shoulder. The tip missed the mark and struck his rib, causing Dennis to shriek in pain. Joseph immediately reined in his horse and tried to see why his brother, now enveloped in dust, had cried out. This gave Lee Shi-tong time to shove away the toolbox hiding his fuse. He didn't think the Kearny brothers would give him a chance to put his cigar to it unless he kept them dodging his horsewhip. Both men had hauled in their horses in anticipation of a second assault.

Lee Shi-tong dropped the tip of his cigar in the direction of the fuse, but couldn't find the end without taking his eyes off the attackers. For the time being, it was more important to keep his weapon active. Joseph spurred his horse forward to re-secure control over the lead mule, unwittingly coming into range of the whip that struck him on the neck, producing a searing sting. Lee Shi-tong took advantage of the moment to concentrate on planting the embers of his cigar against the wick's end. As he transferred his attention back to Kearny, he felt heat from the burning of black powder on his ankle. His boot maneuvered the toolbox back into position, more or less hiding the burning fuse from sight.

The Kearny brothers, now in full control of both mules, moved in close to the Chinaman, where his whip was no longer effective. An eight-inch trail knife sliced at the line lashing a tarpaulin over the powder kegs.

"Get down from there," Joseph ordered while signaling with a revolver for Lee Shi-tong to dismount.

Lee threw a glance back at his partner who appeared frozen with fear, unable to implement their plan and ignite his fuse. Just as well, thought Lee Shi-tong, because he would only attract attention to their sabotage. One explosion would make their point. He thought how foolish to have wasted time rehearsing with him and refocused on the white men, issuing a spate of expletives in Cantonese. Before finishing, a strong arm reached forward, dragging him sideways. He was now off-balance, but not out of the fight. Locked into combat, he dug his teeth into Dennis's forearm to produce an anguished wail, followed with a curse. Another tug and Lee Shi-tong found himself lifted from the buckboard and sailing toward the ground. In the process he grabbed for his assailant and caught him far enough out of the saddle to drag him alongside toward the ground. Dennis Kearny landed on top of Lee Shi-tong. The instant both recovered from the shock, they began wrestling in the dust.

Kearny's men, who were uncovering the tarp from Ho Lung-chi's wagon, immediately lunged forward to assist their leader. At the same time, Ho recovered his wits and did what he had been trained to do and touched the end of his cigar to a fuse beneath the buckboard. What he had lacked in reflex he made up for with dexterity. On first contact, the wick sputtered alive. A moment later he had the burning fuse tucked back under his seat.

On the ground Lee Shi-tong was paying a dear price for his resistance. By now, Joseph Kearny had joined his brother, pounding the Chinaman's ribs and groin and taking revenge for the whipping they had received.

Their cohorts were determined that Ho Lung-chi should not escape punishment. They urged their horses beside the rear wagon and reached for him. He slid sideways to avoid capture and noticed the hissing fuse within view. He threw a leg forward to hook the utility box with his toe. It moved an inch, enough to conceal the fuse. And none too soon because an instant later a hijacker's hand hooked under his armpit and hauled him from the wagon seat. He found himself on the ground like Lee Shi-tong.

It was Dennis Kearny who first recognized that his men had lost control. Assaulting Chinese coolies was no way of accomplishing their goal of regaining the Heckendom. An honest fight between equals was one thing, but torturing undersized Chinese peasants was something else altogether.

"Get out of here," he told both Chinamen, who had failed to stand up, apparently preferring to crawl on the ground like dogs. Prodding boots into their sides gave them encouragement. Once Lee Shi-tong and Ho Lung-chi got up, they wobbled, hacking dust from their lungs. A second attacker ordered them to start making tracks. Lee Shi-tong surveyed his wagon, looking for smoke under the seat. There was none, a sign that in his haste he had failed to ignite the fuse or that it was defective. He took the first steps of retreat, chastising himself for his incompetence. Ho Lung-chi released a volley of curses at the white men in Cantonese, but having run out of nasty things to say, reluctantly followed his companion.

"Let's see what these vermin have brought us," Joseph dusted himself off and called to the others behind him. The tarps were unfastened, but still partially covered the cargo. Kearny pulled back the first canvas to expose barrels of powder, neatly stacked so that they would not roll.

"Well, Jesus be God Christ!" he exclaimed. "You wouldn't believe what these Chinks are hauling."

"Where did they get this stuff?" one of the accomplices asked and then answered his own question. "They goddamn stole it. Even got the manufacturer's labels on 'em. From New York state. No coolie could buy this."

"The stuff's gotta be worth at least seven hundred dollars. We won't have much trouble sellin' it in Moke Hill."

"We're not selling anything," Dennis interceded with the commanding tone he used while addressing dockworkers on San Francisco Bay. "We've already agreed. We're not highwaymen and thieves. Besides, we can't sell powder that's already been stolen. That would make us accomplices in the original crime."

"We ain't gonna sell it exactly. They stole it from somebody. We're just gonna take a commission for puttin' it back on the market."

"We've got to return it to the sheriff in town. That will establish our claim that the Chinks are thieves. Let the law find out who owns the stuff. Neither me or my brother will conspire in thievery."

"That's because we didn't know what they was hauling," one accomplice said. "Now that we do, it don't seem smart to take it to town. Besides, if we turn it in, people will want to know what happened out here. They gonna ask why we ambushed the Chinks. Every man in town would have wanted to be with us, but nobody would want that written up in the papers."

"Let's toss the stuff into a ravine," another accomplice said.

"What a waste," responded Joseph Kearny. "That's a goddamn waste. Better to use it to put Wong and his clan out of business once an' for all."

That idea made everybody stop and think. Joseph Kearny voiced what had been on his mind from the moment he saw the powder: "Let's drive these wagons onto the Heckendom and cause a little mischief. Then there won't be any Chinks left in Calaveras County to bother us. No more of their meddling in these parts."

Dennis fancied the idea of returning the wagons to the Heckendom. The fact that they had caught Chinamen with powder proved their intention to mine deep. If they actually struck a vein, dislodging them might be complicated. State law protected a miner's strike and, as far as he knew, the law said nothing about whether Chinamen had a right to benefit from this. With extenuating circumstances, it might even support a Chinese claim. His brother's plan started to make sense.

To demonstrate his resolve, Joseph climbed onto the first wagon and grabbed the reins. One accomplice mounted the second vehicle, while

Dennis gathered the reins of the two riderless horses and moved forward to lead the new column in the final drive home.

The wagons arrived at the Heckendom well before Ho Lung-chi and Lee Shi-tong, who believed the ambushers would turn the wagons around and move as fast as possible in the opposite direction. Though Lee Shi-tong had convinced himself that his charges would not detonate, Ho was confident that his would. It was just a question of time before they'd hear an explosion somewhere in the hills.

Several coolies at the mine mistook the Kearny caravan for their returning compatriots, whom they expected to be disguised as white men. They could not account for the horses, but there were many things they could not account for and soon there would be an explanation. In Wong's absence they formed a welcoming party near the gate to the mine property. Their greeting ceased as they saw unfamiliar men driving the wagons. Joseph Kearny, in the first wagon, didn't bother to stop. Ignoring the Chinamen by the gate, he steered immediately in the direction of the ball mill. Once inside the mine property, the second wagon headed for the wooden head-frame towering over the main shaft.

More coolies arrived to greet what they also thought were fellow Chinamen and were equally alarmed to find the wagons occupied by white men. It was a bad omen, to say the least. They were jabbering among themselves when the detonating powder keg under Joseph's seat exploded. An instant later stacked kegs behind him blew up. In the flash of an eye, the wagon rose into the air, engulfed in a ball of flames. The mule team sailed up with it, pummeling the log cabin that housed the ball mill and nearby cyanide plant, some two hundred feet away. Fragments from the wagon and its inhabitant rained earthward through thick black smoke, blocking out the morning's sunlight.

It didn't take the second driver long to figure out that his wagon might also be booby trapped. He jumped from the buckboard and hit the ground, half-rolling and half-scrambling as fast as his legs would take him. His timing was perfect. The detonating charge erupted with an angry blast and an instant later the main cargo blew, repeating the previous scene of destruction. Survivors on the ground burrowed into anything that might shelter them from descending debris. Smoke and dust lingered above them far longer than the echo of the blasts.

Dennis Kearny was the first to lift his eyes and survey the battle scene. His brother's wagon had disintegrated. A portion of a mule's hindquarter lay on the ground some twenty feet from him. Another beast had been reduced to singed bone. Other than steel on the wagon wheels, the wagon carriages had all but disappeared. Ground shrubbery was charred black and burning. Dennis screamed as though his tenor voice, cultivated belting out Irish folksongs, would bring his brother back to life. But there was nothing left to revive. Few bones and no flesh.

Frightened coolies approached the scene of destruction, listening to Dennis's golden voice in mourning. When he took notice of this gathering, he addressed the foreigners. "My brother was a mild-mannered man with no prejudice against you Chinks. He often said that what you do in China is your own business, not his. Live and let live, that was his motto. God made different races for a purpose. But the Almighty also put them on their own continents and separated them by a large ocean. When they leave their God-given territories, trouble begins. The good Lord's amply provided for you Chinks in China. You've got no right to be here in California. Leave now before we throw all the rest of you into the sea."

"Let's clean'em out once and for all," said a mounted drifter from Sacramento as he yanked a Winchester from his saddle holster.

The coolies turned and ran for the trees.

"Weasels," he howled, firing a single shot into the woods in the general direction of the fleeing Chinamen. "Come out of the trees and fight like men."

But Wong's unarmed coolies were far too savvy to confront enraged white men with guns. They hid in the forest, suspecting the white men's horses wouldn't follow them through thick vegetation and around deadfall tree trunks.

Three horses survived the explosions. A fourth horse was so badly injured it had to be shot. When it became clear that the white men couldn't pursue them in the forest, the coolies cautiously returned to the mine to help fight fires at five locations. They immediately gathered buckets to fill with water from the wastewater pond beside the cyanide plant. At first the white men looked with contempt at their attempts to salvage mine property. Though the Celestials left empty buckets nearby, none added a helping hand.

The white men remained through mid-afternoon, collecting particles of flesh and clothing. When there was nothing more to do, three survivors mounted their horses and pulled out of the Heckendom property to mourn their losses elsewhere.

Before Mei Yok arrived in California, the thought of not having children obsessed Wong Po-ching. Gregarious by nature, he found many companions in the railroad camps, but made few close friends. His compatriots were largely rootless men looking for an opportunity to improve their failed lives in China. Some were running from bad marriages; others had lost jobs and had dim prospects. Without exception, they had fled from poverty, for why would a well-off man journey such a long way to face an uncertain future? Chinese laborers were loners and runners, drifters and criminals with little interest in family life. Of course, they enjoyed sex as much as any man, but that had nothing to do with family matters.

On occasion, Wong tried talking about family with working white men. To them families meant responsibilities they didn't want and expenses they couldn't afford. Women, they vehemently asserted, were a continuous source of aggravation. In the mountain camps, men were accustomed to cooking their own food and mending their own clothing, with little need for a woman's domestic skills. What Wong observed in the mountain camps confused him. At first these white men fought other men over women, then fought with the very same women they had won. Children arrived, though their fathers often protested that they arrived by accident not design. And when on occasion these kids came to visit the mountain camps, their fathers spent little time with them. Wong's childhood was different because, until his village was ravaged by bandits, he had been close to his parents. In China a family meant ties to the past, an anchor in the present, and a link to the future. He wondered what it was about Gum San that made men look at family differently than he did.

Wong had avoided local Chinese joss houses, empty mine buildings that had been converted into religious shrines used to honor one's ancestry. He found them noisy, and the ubiquitous smell of incense irritated his nose. For a while he toyed with the thought of building a private joss house at the Heckendom. The idea lost its appeal when he considered that any wooden structure was likely to burn to the ground and, without permanence, how could one have a meaningful religion? The notion of being linked to the future preoccupied him. When he thought what best represented durability, a single image returned to mind, that of the giant redwood tree James MacGreggor had destroyed in Calaveras County. In the days preceding Mei Yok's arrival, the giant sequoias were constantly in his thoughts. Shortly before his marriage in San Francisco, he seized on the idea of establishing a family shrine among these mammoth creatures where Mei Yok, like him, would revere their strength and permanence. Eventually she would come to understand why he wanted to build a shrine for the Wong family in the redwood forest.

At the Stockton ferry dock, Wong paid parking fees for the wagon and mules he had stowed, then loaded Mei Yok's meager belongings behind the buckboard. They followed the Stockton road through farmland until it gradually ascended toward Copperopolis. In higher altitudes, a thin powder of snow covered the ground, not enough to impede travel, but a warning of colder weather to come. En route, Wong enthusiastically shared with his new bride what he had learned about Gum San. Normally she enjoyed talking, but she could not organize her thoughts coherently as she took in this unfamiliar landscape. Her silence convinced Wong that his Mei Yok was an extremely good listener, an admirable trait in a Chinese wife.

From Copperopolis the track weaved through foothills toward Murphy's, then rose gently between thick sugar pine forests. Above them, thick cumulus clouds gathered on the mountaintops. As the temperature dropped, Mei Yok shivered beneath her light cotton jacket until Wong wrapped her tightly in a blanket. He had also brought food, a small miner's tent, and camping gear, essentials for travelers on the sparsely inhabited track connecting the mining settlements. Experience in the mountains had taught him that a rapid drop in temperature in autumn meant a blizzard was on its way. In planning for this trip to the grove he called "Big Trees," he hoped to make camp before the sun's rays ceased shining through the dense canopy above and enclose the forest in dark stillness.

The weather did not cooperate. They arrived among the redwoods as low-lying clouds obscured the treetops. Moisture dripped from above, making the forest floor soggy.

Mei Yok's feet sank into a soft, damp coniferous duff. Though she could not see through the heavy mist, she calculated the height of the trees by their massive girths and exclaimed, "Such enormous trees! Nothing so big in China."

"And old too," he added with a sense of pride in the discovery. "Maybe hundreds of years old. Maybe they were born during the Ch'in Dynasty when China was very young, or the Sui."

She looked as though she didn't believe that. "No trees could possibly be that old. A hundred years, perhaps. At the very most, maybe a hundred and fifty."

He absorbed her remark, thinking that he had married a woman who spoke her mind. That was a good sign. But she was still wrong about the giant sequoia, just as Charley Crocker had been wrong about them years before. Together they trekked over to the massive tree he and James MacGreggor had destroyed with nitroglycerin. By now saplings had begun to sprout from the horizontal trunk, nourishing themselves from the decomposing elements of their ancestor. The annual growth circles in the upturned heartwood and sapwood interior were no longer visible. Lady and sword ferns clung to shaded spaces between the trunk and the damp soil beneath. A garden of moss and dark lichen flourished on the rotting bark. Nature's inexorable cycle of regeneration was everywhere.

Mei Yok left her husband to explore on her own the fibrous bark and to run her eyes along the gargantuan trunk. When she returned she asked, "Why did you bring me here, my husband? I thought we would go to your house."

"To see these trees. I have a plan for you and me and our children. Our family will be buried here. In the roots of that giant over there," he said, stretching his arm forward and pointing with a finger as if cracking a horsewhip. "It's from here we shall enter the world of spirits. These trees live for many centuries, Mei Yok. Of that, I am certain. For as long as they live, our souls will be alive in their roots."

His obsession with death struck her as bizarre and she began to giggle. "You paid much money for me, my husband. How is it that already you're talking of dying?"

"No. No. Not now. Of course, not now. Only when the time comes, Mei Yok. I want you to put my ashes in the roots of that tree," he said, pointing again to a redwood surrounded by a half-dozen subalterns.

This notion alarmed her. "What about the Celestial Kingdom? Don't you want to be buried inside the Great Wall?"

"I'm never going back to China. All it gave us was grueling work and hunger. You wouldn't be here now if that wasn't true. In China we did work we didn't want to do. We toiled without reward until we could no longer stand up. China means nothing to me, dead or alive. Gum San's better. Take my word for that, Mei Yok. Here you work hard too, but you get paid and you won't starve. You'll see. Place my ashes in that tree."

"Will we not be buried together, Wong Po-ching?" He had already given thought to that and responded, "Of course. Pick a tree for yourself. Whichever you wish. If you die first, I'll bury your ashes in its roots."

However bizarre, she liked what she heard and did what surprised him. She laughed and pointed to a behemoth in the distance beyond the tree Wong had selected for himself. "Then, Wong Po-ching, I choose that tree over there."

He pouted disapproval. "No. Mei Yok, that will not do. Choose again."

"Why must I choose again? There is no shortage of trees in this forest."

"The one you have chosen is too big. Your tree cannot be bigger than mine. And just as important, we must rest beside each other. The branches of my tree should touch the branches of yours. Our children will take smaller trees around us. And someday the smaller ones will grow big and take their places in this grove."

From his remark about children, she concluded that her husband was indeed serious about burial positions and, in a conciliatory mood, pointed to a more modest redwood beside the tree her husband had selected for himself.

"Promise me, Mei Yok?"

"About what?"

"That you will put my ashes here. You must. It's a wife's duty. I cannot trust the white men in this place, even the few who are friendly. The duty resides with you. Will you see to it?"

"And if we return to China before that, my husband?"

"Never," he shot back, as though the door to his native land was irrevocably shut.

She shivered from the cold and snuggled close to him for warmth. In a low voice she whispered. "Well, maybe?"

"No maybe. Gum San's our home now. It will be the home of our children and grandchildren. Promise me, Mei Yok."

She fixed her eyes on the long stretch of branchless trunk jutting above her and replayed his words in her mind, concluding that a demon spirit of this strange land had possessed her husband. From the outset, she admired his energy. To him nothing seemed impossible. But white people had affected his mind. Yes, that was it. Wong had become infected by white men's thoughts. They had instilled their madness in him.

"Will you?" he insisted.

"I will see that you rest where you wish. For myself, that's another matter. I don't know this place. You will rest here if that's what you want."

He rocked backward on his heels and looked at his new wife. She was more than he had bargained for, with a mind of her own and a spirit of independence. "You'll get to know these trees," he said, "and you'll understand. They talk to me. Someday they will talk to you too."

She helped him set their campsite beside a creek, its banks flushed with mountain dogwood flowers. The tent went up first. A pair of chipmunks dashed across the conifer needles, skeptical of intruders. Wong had never planned for an elaborate honeymoon and had packed no more than the tent, their bedding, two cooking pots, some rice, pork, and smoked squid. The rest he could forage—rainbow trout from the streams, berries from the meadows, and all the pine nuts one could eat.

A small fire cleverly built into a pit outside the tent warmed them against downdrafts of damp air. They huddled together and drank tea, both staring at the giant sequoias and up through thick branches to tiny patches of sky. A double crack of thunder in the distance interrupted their silence.

Wong's response was to cradle his wife in his arms until the first drops of rain sent them scrambling into the tent. It smelled of stale smoke and sweaty bodies, but was dry and private. Wong took the opportunity to study his wife, examining first her forehead, eyes and nose, then her sallow cheeks and sculptured chin. Vertebrae poked out from the rear of her slender neck. She permitted him to lift her tunic from her shoulders, revealing small breasts with ruddy nipples that became erect when he touched them. She swooned, combing her fingers through his hair and gently pressing him against her body.

Rain ran along the tent and began to trickle onto the tarpaulin floor. His hand unfastened the drawstring of her pantaloons and drew them down past her ankles, exposing narrow hips and a smooth stomach. She removed his trousers and ran her hand over his stomach. They stretched a blanket over a bed of conifer needles and sank onto it, exploring the crevices and folds of their bodies. Both seem weightless in the other's arms. A steady patter of rain on the tent canvas punctuated sighs of contentment. Their union in San Francisco's Globe Hotel under the gaze of lecherous spectators now drew to a more natural climax.

As it passed over the sequoia forest, the storm released a clap of thunder at the precise moment Wong released a yelp of pleasure. Mei Yok froze for a moment, caressing her husband.

When they awoke with the first rays of dawn, they laughed aloud. A puddle of water had seeped under the tent and surrounded their bedding like an island.

"I'm afraid," she said.

"Don't worry, Mei Yok. You're not familiar with mountain storms. They come on fast, then leave just as fast. In winter, blizzards blanket everything with thick snow."

The rain had all but stopped, yet moisture from branches towering overhead continued to drip onto the tent.

It took all afternoon to dry their clothing over a fire. The next morning they explored the forest of white fir and sequoia with a few ponderosa pines sprinkled in. They tramped from north to south, eventually making a looping return to the camp. With his knife, Wong bored four holes through the bark of the sequoia he had chosen as his grave marker. He duplicated the identical borings in the bark of the tree she had chosen for herself.

The initial branding completed, they made love again on the soggy pelt between the two giants. Their bodies were fresh, inviting further exploration. During this lovemaking, she felt easier about the big trees witnessing their union. Though silent in voice, the sequoias entered into their lives.

From that moment forward, this place became Wong's sanctuary. Before leaving Big Trees, they stood in silent tribute beside the giant sequoia James MacGreggor had destroyed.

On the homeward journey they were greeted by a black tail doe with two fawns. The creatures leapt before the mules, keeping to the wagon track then suddenly disappearing into thick forest. Mei Yok had never seen a wild animal in China, where any creature worth eating was immediately slaughtered. It tickled her to think that such creatures might survive the hunters. She was already beginning to grow fond of this new country.

CHAPTER NINE

Palace Hotel, San Francisco

Harriet Horn eased into a seat in the crowded ballroom of the Palace Hotel on Market Street and scanned those waiting for the U.S. Senate Committee hearing. She could read on their faces that few thought this was going to be a civil government inquiry into the growing presence of Chinese in California. In the increasingly hostility against the Chinese, she felt alone, except for members of the Chinese Protection League who had come to provide support. It was no surprise to her that fourteen prominent citizens proudly announced in advance how they intended to provide damning evidence how the illiterate, opium-addicted Chinese laborers had crippled employment for hungry white men. To counter this not a single Chinese business leader in the city had been invited to the hearing. Chinese in the import-export, food distribution, and construction trades who did not fit the stereotype and had achieved a higher station in their adopted land were systematically ignored.

On the elevated speaker's platform, Llewellyn Hubbel, chairman of the inquiry and in his first term as Republican senator from California, toyed nervously with a water glass, which Harriet suspected to be spiked with a drop or two of his favorite rye whiskey. The forest of unruly black hair that had distinguished him in his earlier days as the speaker of the California Assembly had thinned to a point where the few remaining strands were now combed horizontally across his forehead. He wore a dapper mohair suit with a fluffy handkerchief in the pocket and a freshly starched shirt, a noteworthy departure from his frugal days as a young state legislator. His purchase of stock in the Central Pacific Railroad had made him a wealthy man, for when he became certain that Leland Stanford and Charles Crocker had artificially induced the avalanche to stop his train filled with legislators from reaching Donner Summit, he acted. Since others were convinced that the CPRR was inexorably bogged down in the Sierra and dumping their shares at deep discounts, he borrowed heavily and purchased as much stock as he could without drawing undue attention in the press.

The moment my father's engineers broke through the Donner Pass, the price of Central Pacific stock stabilized, then began a relentless climb into the stratosphere. In four months Hubbel became independently wealthy and no longer dependent upon a civil servant's niggardly stipend. This freed him from the need to supplement his salary by paying homage to California's industrialist.

Thirty minutes before the hearing was schedule to begin, every inch of space in the ballroom was filled with spectators, reporters, and government officials. Unable to find either a place to sit or stand, many more were turned away and the doors locked behind them. From outside, one could hear angry cries demanding to be allowed inside. Seven San Francisco policemen armed with three-foot-long billy-sticks stood behind shut doors to see they didn't.

Panelist Senator Benjamin C. Wayne from the State of Washington voiced his concern that the police might not be able to control this undisciplined mob. The police chief sashayed behind the panel to assure him that not only were his men prepared to barricade the doors, but to confront any disturbance of the peace with armed officers stationed outside.

Harriet's family had come to fortune manufacturing long-range cannon during the Civil War, over sixty percent of which Confederate armies captured in a long series of victories over Union forces. While her family's foundries in Massachusetts and Connecticut had long since been retooled to make locomotives, Harriett never lost an interest in military matters. As she waited for the Senate hearing to begin, she mentally calculated how many policemen it would take on Montgomery Street to block the number of angry demonstrators purported to be massed there.

"Sounds like the Workingman's Party is planning fireworks," she whispered into the ear of Mabel Dickerson, the imperious-looking president of the Chinese Protection League.

"Inside or out?" Mabel asked over the din of nervous voices around them.

"Both. Everybody knows the Workingman's Party contributes heavily to the Police Department Relief Fund, so I can't imagine policed officers eager to bite the hand that feeds them."

"What about Llewellyn?" Mabel asked.

"He'll wobble. Our new senator deserves an award as Political Hack of the Year."

"The army helped against mobsters in Chinatown," Mabel said, eyeing Harriet with suspicion and thinking that she often overstated issues.

"General Graham took his time dispatching troops from the Presidio garrison. The papers say he won't permit his boys to do the job of the police. And, keep in mind, in the ruckus in Chinatown not a single rioter was arrested."

Senator Hubbel pounded his gavel twice on the tabletop without silencing the audience. It cracked twice more, after which he spoke in a bellowing voice he had cultivated for just such an occasion, "Gentlemen, Gentlemen, Ladies, please...this hearing is now officially open."

Conversations eventually quieted down and, in a display of impatience, the senator declared, "Our hearing for the Senate of the United States of America will now continue. We're here this morning to ascertain facts–"

A heckler shouted, "No more hearings, Senator! You guys have studied the matter to death and the facts are already indisputably established. Fact One: Twenty thousand white men in California are unemployed. Fact Two: Nobody wants immigration from China. Open the doors to this room and you'll see Fact Three for yourselves."

Down went Hubbel's gavel, and at the same time he scowled his disapproval and snapped with annoyance, "Let me remind everybody that this isn't a saloon. We're here to gather information, not listen to people making assertions. Our job here isn't to craft legislation. That's the duty of the Congress, and the Congress of the United States bases its legislation on cold facts. The Senate has appointed me to gather information, and that's exactly what I intend to do, irrespective of who's marching, demonstrating, screaming, or doing otherwise outside. People can march wherever they want. They can put up placards. They can say whatever they damn well please. They're invited to talk to any newsmen who will listen. But they can't disrupt this hearing. No heckling and no shouting and no speeches out of order. Everybody understand? The Workingman's Party has adequate representation to express its views.

We don't need to hear the same statements repeated from ten thousand different people. The sergeant-at-arms is hereby instructed to escort outside anybody who speaks out of order. Do I make myself clear?"

Angry shouts originated from the senator's left. He sniffed, expanding his nostrils like a bulldog to acknowledge awareness of what faced the commission. Opinion at the hearing was divided. Half those in attendance wanted total and absolute exclusion of Chinese from the United States; the other half favored a highly restrictive policy under strong labor contracts. As far as he could determine, nobody was advocating letting more Chinese into the country and only a handful of abolitionists, left over from the heady days of the Civil War and by now largely discredited, favored extending American citizenship to Asian immigrants already here.

A gabardine suit that needed additional tailoring on the shoulders and collar made Dennis Kearny look more rumpled and less upper-crust than he intended. He was seated at a long table in front of Senator Hubbel, Congressmen Korn, Davenport, Eagle, and Bueller, all of whom were fumbling with notes from testimony taken the previous day. Working without the benefit of notes, Senator Benjamin Wayne, Republican from the State of Washington, looked at Kearny through moist eyes sedated by a host of painkillers he took to counter a back injury, the result of a fall he had taken from his horse on an elk-hunting trip in the Rockies.

Senator Hubbel: Now, Mr. Kearny, we will continue where your testimony left off yesterday. Your claim that you and your brother were dispossessed off a mine in Calaveras County…Please continue.

Kearny: Yes, sir. The same Chinamen who ran me and my brother off the mine are still there. They've probably got a dozen more coolies workin' with them since then. Recently they brought a Chinese woman to live on the property. I ask you, what if each Celestial takes a wife? They're a fertile people. That's how their nation across the Pacific got to be so populous. If every Chinaman in California had children, before you know it, this country's gonna be filled with Chinese kids. If folks in the East believe this is a problem for the West to solve by itself, they're wrong. What will stop factories in the East from importin' cheap labor from China?"

Harriet Horn: Sir, Dr. Harriet Horn here from the Chinese Protection League with a follow-up question for Mr. Kearny, if you please.

Hubbel: You're out of order, Dr. Horn. The Protection League has not been recognized. At this time we're not accepting questions from the floor. We follow rules. You ladies will have to wait until I open the floor to questions.

Horn: Rules, Llewellyn, rules! You conscientiously guard the rules to hear only what you want to hear. That makes these hearings a farce. Why haven't you invited representatives from Chinatown to participate? It's less than a half-mile away as the crow flies. How is it possible to gather information about people who could readily speak for themselves but whom you consistently exclude?

Hubbel: Harriet, I'm warning you not to interrupt. If you don't keep quiet I'll have the sergeant-at-arms escort you outside. I doubt you'll get much respect from the mob on Market Street.

Horn: I'll take my chances there if you'll take this panel to Chinatown and talk to some Chinese people. There you'd learn about the unconscionable treatment of Chinese women in this state. The National Woman's League and a half-dozen other women's organizations have written to you innumerable times and you ignore our letters.

Hubbel: That's got nothing to do with pending legislation on Chinese labor, and you know it.

Horn: It's got everything to do with it. If the authorities would permit decent Chinese women to enter this state, we wouldn't have a string of disease-ridden singsong houses up and down the West Coast, from Mexico to Canada.

Hubbel: Without Chinese patrons there won't be any more singsong houses.

Horn: Congress is elected by men for one purpose only, to protect the interests of other men. Sometimes I think that the only reason they suffer women in this nation at all is to make more of their own sex. You know as well as I do, the government encourages Chinese and Caucasian brothels. Women don't frequent these places. It's men who satisfy their lust at the expense of destitute women. And just to keep the truth from vanishing altogether, the majority of patrons in these whorehouses are white and purportedly Christian, not Chinese. As soon as women vote, we'll stop this exploitation.

Hubbel: Harriet, I'm not letting you turn this hearing into a debate over suffrage. Frankly, I wish you'd get married and leave politics to your husband; that is, if you can find one strong enough to corral you.

Horn: Llewellyn, if you don't stop making snide cracks about my private life, I'll introduce a few facts about yours. Then the people of California will learn who's patronizing the brothels and singsong houses in this state.

Amused chuckles broke out in the ballroom.

Hubbel trained his eyes on his adversary. His lips curled into a malicious sneer, as though he were preparing to unleash a tirade. Only an interruption by another speaker prevented him from ordering Harriet removed from the ballroom. "Identify yourself, sir," he said, muzzling his anger in a polite command.

The man who had stood up to speak was lean and well-proportioned, with wavy blond hair that covered his ears. His voice resonated with assurance. "My name is Malachi Snowden, the Reverend Malachi Snowden."

"Your parish, sir?"

"I was at the First Congregational, the township of Mokelumne Hill up in Calaveras County."

"If you're no longer the pastor there, why identify yourself as such?"

"Mr. Snowden was dismissed," Dennis Kearny interjected from his seat. "That will tell you what the citizens of Moke Hill think of him."

"The people of Moke Hill are frightened of the truth," Snowden answered, stabbing the air with the long, dramatic fingers of his left hand. "They uphold my right to speak out from any pulpit in the land. Any pulpit in the entire nation but, unfortunately, not theirs."

The reverend's predicament triggered much laughter.

"Let's hear then what you think the truth is, Reverend," Hubbel said.

"That Mr. Kearny's brother, Joseph, went before the citizens in Mokelumne Hill proposing to run the Chinese off the Heckendom Mine and to string up their leader, a fellow by the name of Wong Po-ching. The old lynch law: hang 'em first and ask questions later. Fortunately I prevailed on the town to invite a friend of mine, a journalist from the *Virginia City Territorial Enterpriser*, to make a private inquiry before they got out their rope. His name's Mark Twain. You may have read his stories."

Representative Andrew Korn, a wolfish looking man with a large, crooked nose that eclipsed narrow cheeks, leaned forward over the panel's table to attract the chairman's attention. "Seems this commission's gotten sidetracked. We're supposed to help other states decide whether cheap labor is really worth the ill will and economic disadvantages to our own people or being surrounded by non-Christian foreigners from China. We're all entertained by Mr. Mark Twain's wit, but he provides sheer entertainment and is nothing but a sideshow. He makes me laugh more than most men, but I don't think he's qualified to testify at a Senate hearing."

"But it is entirely relevant!" Harriet Horn shouted. "Everywhere the Chinese are accused of sexual depravity. That's because they're forced to live without families. Would white men without women act any differently? If there's a Chinese family at the Heckendom, as Mr. Dennis Kearny asserts there is, then we have a test case. Why not find out if Chinese can live like civilized, law-abiding Californians?"

"And put more white men out of work," Kearny shouted. "Twenty thousand are looking for something to do. Most don't have families because they can't afford them. Send China John home and we'll have more jobs for Americans. Give white men good, well-paying jobs and we'll have more Christian families. Even the Reverend Snowden must agree with that premise."

"Every human being's got a right to children," Horn said. "That's stated in the Bible. God granted the Egyptians, the Hittites, the Amalakites, and the Moabites the right to reproduce. Not just the Israelites. If God didn't want them to live on this earth along with good Christians, then He most certainly wouldn't have put them here in the first place."

Kearny interrupted. "In their own country, not ours. If we don't stop them now, the whole place will swarm with these disbelievers. They can live on practically nothing. Who'll hire a white man when a Chinaman works for a fraction of an honorable wage?"

"That's not what happened on the railroad," Snowden replied. "On the Central Pacific the Chinese struck for equal pay with white laborers and they got it. The same thing will happen in other fields."

"The railroad was different. The population's grown since then," Kearny said.

Hubbel's gavel struck three times in quick succession. "This isn't an open debate. From this moment on, nobody speaks until I say so. The chairman determines who has the floor."

"That's why there are no Chinese here," Mabel Dickerson said, ignoring Hubbel and filling the momentary hiatus. "You don't have the slightest idea who these people are. Or what they think. Most white men have never even talked to them."

Kearny cupped his hands like a megaphone. "This hearing's deplorable. Thousands of men outside are waiting to be heard. As long as they're barred, I declare these proceedings null and void. Close up and go home."

The gavel slammed down for silence. A reddish hue suffused Hubbel's fleshy jowls as he shouted, "You'll declare nothing of the sort, Mr. Kearny. I'm the only one who can end this hearing. It's absolutely impossible to squeeze more people into this room. Besides, we already know what your folks think. We saw their handiwork in Chinatown last week. They left four Chinamen dead. They were your henchmen, weren't they, Mr. Kearny?"

"Anything wrong with organizing a political rally? This is a free country."

Hubbel's eyes shifted toward his fellow congressmen, two of whom he knew to be financed partially by funds from the Workingman's Party. "Nothing is wrong with that, Mr. Kearny. But that doesn't give members of a political party the right to murder their opponents."

"Now who's making accusations? I categorically deny that my party had anything to do with what happened in Chinatown last week. I'm not saying there weren't party members in the neighborhood, but the leadership gave no sanction to violence. You cannot overlook strong sentiment against these Chinese and ignore public opinion. Even a Congress that's bought and paid for by railroad barons cannot silence us."

"I resent that accusation, sir."

"Politicians don't listen. Nobody will stop us once we get rolling."

"Your men are responsible for the carnage in Chinatown," Reverend Snowden interrupted.

"Not my party," Kearny responded. "What happened there was the result of popular contempt. Don't say it was perpetrated by a desperate few. Far from that. And don't expect men who can't feed their families to love and respect those who steal bread from their mouths. If you don't believe me, go out on Market Street and look for yourselves."

"But they were still your people in Chinatown last week, weren't they?" Snowden asked.

"Not *my* people. Californians, sir. Unemployed Californians. Travel around the state and you'll find the same sentiment. However Congress protects cheap labor, facts speak for themselves. The Chinese must go!"

A roar of approval rose spontaneously from the audience. When Kearny lifted his arm in response, a second wave of slogans filled the ballroom. Groups around the room started repeating, "Chinese must go! Chinese must go!"

Hubbel's gavel pounded the desktop, its noise immediately lost in the shouting from the audience. The chairman rose and raised his arm for quiet, then tried to wave for attention, but failed on both counts. Seeing the mood shifting against him, he dropped back into his seat and looked at his fellow congressmen who were already whispering to each other in caucus. Experience dictated that there was little to do until the hecklers quieted down. Among themselves, the lawmakers agreed to wait for the storm to pass. In the meantime they exchanged accusations about who was responsible for the current pandemonium.

A medium-sized man in a baggy, cream-colored suit, sporting a handlebar mustache, approached the speaker's table. He turned about face and lifted his chin in a condescending gesture and dramatically eyed the room from left to right, taking time to let the chanters recognize his face. As if he had waved a magic wand, the crowd quieted down. His self-confident expression relaxed into a wide, easygoing smile. His eyes danced with a combination of mischievousness and wit.

Senator Hubbel addressed him. "Mr. Mark Twain, are you not?"

"To my readers. My mother named me Samuel Clemens, sir," he said in a crusty voice.

"The Reverend Snowden told us that you went to Mokelumne Hill to report on the Chinese there. Is that true?"

"If you call a human interest story *reportin'* then it wouldn't be stretchin' the imagination too much to say I was in Moke Hill."

"Can you tell this commission what you found? Briefly, that is."

"No, sir, I cannot. If it could be told briefly, there wouldn't be a need for my story. Storytellers like to spin out a narrative, if you know what I mean. As my readers know, brevity isn't one of my virtues. But, with your permission, I'll try to summarize what I saw and, of course, not interrupt myself."

More laughter.

"Do you purport to be unbiased in this matter?"

"Heavens no. I ain't seen much objectivity between the Mississippi and the Pacific, and I don't intend to start a crusade for it now. Still, I'll be happy to tell you what I learned in Moke Hill."

"Sounds good to me," Hubbel said, feeling grateful to Sam Clemens who, with nothing more than a smile, had calmed down the aroused audience. "Perhaps you can start by addressing Mr. Kearny's statement yesterday that his brother was dispossessed from property in Mokelumne Hill. The Heckendom Mine, to be exact."

"You're talkin' about a gent called *Wong. Wong Po-ching's* his full name. These Celestials got names like Christian folk, but they sound a little peculiar. He showed me documents pertaining to this matter. It's clear as the water of a mountain stream the Kearny brothers ain't got no legal title to the mine. They were just squatters whom the previous owner, Charles Crocker of the Central Pacific, had allowed to oversee the property and do a little surface digging. I doubt any rent ever passed hands. Legal title belongs to a rather notorious fellow in these parts, the old superintendent of the Central Pacific Railroad, Theodore Gallager. This fellow gave Wong a letter allowing him to work the Heckendom Mine for as long as he wants. And what's more, Wong's got the right to keep fifty percent of what gold he can take out. The way I heard it, Crocker deeded the place to Gallager in lieu of a sum owed the superintendent for his work on the railroad. Popular thinkin' in Moke Hill is that Crocker swindled Gallager. It's a *borasca* mine. Dry as a nun's loins. Can't figure out why the Kearnys are so worked up over the place or why a Celestial would want to waste his time mining it."

"Are there Chinese women living there?" Congressman Korn asked to the annoyance of the chairman, who believed his question deflected from the subject under discussion.

"No, sir," Sam Clemens said. "Not women but a single lady."

"A loose woman of the night?"

"No, sir. A married woman."

"A healthy sign," Harriet Horn shouted. "The future's looking brighter already."

"I don't believe I asked for your opinion, Harriet," Hubbel barked, "and we'd all appreciate your letting Mr. Clemens talk. This is my last warning. I don't suspect the men outside like suffragettes much more than Chinese."

"You're bluffing, Llewellyn. You know how I'd talk to just about everybody on the way out, especially all those reporters looking for a juicy story."

"Don't push me, Harriet. Now, Mr. Clemens, if you will."

"Throw out the suffragette," someone called from the rear. "Let her leave with the Chinks."

Hubbel banged his gavel. "Gentlemen, are we the same as that rabble outside?"

"Not a rabble, Mr. Chairman," Kearny stated in a belligerent tone. "If you were on the breadlines like them, you'd understand why they're upset. Reverend Snowden and Dr. Horn speak for the Chinese. But who's upholding the rights of hardworking Christians? You think the men outside haven't got anything better to do than stand in the rain with placards? Does anybody believe they enjoy the indignity of unemployment? Tell you what. If you want to keep the Chinese in the country, then ship them to other states. Let congressmen tell their voters that you're importing thousands of coolies into *their* states. But I know you politicians won't do that. Not one of you would remain a day in office after you allowed coolies into your districts. Damn those who talk about allowing the ones already here to stay. And damn those who want us to admit more into California."

A policeman in a blue uniform scurried behind the congressmen to Senator Hubbel and bent over to whisper into his ear. Hubbel nodded then leaned in the direction of his fellow congressmen. Noise from the crowd outside made it almost impossible to hear. They broke from their conversation to find that the four guards behind the ballroom doors had closed ranks and were putting their shoulders against the panels as though expecting the locks to fail.

"Demonstrators in the hotel lobby," Hubbel announced in a bellowing voice. "Our guards outside don't think they'll be able to hold them back much longer."

"Let the voice of the people be heard," someone yelled from the rear.

"We already know the voice of the people," another person cried near the platform.

As pressure from the lobby mounted on the doors, the guards shouldered their weight and anchored their feet into the floor.

Hubbel stood up and signaled for everybody to listen. "This meeting cannot continue under these circumstances. I'm not going to hold hearings under a threat of anarchy. This hearing's hereby postponed." His gavel struck with a note of finality. Immediately people began threading into the aisles but learned that they couldn't escape through the rear doors without letting the angry crowd inside. It was too late anyway. Despite the efforts of the police, two doors collapsed under pressure and the first of the demonstrators flooded into the ballroom. People scrambled through the seats toward the side exits, overturning chairs and charging into each other.

"I'd be careful if I were you," the Reverend Snowden said to Harriet Horn as they were forced to wait for a passageway to clear. "I've seen angry men before. They work themselves into a state and stampede, without much more sense than wild buffalo."

"And I'd say thank you, Reverend Snowden, if I believed you were in any less danger than I am." She turned to push Mabel Dickerson ahead of her.

"I can take care of myself," Snowden replied. "It appears not. You've already gotten yourself fired from your parish," Harriet said. "Hopefully there's another church for you."

"Not in California. Perhaps someplace far away, where they've never seen a Chinaman."

"If you need a place to stay tonight in San Francisco, come to my home. It's on Laguna Street. Here's my card with the address."

Snowden felt the surge of bodies behind him. To guide Harriet and Mabel Dickerson, he placed his hand on Harriet's narrow waist. The firmness under his fingers appealed to him. Pushing gently, he guided her forward through the throng until they found a temporary place of refuge in a corridor leading from the hotel lobby.

"You know where to find me," she said over her shoulder as Mabel moved forward.

"Married men don't stay in the homes of respectable single women," Snowden said.

"But some married men are also desperate, are they not? And isn't it true that desperate men commit dangerous acts? Take those demonstrators, for example. They're unemployed like you and are out there working themselves into a state of mind where they're angry as overloaded mules. I take it you have far more sense than they do."

As he ushered her onto the street he smiled. "I'll consider your kind invitation as a sign of generosity, whatever other people might say."

"I admire courageous clergyman like you, Mr. Snowden." She gave him her hand to shake. "Now you take good care of yourself, you hear?"

He swallowed a lump of saliva in his throat. No woman in his parish had ever described him as being courageous.

Mokelumne Hill

Wong couldn't explain his premonition to Mei Yok and decided not to try. It had started as a gentle gnawing in his gut and moved toward his stomach. The trip to San Francisco had been his fourth and during each one he had worried that something untoward might happen back at the mine. So far, nothing had. But on this occasion his forebodings crept into the wholeness he felt now that Mei Yok had joined him. Trouble with the shipment of black powder from Mirror Lake was the most likely thing to have gone wrong. Had he not felt the urgency of claiming Mei Yok in San Francisco, he would have accompanied Lee and Ho. He tried to distract himself from this obsession by engaging in conversation with his bride. There was so much to explain to her about her new home. He found himself incoherently rambling from subject to subject.

When a guard who was routinely posted on the outskirts of the mine property failed to greet the wagon, Wong's premonition was confirmed.

As they approached, he listened for the usual noises from camp, but only a few stellar bluebirds were chirping. No voices and no clambor of machinery. Though his mules were exhausted, Wong urged them to pull faster through the camp entrance. The joyous greeting he had expected from his men upon Mei Yok's arrival was no longer his primary concern. The machinery shack beside the adit was gone. The space directly in front of the mine entrance, usually cluttered with equipment, spare planks, and slag removed from the shaft, was empty. Evidence of a major explosion was written all over the singed landscape. But more important, none of the workmen were there.

Wong drove his mules past a charred pit, unaware that Joseph Kearny had been incinerated near the spot. It was Mei Yok who first pointed to the mine cabin where a thin plume of smoke rose from the chimney and drifted lazily eastward. From a distance, Wong noted the damaged front porch, its timbers twisted and torn. A shutter was completely gone from one of the two windows. The mules, made nervous by the smell of exploded black powder lingering in the air, were reluctant to move forward. Rather than drive these beasts against their will, Wong scrambled down from the buckboard, ran forward, then scampered up what remained of the cabin's three plank steps. His arrival was so unexpected that he caught a man with his stocking feet propped up on the stone hearth, his back to the door. A squeak in the damaged hinge quickly brought him to his feet, facing Wong.

The two men stood in silence, studying each other. The Chinaman dressed in ill-fitting miners' clothing that clearly was never tailored for him; the white man in a faded green cotton shirt that hung in loose folds over his trousers.

"Wong, you little bastard," my father howled in greeting, "I've been waiting for you to come back. I wasn't sure you would. Jesus Christ, where's your queue? Where's all your hair? Cut it off, did ya?" A puckish grin swept over Wong's face. "Mr. Gallager!"

"Name's *Theo* these days, partner. Let's get one thing straight from the beginning. Up on Donner Summit I was the superintendent of the CP. The bossman, with authority to run things. And in those days you were a workman. It was proper for you to call me *Mr. Gallager*. But time moves on, pal. Now I'm a timber man from Eureka. No more. No less. Call me Theo," he said while sticking out a hand for Wong to shake, which he did reluctantly. A series of boxing cuffs on the shoulders were Wong's reward for taking my father's hand.

As soon as Dad pulled away he turned toward the open door where Mei Yok was standing. "And I can guess who this might be. You did it, didn't you? Damned if you didn't do exactly what you always said you would. I had my doubts, I don't mind telling you. But bringing a wife from China, why that's something mighty grand! You never cease to amaze me, Wong." My father stepped around Wong in Mei Yok's direction and, for a long moment, examined the bride, starting from her head and working his eyes down over her torso and legs, then back up in the opposite direction. Her presence conveyed her peasant stock, with all her features in various degrees of asymmetry. To be sure she was no beauty, but still more than my father had anticipated. No sign of disease or defective limbs.

"How much did you pay for her, Wong?" he asked.

"Far less than she's worth."

Dad paid Mei Yok a gesture of welcome by nodding his head and smiling warmly. "You know any English?"

"She's only been here a few weeks," Wong answered for her. "She'll learn soon enough. When I came, I didn't speak one word of this language. Now, you see, *Meester Gallager, Wong talkee good English,*" he continued, making fun of himself. "I'm surprised to see you, especially now. I've been away for a few days. What's happened here? Where are my men?"

Father took a final look at Mei Yok before reaching behind her to shut the door. "Beats me. I just got here about four hours ago. Thought I'd spend the night. Looks like some big-time explosives were detonated. Where did you get the blasting powder?"

Wong hesitated, trying to mouth my father's Christian name while studying his sun- tanned skin and imposing ramrod posture. He just shook his head.

"Seems luck's run out all the way around," my father sighed, returning to a chair opposite the hearth. Mei Yok found a place to rest on her heels behind her husband, according to Chinese custom. "I had hoped you'd have things operating around here by now. What happened?"

Wong canted his head and concealed his shame. "Don't know. I went down to Frisco to get Mei Yok, then took a couple of days among the big trees where MacGreggor, Mr. Crocker, and you tested the nitro. I expected my men to be here, but they've left. They're probably nearby and will return as soon as they see my wagon. A lot of powder exploded here, that's for sure. What brings you here, Thee-o?" he asked.

"A fellow by the name of Mark Twain wrote in the Virginia City paper how you and Mei Yok consummated your wedding in Frisco. That was quite a story. Many folks denied reading it, but so many people were interested the newspaper had to print extra copies. Twain wrote all the details. And I mean *all*."

Wong was trying to forget the wedding ceremony at the Globe Hotel, if you could call it that. "Timber business needs money, doesn't it?" he asked with his usual candor.

"Yep. I've got plenty of good trees, but no way of getting them to a mill. I need more logging roads. And that takes big bucks."

Wong seldom laughed in public, but this touched his funny bone and he roared, "You bought that land *sight unseen*, right?"

My father was more curious than annoyed by the outburst. "You could say that."

"And you made fun of me for giving my money to the Yung Wo Company for a bride. *Sight unseen*, you said. A *sight unseen wife*, you called her. Well?"

"Well, so what?"

"Well, see what I got!"

The white man's stern look fell over Mei Yok. In an instant he made an evaluation. "From the looks of things, partner, neither one of us got any bargains."

Wong's good humor failed. He was glad Mei Yok didn't understand the language. His mind returned to the pleasure of their honeymoon in the sequoia grove with rain pelting down on their tent, the warmth of her body against his and the feeling of unity that bound them as a couple when he entered her. "I got a good bargain, Thee-o," he said in a voice that bore no animus.

Father shook his head in some visual signal of disagreement. The fool never had much of an eye for women, certainly not pretty ones. But then, he probably had little opportunity to observe attractive Chinese women, if there were any in China. He changed the subject. "So, partner, tell me, what have you been doing here?"

"Repairing the shaft. I've got three levels open. With vents for air. We need to repair cribbing and girts. Inside the mine we've repaired rails for our carts. The ball mill and cyanide vats still need some work."

My father took note of the expertise in his partner's voice. Powder man, waiter, drayman, whatever the Central Pacific needed him to do, he accomplished all tasks with aplomb. Now he sounded like a seasoned miner, but by the looks of things above the mine, little had been accomplished.

"We got white men trouble, Thee-o. They don't like Chinamen operating a mine. When I came here, a man named Joseph Kearny was working it. Said he had rights here too. I offered him a job. But he didn't want to work with us and left in anger. He returned with men who made me pay unfair taxes. I was afraid they would return with guns, so I sent two of my men to fetch the black powder I stored at Mirror Lake. The white men must have returned while I was in Frisco. I expect the tax collector will come back next month for more money. It would be easier if you stayed here, Thee-o. They wouldn't start trouble if you were here. They won't bother a white man."

"Don't bet on it, friend. Your countrymen haven't gained any popularity in this state. Back on the railroad, I thought Californians might look favorably on what your people accomplished and be more tolerant. But facts don't mean much when people's feelings are raw. From what I hear, politicians in Washington are building a case against your people. Politicians are vote whores. They'll do whatever is necessary to stay in office. As long as they believe you folks aren't wanted in California, they'll pass laws to keep you down. And they won't enforce the few laws already on the books to defend you. Popular sentiment wants your people out."

My father stopped talking to look at Mei Yok, who appeared more apprehensive than her husband. "If I were you, friend, I'd take your bride and jump on the first ship home. The best days for your people are past."

"This *is* our home," Wong declared. "And this is *our* mine. *Yours* and *mine*. I'm not going."

"You may be the cleverest Chinaman in this state, but you're also the most stubborn. Back in Utah, I tried to talk you out of coming here. I knew it wouldn't work then, and from what I see I'm surer now. I gave you ten months to try. Face facts, Wong. You can't be so bullheaded that you don't see there's no future for you here."

Wong gasped, looking at his bride. From the crestfallen expression on his face he sensed what was coming and started to chatter with Mei Yok in Cantonese.

Dad interrupted. "I need money to build timber roads. I had hoped to borrow funds in Frisco, but the bankers wouldn't even talk to me. They say there's a surplus of lumber and they won't lend on the industry until the market changes. Charley Crocker's traveling in Europe and hasn't answered my letters. My only option is to sell this place. You and Mei Yok can come work with me in Humboldt County. That's a given in this deal, you know. Whatever I've invested of my own money up till now goes into the common pot. If we're partners here, then we're partners in Humboldt. Fifty-fifty. Nothing changes, absolutely nothing, but the nature of our business together."

Wong thought hard about my father's generosity. Not one white man in ten thousand would have offered to share his wealth with someone from China because they had worked together on a railroad. "Thanks, Theo," he replied. "That's more than Mei Yok and I deserve. But I don't wanna sell this property, even after everything that's happened. The mine belongs to both of us."

"You've got it wrong, Wong. The law's on my side, not yours. Check the county assessor's office. The land and the mine are recorded in *my* name only. It don't say anything there about you on the deed. Not one word. Technically speaking, you're here only because I grant you permission. That's the way things are in this state. Another hard fact you must accept."

"I'll tell Mr. Crocker. He gave this mine to me but recorded the transfer in your name only because that's the law. You know this, Thee-o."

"Crocker can't stop me. He transferred ownership and the mine's recorded in my name now. Besides, I just told you he's traveling in Europe and impossible to reach. There's no way you'll get him to intervene on your behalf."

"You can't throw us off."

"That's the last thing I want. But California law doesn't recognize the rights of coolie squatters."

"I paid taxes for my men to work here. That's got to mean something."

"Makes no difference. I'm the legal taxpayer, not you. If I can get some fool to buy this place, I intend to share the proceeds equally with you. I hope you know that. I'm not about to leave you high and dry. You got a claim here, even if it isn't a legal one, and I recognize that claim. So don't get me wrong."

Mei Yok listened to her husband's translation, her eyes moist and her forehead furrowed in confusion. She moved alongside Wong and seized his arm, pressing herself beside him so that the couple looked to my father like a statue on Union Square in San Francisco.

"I'm not leaving the Heckendom, Thee-o," Wong emphasized, his eyes fixed upon my father. "If you force us off, then you're no different than other white men."

"I resent that, friend. I gave you a chance on the railroad. And I've given you ten months to find gold here. That's a helluva lot more than anybody else. Now I'm offering you a partnership in my timber business. I paid for the land there out of my earnings and I'm offering half of it to you. All I ask in return is that you roll half of the value of this place, whatever it is, into it."

"You broke your word to Mr. Crocker, who left this place to me."

"I don't think you understand. Not only am I offering you and your wife a good living in the lumber business, but I'm saving you from what's going to happen. I'm doing this *for* you and Mei Yok. And for your children. The mine's a bust and you know it. Stay here and you'll always be a coolie. Your kids will be coolies too, if your neighbors don't shoot you first. You think the white people will let you work this mine? They tolerate you now only because they know you'll fail. Ask yourself what would happen if you manage to find a little gold. Will they let you reap the rewards? Hell, no. They'll steal it from you. And if you resist, they'll kill you. They're like grizzly bears who eat the prey killed by wolves and coyotes. They'll let you do the backbreaking hard work and take all the risks, then steal what you manage to take from the ground. That's a cold fact you can't seem to get through your thick skull. Let's put our money in logging roads where we can make some real cash. And with me to protect you, you and your family will hold on to it."

"I don't want to cut down trees. It's wrong to cut down old trees. Smaller pines and firs, okay, but not redwoods. Not the giant sequoias."

"If I don't claim the forest, some other fellow will. That's progress. The first one gets the reward, the second one doesn't."

"Didn't I help you in the mountains, Thee-o?"

"You understood powder on the construction line, but below ground you're just like any other daffy miner living on a prayer." He focused on Mei Yok and said, "Look, partner, I'm trying to do something for *all* of us."

She lifted her lips to Wong's ear and whispered in Cantonese. She had been in Gum San for less than two weeks and had already come to understand something about white men. One principle governed their actions. Money. Theo Gallager was no different. Wong gently disengaged himself from her embrace and stepped near the hearth. With his knife he cleared mortar from horizontal stones until he worked a facing stone free. From a hollow pit he extracted a small leather pouch and tossed it at my father.

Dad caught it with his left hand, exclaiming, "What's this?" Before receiving an answer he opened the drawstrings and extracted two small blocks of gold, far heavier and larger than those seen in banks. About three troy ounces each, he guessed, passing it from hand to hand as though on a gold scale. "Where'd you get these?" Wong said nothing until my father read the inscription on each of the gold pieces. One had a Chinese sinogram that made no sense to him. The other possessed English initials, T and G. "What's this?"

"Our profits so far. We agreed to share what gold I got from the mine. Half belongs to you, Thee-o. I put your initials on yours. The Chinese is for my family. So far that's all there is. No more."

Dad reexamined both gold castings. "You got this stuff from our mine?" he asked, sounding incredulous.

"No," Wong said, shaking his head.

"You stole it from local prospectors?"

"No. The dust came from old mine tailings down by the stream. When I came here, I found them left by previous miners. To test our mill, I put the leftover dregs through a fresh cyanide process. The previous miners left behind gold in the ore they took out of this mine. I brought the dust here and smelted it into blocks for easier handling."

Father tossed one of the gold pieces into the air and snatched it with his fist. "We won't get rich refining somebody else's tailings. That's like a lizard drinking water from a cactus in the desert. He extracts only enough moisture to waddle to the next cactus."

"You're forgetting where that ore came from." Wong pointed with his index finger in the direction of the main shaft. "The vein must have been rich enough to make the early miners careless. We need to dig below level three."

My father's eyes fell over the gold pieces in his palm, weighing them a second time. He flipped one after another at the Chinaman who caught both as if he were catching a ball. Wong tossed one back at my father. "That's yours. First payment from the Heckendom."

Dad transferred it from his left hand to his right, then studied the crude inscription, T. G. "No," he said, lifting his chin and twisting his head to grin at Mei Yok. The gold piece went sailing back in Wong's direction. "Both belong to you. My portion is a wedding present to the newlyweds. *From Theo Gallager to Wong Po-ching and Mei Yok.* May God bless you both."

The gift softened everyone's feelings and, for the moment, they agreed not to argue further. That gave Wong and my father a chance to survey the damage to the property before sundown. They left Mei Yok in the cabin and together ventured outside in silence, kneeling from time to time to examine residue from the blast, slowly gathering evidence of two massive explosions. Whether they were the result of an accident or had been deliberately detonated by Wong's men or his enemies, they couldn't determine. Darkness drove them back to the cabin where Wong and Mei Yok seized the opportunity to become hosts. The two jabbered at one another in Cantonese making plans to offer my father their hospitality. But first they had to unload their wagon and care for the mules. In the morning they would begin looking for the workmen.

A half-hour later, Mei Yok was cooking a supper of salted codfish and green squash purchased in Oakland en route to the mountains. They had cleaned up and were preparing to go to sleep when Lee Shi-tong and Ho Lung-chi returned, claiming that they had waited to make sure no white men remained behind, then snuck back to camp. They told Wong in Cantonese how the Kearnys had ambushed them on the Barnston Road, how they had set booby traps according to the original plans, then watched the white men drive the wagons to the mine. The ruined camp spoke for itself.

"Anybody hurt?" Wong asked.

"Not sure," Lee Shi-tong replied. "We heard two big explosions, but were afraid to come close."

"That's a bad sign," Wong said to my father in English. "If white men are hurt, they'll come for revenge."

Dad cupped his fist to his lips, belched, and nodded his agreement. "It sounds as though they're determined, partner. You can fight them off once or twice, but if they keep coming, eventually they'll bury you. Time to call it quits. If we sell the land, we'll get some money. It will be worth more if we sell before they set charges inside the mine."

"I'll fight, Thee-o."

"With what? Do you have guns? Your men are scattered all over the countryside. How about the law? Can you get protection from the sheriff? That's what he's paid to do, right? Protect the citizens. Only one problem, friend, you're not a citizen. The law won't lift a finger to help Chinamen."

"We got plenty of black powder."

"Did it do any good in the last encounter?"

"We still got this place."

My father turned away with a sigh of disgust. He saw the future clearly, but couldn't break through Wong's stubbornness. At the moment, he couldn't think of anyone he knew who possessed Wong's single-mindedness. This he recognized as a virtue that placed Wong above his countrymen. But it was also a flaw destined to destroy him.

Mr. Daniel Gutherie, Editor
Territorial Enterpriser
Virginia City, Territory of Nevada

Mr. Samuel Clemens   17 April 1870
16 Natoma Street
San Francisco, California

Dear Sam:

No. No. No. I'm not kidding, Sam, so hear me clearly. You're poking your nose into something much bigger than you appreciate. You can't threaten men's livelihoods and expect them to be rational, much less charitable. The public won't buy your crusade to help a Chinese couple in a remote mountain camp. Let me remind you, I'm in business to sell newspapers, not to redress the wrongs of society. If I can help a few lost souls in the process, I'm happy to do so. But I won't champion a cause guaranteed to destroy the paper that my family has toiled so long and so hard to build.

Don't mix the welfare of a few Chinese miners in the Sierra foothills with an economic recession and men in dire need of work to support their families. You know as well as I that a few thousand Chinamen working for low wages aren't going to turn this foul recession around. But you can't expect our readers to accept that, even authored by your pen.

I admit our readers loved your story about the Chinese nuptials. But this is different. The former was a human-interest story that didn't touch their money pockets; the latter is an unpopular discourse on economics.

Sam, don't bother to write this story because I promise you I won't print it. End of discussion. Just give me something light and funny. We all need a chuckle.

Daniel

Dear Dan:
21 April 1870

Oh come now! Will the Territorial Enterpriser stand silent at a lynching? This fellow Kearny's a spectacular orator who knows how to whip up a crowd. He possesses a sharp, compelling tongue. He's firing up the rabble in Frisco on a statewide campaign against the Celestials. They've already managed to murder four hapless Orientals. Politicians are so scared they keep their mouths shut, a most unusual occurrence, I might add. The police claim they have only one interest, to protect Kearny's freedom of speech. What about the Chinese right to earn a living? Or just to stay alive? This Irishman's fury is destined to become a conflagration.

There'll be a lynching in this mountain camp. Then more and more lynchings until the Celestials flee in panic. Shame on us. Shame on you. Shame on the citizens of California. If we don't embarrass the politicians and expose their duplicity, timidity and hypocrisy, who will? Dan, set your headline now and beat the Sacramento Union. Here it is:

VIGILANTE LAW NOW GOVERNS CALIFORNIA!

Sam

CHAPTER TEN

Pacific Heights

"What a surprise! Theodore Gallager," Harriet Horn greeted my father as she ushered him into the foyer of her Pacific Heights home, revealing her satisfaction with his unexpected visit. Their last meeting near the railroad camp at Alta had ended unpleasantly, as had all their previous meetings. Often, she had mentally replayed their interchanges and come to the conclusion that their conflict was as unfortunate as it was unnecessary. In order not to let men she found attractive become her suitors, she made a habit of alienating them. But my father, she had come to believe, was different from the others. However much she had tried to forget him, the memory of their encounters kept creeping back into her mind. Somehow he had gotten past her defenses, stirring a strong desire to see him again. The immediate duties of her medical practice kept her from inviting him to visit; that coupled with a certain conviction that, after having treated him so shabbily in the past, he would decline the invitation. But suddenly he was standing in her home foursquare before her. She reached forward to take his hand, her fingers bleached white from frequent scrubbing before surgery with calcium chloride. No matter how many expensive creams she applied, the disinfectant left her skin rough and unsightly, a constant embarrassment.

"I'm so pleased to see you again, Mr. Gallager," she said.

"It's Theo, please," he corrected, awkwardly holding onto a package first with the left then the right hand while allowing Diego Montera, Harriet's Mexican domestic servant, to slip a deerskin jacket from his shoulders. "I've come to return your revolver. I'm afraid I'm almost a year late. My apologies. Rude of me not to have returned it sooner, but I hope you understand how occupied I was in the mountains. If it's any consolation to you, I put this pistol to damn good use."

"I don't want to know how many people you intimidated with it, Theo. Please don't tell me how many men you shot."

"No dead or wounded men, if that's what you're thinking. I saw enough killing of my friends and foes during the war and want no part of it. But I confess to using your revolver for some judicious coercion during my last months on the railroad. It wasn't easy keeping to our schedule, yet that's all past us now. These days I like to pack your gun when I'm alone in the forest. It gives me a sense of comfort. Once it saved my life just outside of Arcadia where I found myself between a black bear sow and her cubs. She came after me with a vengeance and kept coming. Had to shoot her. One of us was going to get hurt and I didn't want it to be me. Here," he said and pressed the package forward.

She weighed the weapon in her hands like dust on a gold scale and smiled warmly. "Frankly, I had forgotten about this. I bought myself a replacement for personal protection, but I never carry it with me, so I guess I no longer feel the need. It sounds as if you will make far better use of it than I. It would give me great pleasure to know it protected you. Only please don't shoot any more momma bears. Do promise me. But then, you didn't come to San Francisco just to return my Colt, now did you?"

"I have business in the city," he said.

"And what business might that be? Last time we met you were intent on building a railroad which, from all the publicity, you succeeded in doing quite admirably. I read in the papers what you said at Promontory, Utah, and saw your picture. Your words sounded like those of the man I met on the steamship *Japan*. I confess to feeling enormously proud of you, Theo. You didn't start out as a friend of the Chinese, but you remained open-minded. I wanted to write my congratulations, but feared you had received boatloads of letters from women far worthier than me. I can imagine how many female admirers you have."

"I could tell you lies. But the truth is that most people wanted to skin me alive. The few letters forwarded to me in Eureka, where I went after Promontory, were as angry as that black bear I killed. They accused me of being a disgrace to honest Christian workingmen who asked for no more than to make an honorable living. Governor Stanford and Mark Hopkins haven't talked to me since. Charley Crocker confidentially admits that I was right, but was furious with me for having said what I did in public. I don't think he would have minded my outspokenness any place but Promontory, which was crowded with newsmen from all over the nation, along with a few from Europe. He said my remarks amounted to a public relations fiasco for his railroad."

My father strolled beside Harriet through a lofty foyer with a magnificent mahogany staircase that circled from the mezzanine to the hardwood floor. A glint of sunlight dashed through stained-glass windows bordering the stairs and reflected through Harriet's reddish brown hair. The faintest whiff of perfume from her body tickled his nostrils. "You live well, I see," he said, allowing his eyes to survey the luxury.

"I confess it," she replied, angling toward him, her hand on his arm to squire him into an adjacent sitting room. A friendly smile exposed large and well-positioned teeth that he had failed to notice in the mountains.

"You didn't amass such extravagances from the practice of medicine, I hope. If you did, I'd say you've been fleecing your patients. You must have married since we last met." A wry laugh greeted his words. "You don't know me, Theo. I envy friends with families, women with their husbands, some faithful, but I fear the majority not. A few of the philanders have come secretly knocking at this door, but I'd have nothing of them. There's something sacred in matrimony. But that's for others, definitely not for me. I didn't leave suffocation by my family in Massachusetts to become imprisoned by a husband in California."

A conspiratorial look flashed across Dad's face. Perhaps the fear of suffocation was the reason why he had not married either.

They entered a spacious sitting room with lounges and chairs in a semicircle around a low table topped with a horizontal slice from a giant redwood trunk, polished to a high sheen. Father identified the redwood immediately, noting to himself a novel use for the timber he intended to merchandise in great quantities.

"*Imprisonment's* a powerful word," he said, picking up the conversation and shooting a playful smile at Harriet. "I'm no expert in such matters, but I can't recall any married people complaining that they were incarcerated by each other. Though I must confess I haven't spent much time with married people. Is your freedom so important to you?"

"That. And my medical practice. You could say I value them both equally."

"Come from a medical family, do you?"

She spoke Spanish to Diego Montera who had followed them into the sitting room, seeking instructions about refreshments. Then she ushered Dad to a sofa lined with puffy satin pillows in bright pastels and sat down beside him, unlike the custom for women in San Francisco society who were trained to sit at some distance across a room from unmarried men. "The truth is that there are no doctors in my family. We've been in the foundry business for two generations. My grandfather started the foundry with a fellow immigrant from the Rhineland and passed it onto my father and uncle. They began casting iron cannon for export to Europe just before war broke out in the South. Their timing was impeccable. Federal forces bought our cannon as fast as we could cast them. I hope I won't annoy you when I say it was the incompetence of Union generals that made the family wealthy. We sold our cannon exclusively to the Union Army, which then rapidly proceeded to lose them in battle to the Rebels. After every encounter, we received fresh orders for replacement napoleons and parrots. Unfortunately our guns spilled both Yankee and Rebel blood, terrible for all those dead and wounded young men, but good for the family's fortune. Before hostilities ended, my father wisely reinvested his profits in manufacturing locomotive parts, once again with superb timing. As soon as soldiers no longer needed our guns, engineers like you started laying railroad track just about everywhere in the nation. While few battled with the mountains as you did, all that additional track created a raging demand for locomotives. There's hardly an engine in the country without parts manufactured by AtlanticNorthern Industries. Ever hear of ANI, Theo?"

"Of course I have. And I've even fired off a few of your pappy's cannon in the Tennessee Valley, but thank God I wasn't cut out for the artillery. The Central Pacific bought plenty of Atlantic-Northern parts, though that wasn't my department. It mystifies me why you left a thriving business to live in a God-forsaken place like this."

She pouted a little at that remark and canted her head sideways in a girlish manner, resting her hand back on my father's arm. "Why this place is not *God-forsaken* at all. Quite the opposite! California *is* God's country. Everybody in my family thinks that I've lost my mind. I guess

I've always been something of a rebel, but I love the West. I'm an only child with no brothers or sisters, no nieces or nephews back home. I write to my family that someday I'll return to Massachusetts, but I doubt that's going to happen. I'll visit perhaps, but I'll never move back there. I've dropped my anchor here in San Francisco, Theo. And when the time comes I want to be buried in California."

He found himself staring into the hazel-green eyes whose sparkle he had overlooked in the mountain camp. "You've made a name for yourself in the city, I hear."

"After years of struggling, my medical practice is finally started to grow," she said. "At first male colleagues wouldn't let me do anything but deliver babies and care for sick children. When I finally proved myself, they let me treat women for female problems. Menstrual cramps. Menopause. Incontinence. Men wouldn't come to my clinic and my esteemed colleagues wouldn't refer them. But that's begun to change now. These days I get a few old men."

That didn't sound odd to my father, who personally avoided visiting doctors whenever possible. Perhaps if he had had the opportunity to choose a physician as pretty as Harriet Horn, he might have reconsidered. "So now that you have male patients, do your colleagues accept you into their associations?"

"Not quite yet."

"So where has it gotten you?" he said, sounding puzzled.

A thoughtful grimace came over her face. "Now that they let me examine old men, a practice once absolutely taboo, they let me mention parts of the male anatomy. In medical discussions I'm now allowed to say *penis*. That's some progress, wouldn't you say?"

Dad was taken back by her candor, a quality he found irresistible in other women. He cleared his throat, grasping for something intelligent to answer and coming up with nothing except, "It's hard for me to believe you're not married, Harriet. Don't tell me you don't have to fight off suitors."

Her eyes fell to her lap and when they returned to him there was resignation in her expression. Her voice was softer. "Lots of them. But not many good ones. They're drinking men, womanizing men, bullying men who bring out the worse in my personality. So I gravitate toward feminine, foppish men who amuse me, but who are safe enough because

I cannot conjure up feelings for them. The few I don't offend are unlikely suitors. There are few like you, Theo."

Few like you, Theo. Had he heard right? This was the second time her candor had caught him unprepared, causing his tongue to stick to the roof of his mouth. He wanted to respond but no words came. Harriet's speech was always direct. She gave the impression of someone whose words were not far from her thoughts, a characteristic he greatly admired.

"Does that surprise you, Theo?" she asked, finally breaking the silence. "Or do I misjudge you? I formed a good impression of you aboard the *Japan*. How I've laughed over that incident. If it wasn't your most sanitary moment, then certainly it was your noblest. I'd say you're too shy to be a womanizer. Too responsible to be a drunkard. Too confident to bully women. And you are certainly not foppish. You'd be a catch as a husband, but you, like me, are too clever to get snared. We're kindred spirits, you know, because neither one of us will be harnessed like an ox."

"I was thinking the same thing about you," he commented, blushing red.

Diego Montera arrived with a tray topped with biscuits and tea that Harriet poured from a silver urn like an English lady, milk first followed by dark black Indian tea. It wasn't my father's favorite choice in beverages, yet he was determined to hide that from his gracious hostess.

Harriet leaned back against the cushioned sofa and studied his pretense. A wide grin spread across her lips and punched dimples in her cheeks. "So, Theo, what really brings you to San Francisco? Certainly not me."

He set his cup down on the table but hit the edge of a coaster. The cup spun around in the saucer, splashing the tabletop with hot tea. She leaned forward and in a single motion snatched a napkin to wipe up the spill. "Not to worry. Not to worry. Now, tell me, why are you here?"

"Charley Crocker gave Wong Po-ching an old gold mine in Calaveras County, which he deeded in my name, so the two of us became partners. Wong's been up there working it. The only gold he's found comes not from the mine but from old tailings left during the big strike. I need cash for my business in Humboldt County. I don't think the mine's worth much, but I'm putting it up for sale."

"Aren't Wong Po-ching and his new wife still there?"

"Yes."

"Ever read the *Virginia City Enterpriser*? Mark Twain has been writing stories about them. He makes me laugh at one line and cry at another."

"Wong and I go back a long way. He's not happy about me selling the Heckendom."

"Where will they go? His wife just arrived. I'd hate to think of her returning to China after such a long voyage."

Father shook his head. "I don't think it will come to that. Wong can work with me for as long as he wants. We're partners in the mine and, as far as I'm concerned, he'll be a partner with me in the lumber business. That is, if I can raise some cash to cut new roads into my acreage."

"You're betting on timber over gold, are you?"

"There's a voracious appetite for lumber in the West. With some capital, I'll supply a portion of that need. My forests are mostly composed of coastal redwoods. It's the best timber in the world for foundations. Termite-proof, with a great natural resistance to fire. People are beginning to appreciate these qualities. You can see for yourself what's happening in this state. Folks used to throw up shacks and sheds, with little concern for quality. But that's changing. People are now thinking of sticking around, so they want buildings that will last for decades. That's where redwood comes in. And those trees grow big. Real big."

"What do Wong and Mei Yok think about leaving the mine?"

"Wong's got to be realistic. I don't know if there's any gold left in the Heckendom.

But I know for sure that white men in Calaveras County won't let him keep it. You probably read in the papers that explosions happened at the Heckendom Mine. Dennis Kearny's older brother, Joseph, was killed in one of them. The white people at Moke Hill think his death was caused by Wong's Chinamen, though there's good reason to believe Joseph was responsible for his own death. It really doesn't matter who's guilty. Dennis won't let his brother's death go unavenged. Wong's prepared to fight, but he underestimates the enemy."

"Well, I'm with him," Harriet responded. "A fellow like that should be allowed to succeed. He's a credit to his countrymen."

"If he fights, he's a dead man. I want him in the lumber business with me, not buried in the mountains. He's got a wife to support. My guess is that children will come real soon."

Harriet laughed aloud. "You're a practical man. So tell me, who's going to buy your property?"

"The most logical buyer. The Kearny family. They seem to want it. His brother lost his life fighting Wong to get it. I wrote to Dennis offering to sell the mine at an excellent price. He didn't bother to answer my letter, but I know he's leading a demonstration on the waterfront tomorrow morning. If I can find him, I'll arrange a time to talk about selling him the mine."

"Negotiating with the devil himself," she added. "The newspapers say he's a dangerous firebrand who advocates 'judicious hangings' for politicians who don't support the Workingman's Party. I think it's a humorous choice of words, but he claims he's dead serious. In any case, his message has a certain appeal. I don't think there's a single Californian who wouldn't like to see a few of his favorite politicians strung up."

"I don't intend to oppose or support him. All I want is to raise cash."

"Good luck, though I can't say I favor uprooting Wong and Mei Yok. They deserve a chance to make a life for themselves. And it goes deeper than the Heckendom. People in this state must see what the Chinese can do. Wong's the person to show them. I've promised a U.S. Senate committee to investigate health conditions of the Chinese workmen in the Sierra. The Protection League will underwrite my trip, though I'm not particularly interested in what it costs. Now that I know where Wong is, perhaps I could visit with him in a couple of weeks. I pray things will have improved."

"You and Sam Clemens and your do-good friends from the Protection League only encourage them. They don't have weapons to defend themselves. There will be bloodshed and it won't be white men's. There's nobody to protect them."

The conversation lasted more than an hour and a half. My father, not considering himself much of a ladies' man, could hardly remember such an animated discussion with a woman, though his contact with educated women was, admittedly, quite limited. He rarely if ever sought out their company. Harriet Horn, on the other hand, found his pragmatic approach refreshing. He was clearheaded and forceful in his views. She judged him to be a man of simple tastes, completely immune to the stuffy values of urban Californians.

When it was time for him to leave, Harriet blocked his way to the front door where Diego Montera returned his deerskin jacket. Instead of stepping aside, she tarried for what seemed a long moment of reflection. "Theo, you said that there was nobody to protect Wong and Mei Yok. Perhaps you can. Take my .44," she said, picking it up from a side table where she had put it. "You'll make better use of it than I." She placed it in his hand and with her own fingers carefully curled his fingers around the barrel.

"I'm not going to protect Wong and his clan, if that's what you have in mind," he said. "It's a losing cause. And I don't fight losing battles."

"That doesn't sound like the Theo Gallager I know. You protected Wong many times before, and I'll wager you won't let him down now. Anyway, it would make me feel better to know you had my gun on your hip. In a symbolic way, perhaps I can protect *you*."

"What should I say, Harriet?"

"Say that you'll come back and see me again. Soon too. Maybe we'll meet at Mokelumne Hill."

He liked what he heard and smiled. "I have to sell the mine first."

"Hope you don't, for Wong's and Mei Yok's sake, that is. And one more thing before you go, Theodore Gallager."

He had slipped into the doorway and stopped to pivot back.

"Above all, don't go getting yourself married off. At least not before you give me fair warning."

"You said you weren't the marrying type," he shot back.

"That's precisely what I said, and I'm not. You could say I'm a confirmed spinster. But that doesn't mean I'm prepared to sit back and watch another woman snare you. Now get going, Theo, before I say any more foolish things. And don't get lost in Humboldt County. Visit me again on your next journey south."

Embarcadero

The barkentine *Magellan*, 194 feet in length, 39 feet wide, and displacing 899 tons, was anchored offshore, east of the Brannan Street Wharf. Normally a Saunders and Kirchmann ship like the *Magellan*, distinguished by its square-rigged foresail and schooner mainsails, would be eased into the dock by a team of three steam-driven "donkey-engines." But this was not a normal morning. Angry men, marching along the waterfront with placards saying **No More Chinks in Calif**, forced its skipper to lay anchor nine hundred leagues offshore and await instructions from Saunders and Kirchmann, Ltd., the owners. The captain had taken pains to hide the presence of 461 Chinese coolies in the ship's hold, yet word had somehow slipped out. That wasn't unusual. Secrets travel poorly aboard a ship. A mob onshore, organized by the Workingman's Party of California and composed mainly of unemployed longshoremen, numbered many thousands. In an angry mood, they were noisy and rowdy.

Hacks and drays were waiting on the docks for drayage from the *Magellan* as Dennis Kearny wove a path through these parked vehicles, determined to hold his men on the docks for as long as it took. Sooner or later, *Magellan* would have to weigh anchor and sail back through the Golden Gate. He had intended to make an example of this vessel to discourage other shipping companies from transporting Chinese workers to California. Given the current climate, state politicians feared opposing the Workingman's Party. Many supported a federal bill circulating through the labyrinthine corridors of Washington to formally exclude more Chinese workers from America. To accelerate passage of this legislation, Kearny wanted to bring the Port of San Francisco to a standstill.

"The name's Sam Clemens," the newsman and raconteur said by way of introduction while muscling through Kearny's bodyguards to gather a few quotes from the labor leader. "May I ask you some questions?" His presence at the demonstration was not unwelcome, for recently he had begun to command a vast national readership.

"So long as I'm not obliged to answer," Kearny said as he kept walking at a brisk pace, forcing Clemens to trot after him, two steps for each of Kearny's. "I know who you are, Mr. Mark Twain. Just about everybody does these days. I can't say I like what you write, even though on occasion you make me laugh. You're dead wrong about this Chinese problem, you know. You're poisoning people against honest workingmen in this state. It's a surprise to see a man of your intelligence championing a discredited cause. You make the subject of unemployment into a joke, which, I assure you most solemnly, isn't funny."

"Grown men paradin' about and yellin' slogans against a handful of Asiatics strikes me as mighty peculiar, Mr. Kearny. And it's damn inhospitable, if nothing more.

Magellan can't sit out there forever. What are you planning to do when she disembarks her passengers?"

"I got no quarrel with the ship or her owners. *Magellan* can dock any time she wants. Offload any cargo she's carryin'. That is, with the exception of Chinamen. We'll stop the disembarkation of Celestials on California soil."

Kearny suddenly broke off the conversation and turned to one of his lieutenants who was trailing along. "Kevin, I don't want innocent people getting hurt, you understand? Especially those ladies over there from the Chinese Protection League. You see them? The ones with big red bands on their hats and those silly-looking white scarves? You can't miss them in a crowd. Their noses are twice as big as normal ladies'. Probably because they always gettin' 'em stuck in other people's business. Move 'em away from the pier where they won't get hurt. Gently, that is. We can't afford bad publicity over this."

"No law prevents Celestials from coming here to work," Clemens stated in the raspy voice of a dedicated cigar smoker.

Kearny stopped and pointed an intimidating finger at the reporter. "That's cause people outside of this state don't understand what's goin' on. Chinese aren't taking *their* jobs. I promise you, the day Chinamen show up to work in New England factories, federal law will change mighty fast. This isn't high moral ground here, Mr. Clemens. And this pier you're standing on is no church. White men gotta feed their families. We're not talking the lofty language of Heaven. The law of the jungle is bread, sir. Nothing more sophisticated than bread. Now go and print that in your paper."

"They said the same thing in Philadelphia and New York when your kinfolk landed from Ireland. That's how your parents got here, Mr. Kearny. We've got plenty of space for people in this land. Last time I looked, this was a free country."

Kearny's gaze shifted in the direction of the anchored bark, her horizontal sails on the forward mast rolled tight with only a small mizzen unfolded to keep her from shifting in the erratic winds. "Now if you'll excuse me, there's a steam launch ready to take me to the *Magellan*, whose skipper needs some educating about what's waiting for his passengers ashore. And if you're not feeling a yen for some old-fashioned violence, I'd advise you to move away. And mighty fast too."

"Are you Dennis Kearny?" a stern, crisp voice called from the rear.

"That's what my father named me," he replied and turned to find a uniformed police officer, flanked by four constables in dark blue jackets with shiny brass buttons. All sported bushy handlebar mustaches and were wielding heavy wood truncheons they held diagonally across their chests.

"Lieutenant Jeremy Wellington. S-F-P-D," he said and pointed to his officers with the end of his billy-stick. "We're worried, sir. Your men are in an angry state. Nobody controls the emotions of a mob. We've seen some guns too. The city doesn't want trouble, Mr. Kearny. We will not tolerate violence."

Kearny regarded the police officers with annoyance. "Nothing's gonna happen, as long as that bark doesn't unload any Chinamen. If you want to prevent violence, then stop the captain from putting more Celestials on the San Francisco docks."

"We can't do that. The owners have a license to dock and offload. The license doesn't specify what *kind* of cargo. We have no control over the steamship company."

"Dennis Kearny," a new voice interrupted the policemen. My father stepped beside Sam Clemens and greeted Kearny with a tilt of the head and a practiced smile that could win affection from most people.

"I know you, don't I?" Kearny asked.

"Don't suspect you do. But you might have seen my picture. About a year ago. The Central Pacific Railroad. "

"Yes, yes, of course. Your people on the railroad brought Chinese here in the first place. It was a bad idea then and a worse idea now. I don't like you, Mr?"

"Gallager. Theodore Gallager. Whether you like me or not, I have a business proposition for you."

"You hear that, gentlemen?" Kearny addressed Clemens and the police constables. "A couple thousand men are on piers along the Embarcadero. There's a launch waiting to take me to *Magellan's* skipper. And this Hibernian's got a proposition! Now can a man from Cork turn down a compatriot from Eire? Let's hear it, Gallager. But be quick, man."

"I want to sell at a good price the Heckendom Mine in Calaveras County. Interested in buying?"

Kearny stalled for a moment, shifting his focus from events on the bay to my father's proposition. "The one near Mokelumne Hill? Surely you're joking, Gallager. My brother, Joseph, was killed there. Are you the new owner? How did you get it from that gang of Chinese usurpers?"

"I didn't seize it, if that's what you're implying. Wong Po-ching and I own it as partners."

"Then you own half a *borasca* mine. Give me one reason why I should buy a barren, paid-out property like that."

"For the same reason your brother tried to steal it from my partner. If he hadn't attempted to run the Chinaman off, he'd be alive today. You know that."

"The Chinaman stole it from Joseph first."

"Your brother never owned the mine in the first place. Charley Crocker let him work it.

I read the documents. Crocker later deeded it over to me. And I made Wong my partner. I gave him permission to operate the place in my absence. Check the land registry. I'm the legal owner of the Heckendom Mine."

"Even if that's true, a Chinaman can't be a partner in a mining venture. He can't stake out a claim and he can't register nothing. He's got no standing before the law."

A longshoreman trotted up to Kearny and announced, "They've lowered a longboat on *Magellan*'s starboard. It's too far away to see who's in it."

"Then watch carefully, Mr. Jackson. Tell me if you see any Chinamen aboard. If so, we'll stop it *before* she comes ashore." To Clemens and Father he said, "Now, gentlemen, a launch is waiting. Gallager, keep your mine. I don't want it at any price. It would only bring back bad memories."

"No law says you have to buy, Kearny. That's your decision. But I'm warning you and your henchmen to stay away from Wong Po-ching. Wong's my man and can work it until I find a buyer. You might want to reconsider, just to get rid of him."

"Now that's an interesting idea I'll take under consideration."

"Sir," a junior officer aboard the launch yelled through a cloud of escaping steam from the boiler, "ready to shove off. If you're gonna talk all morning, we'll lower the steam pressure. Can't keep the engine running like this without flushing seawater through it to cool down."

"Somebody with better eyes than mine just spotted Chinks aboard the longboat," Jackson howled at Kearny.

"Time to see they don't land," the Irishman snapped and, in a passing instant of reflection, turned on Father. "My brother's blood ran at the

Heckendom. Your China John won't mine it, Mr. Gallager. That's a promise from me to you." He paused for an instant on the top rung of the ladder descending to the launch. "And you, Mr. Mark Twain. No humorous stories about what's happening here. Tell the truth. Tell it without your usual embellishment. No jokes."

Clemens said. "Not much point in that. Don't see a single man on this pier who knows how to laugh. And, for that matter, I'm not convinced there are many more who know how to read."

As the longboat, rowed by four oarsmen from the *Magellan* crew, approached the Saunders and Kirchmann dock, Kearny's launch, now under full steam, powered out to intercept it. Over the chugging of its engine, men in the launch shouted warnings to turn back, which oarsmen in the longboat misunderstood as a friendly challenge and increased their pace. The launch maintained its throttle, belching puffs of steam into the westerly air currents. Demonstrators on the docks viewed the pursuit along open water as a match between human brawn and modern technology, and they were universally betting on the steam engine. They set down their placards and yelled encouragement to Kearny's sailors. Conspicuously absent were cheers for the Chinese.

The longboat had less water to cover to the dock but could not match the speed of the motorboat. When the launch came within shouting distance, Kearny warned *Magellan's* oarsmen through a megaphone. No officer from the vessel was aboard, thus the crew had no authority to turn back. Instead they set a furious pace with their oars, in near-perfect precision. The launch closed in, almost cutting through the starboard oars. Kearny rotated his torso toward shore to judge the distance then barked orders at his pilot to turn eighty degrees in preparation to ram the longboat. The order caught the motorboat's pilot by surprise. While running parallel to the longboat, he hesitated until Kearny repeated the order. A quick turn of the rudder drastically altered the launch's heading. A few seconds later, its bow slivered through the longboat's port oars, splitting them like broken matchsticks. The longboat's wooden siding became the next target. The launch's high bow then sliced through the gunwale, puncturing a hole almost to the water line. The pilot of the launch immediately threw his gears into reverse, effectively stopping forward motion before severing the longboat in two. For a short time the two boats remained entangled, their hulls emitting groans and screeches.

At one point it looked as if the launch's engine lacked sufficient power to disengage. But the pilot adroitly rocked his vessel free by shifting from forward to reverse and back again.

Seawater rushed into the disabled longboat. Chinamen, the majority of whom did not know how to swim, howled in their native tongue. Their cries were easily drowned out by thunderous cheers from the docks. Coolies seated in front where their longboat's bow had been punctured scrambled back into the stern into space already crowded with panicked countrymen. Though it was clear that the vessel from *Magellan* would not stay afloat for long, the men in Kearny's launch offered no assistance.

As the two craft separated, a Chinaman managed to leap onto the gunwale of the steam launch, but was met by two crewmen who pounded him with their fists until he tumbled into the chilly water where, unable to swim, he thrashed wildly on the surface. The launch continued in reverse before shifting back into forward gear. Whether the drowning coolie sank or swam made no apparent difference to the crew.

As soon as it became clear that their countryman in the water would receive no help, the Celestials in the overcrowded stern started flailing their arms and wailing for help. Eventually they caught the attention of the lookout aboard *Magellan* who reported immediately to the officer of the deck. On orders from the bridge, sailors aboard the barkentine hastily prepared to lower a second longboat to stage a rescue.

While demonstrators on the docks were celebrating, Dennis Kearny flung his arms over his head in a signal of victory. He had accomplished exactly what he had promised; he had stopped this boatload of Chinese from setting foot on California soil.

After assessing the deteriorating condition of the Chinese in the longboat less than a thousand yards from the docks, my father jumped onto an empty dray wagon to organize his own rescue. It took a great deal of shouting to convince those nearby that he was not adding his voice to their victorious cheers and that he was, in fact, exhorting them to counter the violent attack by their leader. Hostile mobs were not new to Father, nor did they intimidate him. "Who'll help me save these drowning men? God only knows if they can swim," he bellowed. "If we move quickly we might get them before their longboat sinks. Any volunteers?"

Providing help was the last thing on anybody's mind. The men of the Workingman's Party were at war with the coolies, and who in his right mind would volunteer to give aid and comfort to his enemies?

"I didn't hear any voices," Dad demanded.

"Chink lover," a heckler shouted from the mob.

"I'll help," Sam Clemens answered in his characteristically raspy voice. What his voice lacked in volume his presence added to the seriousness of the mission.

"Y'hear that, you unworthy sonavabitches? Mr. Mark Twain here won't let fellow beings drown without lending a hand. Follow him and I promise he'll lead you through the Pearly Gates." My father turned on the driver of a nearby dray. "I'll get a line on that longboat if you'll haul it back. Will you put your mules to service, man?"

The drayman looked around for support. Angry faces dared him to accept.

Dad jumped down from his dray and stepped over to the hauler, placing his hand on a coiled line beside the wagon. "Attach one end of this to your rig. I'll take the other." Before receiving a verbal commitment, he challenged a second drayman parked alongside. "Add your line to this man's. We'll need a few hundred yards. Then help him make room to pull away from the water. As soon as I get the longboat secured, I'll signal with my arms for you to drive your dray back from the dock, pulling the longboat ashore."

My father pointed to a dinghy moored below the pier. "Mr. Clemens, if you please, get that boat free. Will you help row me out there?"

By this time the steam launch transporting Dennis Kearny was returning to the dock. The labor leader stood in the bow waving in victory to his supporters. But Dad had dampened some of the crowd's enthusiasm and the response was less robust than Kearny had hoped.

At this point my father squared his lines from the dray wagons and had begun moving along the dock. Sam Clemens, far from being an agile man under the best of circumstances, had managed to clamber clumsily down a rope ladder to the dinghy and installed himself there with two stubby oars. His cream white jacket was beside him on the seat and his signature black string tie was draped across his chest. He was chewing ferociously on an unlit cigar wedged between his teeth. No sooner had he settled himself into the frail craft than the rocking waves made him woozy. His naturally light complexion turned a sallow gray. But an expression of determination came over his face: He refused to let a touch of seasickness deter him while Chinamen were facing death in the water.

Dad's eyes shot out along the bay to assess the longboat's plight. Beyond that, he could discern the silhouette of a second longboat being lowered from *Magellan's* starboard.

Clemens was more powerful at the oars than his scrawny appearance indicated. He bent his back far forward to pull with maximum power, dragging the line being fed from shore. His strokes were long and deep in the water. Performing before a large audience of muscular men on the dock appealed to him. Father caught his eyes scanning the reaction of the skeptical crowd onshore.

Off came my father's boots and jacket. His plan was simple: to dive into the water and tie the end of his line to the sinking longboat, then signal for the dray wagons to pull backward, hauling the disabled boat filled with Chinamen to shore. Before diving into the water, he turned around and saw that Kearny's launch had swung back away from shore to threaten the longboat with a second attack. A small dinghy could hardly compete with a powerful steam engine in a race. Nevertheless, he encouraged Clemens to row as fast as he could. In preparation for his dive into the water, Dad secured the end of the line in a double coil around his waist.

When the dinghy arrived within swimming distance, the line circling my father got caught, hindering his dive overboard. Clemens leaned forward to help free the snag, but that forced him to stop rowing while Kearny's motor launch was racing to ram the longboat, or perhaps sink the dinghy. Since every second was critical, Dad took a chance and dove overboard before the line around him was fully untangled. For a moment it appeared to be dragging him underwater. Air bubbles broke the surface, but there was no sign of the swimmer.

Clemens was about to start hauling in his end of the rope when Dad's head popped into view. They exchanged calls before my father started to swim in the direction of the panicking coolies. The icy bay water, not more than fifty-two degrees Fahrenheit, contracted blood vessels in his ankles and wrists, causing excruciating pain. His fingers lost all sensation. Experience swimming and bathing in the cold lakes of the Sierra had taught him that the pain would disappear once his blood started circulating at his extremities.

The cold soon proved subordinate to the weight of waterlogged line stretching from the Saunders and Kirchmann dock. Only the sheer strength of his kick and the power of his strokes kept him afloat. Rope chafing against his skin was annoying but less dangerous.

Though the coolies could not communicate in English, they watched my father's approach and understood his plan. Two younger Chinese inched toward the sinking bow to lend a hand over the gunwale. But once there they began to argue. The bow dipped too low in the water and any line attached to it might drag the vessel under the surface, flooding the stern. After considerable confusion, both young men decided to wade back through their compatriots to attach my father's line to the stern. To make room, three coolies had to jump into the water and hold onto the gunwale. When Dad swam alongside the longboat, he found several sets of hands ready to secure his line.

Once satisfied that all was ready, my father cried out to Clemens. "Signal ashore to heave in. Slowly, so that we can get the vessel turned in the right direction. Watch that damn launch on your tail! Stay between the launch and the longboat."

Clemens snatched his white jacket and half-stood on the seat to wave it at those on the pier. Near-sighted, he could not tell whether men at that distance were properly interpreting his signal; the line remained slack. Men appeared to be moving in the distance, but not the dray wagons or their mules. The coolies were the first to notice the slack tighten as the vessel's stern eased over in the direction of the dock.

My father did not try to enter the longboat, but rather swam twenty yards away to provide turning room. Sam Clemens forward-paddled his oars to maneuver the dinghy for a pickup.

The line suddenly emerged on the water surface as mules ashore took up the slack and hauled. Just at this moment the steam launch arrived nearby, with Kearny standing in full view beside his helmsman. Father yelled for him to go back, but he answered that he had no intention of retreating. Quite the contrary, he directed his helmsman on a new heading to collide with the longboat a second time. From the distance, a thousand voices rose in unison. Clemens stood in the unstable dinghy to determine if these voices were encouragement for Kearny or for the Chinese coolies. My father reversed direction, swimming back swiftly toward the longboat.

At the last moment, Kearny's launch veered forty-five degrees to sever the line Dad had just established with the shore. Frightened coolies had stood up to witness the second collision. The jolt was so severe that four of them lost their balance and tumbled into the water. The remaining passengers attempted to stabilize the crippled vessel without success. Six more eventually spilled overboard. Flooding water surged in from the bow to the stern.

Dad swam in close to help stabilize the floundering craft, but the weight of those still aboard was so poorly distributed that the longboat turtled over, pitching the remaining coolies into the water. He found himself trapped in a narrow pocket of air beneath the overturned vessel. My father neither saw nor heard Sam Clemens call to him. Coolies thrashed about in the froth, frantically grabbing flotsam. A patch of blood rapidly swelled over the water's surface.

Father's head suddenly rose through the tumultuous water. He coughed hard to clear his lungs. A bloody hand in the air signaled that he had been injured. More blood colored the water around him. Rather than swim in the direction of Clemens's dinghy, Dad turned toward the longboat. Two coolies nearby needed a tow to the floating wreckage. Another was splashing in the water, barely staying above the surface. Helping the drowning Chinaman proved more difficult than Dad expected. The terrified man tried to climb on top of him. Normally he would have overpowered a smaller man, but his injury had exhausted him. It took all his remaining strength to extricate himself and paddle from the desperate man's grasp.

Fortunately by this time the second longboat from *Magellan* had arrived in the vicinity and begun throwing flotation rings to those in the water. Dad seized one and pushed it in front of himself, then dove underwater and emerged behind the drowning coolie he had just abandoned. The man was coughing water, but once buoyed by a floating ring his thrashing ceased.

My father instructed the coolies holding to the wreckage how to stay afloat by wedging flotsam under their armpits. Meanwhile *Magellan's* boat plucked from the water stragglers carried away by the current. Crewmen aboard the mother ship dropped an additional dinghy into the water to search for men who had disappeared. Chinamen wailed aloud when they realized that Kuo Man-shang, Lou Wing-on, and Lin Bao-shi could not be found. Their turmoil was so great that none noticed an expanding ring of blood near my father. The last swimmer to be hauled into the rescue longboat, he was barely conscious. The sailors concluded that though he had survived the loss of blood, the freezing water was certain to kill him. The seaman who commanded the longboat headed not to shore but back toward *Magellan*, where he reckoned the reception would be friendlier.

An hour later, *Magellan's* crew delivered Father and eight injured Chinamen to the dock for emergency medical attention. Lying in a makeshift stretcher, my father's breathing was stable, though his normally ruddy complexion had turned almost blue-white from cold and his eyes were lifeless. Mabel Dickerson from the Chinese Protection League, whose team had planned to offer medical assistance to the Celestials, moved immediately beside the stretcher. Without asking for permission, she took charge of my father and the injured coolies in the dock area, keeping them warm and elevating their legs above their head to prevent them from going into shock.

The Protection League's signature red hatbands and oversized white scarves suddenly appeared throughout the crowd. They wrapped the shivering Chinese in wool blankets and commandeered a small bonfire that the demonstrators had made for boiling water. A half-hour later, an ambulance crept onto the pier to transport those needing medical attention to a nearby seaman's hospital. To the injured Chinamen who could control their fear long enough to eat and drink, they served hot tea and biscuits. Two open wagons from the Seafarer's Hospital on Folsom Street approached to carry the injured coolies who did not need to ride in the ambulance.

Dickerson scribbled a note and addressed a young man who worked for the league. "Take this immediately to Dr. Harriet Horn. You know her home on Laguna Street, near Gough, I presume. If she's not there, go immediately to St. Francis Hospital. Department of Surgery. She'll be there. Tell Dr. Horn that Theodore Gallager's been badly injured. We're taking him to Seafarer's Hospital. Several Chinese also need medical attention, but their injuries are not as serious. We'll need her help there."

As soon as the young man left, she knelt on the ground beside Dad's stretcher and spoke in a full, commanding voice. "Can you hear me, Mr. Gallager? We're taking you to a hospital. I've sent for Dr. Horn."

He nodded his head, but said nothing, nor did he open his eyes.

"Talk to me, Mr. Gallager," she said. "I need to know which limbs you can move and which you can't."

From deep in my father's throat came a gurgle. Rather than speak, he lifted each leg, then contracted his fingers into a ball and opened them.

"He's lost blood," Dickerson said to one of her assistants. "Keep his legs above his body so the blood will flow back to the heart."

"Can we put a tourniquet on him?" another assistant asked.

"Not with a wound to the groin. We'll have to remove his trousers to stop the hemorrhaging." To a woman near his feet she said, "Okay, take 'em off."

"What?"

"The trousers, of course."

"Here? In public?"

"You know a better place to prevent this man from bleeding to death?"

Fortunately my father had discarded his boots before entering the water, but his trousers stuck to his legs. Two women pulled from the feet as gently as possible so as not to cause additional injury. Meanwhile Mabel readied bandages and a disinfecting chloroform spray supplied by the ambulance driver. When the women finally worked the trousers off his legs, Mabel cut away his soiled underwear to expose the wound. Salty seawater had cauterized it, but an open gash in his groin was still oozing blood. The scrotal sack on the right side was crushed. Without embarrassment, she lifted his penis with a cotton bandage and first sprayed the crushed right testicle with carbolic acid from an atomizer, then disinfected the entire groin. Next she liberally doused the open wound with calcium bromide powder and not very gently administered pressure to the region with cotton. The bleeding slowed but did not stop. A thick pressure dressing was applied on top of the cotton. The first aid complete, the next objective was to keep her patient warm. Someone produced two heavy military blankets. Mabel trotted alongside the stretcher-bearers as they bore my father to the ambulance.

"We're not about to let you take these Chinese off like they're dignitaries," one of the demonstrators called out as they approached the ambulance. "You can do what you want with Gallager, but you're not taking these Chinks from the dock. They're going back to the *Magellan*."

"You'll do nothing of the sort, Mr...Mr...I didn't get your name."

"Then use mine," Dennis Kearny said, stepping through the cluster of spectators and throwing a menacing gaze over Mabel's army of female assistants. "Use the name of Dennis Kearny. What this man says is absolutely correct. We're sending these Celestials back to the

Magellan. Her skipper can take them wherever he wants, so long as it's not California."

"They're sick, cold, and frightened to death. You'd send human souls back on the high seas in such a condition?" she bellowed.

"They wouldn't be if they had stayed in China where they belong."

"I don't have time to argue with you, Mr. Kearny. You already got what you wanted. Only a handful of these men have landed. They need medical attention and I intend to see that they get it. Mr. Gallager's in critical condition and most likely won't make it. If he doesn't, I'd hate to be in your shoes. Enough people witnessed your handiwork. As far as I'm concerned, you deserve to hang alongside the ghost of John Booth. And I promise you, Mr. Kearny, if Mr. Gallager doesn't survive, my league will do everything in its power to see you prosecuted for murder, cold-blooded murder."

Kearny's bodyguards formed a phalanx in front of the ambulance. Others took positions beside wagons now filled with coolies.

With an eye on this hostile movement, Mabel said, "If you try stopping us, you'll have to lay hands on me and my women. Even your goons won't manhandle respectable ladies. We're going to take Mr. Gallager and these Chinese for medical attention. Stop us, and we'll see that the authorities also charge you for molesting us."

A dash of blue uniforms suddenly appeared, a dozen of them from the San Francisco Police Department. In clear view were several Henry repeating rifles.

"That's the way it's gonna be," Lieutenant Wellington announced in a no-nonsense voice.

"You're out of line here, Lieutenant," Kearny cut him off. "You know that the city fathers support this demonstration. The mayor and just about everybody else wants Chinese exclusion. He'll be here shortly to make a speech."

"We may be out of line, as you call it. But we have eyes. As Miss Dickerson just said, the Workingman's Party's done a lot of damage this morning. Three coolies are still missing. We'll file formal charges against you. I won't promise that the city fathers will move on our charges, but I seen what I seen, and I'm filing them. Put a hand on these women and you're going right to jail. Understood? Once you're behind bars, you can hire a lawyer and have your day in court. But you'll be behind bars, Kearny. And in my jail."

"What happened on the water was an accident," Kearny said. "Everybody saw a good-natured race over the water. It wasn't our fault that the longboat turned into us at the wrong time. We were returning to help and my launch accidentally ran over the towline. None of this would have happened if the longboat hadn't made an aggressive turn."

"You haven't been charged just yet." Lieutenant Wellington signaled for those gathered around to make room for the ambulance. "Save your story for the district attorney."

"We'll continue this at the hospital," Kearny pledged.

"I don't care where you go, but for the time being I don't want to see your people lay a hand on these women. You've got some tough thugs, but my men also know how to break bones. I've got the law on my side, Mr. Kearny, and it says your demonstration is over. Over. Get that? Disperse your men immediately. Ladies, please take these injured Chinamen to the hospital. My officers will help in any way they can. Consider them your escort."

To Kearny Wellington said, "You'd better pray for Mr. Gallager. Nobody likes Chinks around here. And that includes me. But everybody admires a courageous man. And killing a man like Theodore Gallager will get a lot of people mad as hell."

CHAPTER ELEVEN

Seafarer's Hospital

When he arrived at the Seafarer's Hospital, my father was unconscious. His blood had soaked through one of the two blankets covering him. An attending surgeon transferred him to a gurney and, with the aid of orderlies, rolled him directly into the operating room. Four confused Chinese coolies straggled alongside, chattering in a language understood only to themselves and adding to the general confusion. A young surgeon still in training triaged Dad's injury and immediately administered smelling salts, then ordered his attendants to strip the soaked dressings from his body. While contemplating the medical problems, he barked, "And calm down these jabbering Chinamen before they drive me crazy. See if anything's wrong with them, but get them out of here. Put 'em in the recovery room. Or take 'em to the inhalation room or the cafeteria. Any place but here."

Clarence Dunnagan, chief of surgery at the Seafarer's, poked his head through the operating theater door, searching for the young surgeon. Not much over five feet in stature, Dr. Dunnagan was dressed in the suit of a lawyer, not a physician, and carried himself with the air of a junior Napoleon. Massive gray whiskers covered his cheeks. He snapped at the young surgeon, "There's trouble on the street outside, Alexander. All physicians and staff must vacate the building immediately. And that means you too."

"Can't do that, sir," the young surgeon replied to his superior. "I've got a man here who's in shock. He's bleeding, but I don't exactly know why. They gave him first aid on the dock."

"From the wharf? If he came with the Chinamen, all the more reason to stop. The orderly will take care of him until we settle things outside."

"There's nothing outside compelling enough to leave a patient in this condition."

Harriet Horn, in a navy-blue traveling cape with the hood thrown back over her shoulders, her red hair massed in a tight chignon behind her head, brushed past Clarence Dunnagan and the orderlies at the door and stepped into the operating room, announcing herself to the young physician. "I am Dr. Horn. I don't think I know you."

He glanced up long enough to take in Harriet's presence. While few of San Francisco's doctors knew him, every practitioner of medicine had heard of Harriet Horn. Her reputation as an irreverent but competent physician with a foul mouth that often embarrassed good company had preceded her. He felt both honored and intimidated to have her in surgery with him. "I'm Horace Menitoff."

"If you must go bargain with street rabble outside, then go. You may leave your patient in my care, Dr. Menitoff," she said. "It's a sad day when a mob dictates to the medical profession what we can and cannot do."

Dr. Dunnagan bellowed from his position half in and half outside the operating room, "All surgeons are gathering to meet with the city fathers outside. We have no responsibility to care for these Chinese and their friends."

Menitoff hesitated. A duty to his patient was unquestioned, yet his career rested in the hands of the surgical committee. And Clarence Dunnagan was a ranking member of that committee. To disobey him would guarantee his junior position and junior pay for many years to come. Most likely he would be banished to a surgical post in a rural community hospital, or worse, be compelled to enlist as a military surgeon. Dunnagan was known to use his senior position to sidetrack the careers of more than a few young physicians who crossed him.

"Maybe all the *male* surgeons must pass muster on the streets," Harriet added, "but not *all* surgeons. *This* physician is staying right here. Go, Dr. Menitoff, go and join your cohorts in the gutter. I'll manage here until some of our esteemed colleagues come to their senses and return to help."

She knew she had made a mistake the moment she dropped her eyes over my father. Much of his strength had already slipped away. His eyes were closed and his breathing weak. She took a pulse reading. Her hand moved in a tender, circular movement over his forehead and slipped down along the cheek. News about his exploits at the Saunders and

Kirchmann wharf was already all over San Francisco. She had heard how he had swum out to rescue Chinese laborers and was injured when an oarlock on their capsized longboat impaled his groin. Feelings that she had controlled during her dash from St. Francis Hospital in a hansom carriage suddenly erupted. Here was a man without particular affection for the Chinese, but one who could not tolerate violence deliberately perpetrated against them. She had long known that Dad wasn't the kind of man who would let other men drown in the bay like animals, even if they were Chinese. For the first time in her memory, words of affection slipped from her lips without her routine censorship. "You lovable fool, now we're going to have to fight like hell to keep you with us a bit longer."

There was something about Theodore Gallager that had penetrated the shield she had built up around her feelings. Perhaps, she had once speculated, it was because he had never presented himself as a suitor. Far from being a sad, lonely man, he appeared both aloof from others and enormously secure in his own company. That, oddly, paralleled the way she thought of herself. And in addition, he appeared to live on the edge of possibility, exactly where she found that her own life was most invigorating.

The practice of medicine had taught her to mistrust men. For years colleagues had refused to acknowledge her competency in medicine, steadfastly resenting the very presence of a woman in a profession they believed was properly filled only by other men. With the greatest reluctance they would refer to her attention female patients who couldn't afford their fees and, when they were too busy taking care of paying patients, would refer vagrants and beggars requiring elementary treatments. By monopolizing the challenging medical cases, they effectively denied her the chance to increase her knowledge and experience. Such ostracism carried over into her social life. The wives of her colleagues, many jealous of her talents or, more honestly, fearful of her beauty, made sure she remained a pariah, never invited to their homes. Her reputation as an aloof, mysterious woman fueled malicious rumors about promiscuous affairs with both males and females.

Mabel Dickerson, who had silently entered the operating room, stepped alongside to interrupt a moment of reflection. "Thank God you're finally here, Harriet," she declared. "Your cowardly colleagues are talking with the politicians on the street. Can I be of help?"

"From the looks of this, I'm going to need lots," Harriet replied, her words heavy in her throat. She took a deep breath, acknowledging that my father had not requested her to be his surgeon, nor was she officially accredited to the medical staff of the Seafarer's Hospital. But this was an emergency and the hospital doctors had abandoned their posts, to her mind violating one of the most sacred tenets of medicine. She was in no mood to quibble over medical technicalities and immediately began removing the groin dressing Mabel had applied on the dock. Step one was to wash her hands with a solution of diluted chlorine and bromine at the scrubbing basin.

"Your colleagues are cutting a deal with the lily-livered politicians who run this city. They haven't got the guts to stand up to Kearny and his rabble."

Harriet's face filled with frustration. In the corridor outside, she had seen the sorry condition of the Chinese coolies, who were also being ignored. "Can our women assist with those Chinamen outside while I attend to Theo?"

"Of course. We've already triaged them. All have diarrhea. Some TB. But that can wait. Mostly they're cold and scared. My guess is that they've never seen a hospital before."

"Okay, warm them up. Get liquids into them. If emergencies arise, let me know. Is anyone on your staff qualified to help in surgery? Any trained nurses?"

"Me. I served in Virginia during the war."

Harriet pointed a pair of steel scissors at Mabel. "Do you have any idea what you've just volunteered for? This isn't going to be pretty."

"I put those bandages on Mr. Gallager at the wharf. I saw many good men die on the battlefield. In those days, we didn't have clean hospitals and were forced to do some primitive operations. If you can take it, Harriet, so can I."

"I don't have an alternative. You have."

"Give me a minute to get the coolies cared for, then I'll be back," Mabel said. The moment Harriet nodded approval, she made a quick exit.

With her scissors, Harriet carefully stripped the dressing from my father's midsection and examined an open wound buried under his pubic hair. The puncture sliced through abdominal muscle, exposing the lower bowel. The severed muscle needed to be sutured, though it occurred to her that this wound should not have produced the quantity of blood the blanket had absorbed. There had to be more hidden damage. She then unwrapped the remaining bandage from his genitals and for an extended moment examined the flaccid penis, mercifully spared by the oarlock. With her left hand, she lifted it vertically for a better view of the damaged scrotum beneath.

The oarlock had punctured the scrotal sack and crushed the right testicle against the pelvic bone. Blood diluted with seawater continued to ooze from a ruptured vein. Step one was to find a surgical clip among the paraphernalia of the operating theater and stop the bleeding. Had the oarlock punctured the artery, far more blood would have been lost, most probably causing the loss of life. She still couldn't see how far the oarlock had penetrated and was forced to probe the damaged testis with her fingers. The epididymis and the vas deferens above it were completely destroyed. With a sense of despair, she examined the left testicle. Seminal vesicles and epididymis on the left side felt firmer to the touch and seemed to have escaped damage.

While she had no experience operating on male genitalia, it was clear that removal of the crushed right testicle was a medical necessity. She held back emotion and ground her teeth in determination. During her career she had performed several life-threatening surgical operations for impoverished patients on vital organs, but never on the testes and certainly never on someone for whom she had feelings. It was not lost on her that an error removing a testicle from my father would deprive him of sexual function. Incontinence was also a strong possibility. And he was almost certain to become infected. Without rescrubbing her hands, she dared not wipe away the tears that partially clouded her vision or moisture that had accumulated on her forehead.

Mabel Dickerson whisked back through the operating room door.

"Good job in getting him this far, Mabel," Harriet remarked, her eyes still studying the wound. "His right testicle's completely crushed. It's got to come off. Did you happen to see Dr. Frost, Dr. Jeremiah Frost, outside?"

"I don't know him."

"Could you find out, please, if somebody around here does? And in a hurry too. Frost is an expert with orchiectomies. I'll prepare Theo, but I need someone with experience. Hopefully you'll locate him or another surgeon before I start. Tell him it's an emergency. I'm going to put Theo fully to sleep and clean the damaged area. There's got to be an ether inhaler somewhere in this OR. As soon as he's had enough, I'll make an incision in the scrotum. I want an expert to cut and tie up."

"Is there no way to save the testis?"

"Too far gone. If we don't take it off immediately, the left testis will swell up like a sunflower. Then he won't be able to pee without a catheter and that's sure to cause infection."

"What if I can't locate another surgeon?"

Harriet lifted her eyes to meet Mabel's and grimaced. "Then get back here on the double to help me. I've never done an orchiectomy and never observed one performed. But if there's nobody more qualified, do you have a better suggestion? Believe me, I'd love one. I'll be working on instinct, Mabel, not experience."

"I'd hate to be in your shoes."

"Pray for help."

Ten minutes later Mabel returned to find Harriet still involved in the surgical preparation. "No luck, Harriet. I couldn't locate Dr. Frost. The good constable who helped bring Mr. Gallager and the Chinese from the wharf said he'd continue the search. He's got thirty men in his detail. They have bullhorns. He assured me that if Dr. Frost is anywhere nearby, they'll find him."

"Can't wait, Mabel. Scrub in quickly. Use that bromine solution at the basin. There's a gown behind the door. I've already got a scalpel steam-cleaned. We'll need some dressings. And plenty of small sutures. See what you can find in the cabinets."

Harriet carefully cut a three-centimeter incision in the soft tissue of the scrotum, daubed the open wound with bromine to seal the severed capillaries, then peeled back the epidermis and pinned it with small surgical clamps. Next she disinfected the wound site, this time with a carbolic acid spray. Mabel stepped alongside to provide additional surgical instruments. She took note of the sweat beading on Harriet's brow and wiped it away with a cotton dressing.

"Ever see a testicle like this before?" Harriet asked without taking her eyes from my father's wound.

Mabel chortled one of her light laughs. "Not from the inside. But I've had the good fortune to see my share of healthy ones from the outside."

Harriett's eyes lifted the over rim of her glasses with a conspiratorial look.

"And yes," Mabel finished her thought, "exactly where the Good Lord put them."

Harriet's attention returned immediately to her hands, announcing her next procedure. "Now I'm going to remove the scrotal contents and cauterize as high as possible. I've also got to tie off the veins. If I recall my lessons in anatomy, the lymphatic system drains into the superficial inguinal nodes. We've got many blood vessels and nerves to contend with. When I get them all tied off, I'll then surgically remove the spongy part of the testis from the epididymis. Eventually we'll sew the scrotum back up."

Since most of the hospital staff was out in the streets, no one was guarding the operating room door. Lieutenant Wellington from the San Francisco police poked his head through it to find Mabel standing beside Harriet. "Sorry to disturb you, ladies, but we've found our Dr. Frost, who seemed a bit reluctant. So we used a little persuasion." Noise of a scuffle from the hallway filtered into the operating room. Wellington turned away from the door to evaluate the disruption behind him before saying in a mischievous tone, "No, I wouldn't exactly say Dr. Frost volunteered his services, but then I don't think he liked the idea of a week in my poke either, if you catch my drift."

"As long as he's here, send him in, Lieutenant. I need his expertise," Harriet cried.

Two uniformed constables rough handled Jeremiah Frost into the OR. He tripped but recovered before bumping into Mabel Dickerson's backside.

"I could use your help, Jeremy," Harriet said, getting right to the point. "I've gone about as far with this orchiectomy as I dare without doing major damage to this poor man. I know this is a bread-and-butter procedure for you. Please scrub in and help me. Or if you don't want to pitch in then just tell me what I should be doing."

Frost was about to lodge a complaint about the treatment of a professional physician when he smelled carbolic acid. At home at an operating table, he bent over to examine Harriet's work. She pointed out the steps she had taken in preparation for surgery and the procedure she intended to perform.

"Ever done a castration?" Frost asked, bending over still further for a better view.

"You know damn well I haven't, Jeremy. Your good old boys' club has deliberately excluded me from this kind of work."

He ignored the remark and bent over my father for a closer inspection. "So far, Harriet, your instincts look pretty good."

"Go ahead and scrub."

"Why? You're doing just fine. So far, no mistakes. I'll make a few suggestions. Since you're right on track, the operation is all yours."

"Can I save his potency?"

"If you cauterize all the nerves very carefully. And if he doesn't get infected. But you'll have to work fast. Reach up along the vas with your finger. When you get up as high as you can, slip the scalpel in with your free hand. Put a clamp on it immediately. We'll go back in a few minutes."

"Like this?" Harriet said.

"Higher."

Harriet concentrated on following Dr. Frost's instruction while saying, "Theo Gallager thanks you, Jeremy,"

"Who's Theo Gallager?"

"The guy whose testicle I'm about to remove. I guess you didn't hear what he did this morning on the bay."

"Don't chatter. You must work close to the lymph nodes. And you don't have all the time in the world to do it. So move to your left. And catch that vessel before you go on."

Harriet stopped talking and leaned far over my father. With minute movements she severed the damage testicle, placing it gently in a dish for Mabel to remove. After cauterizing the wounds, she returned to reopen sealed ducts and reconnect the vas deferens. Then more suturing. When it was over, her eyes were tired and her back ached. Dr. Frost enthusiastically congratulated her on her first orchiectomy. The patient was destined to wake up from the anesthesia in considerable pain, but hopefully no infection would seep in.

After Father was moved to the recovery room, Harriet thanked Jeremy Frost. He then inquired about Theodore Gallager and she related what she had leaned about his help to the drowning Chinese workers. While my father was recovering she intended to look in on them, wherever they had been taken in the hospital.

Outside the operating room, Dr. Frost's demeanor became solemn. He regarded Harriet with heavy eyes and said, "I'll have to explain matters to the hospital's chief of surgery, Clarence Dunnagan. That's a given, you understand. He's not going to be happy about you're coming into his hospital and operating without permission from the surgical board."

For a brief moment Harriet looked remorseful. But that moment passed quickly, for she said, "If Clarence Dunnagan's staff hadn't violated their Hippocratic oath and left a patient in dire need of attention, I wouldn't have had to. Tell Clarence if he wants a fight, he'll get one. I'll drag him and his hospital through a legislative inquiry in Sacramento. We've been bruising for this fight for years, so I'm warning him through you: don't provoke me. I've got friends in the Legislature who won't like the idea that doctors abandoned a patient on the operating table. Theo Gallager's already a hero in this state. Once word gets around about his exploits on the bay, the public will likely want to drown Clarence in a public execution near the Embarcadero."

"Let's hope it won't come to that, Harriet. You did a fine job in there. I'll do what I can to appease Clarence. I'm sure Mr. Gallager will be grateful too."

The following afternoon, Harriet, in a clean medical smock borrowed from St. Francis Hospital, entered Father's room to find him propped up in bed on a pillow. Bouquets of flowers were everywhere. The nurses had shaved his face and combed his hair. His face was sallow, but there was a small, playful glint in his eye. She stepped to the bedside and took his hand in hers.

"The nurses said you saved my life," he said. "Last thing I can remember is being on the dock, then everything went dark. I thought I was finished. I feel like a man who slept through a century to wake up in a new world. The nurse said you would explain everything to me. I'm numb below the waist. I can't move much either. What's gone? What's left, Harriet?"

Big dimples emerged behind a warm smile. "Everything essential, Theo. Don't worry about that. I know because I was your surgeon."

"You?"

Her eyes roamed the room. "Yes, but not by choice. My God, you have a lot of flowers. You must have many admirers. When you were injured, Mabel Dickerson, you remember her from the Chinese Protection League, brought you here along with five coolies who required immediate medical attention and another eight in need of first aid. Thousands of unemployed men followed, threatening to burn down the hospital if any Chinese received treatment. The mob intimidated my venerable colleagues. The bloody cowards abandoned the building. Not a single doctor remained at his post. Mabel notified me and I came as fast as I could."

"What happened to *Magellan*? Did the Chinese get ashore?"

"The newspapers reported that she sailed back through the Golden Gate, her decks crammed with coolies. Last I've heard her destination was a secret. There's speculation she's headed south to Monterey or San Pedro. Maybe Mexico. The Protection League's hired a lawyer. There'll be a suit filed against the Workingman's Party and maybe against the steamship company too. I doubt it will do much good. Judges in this city are elected by you-know-who."

He reached up for a firmer hold on her hand. "The nurses wouldn't say what's wrong. I know there are bandages on my bottom. One nurse told me about a catheter between my legs. I'm missing vital parts, aren't I?"

Harriet dropped her head closer to his and spoke in a clear, but low voice. "A longboat capsized over you. Your right testicle was mangled by an oarlock. I tried to save it, but couldn't. It was too badly crushed and there was lots of bleeding. I removed the damaged testis and sealed up the artery and vessels. There was no alternative, Theo. If it wasn't removed, it would have caused gangrene and infection. Dr. Jeremiah Frost joined me midway through the operation. He routinely performs surgery for cancer of the testes. Sometimes he operates on sex offenders. He supervised what I did."

"What about my left side? Is that gone too?"

"Absolutely not. I did a thorough examination. Whatever crushed the right testicle spared your penis and left testicle. You're not out of the woods yet, my friend, but with some luck you should function pretty well. Your plumbing system will be fine, but you'll have a catheter for the time being. You shouldn't have trouble peeing, if that's what you're worried about. When you're ready, we'll take off the dressing and I'll explain why things look the way they do and exactly what I did down there. Inside and out."

His eyes left her and swept the ceiling. "Guess I'm not the man I used to be."

She swallowed. "In whose eyes, Theo? Certainly not mine. There are at lease thirteen coolies alive today because of what you did. The way I heard it, there were thousands of angry men on the docks, waiting for these Chinamen to drown. You were the only one with any feeling for Asian members of the human race. That's the kind of man I admire."

"I didn't mean it that way," my father blushed. "I meant sexually. I'm a eunuch now."

She leaned far over him and kissed his forehead, then pulled back only enough to look at him squarely in the eyes, keeping her lips close to his. "They make eunuchs by castrating both testes. You've still got one. A man of your strength doesn't need two. One's enough. You've probably got more juice in your left side than most men in both."

He let out a mocking laugh. "Is that Doctor Horn or just my friend, Harriet, talking?"

The question caught her off-guard and she straightened up, pondering an answer. It came slow, but with conviction. "Both, Theo. Both."

"You make me feel good, but I can see what's coming. I'm not likely to become a father. Sounds like I'm finished in that department."

"The minute you leave this hospital, hordes of women will be trying to climb in the sack with you. They won't give a thought to what's between the legs of Theodore Gallager. They'll just want to sleep with you because of the total man you are. And they'll be thrilled to make love with you under any conditions."

"What's left of me?"

"I tied up your scrotum. I could have inserted a prosthesis, a small steel ball or something, to balance out the pouch, but it's too dangerous. You'd have potential urinary problems or persistent pain. As it is, the right side of your scrotum is empty. The left side looks quite natural and should work just fine."

He puckered his lips. "When I met you aboard the *Japan* I never imagined you'd know me so intimately. Both inside and out."

"Do I see a modest man? Or a shy one?"

"A little of both. You were here when I needed you, Harriet. Thanks. I couldn't have asked for anyone better. Of course, I'll pay your fees."

"Fees? My God, I never gave that a single thought. We're friends, Theo. No power on this planet would compel me to charge someone who just saved thirteen lives. The citizens of San Francisco should reward you handsomely for lifting us all above the rabble."

A nurse cracked the door to the room and poked her head inside. "There's a delegation of Chinamen outside. Not coolies, but men from Chinatown. Merchants, I think."

Harriet turned on her. "Nobody may disturb my patient. He needs rest and quiet and he can't get that with every Wing, Louie, and Gee visiting him. They'll have to come back in a few days."

The nurse closed the door, but reopened it a few minutes later. "They've brought gifts for Mr. Gallager."

Exasperated, Harriet said, "That's very considerate, but they'll have to leave them outside the room. Mr. Gallager will acknowledge this generosity as soon as he has the strength."

"Begging your pardon, Dr. Horn, but there's a particular Chinaman here who absolutely insists on seeing Mr. Gallager. He won't take no for an answer. He's dressed in workman's clothes, not like the merchants. Speaks perfect English. He says his name is Wong Po...something. I didn't get the rest."

My father heard the name and tried to sit higher. Pain in his groin forced him back to his original position. "That little sonavabitch." His voice was weak. "Harriet, if it's Wong, I want to see him right away. I want to see my partner."

The tall Chinaman was dressed in mountain clothes with high leather boots and a sheep's wool jacket in forest green. He plowed into the room with a wide grin and a thick bunch of white carnations in his hand.

"How the devil'd you find me, Wong?" Dad could barely lift an arm to shake his hand.

"The Chinese telegraph. That's the Chinese rumor mill. I learned of trouble on the bay on my way here to fetch three new miners from the *Magellan*. Only I stayed too long in Moke Hill and missed the ferry from Stockton. I arrived at the Saunders and Kirchmann Wharf after the trouble was over. Everybody was talking about you. You're the only white man dumb enough to do something like this, Thee-o. There isn't a Chinaman in California who expected you to sacrifice yourself for new workers from China. You've already done enough for us. You didn't have to go out and get yourself hurt. There are men on the streets who want to kill you. But many more promise to hang anyone who tries. Chinese merchants are going to hold a parade in your honor. To hell with the damn Workingman's Party."

"So there's no mistake, let me set the record straight. I didn't go to the Embarcadero to help your countrymen. If the truth be known, I went there to talk with Dennis Kearny about selling the mine. When I got to the docks, I didn't intend to save anybody. It just happened that way. And I don't want a parade. What I did doesn't warrant that. "

"That's not for you to decide. I heard you were hurt real bad."

"Mostly to my pride, I guess. Dr. Horn patched me up. I'm not checking out on life just yet. God, it's good to see you, Wong. Good news for you about the mine, news you're gonna like. Kearny was the most logical buyer for it, but he turned me down cold. I misread him, figuring that since his brother wanted the place so much he would be interested. So as much as I need to sell it for cash, I haven't found a fool who wants to buy. At least not yet."

"How's your wife? I think her name's Mei Yok, yes?" Harriet asked interrupting a conversation she knew would lock her out if she permitted it.

Wong's eyes danced. "Getting big. Around here," he drew a semicircle around his belly.

"She's pregnant?" Harriet asked.

"Yes, Ma'am. The baby will come soon. We're making preparations in the mine cabin."

"Do you have a midwife or a doctor?" He shook his head, no. "The doctor in Moke Hill said he would like to help, but would lose all his patients if he delivered a Chinese baby. But he wrote out instructions about what to do when the time comes. Trouble is, only Lin She-an can read a little English and he can't make out what the doctor wrote. We're waiting for you, Theo, to read it for us. There's an Indian midwife who I think might help. But she smokes something that makes her crazy. When the time comes we can't be sure she'll be in any condition to do much."

"We'll have to work on that," Harriet said. "I don't know what I can do, but I'll think of something."

"How are things at the mine?" my father asked.

Wong extracted an object from his trouser pocket and handed it to his partner. A piece of quartz laced with a small vein of genuine gold, not fool's porphyry.

"This from the Heckendom?"

"Not the levels you're familiar with. We blasted a new chute below level three and just started to haul out black slate when we ran into this." A huge smile suffused Wong's round face, "There's gold there, Theo. Lots of it. I always knew it."

"Rock or diabase?" Dad asked.

Wong hesitated. "Mostly diabase."

"That's dangerous stuff, friend. The mountain isn't stable. Quartz or no, you shouldn't be blasting. Dig it out by hand if you must. Don't use powder in that stuff. Any more trouble with the neighbors?"

"They stole some equipment, but nothing more serious. People are still talkin' in Moke Hill about revengin' Joe Kearny's death. But, so far, no shooting."

"If they learn you've hit a vein, trouble's guaranteed. I'm telling you, Wong, they won't let Chinamen succeed. Wait till I'm well enough to help."

"I can't wait. I need cash to pay the foreign miner's tax. And I haven't paid my men for months. You can't keep working them without pay. They may leave any day now. The tax collector, Mr. Sickles, will return in two weeks for more taxes."

"Then for God's sake, keep your men away from town. The minute white men learn you're tracking a vein, they'll come after you. We'll have a repeat performance of what happened before. Keep your men out of sight."

"Tell Mei Yok that I'll try to visit before she delivers," Harriet said. "For the time being, I've got my hands full with medical matters here. Theo's now one of them." She turned her attention to her patient, saying, "If you want, you can recuperate at my house where I can keep an eye on you. The catheters will need attention." To Wong she said, "If you or Mei Yok need either one of us, don't hesitate to ask."

She took from her smock pocket a notebook and scribbled her address, then handed it to Wong. "Can you read this?"

He looked at the note and shook his head from side to side. Then he wrestled with the letters and read aloud. "*L -A- G- U- N -A Street. Number 3 4 1.* I'm learning. There's not much time, but I try to read every night with Lin She-an."

Wong touched Dad's hand. "Get well, partner," he said while pulling away from this gesture of affection. "We'll be rich by the time you return to the Heckendom."

"You already got a wife and a child on the way. What do you want so much money for, Wong?"

"For my family, Theo." Then he used the slang my father noticed creeping into his speech. "California ain't cheap. We'll make a bundle together. As soon as we start mining that vein."

Father canted his head. "I appreciate that, friend, but I can manage with what the Good Lord has already allotted me. Don't get yourself in trouble for my sake. Don't write off the lumber business. Remember, I want you to be my partner up north."

Wong shook his head mildly and pressed his lips tightly together. This was not the right time to argue about cutting down old-growth redwoods. He had contemplated other occupations, but lumbering was never one of them. Timber was a necessary evil of modern society, but he couldn't see himself contributing to the destruction of a thousand-year-old forest.

While a nurse fed my father a diet of bean soup and berry juice, Wong stayed in the hospital room. When it was time for him to go, Harriet ushered him through the hospital corridor to a back door where he could slip past hostile Workingman's Party members still milling around the neighborhood.

Laguna Street, San Francisco
October 1870

On Sunday morning, a crisp, westerly wind from the Pacific swept the city clear of fog and breezed through the open front door of Harriet's home where Dad had agreed to recuperate. A minute later, Diego Montera brought a calling card to him where he was resting on the living room sofa. He was fully dressed, looking chipper and no further in need of a catheter, which weeks before required him to carry around an awkward and embarrassing urine bottle. At the moment Harriet was reading a medical journal, jotting notes in the margin, with reading glasses low over her nose. Father displayed the card, though he knew she could not read it from the distance.

ROGER HERST

CHARLES CORNELIUS CROCKER
INVESTMENTS
SAN FRANCISCO, CALIF.

It was unlike Charley Crocker to wait for a formal invitation to make a social call. While Father absorbed the thought of a surprise visit by his ex-employer and just about the wealthiest man in the West, Crocker barged through the sitting room door, arms outstretched in greeting and an infectious smile on his lips. Mary Crocker, his overweight, overdressed, and over-powdered wife, tagged behind him like a trained hound dog on a leash.

"Well, well, well, my boy," he pounced on Father, who barely had time to scramble to his feet, "so there's something on this earth to slow down even the irrepressible and indefatigable Theo Gallager. Mary and I were returning from Holland when the story about the *Magellan* hit the papers. The episode was completely unnecessary, you know, and I don't mind telling you how foolish you were. Everybody concedes that Kearny went too far. Yet this Chinese matter doesn't want to go away. The minute I read the headline, I knew you'd be involved."

Almost as an afterthought, he turned to acknowledge Harriet who rose to greet Mary. "And this must be the infamous Doctor Harriet Horn," he said, pivoting to face Harriet, who removed the glasses from her nose and angled her head in acknowledgment, though she had wondered what he meant by the word *infamous*. A courteous smile punctuated shallow dimples in her cheeks. To Harriet he declared, "Of course you know my wife, Mary. Or at least you've heard about her. These days she's famous for buying up everything that isn't bolted down in England and France. When all the articles she purchased finally arrive in San Francisco, I fear the additional weight on the city's bedrock will prompt an earthquake. If that doesn't happen, it's sure that their sheer poundage will cause several neighborhoods to break from the mainland and slip into the bay."

"What an honor," Mary said, ignoring her husband's ribbing and approaching Harriet with both hands outstretched. "If we had more professionals like you, Dr. Horn, women could take their rightful place in this society. And Theo, how wonderful to see you in good health. The papers said you had a serious injury."

Crocker handed a box of Swiss chocolates to my father. "I warn you, young man, they're addictive. Chocolates have always been my ruination,

-274-

you know. And you can see for yourself, I've lost the war against fat." To Harriet he said with his customary penchant for dropping famous people's names, "Mark Twain wrote that you've performed a miracle on my boy, Theo."

"No miracles, I assure you, Mr. Crocker. Anatomy's a precise science. Surgeons just cut and sew. It's like tailoring. If we do it right, the body restores itself. In modern medicine, there's no room for miracles, divine or otherwise."

Crocker's face bore an expression of omniscience. "You miss my meaning, I'm afraid. What I was suggesting was that you didn't have much help at the hospital. My spies tell me that in the midst of the operation your colleagues deserted you."

"One doctor added valuable advice. And the Chinese had other friends. Mr. Clemens, for example. You probably read how he helped Theo on the bay, at great peril to himself. We were both surprised to learn that despite all he wrote about boyhood life on the Mississippi River, he's not much of a swimmer."

"They wouldn't touch a cult figure like Sam. Most men threaten with their fists; Sam, with his pen. After all, the pen is the deadliest rapier of all."

Harriet signaled Diego Montera, ordering tea and sandwiches. Everybody took their places around a low coffee table.

"Any news from Wong Po-ching, Theo?" Crocker asked after they had settled down.

There was a shy, reticent tone in Dad's voice. "He's still at the Heckendom, with thirteen or fourteen coolies. Wong came down from the mountains to see me in the hospital. It isn't safe for a Chinaman to be traveling alone on the open roads these days. He's got a wife now and a baby on the way."

"Why am I not surprised? Success was stamped on that man's forehead. If he comes to the city again, I want you to bring him to my house, you understand? That's an order, Theo. Maybe I don't want to know this, but has Wong had luck in that old mine? If you tell me he's hit a vein, I'm going to feel I made a mistake by giving the mine away. No, that's not really true. I'd be delighted to have you fellows strike it rich."

"The neighbors have been mighty unfriendly. You probably read Twain's articles on the subject. Wong's enemies have stolen just about everything above grade. Some blew up the head-frame and ball mill.

Dennis Kearny lost his brother in an explosion on the property. Most people think that's why his brother's on a rampage against all the Chinese in the state."

"But is there any gold there? That's what I want to know," Crocker said, still thinking about what he might have given away.

My father thought about revealing what Wong had told him and fibbed. "Once Wong starts bringing ore to the surface, he'll have something. Up to now, it's all preparation."

Crocker smacked his knees with the flat of his hands. "If I were you, I'd sell the place for anything you can get. You know I'll always find work for Wong. I offered that to him in Utah. Nothing's changed since then. And I'll hire you any day you'll work in one of my enterprises. At a generous salary too."

"I prefer to work for myself," Father said without sounding arrogant. "I wrote you about my timber business."

"Your letters were forwarded to me in Europe," Crocker replied. "You know I'm a terrible letter writer. I get hundreds each week. Most asking for money for one silly idea after another. I have no time for writing, particularly when Mary and I are traveling. But just because I didn't answer yours doesn't mean I didn't read it. I planned to talk with you face to face rather than start a correspondence. You wrote how you wanted money to build timber roads. You're talking to someone who understands this, Theo, since timber roads can't be much different from railroads. If you're in the timber business you gotta move products somehow. If you can't get your wood to market, you got nothing to sell. That's how I got my start in dry goods. I made sure my shelves were stocked. And to keep them stocked, you have to control the means of delivery."

Diego arrived with a tray and set it on the table in front of Harriet. She poured tea with the grace of an English lady, genteelly passing cups to her guests.

"You didn't learn how to serve like that in San Francisco," Mary Crocker observed, glad to steer the conversation away from business.

"No, I didn't, Mrs. Crocker," Harriet answered. "I grew up in Massachusetts and learned about serving tea at the Boston Finishing School. In those days, it was essential curriculum for girls of good breeding. Unfortunately they didn't teach us much more than how to pour tea there. After all, what else did a girl from a wealthy family have to know in order to become the duteous wife to a wealthy husband?"

"That was a better education that I got," said Mary Crocker. "I was forced to learn the skill on the job, so to speak."

"Indeed," Crocker huffed then returned to his ex-superintendent. "You know I never come to a meeting like a mendicant, with an empty rice bowl in hand. I'm prepared to help you create a business in Eureka, or wherever your timber business is."

Dad looked to Harriet in surprise. Until that moment, he assumed that his unanswered request by post meant rejection.

"My spies tell me that the banks have turned you down. That shouldn't come as a surprise. Bankers possess all the imagination of garden slugs. Most have absolutely no instinct for business. That's why they trade money rather than something more substantial. Fortunately I'm no banker and, as you well know, I never, never lend money. And for your information, Theo, I don't intend to start with you, no matter how long we've known each other."

My father's optimism faded.

Crocker continued as if he didn't notice this disappointment, which he did. "If I put up money for timber roads it has to be in the role of a principal, not a lender. Yes, Theo, I'll bet on you. But I want a piece of your action. I'll buy a percentage of your timber business, then as a partner pay for what's needed to make it successful. You put in the muscle and I'll take the financial risk."

"I never gave that a thought, Mr. Crocker," Dad sounded dubious. "Nor have I the slightest idea how to structure a deal like that."

Crocker seized Mary's hand and stroked it in a public display of affection, slowly moving his eyes in my father's direction. "People say I'm coldhearted. I like to think of myself as pragmatic. Sure, I like making money. And yes, I like to own things, particularly things that make money for my expensive wife. But I also like men who know what they want, then go after it. It's not the timber business that intrigues me. To be honest, I don't intend to learn much about it, but if it makes money I may well change my mind. If you say it's going to be profitable, Theo, then that's good enough for me. I'm investing in you, my boy, not trees."

Dad mopped his brow with the back of his hand. "I'm flattered, but I still don't know how we'd divide the ownership."

"Let me make it easy for you. Real easy. Give me just two figures. Tell me how much you'll need for those roads. Then double the figure so you'll have plenty of cash to do the work right. Nothing can be worse for a growing business than to be undercapitalized, as we were on the railroad. Then tell me what percentage of the business you think that's worth. I'll listen to whatever you propose. Then, if I like what I hear, we shake hands. I don't want to negotiate with you because I know you won't cheat me. I'll instruct my lawyers to draw up the papers and deposit the money in an account for you to draw on. You manage the business. I'll probably be in Europe or somewhere else outside the state. Once a year, you draft an income statement. Send it to my business manager. If we make a profit, send a check for my share. If not, explain how much more I'll need to prime the partnership to make it profitable."

Crocker dropped Mary's hand and stretched his toward my father. "How does that proposition sound to you, my boy?"

"It sounds fair enough, but I've got to think about it a while."

"I reckon you'll make a decision by the time Dr. Horn pours me a second cup of tea. And if that isn't enough time, I'll have to eat some of your Swiss chocolates." He turned to the box he had brought, unfastened a string and offered my father and Harriet their choice. Harriet declined. Mary was tempted but at the last moment pulled back. A large chocolate-covered nugget slipped quickly into Crocker's mouth before he replaced the box on the table.

After a second cup of tea, Dad escorted the Crockers to the front door and placed his hand on the stout man's shoulder. "I like the proposition," he said. "A wealthy partner's a valuable asset. As soon as I've played with some figures, I'll send you the numbers you want."

On the doorstep, Crocker thanked Harriet for her hospitality. He paused a long moment to study her features before letting his eyes drop down over her figure. An indiscreet grunt of approval eased from his lips. To my father, he said, in a voice loud enough for all to hear, "You got a good friend here in Dr. Horn. Don't take her for granted, Theo. Women of this quality don't come around often. Right, Mary?"

Crocker's coachman descended to open the door for his employer. Mary mounted the step first and climbed into the cab. Her husband placed his foot on the mount but suddenly stopped and turned, signaling for Dad to approach him for a final word. Moving forward toward the carriage enervated my father, who rejected Harriet's helping hand.

"You know the state is planning an inquiry about events on the wharf." Crocker kept his hand on the coach door. "Woman from the Chinese Protection League have hired a very expensive law firm to represent the Chinese and they want me to underwrite its exorbitant fees."

Father grinned, sure that Crocker had turned down the request. There wasn't a chance in hell that the railroad magnate would pay someone else's legal expenses. Especially not for the Chinese Protection League.

"Of course, there was a time when I wouldn't have given a red cent for such a legal defense fund. But these days I'm older and, as you can readily see, I'm much closer to my Maker. If the truth be told, and I *never, never, never want you* to repeat it, we didn't give our Chinese in the Sierra an entirely fair shake. You could argue I gave them a shake, but not a fair one. We owed them more than their wages, which weren't all that bad, but not all that good either. Their services were invaluable. So I've agreed to underwrite up to five thousand dollars for legal expenses. But I fear that even the best lawyers in the West won't put Kearny and his gang on the gallows where they belong."

"Supporting the Protection League could be dangerous," Dad said. "We're dealing with unscrupulous men. Violence is their stock-in-trade."

"Oh, they won't touch a man like me. If I wanted, I could squash them like the spiders they are."

"Then why don't you?"

Crocker pouted. "You don't stay rich by being impractical. I'm prepared to let the law take its course. That's better for everybody. Chinese immigration is bigger than a single incident on the bay. The country's gonna have to decide its future. Not just the State of California, but all states of the Union. I'm sure you'll receive a subpoena to testify at the inquiry, Theo. I can't imagine one without your testimony." Crocker climbed into the cab and clumsily dropped into the seat near his wife.

My father remained beside the open door. "I'll look forward to telling the panel what I saw. It's time the state punished lawbreakers like Kearny."

"I wouldn't be optimistic about that if I were you. The state isn't gonna punish anybody. The inquiry's nothing but window dressing."

"The police saw everything. Lieutenant Wellington knows. There were plenty of newsmen. Sam Clemens, for example. There were thousands of witnesses."

"Politicians aren't interested in the truth; they're interested in staying in office. And they're not about to take an unpopular stand. Whether you and I and Dr. Horn and Mary agree or not, most citizens applaud what Kearny did. They won't say so in public, but behind closed doors they probably have a single regret, that you helped thirteen more coolies enter the state. You may be a hero to some, Theo. But I wouldn't trust the majority. Be prudent about what you say at the inquiry."

"I can take care of myself."

Harriet approached the carriage and stood beside my father, her hand steadying him.

"You hear that, Dr. Horn?" he asked, drawing Harriet into the conversation. "My partner thinks he can fight the world. And he has the audacity to believe he'll win. What he needs is a good woman to dampen some of his wild ardor and offer some protection."

Harriet's smile lit up her face. "He's too weak to get into much trouble for a few weeks. After that, I'll see what I can do."

"I say, the sooner we get him to the forests in Humboldt County, the safer he'll be."

The subpoena Father expected from the California State Board of Inquiry arrived in less than a week.

Venue: San Francisco City Hall.
Time: Wednesday noon, the 16th of October.

Newspapers carried the names of a dozen witnesses similarly subpoenaed and named my father and Sam Clemens at the top of the list. It was damn inconvenient timing. First, Dad was in no physical condition to testify at a long inquiry in the foul air of City Hall, notoriously polluted with odors from unwashed bodies and stale cigars. Second, he wanted to forget what had happened on the bay and focus his attention on his timber business. Crocker's money was a windfall, permitting him to accomplish what he had set out to do fourteen months before. Harvest timber.

Crocker's attorneys were quick to draft a partnership agreement. In deference to my father's injury, they delivered the documents to Harriet's home and stayed behind to explain the fine points of the agreement. Space for their client's contribution to the partnership was conspicuously blank, as well as the percentage of ownership this sum would represent. Dad was extremely uncomfortable when people fawned over him, and he didn't like important men coming to him. Thus, when an additional meeting became necessary, he volunteered to visit the law firm's chambers on California Street.

Reporters eventually tracked him down at Harriet's home and badgered him about *The Magellan Affair*, as it was dubbed. They pieced together a fairly accurate picture of his role in the rescue attempt then, with journalistic embellishments, wrote sensational stories meant to sell newspapers. My father was so disgusted by their departure from the truth that he even refused to say hello to the reporters camped outside Harriet's home. Their presence on Laguna Street drew attention to the fact that he was recuperating in the home of an unmarried woman. With her normal bravado, Harriet brushed off the inevitable gossip, though the invasion of privacy incensed my father.

Shortly thereafter, Charles Crocker sent my father a receipt for eight thousand dollars deposited in the Wells Fargo Bank and Trust Company on Montgomery Street, for twelve percent interest in the Gallager-Crocker Partnership. Crocker's accompanying note said the money was a mere down payment to begin construction of timber roads.

During Dad's recovery, Harriet returned home from the hospital each evening to dine with him. Rather than give San Francisco's gossipmongers something to talk about, they elected to eat alone. After dinner, Diego served coffee in the parlor, where they discussed modern medicine and California politics. Harriet made certain my father went to bed early.

One Saturday morning after Harriet had left to make hospital rounds, something unexpected shattered their routine. My father was seated at the dining room table working on maps of his timber forests when a sharp sound from the front room startled him. He limped forward from the dining room to investigate. Shattered window glass covered the floor and fog-cooled air circulated through the broken pane. Diego arrived a moment later and shuffled forward to retrieve a brick that had bounced from the couch and come to rest on the Trabiz carpet. A knotted cord secured a note to it. Father unfolded the paper to read:

A Warning to Theodore Gallager

Testify at the Inquiry and you'll lose *your remaining gonad. Or Dr. Horn.*
One or the other, it's your choice.
Concerned Citizens

Threats like this fired Dad's fighting spirit. He would have hurled the brick back into the street had he seen the perpetrator. That the cowardly author had hid behind the anonymity of "Concerned Citizens" made him that much angrier. The actual rock thrower meant nothing to him. To ignore the subpoena and not testify was unthinkable. Intimidation only fueled his determination. When his initial anger subsided, he thought about how to protect Harriet. Somehow he'd find a way.

His first priority was to repair the broken window, hopefully before Harriet returned. In this, Diego proved to be invaluable. In addition to being a servant, he was a craftsman who kept a variety of construction materials in the basement. Among them was a piece of replacement glass, albeit one that did not match the other panes in color or clarity. He reckoned that if Harriet returned after dark she might not notice the difference, at least not until the morning. Diego was instructed to cut and install this glass immediately. Later on, a professional glazier could replace it with a better match. By then my father would have a plan in place.

The conspiracy with Diego not to tell Harriet what had happened worked. She arrived home after sundown and, tired as she was, failed to notice the repaired window. The following week, after she left the house, he would have a gun dealer make a sales call on the Laguna Street residence and purchase from him a brace of pistols.

On Sunday morning, the day after the rock-throwing incident, Harriet made a picnic lunch and ordered a buggy to take them along California Street west to the Cliff House overlooking the Pacific Ocean. This majestic Victorian building with restaurants and a ballroom clung to a cliff, seemingly poised to plunge down two hundred feet into the frothy surf below. They left the buggy near the beach where they could look northwest past the Golden Gate along the California coast. A lone steamer, its stack belching coal smoke into a gusty wind, pounded against an outgoing tide toward calmer water inside the bay.

They removed their shoes and walked together in the surf. There was still pain in my father's groin, though each day he felt strength returning to his legs. And each day physical exertion fatigued him a little less. Together they gazed out over the rolling waves and watched white and gray gulls dart through the sea spray, riding air currents to shore, then dive along the water's surface, fetching herring in a series of graceful acrobatics.

"Did you buy a new pistol, Harriet?" Father asked as their shoulders touched and stayed close together.

She enjoyed physical proximity with him and spoke over the din of the waves. "I never thought I needed one after I gave you my Colt. I still have a Derringer, which I take when I'm nervous."

"A mere pee shooter, Harriet. You won't stop anybody up to real mischief with that. I've just ordered from a gunsmith two new .36 caliber Dragoons. They should arrive tomorrow. From now until the inquiry, I want you to carry one at all times."

She turned, blocking his forward movement and forcing him to stop. The wind caught strains of hair from beneath her bonnet and blew them across her nose. He reached up instinctively and moved them back to the side of her head. "Do you intend to shoot someone?" she asked.

He grappled with the thought of telling her about the threatening note he had stashed in the breast pocket of his pigskin jacket.

"You're not the kind of man who needs to intimidate people with guns, Theo."

"You obviously haven't noticed the new glass in your front window. This came through it yesterday," he said, handing her the note.

She carried reading spectacles tucked into her sleeve and took a moment to adjust them on her nose.

"That's why we're going to need heavy firepower."

"What about my old .44?"

"I left it with Wong at the Heckendom. Kinda figured he would need it more there than me. But it looks like we're going to need our own artillery. I'm scheduled at the inquest on Wednesday. Nobody will harm us *before* that. But *after*, I'm guarding you like a hawk. No one will get near you."

"What about you, Theo?"

"I have no intention of surrendering my left testicle."

She took his arm and gently turned him to continue walking. In the meantime the tide had receded, presenting moist, dark sand to walk on. She skipped over seashells as her toes sank into the water-saturated beach. "What will you gain by testifying? Do you really think your testimony will make a difference?"

"No. If the police haven't filed charges by now, my testimony probably won't do anything. Kearny is still making rabble-rousing speeches. If you can believe what he says, he wants to lynch politicians who support the Chinese. He's got everybody frightened. My bet is the law won't charge him with anything more serious than a misdemeanor. The police will probably slap his hands with a disturbing the peace violation."

"Then why put us both in harm's way?" Dad pondered that, glancing down to watch their toes disappear in the sand. "Somebody's got to speak out. I was there. I didn't see everything, but I saw Kearny deliberately ram that longboat. And I saw his men, directly under his orders, refuse to help the drowning coolies. We know who buys and sells the judges in the courts and we know our politicians won't protect Chinamen. I take those as the brute, unpleasant facts of human behavior. But that doesn't mean I shouldn't tell what I saw. Maybe the press will publish the truth. Many Californians already know what happened. It's sad that they're not outraged by this kind of mob violence."

"Is it worth fighting those thugs?"

"They're bullies. They're only testing me."

"You don't know that for sure. Can we get police protection?" "Most of the police support the Workingman's Party. My guess is that the majority of our law enforcement officers are members."

When they came to a small rivulet running from the city into the ocean, they turned and worked their way up the beach, where their feet sank still deeper into the sun-warmed sand. She took a sack filled with lunch from Dad's shoulders. On the top was a slick cloth for sitting. Two large driftwood logs served as backrests. Between them, she laid out cuts of cold chicken, slivered cucumbers, thin slices of wheat bread smothered in butter, little yellow and red apples and a bottle of Burgundy wine from Napa County.

His eyes were fixed on the shape of her toes silhouetted against the surf. The opportunity to study this part of the feminine anatomy seldom presented itself. Pointed shoes that were currently the fashion didn't seem to disfigure Harriet's straight toes, which were speckled with sand.

"Toes are strange, aren't they?" she said when her attention returned to him. She wiggled them, kicking sand into the air. "I mean you would have to think they couldn't support our weight."

"Not yours, Harriet. When I was lying in bed for a week, for some odd reason I kept wondering about your feet. Hard to know someone when you can only see a fragment of their flesh. Like your face and hands. You've got very pretty toes."

"Thanks, but my hands are gruesome. The fate of a surgeon constantly scrubbing in carbolic acid solution. I apply all manner of creams, but they only make the skin look worse. I'm delighted you see redeeming beauty in my feet. But tell me what about them appeals to you?"

"Most, I think, because they belong to you. And that they aren't covered with stockings or shoes. And that they're exposed so I can see them."

"And so are yours, Theo."

"True, but you already know everything about me. I've been on your operating table, remember? You know me from inside and out. My feet are just the extension of everything else."

"So are mine."

"But aside from your face and hands, they're the only flesh I know. The rest of you is hidden away. Sometimes, my imagination runs wild and I try to imagine the real you under all your silks and taffetas and cottons and all those nice things you wear. So I guess I've answered your question. Now you know why I like looking at your feet."

Harriet put down her cup and inched sideways against my father until she was close enough to stretch over to him and plant a soft kiss on his cheek. Her lips remained near him where she whispered, "I think I understand what you're saying and if I'm right, this can be rectified. Above all, Theo, I want us to be on equal footing. A surgeon has an advantage because I examined you in the name of science. And I did. You've a right to feel that's unfair. I concede it."

He laughed. "Not to worry. In the scope of things, it's a trivial injustice. You saved me from bleeding to death."

"No need for that. I mean what I said about being on equal ground. People like us can only be friends when there are no advantages. When we go home, I'll take off my clothes. All of them, if you want, because I want you to know me as I know you. As absolute equals."

He was staggered by the suggestion. In all his life he had never met a woman like Harriet Horn. There was shyness in his voice when he said, "Yes, I think I'd like that very much. But it isn't advisable for two reasons. First, I'm not sure I could remain a gentleman. And second, I'm sure your friends wouldn't think that's a very ladylike thing for you to do."

She planted a second kiss on his cheek, this time lingering longer with her lips against his flesh. "As to your first concern, if I thought you were not a gentleman, the idea would never have occurred to me. And as to the second, I don't care what my friends say. They're not going to know because I have no intention of telling them. This is between you and me, Theo."

CHAPTER TWELVE

The Mine

Powell Street in Chinatown was crowded with Asians in brightly colored costumes, scarlet red pantaloons and yellow tunics, chartreuse shoes and Oriental masks, celebrating the arrival of their countrymen from the *Magellan*. Torches burning on stakes illuminated musicians playing a combination of strident string instruments, flat Chinese drums and pipes, none recognizable to Caucasians and, to the Western ear, barely synchronized. Each half-hour an enormous green and yellow cloth dragon conveyed by a dozen men danced through the crowd, spewing fire from its open mouth. Firecrackers exploded wherever young men could find space to ignite them. An odor of spent gunpowder, mixed with the aroma of Oriental spices, permeated the air.

Chinese in San Francisco had never before celebrated the safe arrival of their compatriots because their leaders feared anything that might provoke the ire of white men. But Kearny's attack on *Magellan's* passengers had unleashed a wave of hitherto silent resentment. Even cautious community leaders were now prepared to rethink their previous decision and admit that their policy of appeasement had failed. Chinatown's elders needed to inspire their dispirited countrymen, who had come to believe that white men would never support their claims for fairness. They planned to turn a public relations disaster at the wharf into a victory rally to honor the bevy of fellow Chinamen who had scrambled ashore. There was nothing like a colorful and loud rally to generate a feeling of solidarity.

My father stood on the makeshift grandstand, surrounded by Chinese merchants, listening to fiery speeches in a language he could not understand. The audience would cry out and stamp its feet the moment a speaker paused. And when one of them lifted his arm in a flamboyant gesture, folks howled approval, mimicking the speaker. Finally an elderly dignitary with a thin mustache and pasty eyes opened his palms toward the audience, requesting silence, which wasn't something the rollicking Chinese gave willingly. It took several minutes for everyone to quiet down before the dignitary started speaking in English.

White policemen stationed at strategic locations in the Chinese quarter provided only nominal protection against an attack by angry whites. Dad's hand brushed along his waist to finger the new .36 caliber Dragoon tucked under his jacket. He insisted that Harriet carry her new revolver in her medical bag, though he had yet to find a safe place where she could practice firing it. That she knew how to shoot the older Colt .44 was a good beginning.

"Meester Theodore G'allag'r," the new speaker signaled him forward to the lectern while continuing to address his audience, "is responsible for saving thirteen Chinaman. No other white men willing. Meester G'allag'r now in danger. Some white men say he the living devil. Some say they kill him and send his body to China for burial."

A variety of verbal hoots and cheers arose from the spectators. Dad had no idea what this signified.

Wing So-chien, president of the Confederation of Benevolent Associates, stepped forward to place a beaded necklace around my father's neck. From it hung an obsidian medallion imprinted with the head of a fierce-looking dragon. The president spoke English with only traces of a Chinese accent. "Theodore Gallager, the Chinese community in California honors you for your help on the bay. It was an unparalleled act of courage for which you have sustained bodily injury. In California, we Chinese have few friends and many, many enemies. And when we find a rare and precious friend like you, he is especially cherished. The Chinese people are renowned for many vices, and our virtues are seldom acknowledged. But among our virtues is that of long memory. We do not forget. We do not forget friendship. We, the Chinese in San Francisco, will not forget who stood with us during our hour of peril. We, the Chinese of California, have found a white brother who is now a member of our family. We know of your injuries during the rescue and deeply appreciate your sacrifice. We wish you a full and speedy recovery."

After a translation into Cantonese, the crowd broke into spontaneous applause. The band played a few bars of discordant music, ending with an extended roll on the drums. A salvo of firecrackers crackled in front of the bandstand.

When the crowd quieted down, president Wing So-chien continued in a subdued voice, looking at my father. "Mr. Theodore Gallager, threats have been made against you. They are probably instigated by the same people who oppose our presence in this state. This is very distressing. My countrymen have given me authority to provide you with a Chinese pledge. From now on, your enemies are our enemies and your friends are our friends. We offer our lives to protect you. Never hesitate to call upon us."

Dad's heartbeat increased. Harriet had tried to dissuade him from accepting an invitation to the celebration, contending that no honor was worth exposing himself in a crowd where an assassin might hide. But it was his inclination to defy dangers he could not quantify. When he had jumped into the bay, it had never occurred to him that he was doing anything more than preventing fellow human beings from drowning. After all, he didn't even know the names of the men he was helping. As individuals they were complete strangers, not men of the Mongoloid race but only men of the human race. He sensed that his action, however spontaneous, had kindled a fire in this silent community of hardworking immigrants. And he knew that white men would take them seriously only when they demonstrated their willingness to defend themselves.

Harriet spoke while taking Dad's arm and guiding him through milling bodies toward a waiting buggy. "I'm so proud of you, Theo. While Wing So-chien was talking, I watched faces in the crowd. They respect you. Few men get an opportunity to be heroic. Most never rise to the occasion when they do. But you did and these undervalued and hated peoples have recognized your heroism and honored your sacrifice."

The tension and noise had tired Dad out and he limped along silently beside her.

"Let's go home, Theo. This hero needs his rest. And his surgeon needs to keep a promise to her patient."

"On equal footing, Theo," were the last words Harriet said before her robe dropped from her shoulders. She was standing in her bedroom, a foot from the bed. My father, for want of a better place to put himself, had awkwardly backed up against her desk, six feet away, and leaned his backside against the edge. The urge for physical intimacy with Harriet had been stirring inside him almost from their first encounter aboard the steamship *Japan*. But he had successfully suppressed the desire, looking to other women to satisfy his manly instincts. He had taken seriously her declaration about maintaining her independence and he admired how she distanced herself from suitors he knew often hovered around, seeking every opportunity to woo her affections. Once she had become his physician, he elevated her even further beyond his own reach, careful not to approach her in any manner that might compromise her position.

When he first learned that she had operated on him at the Seafarer's Hospital he had felt embarrassed, somewhat violated. But that lasted only a short time, for he had begun to think about what had happened not as an embarrassment, but an honor. He had become accustomed to the idea of her operating on his privates and never thought of it as an advantage in her favor. On the beach, when she brought up the subject of undressing before him to level this perceived advantage, he didn't take it seriously. Like sand dispersed by the winds, it was no more than fleeting conversation.

But Harriet had not forgotten. Suddenly she was standing before him in the flesh of Eden, as God had fashioned woman. Her alabaster skin was evenly mottled with light freckles. Her breasts were firm and slightly pointed; her nipples, brown-pink, reminding him of a porcelain statue of a mythic goddess he had once seen in a Cincinnati art museum. Around the waist she was slim, but her hips spread wider than he imagined while admiring them under layers of taffeta.

She noticed his eyes barely focused on her. She lifted her chin and spoke, "Is this a modest gentleman before me? Or my lover?"

He wrestled for words. "I'm not used to this."

"Neither am I. Take your time, Theo. I worked on you at the hospital for several hours. You're entitled to equal time."

"Are we counting?" he asked, wondering whether his feelings were aesthetic, prurient, or sexual, and immediately concluding they were a combination of all three.

"There's more to see. I want you to know everything about me, both inside and out," she said, rotating to expose all sides. After pausing for an instant with her back toward him, she rotated to reface him.

"Doctor Horn, *perdóname, por favor.*" Diego Montera's voice in Spanish passed through the bedroom door at the same time he rapped hard. "Doctor Horn, *Discúlpeme por la interrupción* . You told me not to disturb you. But there's a gentleman here who says it's an emergency. He *must* speak with you immediately. I tried to make him wait, but he absolutely insists it's extremely urgent."

Harriet's look of exasperation fell on my father. For an instant it appeared as though she would resist this interference. But a moment later she snatched the robe she had let drop to the floor. Father stepped toward her to help secure it around her shoulders. In her bare feet she marched to the door and spoke through it. "Who is it, Diego?"

"Says his name is Malachi Snowden. He says you know him from a meeting in town."

"The Reverend Snowden?"

"*No lo conozco, Doctor.*"

She touched Dad's outstretched fingers then moved to find a pair of slippers. "All right, Diego. Tell Reverend Snowden I'll be right down." And to my father she said as the door cracked open, "Sorry. This shouldn't take long. I want to finish what we've started."

My father knew the moment had passed and probably would never return. His grimace revealed a moment of utter confusion. In a way, he feared repeating what he had just seen. But in another, perhaps stronger way he wanted to wrap his arms around Harriet and make love to her. But in his shyness, that day seemed far away.

She paused before leaving him behind in the bedroom and looked into his eyes, a hand on his forearm. "If you're thinking Reverend Snowden's a suitor, I promise you he isn't. He's a friend of the Chinese who stayed here after the riot in Chinatown to attend the congressional hearing at the Palace Hotel. He had nowhere to go, and I invited him to stay in my home. He's got a wife and children somewhere near Mokelumne Hill. Last I heard he's a churchman without a church." She planted a final kiss dead center on Dad's lips before ducking through the door.

Malachi Snowden was pacing nervously in the foyer at the foot of the mahogany staircase. Blond-gray hair that sat in a heavy mop on his head was disheveled. Three days of whiskers bristled on his cheeks. His eyes were moist and bloodshot, as though he had been drinking. He wore mountain clothes and muddy boots. No clerical collar circled his throat.

"Good day, Reverend. Your visit is unexpected. I had no idea you were in San Francisco," she said, greeting him with an outstretched hand that he took.

He had anticipated more formal dress to receive him and was surprised to find her in bedroom attire. "It's wonderful to see you again, Miss Horn, I mean Dr. Horn. I don't refer to myself as *Reverend* anymore. I lost my pulpit. People in Moke Hill have no Christian love for the Chinese. Even less for a pastor who promotes their cause. I haven't tried to find a new parish and am now supporting my family by doing odd jobs around the camps."

"Have you also lost your faith, Mr. Snowden?"

"In a manner of speaking. Only a strong faith is worth losing, you know. Many people believe finding God is the ultimate human experience. This may sound odd, Dr. Horn, but for me, it was losing Him."

"Is that why you came here?"

"No. I came looking for Theodore Gallager. He's Wong Po-ching's partner at the Heckendom mine. There's big trouble on the property. Mr. Gallager's got to come right away. It's an emergency. Wong and eleven men are trapped deep in the mine. I've tried to raise men to dig them out, but nobody is willing to lift a finger on their behalf. Time's critical. The Chinese trapped in the mine can't last too many more days underground. I thought you might help me find Mr. Gallager. Where else can I turn?"

Harriet absorbed the onslaught of his words, her hand pawing at her own lips in a gesture of contemplation. The flush of skepticism, which normally made her cautious, evaporated when she considered Snowden's credentials as the only practicing Christian she knew in the Mokelumne Hill district, a man who had sacrificed much for his convictions. The question arose in her mind about the impression it would make if she produced my father on the spot. She was clothed in no more than a bathrobe. Assumptions would be made.

"If I told you that Theo Gallager was staying here in this very house, would that surprise you, Reverend Snowden?"

"It certainly would. But it would also make things a lot easier."

She turned to Diego who had come to await her bidding. "Fetch Mr. Gallager. Please ask him to come down to the sitting room. If the Reverend Snowden says the matter's urgent, so it must be. Then bring our good friend something to eat and some tea. It looks like my favorite pastor is very hungry and thirsty."

"Malachi," he corrected.

"You're the Reverend Snowden to me, sir. To my mind there's no one more deserving of that title than yourself, despite what your parishioners might think."

When Father entered the sitting room, Snowden was on a couch, his head dipping toward his lap and his hands cupped over his temples, massaging away a headache. Harriet was arranging a plate and a cup on the table in front of him. He rose and stepped around the table to greet my father with both hands outstretched. "I've read about you, Mr. Gallager. Wong Po-ching speaks highly of you. He never calls you by name and refers to you only as *my partner*."

"Is he all right?"

"No. A rumor circulated in town that Wong hit a rich vein. Rich but very deep. Local miners and drifters went crazy. Chileans and Spaniards. Welshmen and Norwegians. They couldn't stand the thought of a Chinaman succeeding when they were failing. A mob, calling itself *Posse Comitatus*, mounted an attack on the mine. Said they were out to take revenge for the death of Joseph Kearny. This wasn't like earlier attacks. They came with rifles and blasting powder and caught Wong and his men deep inside the mine, then set charges around the head-frame. They blew out the new adit Wong had just constructed. Everyone who was inside the mine at the time is trapped below ground. Twelve men altogether, I believe. They're trying to dig themselves out at this very moment, but conditions must be awful."

"I warned him that the locals wouldn't let him succeed. Air? How are they breathing?"

"You know Wong. Air in a tunnel is always his first priority. Before he started blasting out level four, he opened a new vent to level three. He must have anticipated something like this because he also blasted out auxiliary vents from the first and second tiers. He's a cautious miner and stashed food, water, and fuel down there in case of disaster. So for the short run, they'll probably survive. But they can't get out without help from above."

Snowden unhitched his shirt pocket and pulled out a map. "I drew this on the steamer from Stockton. I'm not much of a mapmaker, but it'll give you an idea. You probably already know the top levels."

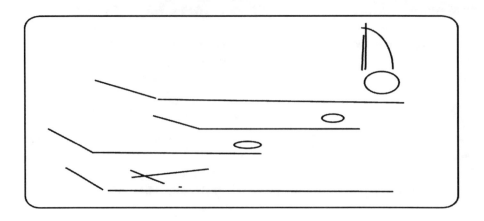

Dad recognized an approximation of the Heckendom Mine below grade. The top right represented the destroyed adit and entrance. The lower left, the bottom level where Wong and his crew were following a vein of gold in a quartz deposit. How much of each entry had been destroyed by the blasting was not shown, but Dad assumed the worst. Otherwise Wong and his men would have worked their way to higher levels rather than remain on level four.

"Is there any way of communicating with them?"

"Lee Shi-tong, Wong's foreman, ran off when the attack started but came back. He's a small fellow who crawled down to the level three vent and called out. Someone answered. He reported one man's badly injured. Another's dead."

"What about Mei Yok?" Harriet interrupted. "Is she at the mine?"

"No, Ma'am. I don't know where she is. In the chaos, she disappeared. Lee She-tong said she was due to deliver a baby any day. Maybe the attackers took her. Maybe she has escaped. Lee's frightened to leave the mine unattended and won't search for her. I've tried to get the few who still consider me their friend to help, but there's no interest in a pregnant Chinese woman. Everyone is afraid of reprisals."

"She'll never survive in the mountains in her condition," Harriet declared.

My father glared at her, processing a host of thoughts, then barked at Snowden, "Who's heading the rescue?"

"No one. Wong had three men topside when the Posse Comitatus arrived. They ran away. Only Lee She-tong's returned. I've pleaded in every tavern in the vicinity. No volunteers. I wouldn't be surprised if some of the men I spoke to participated in the attack. If you can't help me raise a rescue team, then Wong's completely on his own."

"What about neighbors? Surely they'll help. There have to be some God-fearin' people around."

"None. Not one man. Good Christians are timid. They won't risk their families or their jobs. The Posse Comitatus scares everybody."

Dad turned to Harriet. His eyes searched hers for understanding. She planted her hand on his, sensing his thoughts. Snowden noted this sign of affection and swallowed deep. As a married man he had always been true to his wife, Susan. Yet time had eroded their passion and he harbored fantasies of romance. From the moment he had heard Harriet Horn speak her mind before Senator Hubbel's inquiry, she became the focus of these fantasies. Not for an instant could he entertain the possibility of carrying on a real affair with her, yet she was constantly in his innermost thoughts. Any man in his right mind would find her attractive. Theodore Gallager was an obvious candidate for her affections. He felt traces of envy for my father, but no hostile jealousy.

"I must go to Wong," Father stated, his voice exuding an unequivocal urgency that dared anyone to argue with him.

Harriet shot back, "You'll do nothing of the kind, Theo. Listen to your physician. You haven't got the strength. You can't do any good if you get sick. You could start bleeding again. And that is certain to cause an infection. What happens if you can't urinate? You simply can't travel in your condition. And you certainly can't dig anybody out of a damaged mine."

Snowden looked dazed by the revelation of Dad's serious medical condition.

"Who else will rescue those miners?"

"How should I know? Will you and the good reverend here dig him out with your bare hands?" My father considered that for a long moment before offering a solution. "Then I'll buy the help we need, Harriet. I never saw a mountain man who wouldn't roll up his sleeves for a healthy wage. We'll need at least a hundred men below grade. Perhaps another sixty to support them above ground. Can you find a hundred and sixty hungry men, reverend? Men who will work for *double* wages? And who will rent us their gear?"

"Malachi, Malachi, Malachi, Mr. Gallager. It's Malachi. Just Malachi."

"All right, Malachi. Can we raise a couple hundred hands for double wages? Say for ten dollars a day?"

"For that kind of money you could hire an army."

"Just snatch the money from the air, will you?" Harriet said, sounding dubious.

"I've got Mr. Crocker's installment of eight thousand dollars for the timber roads. All I need is a transfer agent. Where's the nearest Wells Fargo agency to Moke Hill, Malachi?"

"San Andreas."

"Good. We'll stop there on the way to the mine and pick up an installment of cash."

Harriet shook her head. "That money's for timber roads."

"I'll raise more later. Wong comes first."

Harriet inched back to look at Dad as her brain processed what was happening. The man before her was impulsive and stubborn; it was unthinkable for him to abandon his partner in a mine, just as it was unthinkable for him to stand on the docks and watch Chinese workers drown. And it was equally unthinkable for him to squirrel away money when a friend was in need. "Then I'm going with you, Theo," she announced.

"That's too dangerous."

"For you, not for me! You're a sick man. If you're going into the lion's den you'll need a physician to look after you."

"The men who did this won't let us rescue Wong without a fight. Shooting is inevitable. I'm taking my Dragoon and not just for intimidation. My new friend, Malachi, has just been appointed my bodyguard. For the sake of mortal sinners like me and Wong, the good reverend may have to kill some foul men. What say you, Malachi? Is this not the Lord's true work?"

"The Lord fired me as His spokesman. I have no further authority to speak in His name."

"Beg your pardon, Reverend Snowden," Harriet said. "God's self-appointed deacons on earth, not God Himself, fired you. And for all the wrong reasons too. You're still our clergyman. Isn't that right, Theo?"

"Absolutely," Dad added with only an instant to ascertain whether he agreed or not.

"I need twenty-four hours to transfer my hospital patients to colleagues," Harriet said. "I can't leave the city without seeing that they're properly cared for."

"Malachi and I can't wait another day. If you're determined to come, which I hope you aren't, you'll have to follow us on your own. There's a steamer to Stockton at five every evening. We're gonna be on it this afternoon. We must be on the early morning stage to San Andreas. Do you have transport in San Andreas, Malachi?"

"I left a wagon. An old mare. Not very fast, but she's reliable enough."

Harriet interjected, "Then I'll come tomorrow. Day after tomorrow at the very latest. I'll catch a stage to Mokelemne Hill and hitch a ride from there."

"I'd worry less if you stayed here."

"And I'd worry more. There's an injured man with Wong. When you get the others out, they'll be dehydrated. Perhaps some will have broken limbs. Lack of food, air, and light causes many physical maladies. They'll need a doctor. I'll bring medicines and supplies. We'll have to find Mei Yok. She'll need female companionship. If the baby isn't born yet, I can help. Delivering babies is my specialty."

She turned to climb the staircase for more clothes, but stopped on the first landing. "My God, I just thought about something! What about the inquest, Theo? We almost forgot your subpoena."

"That's the least of my worries. I'll send Diego with a note to Mr. Hampshire, Crocker's lawyer. Let him file for a continuance. Or better yet, I'll write my account on the steamship to Stockton and post it back to Mr. Hampshire in the morning. Let him read it at the inquest."

"That will enrage the Workingman's Party and they'll come after us at Mokelumne Hill. They still want your left testicle, Theo. And a part of me too."

"Let'em come, Harriet, we'll be waiting. Wong and I are creatures of the mountains. We don't fit in the city. Whatever their numbers, they'll be fighting on our turf."

The paddle-wheel steamer *Joshua Lawrence Chamberlain* departed from the Filbert Street Wharf and, after traveling north through San Francisco Bay, headed south into the San Joaquin River toward Stockton. From there, my father and Malachi Snowden rode by stage along a dusty track, north of Gopher Ridge to San Andreas where, after being shuffled through two echelons of bank officials, they converted to cash most of Crocker's advance payment for roads in Humboldt County. Snowden interrupted his journey at Mokelumne Hill to recruit local workers, while Dad continued on to the Heckendom in the minister's wagon.

Malachi Snowden possessed a wide network of friends and associates from his days at the First Congregational Church in Moke Hill, people who admired his intelligence and integrity, even if they didn't agree with his social positions, especially regarding Chinese workers. Through them, he broadcast word there were jobs available at the Heckendom, jobs that paid double wages, not just room and board but also an eye-opening promise of a bonus if they succeeded in rescuing the buried miners. The call to work passed by word of mouth, faster than a rumor of a gold strike. Unemployed men bivouacked in the mountains never even bothered to head for town for confirmation. Instead, they set off directly for the Heckendom.

Once at the mine, there was no time for my father to recover from the fatigue of his journey. Urinating produced a violent fire in his groin and when his bladder was flushed he was left with a pulsating pain. Still, the urgency below ground forced him to concentrate on the conditions faced by Wong and his cohorts. He established his headquarters in the mine cabin just in time to greet the first eager workers as they entered the camp. Snowden arrived late in the afternoon and, by evening, what had begun as a trickle of recruits turned into a flood, filling every available job. Late arrivals in the wee hours of the next morning were given the option of returning home or remaining at the mine as standbys with reduced salaries paid by the Heckendom. Stragglers who entered the property after daylight had to be turned away.

Miners, lumbermen, and drifters were surprised to find their bossman crippled with pain and obliged to lean on the handle of a pickax to stand for any length of time. Still, Dad's reputation as the superintendent of construction on the Central Pacific preceded him to the mining camp, where these men learned firsthand about his iron determination. His rescue plans were delivered in a crisp, decisive voice, conveying unquestioned certainty in the mission. To the boss, it was not a question if the miners could be rescued but just how fast.

In the army Father had used men from a dozen regiments to build bridges under hostile fire for General Ambrose Burnside before the disastrous defeat at Fredericksburg. Later his engineers cut roads and laid pontoon bridges during multiple battles in what they later called *the Wilderness*. When laying Central Pacific track in the High Sierra, he had organized unskilled workmen into specialized teams. Now he calculated the similarity between soldiers, miners, and railroad laborers. They possessed an instinctive sense about those who gave orders. When inspired, they performed their jobs; but when uninspired, they languished or rebelled. There wasn't the slightest doubt in his mind that to save the lives of Wong and his compatriots he could not afford to let these men become discouraged or lazy.

Malachi Snowden slipped easily into the role of foreman. Men who were prone to thinking of him as a man unworldly and impractical were in for a surprise. Crisis at the Heckendom quickly proved them wrong. Few could outdo him for strength or endurance with a pick or shovel. From the opening moments of the rescue, he set and maintained a rigorous standard of work production. Among other responsibilities, Dad made him paymaster, entrusting to him five thousand dollars in cash withdrawn from the Wells Fargo Express Office in San Andreas. Laborers received ten dollars at the end of each day; five dollars of which was withheld until the rescue operation was over. Every man who genuinely contributed to bringing Wong and his comrades to the surface dead or alive could look forward to a one-time bonus of twenty-five dollars!

In exchange for generous wages, expectations were high. Father made it clear that miners must work until they didn't have an ounce of strength left. No alcohol. No gambling. No time out in camp. No Sundays off. The latter was easy to enforce since everybody acknowledged that the buried miners would die if the operation continued more than four days.

"You can't go into the mine in your condition, Theo," Snowden warned. "It's too dank and hot. You shouldn't breathe foul air. Dr. Horn wouldn't permit it."

"Seeing she's not here, she can't forbid anything. A blind man is ineffective. I must know exactly what I'm dealing with as we go along."

"Why add your tragedy to theirs? I know something about God and I can assure you the Almighty isn't asking for you to go into this mine."

"Well, I hope the Almighty is looking the other way for an hour or so, because I'm going down. We must get water to the men below. I've ordered Lee Shi-tong to thread a hose through the vents from level three to level four. We'll set up a reservoir on level three and feed it by hand with buckets. If we can get water to drip down on Wong's men, they'll be able to lap up some. If they can't see in the dark, they'll be able to hear the trickle and feel for the moisture. Once we start hacking at the slate above them, they won't hear a thing but picks and hammers. With some luck we'll find a safe place to blast. Too bad Wong isn't working with us because he always knows exactly where to plant charges for maximum effect. I could use him now."

"Dr. Horn should be here tomorrow. She'll be furious with you."

"By that time I'll be topside. Harriet will have more important things on her mind. She'll have to revive some ghosts."

Lee Shi-tong mounted the three steps into the mine cabin and gave a thumbs up signal that he was ready with the hose. "Water line at the head-frame. Men pump from high stream. Much pressure. Maybe too much."

"That's good, Lee. Light the lanterns. We'll enter the mine in ten minutes. Any sign of Mei Yok?"

"Lee send Fu Cha to look in mountains. No sign Mei Yok."

To Snowden, my father asked, "Any chance the Posse took her hostage?"

"That's what I'm afraid of. If she's hiding, why hasn't she returned? You'd think she'd come in for help if she's ready to have a baby."

"I don't think she's ever been anywhere but here," my father said while grimacing as a new thought entered his mind. "Except, except for her honeymoon with Wong. He told me they celebrated together in the redwood grove in Calaveras. The place is special to him. My guess is that Wong took her there several times and made her learn the route. Maybe she went to the big redwoods thinking her husband would join her later. She probably doesn't know Wong's trapped. Is there someone we can send to search the redwood grove?"

Snowden pondered the possibility. "I have a friend in Arnold. I officiated at his daughter's wedding in our church. He's a small man with a bad leg and couldn't help us dig in the mine, but he's got a big heart. He'll do what I ask of him. I'll send a message off to Arnold right away. If Mei Yok builds a fire, he'll find her."

"Could she have her baby there?"

"Alone? God, I hope not."

My father instructed Snowden about how he wanted the tools and machinery readied. Next he concentrated on selecting men to follow the ore tracks through level one. He then consulted maps of the mine, hoping they were accurate enough to plan the assault on level two. After considering several ways to open a passage to the trapped men, he chose the shortest but the most dangerous—through the vent hole Wong had cleaved. As a general rule, miners avoided chiseling through vulnerable conduits where a collapse would deny air to those surviving on a lower level. There were two safer ways, but both entailed far more digging. Time was of the essence so Dad was forced to sacrifice safety for speed.

He was comfortable with maps. On an oversized table near the mine entrance, he tracked a new diagram, specifying the local vent holes, crosscuts, and access points, as well as the passageways from level to level. Men with below-grade experience were assembled into pick-and-hammer teams to break down the face rock. Less experienced men became muckers--to shift loose rock into unused neighboring shafts. A third team was assigned to lay track for the mule-driven ore carts. Dad relied on Snowden's friends to recommend squad leaders. His days in the military had taught him the value of a clear chain of command. When every second counted, squabbles over authority could be fatal.

Small in stature, extremely nimble and knowledgeable about the mine from his days working beside Wong, Lee Shi-tong became the team's forward scout. He was asked to wriggle through the airshaft between levels two and three and make his way through fallen gangue rock to the airshaft above Wong's men to tap a rescue message in Cantonese: "Rescue coming. Rescue coming." Every ten minutes he moved to a new position where his message might be heard below.

After two hours he returned to report to my father the unhappy news that he was unable to hear voices or receive signals in response to his tapping. Many wondered aloud if they were unable to elicit a response from the trapped miners below why they should continue digging. Dad refused to be discouraged and sent Lee back to tap new signals and report every twenty minutes. Just when he was about to return to my father with a fresh report, he heard a weak response from level four. For ten minutes, he searched for a fissure in the ore to call to the spot from where he believed the tapping originated.

"Is Wong alive?" Lee howled in Chinese through a fissure in his loudest voice.

"Hope so," came a far weaker reply in his mother tongue.

"Can he talk?"

"Yes, he's talking now. I'm Wong. How many men are digging?"

"One hundred. Many more are aboveground."

"That can't be possible."

"Yes, it's very possible. Mr. Gallager's here. He brought many men to the Heckendom. Are the overhead laggings strong enough for blasting?"

"No. They're ready to crumble."

"So we won't blast."

"Yes, you must blast. There's no time left. My men are injured and weak."

"Be patient. I'll go for Mr. Gallager now."

"Did Mei Yok have her baby?" Wong asked.

Lee Shi-tong paused to catch his breath before lying, "No. Not yet."

"Good. Tell Gallager to take care of Mei Yok if I die. Tell him there's a lot of gold here. My share goes to Mei Yok and our baby."

"Tell him yourself, Wong. We're cutting through to level four. Stay alive, my friend! We'll come to get you, don't worry about that."

Hendrik Schloesser was a miner from Silesia with experience in quartz mining up and down the Mother Lode. A deep digger who never feared working far from the surface in tight shafts, he volunteered to lead the assault team. Rock facing him in the forward shaft was as hard as any he had come across in the Sierra foothills, yet that inspired him to extreme exertion. Layers of sweat on his neck and face attracted a thick coating of brown dust. His eyes squinted at my father, who leaned with his rump against the map table at the mouth of the mine.

Schloesser grunted, slurping water from a bottle with a wide rim. "I reck'n a week to cut through to level four."

"Those Chinamen haven't got a week. One day, maybe two at most. Your men can do it if they press harder."

"No, Gallager. Hard rock and picks are mortal enemies. There's only so much air for our lungs. Tailings clog up the air passage. So if we manage to cut through in a week, you won't find anyone alive. That's for sure."

"And if we use powder?"

"Well, that's another story now. If the charges were placed just right, we might break through in time. But then, if we make a small error, we'll suffocate those little bastards below."

Father's eyes focused on the mine adit. The distant, aloof manner in which Schloesser delivered his judgment was annoying. None of the hired hands seemed to give a damn about the lives of the Chinese miners. If white men had been trapped the story would certainly be different. He knew it was too late to educate his men. He could only hope to keep them engaged.

Snowden trotted down a dusty trail to the mine entrance. A gentle wind cut across his face and blew blond hair across his eyes. "Theo, the trail lookout signaled ahead. There's a wagon approaching. Two women. Could be Doctor Horn."

Dad lifted his weight from the table and peered past the mine cabin, but it was too far to see anything. "Didn't the guard stop them? No sense in putting one out there if he's not going to stop anybody. The Posse could be coming back to finish its dirty work. The wagon might be filled with explosives."

"Two women," Snowden repeated, looking through a cloud of dust in a clearing.

"You know anybody here who's good with dynamite, Schloesser?" my father asked, turning his attention back to the task at hand.

"Nobody's ever good with dynamite, Gallager. You know that. Packers are either mediocre or poor. The decent ones are alive; the poor ones, dead."

"But among those working. There's got to be somebody who stands out."

Schloesser squinted, his gaze moving from my father's chest to his eyes where they settled. Thick, dirty hands pawed at his cheeks. "Me," he said.

"Are you prepared to set the dynamite?"

"If the price is right. It's gonna cost an extra hundred dollars. And you're taking responsibility if we kill those little runts. It's you're responsibility, not mine."

"I can see the wagon," Snowden exclaimed. "Coming at a mighty fast clip."

"Get my pistol, Malachi. And quick too. I've got a bad feeling about this. And Mr. Schloesser. Thanks for your honesty. I want you back here in forty-five minutes with a progress report. I'm going down there to see for myself. I'll know then if you're the right man for the job."

Malachi Snowden helped Harriet and Mabel Dickerson from the wagon. A camp hand took charge of their horse team and led it back along the trail. "Stop at the cabin and unload the wagon," Harriet ordered the hand. "Be very careful because it's filled with medical supplies."

Dad was engaged in an argument with several miners near the adit when Harriet and Mabel approached. He threw a stern glance their way to indicate his irritation, and resumed the heated conversation.

Harriet waited until he was finished then, leading Mabel, stepped forward, planted a kiss on his cheek and, with her hand on his arm, turned him toward Mabel. "There's going to be more work here than I can handle. Mabel's got excellent experience. If there was anyone responsible for saving your life at the wharf it was she."

"And I've already expressed my gratitude, Harriet. Miss Dickerson, thanks for coming to help. The way things are going below we're not going to need either of you. At least not with live bodies."

"How's my patient holding up?" Harriet asked.

Dad threw open his hands to convey that he was coping.

Muckers drove a train of mule-driven ore carts filled with chipped detritus rock behind the ladies. The noise of steel on the rails made it difficult to hear. Men were hollering. Another team of muckers emerged from the mine entrance, pushing a second set of carts by hand.

"Mei Yok's not here, Harriet," my father barked at the ladies. "Lee Shi-tong said she was about to have her baby when the attack occurred. She may have been taken away. Or escaped. The only place I can think of looking is in the redwood forest. She had her honeymoon there ten months ago. It's six miles from here as the crow flies. By track about twice as many. I haven't had time to search. Malachi's sent a friend." Harriet's medical training had taught her the value of retaining her composure under severe stress. "When do you calculate making contact in the mine?"

"No telling. We only have a day, two at most. We'll make it quick or not at all."

Harriet said, "I could look for Mei Yok in the redwoods and be back just about the time you bring the men up. Mabel can stay behind to help in an emergency."

"You can't go alone. The Posse's out there waiting for me to make a mistake."

"I have my .36 caliber and I know how to shoot it," she said and reached under her jacket for a holster and with a series of jerks produced the Dragoon. "Perhaps the Reverend Snowden will accompany me."

"I need him here. I'm not in favor of you going, Harriet. I've got four guards out, twenty-four hours a day. The Posse will be back. It's just a question when they want to strike. There's no use kidding ourselves; several of my new workmen are bound to be spies. The minute you leave the mine word will get out."

"If there's a baby, Mei Yok's going to need help. She can barely speak enough English to ask anyone to give her a hand."

Dad was distracted by a commotion inside the mine. He needed time to mull over the proposition, time he didn't have. "Harriet, you're the most headstrong woman I've ever met. I can't keep you here against your will. It's a free country, though certainly not for those bastards marooned below. In the army, we always sent out scouts and pickets. But here, I'm blind."

He was about to investigate a commotion near the adit when he suddenly turned on Mabel. "Miss Dickerson. We'll need a hospital. Please assemble your equipment in the mine cabin." And to Harriet, he said. "Lee Shi-tong goes with you. He's a good man—smart and tough. Wong once mentioned the north grove of giant sequoias. Look there first. Take warm clothes and some grub from the mess. I want you back here by nightfall tomorrow. Otherwise I'll have to send someone after you and I haven't any got spare hands. If you don't find Mei Yok, come back immediately. Don't look for a needle in a haystack. And stay out of sight."

Harriet surveyed the path leading up to the mine cabin. "You wouldn't have any milk by chance, would you?"

"In a mining camp? Are you out of your mind? We've only got water. And I'm certain some of the boys are brewing beer though they're not supposed to. This isn't a nursery."

"Just thinking ahead. If Mei Yok can't nurse, her baby will need a milk substitute. Starvation kills infants in remote places. I brought medical instruments for a delivery. But no milk."

"You'll have to improvise. Get back here as soon as possible. We're going to need a doctor tomorrow evening. Say, did you ever practice shooting that new Dragoon?"

"Not yet. I'll take a few shots on the way."

"No, don't do that. Shots will attract attention and attention is the last thing you want. Get in and get out as quickly as possible. I want to see you standing here before sundown tomorrow, understand?"

CHAPTER THIRTEEN

Redwoods

The rugged, tree-rooted track to the redwood forest in Calaveras County favored mules over horses and dictated the team Lee Shi-tong hitched to the wagon Harriet had rented at the coach station. As she and Lee Shi-tong left the Heckendom to find Mei Yok, they immediately felt themselves under the watch of sinister eyes. On more than one occasion Harriet spotted the yellow color of human clothing moving through a stand of Douglas fir paralleling the track. While her eyes might have erred, her ears heard the sounds of men traveling through the forest, the snort of a horse with heavy hooves on dry twigs, a muffled human cough, and whistling signals that did not belong to any known species of birds. There was nothing for her to do but grit her teeth and press on, often seeking the assurance found in the wooden stock of her revolver. Several times the thought of returning to the Heckendom crossed her mind, but each time she rejected it. My father already had his hands full and it was essential to keep all his men working on the rescue. Perhaps, she thought, the men following her in the forest hoped to trade on her fears. If so, she was determined not to let them get the better of her.

By the time she and Lee Shi-tong arrived at the redwood grove, all doubt about being followed had vanished from her mind. Nor did she doubt the sinister purpose of those tailing her. Twice she called out in her loudest voice for the men to approach on friendly terms and twice no one accepted her invitation. She thought about appealing to their compassion for a pregnant woman in labor, but knowing how these men feared Chinese children in California, she rejected that idea. If at all possible, it would be best to conceal the purpose of her expedition.

A timeless silence pervaded the Calaveras redwoods as Harriet and Lee Shi-tong turned their mules from the track into the forest of towering trees. A canopy of high branches and leaves cut off sunlight filtering down. Massive sequoia trunks reminded Harriet of columns supporting the Parthenon in Athens. Surrounding forest vegetation—sugar pine, white fir, incense cedar, and ponderosa pine—were mere courtiers to these regal redwoods. Closer to the forest floor, mountain dogwoods and hazelnut vied for space and the scarce light.

The track narrowed into a trail, barely passable for a wagon. Lee Shi-tong was forced to slow down his animals and creep carefully through a graveyard of fallen giants, victims of the saw and ax some twenty years before when drunken, unemployed mountain men had cut down these ancient trees for no other reason than to demonstrate their prowess over nature. Pretty much immune to fire, these fallen redwood trunks lay rotting on the forest floor. In nature's inexorable cycle of regeneration, young saplings had begun to take root around them.

In the northernmost grove, Harriet attempted to locate Mei Yok by firing her Dragoon into the air; the shot echoed for a long time in the stand of trees. She then called Mei Yok's name aloud, encouraging Lee Shi-tong to allay her fears by offering words in Cantonese. When it became obvious that they could barely move in the forest, they packed food and medical supplies and set off on foot to follow narrow deer and bear paths through the trees.

At the first natural parting of this path, they agreed to split up and search different routes, returning to the wagon within two hours. Harriet planned to fire her pistol once if she found Mei Yok, twice if she encountered trouble and needed help. Lee Shi-tong agreed to howl as loudly as possible in Cantonese if he ran into trouble.

A sliver of sunlight glimmered through the canopy as Harriet slogged over ground covered with dried leaves and conifer cones, frequently calling Mei Yok's name. Muffled in the distance and echoed slightly by the surrounding gargantuan trees was Lee Shi-tong's high-pitched voice. Harriet could not shake a nagging sense of futility at searching for Mei Yok in such a large forest, particularly since there was no certainty she was even there. At the same time, trees that rose from the forest floor, towering some 150 feet into the air before their lower branches commingled in the high canopy, enchanted her. From time to time, gray squirrels scampered along the carcasses of downed redwoods, seemingly curious about the intruder.

As they moved in opposite directions, Lee Shi-tong's calls for Mei Yok became softer then stopped altogether. Harriet glanced at a watch, calculating how far she could go before being obliged to turn back. Every three minutes she stopped to listen for a possible response to her calls. The grove's tranquility seduced her into a dreamy disengagement, so silent and ethereal were her surroundings. Was this grove really part of the world she was familiar with? Or was it an antechamber to God's very presence?

At noon songbirds in the midlevel of branches became inordinately quiet. In this silence, Harriet became aware of a peculiar noise. At first it sounded like a chirping but as she strained to hear, it took on qualities of a human moan. Surrounding trees acted like a sounding board, reflecting the same noise from different locations. She knew that in their mating rituals chipmunks and squirrels made odd chirpings. But this was the wrong season for that. Birds sang but did not groan.

Her throat began to feel the strain of continued calling. For the first time she became aware of fatigue in her legs. Unfortunately the odd sound was inconsistent and without rhythm. When she believed she was nearing its source, it suddenly stopped and she was forced to wait. The forest scrambled sounds, undermining her confidence in a mental compass. She advanced in one direction only to hear the sound behind her. And when she backtracked, it sounded as though it were originating from where she had just come. Confusion eroded her patience until she almost stumbled over Mei Yok at the foot of a redwood she had chosen on her honeymoon with Wong to be her gravesite. Her body was coiled in a cavity hewn from the base of the tree and covered with shredded needles and conifer cones. Only the crown of jet-black hair was visible above the edge of a cotton blanket. Harriet fired a shot into the air to alert Lee Shi-tong then dropped to her knees beside Mei Yok.

Carefully she removed the blanket. Mei Yok was naked below the waist. The problem was easily apparent. A portion of an umbilical sack protruded from between her legs. Alone in the forest, she was attempting to give birth but nature had unkindly turned the baby in an unfavorable position. Had the infant come out head first, she might have been successful. But little feet preceded the head, reversing the customary birthing process. The child was stuck in the birth canal. Labor must have started long before and Mei Yok had obviously expended all her strength trying to expel the infant. At some point she had lost consciousness.

Harriet brought her head down over Mei Yok's belly to listen for the baby's heart. Simultaneously she planted fingers on Mei's throat to monitor her pulse. It was very weak, yet to Harriet's surprise, the small heart of the unborn child was beating.

To save mother and child, Harriet was forced to move very fast. There was no time to wash her hands or to prepare her instruments. Her first step was to unravel Mei Yok so that she was lying flat on her back. The next was to work the umbilical sack back from the walls of the vaginal opening in order to get her fingers around the baby. Mei Yok's birth canal was extremely small and there was little room for rotation. To make matters worse, the child had become tangled in the umbilical cord that could easily strangle its air supply.

Experience told Harriet that no matter how fast she worked there was little hope of saving Mei Yok's life. The baby's was even more problematic. Her concentration was broken by Lee Shi-tong's voice calling out for directions.

As soon as he appeared from a stand of white fir, she said, "Mei Yok's giving birth. There's a creek over to the right. Get some water quick. You'll find a tin cup in my pack."

He approached hesitantly, as though he had no right to be in the presence of an unclothed woman, especially another man's wife.

"She's very weak," Harriet said. "I'll be lucky to get this child out in time, if I can get it out at all. Don't stand there, man. Get the cup. Yes, you can come closer."

He inched forward and reached down for her pack, his eyes consciously avoiding Mei Yok's pelvis.

"I'm having trouble maneuvering the baby into position," Harriet gasped in frustration. "Before you go, reach into my bag again and hand me the knife. It's wrapped in clean cloth. Don't touch the blade. I'm going to cut the soft flesh around her vaginal opening to give my fingers more room. It will be bloody. Before you go, talk to Mei Yok in your language. Tell her I'm delivering her baby. Tell her everything will be all right. If you can, make her relax."

Lee Shi-tong dutifully spoke at Mei Yok in Cantonese, but there was no response. He shook his shoulders and repeated an effort to stir her, again without success. With that, he decided to do something constructive and fetch water from the stream.

As soon as he had left, Harriet made incisions in Mei Yok's labia. Blood flowed over her fingers. It had to be painful, but the mother seemed beyond pain. The baby was different. When she could get her fingers around the infant, it felt alive. If only she could turn the baby around.

A few moments later, Lee Shi-tong came running back, the tin cup face down and empty. "Men in trees near creek. I heard them talking. Six maybe seven. They say your name."

Harriet processed this new information while easing the baby's head into position. She wanted to snatch her Dragoon but both her hands were occupied. The infant's crown suddenly peeked through the birth canal. A few moments later, its head exited. Once in the correct position, with the head beyond the now enlarged opening, the final extraction was routine.

The infant entered the world with a healthy cry. It was a boy, drenched in amniotic fluid. A glance at Mei Yok told Harriet that at the very moment a new soul was entering the world another was in the act of departing. Harriet placed the baby on the mother's belly and with the knife cut the umbilical cord, separating the placenta. She didn't have water to bathe the infant and no time to do it anyway. She freed the blanket that had warmed Mei Yok and immediately wrapped it around the newborn.

To Lee Shi-tong, she said, "Quickly now, take this child to the wagon. Move quietly. I'll make noise here and distract those men from the Posse. If they're unfriendly, I've got my revolver. Go immediately to Mr. Gallager. Tell him to send help if he can. I'll stay with Mei Yok."

Lee Shi-tong started to shake when Harriet planted the bundled child in his arms. "Tell them to wash the baby right away. Give him some clean water boiled with sugar. Then get some goat's milk. They've got about a day before this little one will begin sucking for nourishment. Keep the baby warm. If there are women near the camp, give the baby to one of them. They'll know how to care for him."

"You come with me, Missy," Lee Shi-tong protested.

"Mei Yok can't travel and I can't leave her here to die alone. Besides, the Posse men have horses and will overtake our mules. I've got to distract them while you escape. One way or the other, I'll get their attention."

Harriet reached into her bag for the Dragoon then dug deeper for a box of cartridges. About twenty shells—enough to keep the Posse at bay for a long time.

Lee Shi-tong back stepped with apparent trepidation. Harriet was on the ground again, her head no longer between Mei's legs. Her ear was on the patient's chest with her fingers clutching the wrist for confirmation of her pulse. She rocked back on her heels, closed her eyes and breathed heavily, her lips moving in a petition to the Almighty.

She lifted her eyes to find Lee Shi-tong paralyzed where he stood. "Go!" she barked at him with uncompromising severity. "They'll get us all if you don't move your bloody ass now."

Mountain Valley

Lee Shi-tong arrived at the Heckendom after nightfall and immediately took Mei Yok's baby to the headquarters cabin. Cooks outside were broiling venison on open grills and boiling rice in iron pots over their campfires. Inside, maps and diagrams covered every inch of available space, the tables and chairs, the fireplace mantle and two settees against the far wall. There was no place to put the child. Lee Shi-tong felt a sense of urgency in seeking care for the newborn. He ordered the cooks to boil water and to mash softened rice to feed the infant when the time came.

The rescue on level four had just entered its critical phase. In an act of desperation, the miners had set powder charges to blast away at air vents just above Wong and his men. My father was at a temporary command post on level three, overseeing the detonations.

Upon learning of Lee Shi-tong's return, Malachi Snowden came running to the cabin. He scrambled up the wood stairs, howling as he reached the platform. "Where's Dr. Horn?"

"In forest," Lee Shi-tong replied as Snowden burst through the door. "She told me to bring baby back quick. Get help from Meester Gallag'r."

"Is she all right?"

"Bad men in forest. She has gun and bullets."

"Did you hear shots?"

"No."

"Whose baby is this?"

"Mei Yok."

"Is she with Dr. Horn?"

"Mei Yok had big troubles with baby. Dr. Horn told me to wash it then give it water with sugar. I know that China baby eat rice soup."

Malachi quickly sorted through the information from Lee Shi-tong, ordering priorities in his mind. First, he must organize a rescue party to leave for Calaveras as soon as possible. No waiting until sunrise. Second, they'd have to figure out what to do with the baby, though Wong would undoubtedly figure in that decision, if and when he emerged from the mine. Since my father was occupied underground, Malachi took responsibility to act on his behalf. He said to Lee, "I saw a few prostitutes in the gully behind the storehouse. Take the baby to them and promise we'll pay handsomely to care for it. Then come to the head-frame. I'll fetch Gallager from below."

Level three of the Heckendom was hot, crowded, and noisy, its air thick with dust. Miners were advancing in extremely close quarters against face rock, chipping away at a feverish pace. Simultaneously, my father, Schloesser, and two additional sappers were carefully packing the tight air vent leading to level four with explosives and laying out the fuses. Their hope was that the blast would enlarge the conduit enough to thread a small man into the lower level and assess the situation below. Or better yet, large enough for Wong and his men to crawl out themselves, with or without supporting lines. Controlled destruction was what they talked about, but nobody believed it was achievable without a strong streak of luck. Even the most experienced of them could not predict with any accuracy what such a blast might do.

Oil lamps burned at several intervals, but the movement of men crossing their paths created an eerie light. Malachi Snowden elbowed his way through a pack of sweaty bodies toward the air vent, swearing to himself. He knew Father's health was precarious above ground; in the terrible conditions of a mine, they would only deteriorate. Moreover, he had noted Dad's mounting impatience. His system could barely absorb the black coffee he kept drinking to keep himself alert. It would have been far better for his health to remain in the fresh air, but Dad was not the kind of man to shy away from the front lines. As an engineering officer in the Second Pennsylvania, he had seen combat in two major battles in Virginia and participated in five bloody skirmishes in Tennessee. And as the superintendent for Charles Crocker, he was never far from the most dangerous construction. Snowden could not conceive of him topside during the final assault on level four.

"Theo," he called above the din of picks and shovels in a brief, clear sentence. "Harriet's in trouble at Calaveras. Lee Shi-tong says strangers are nearby. They found Mei Yok and Harriet delivered her child. Lee brought the baby back. But Mei Yok is in a bad way, may be dead by now."

My father released a roll of fuse lines and crawled backward to a place where he could see Snowden before exclaiming, "Poor Wong."

"We gotta help Dr. Horn immediately. Lee Shi-tong said he thought those strangers were unfriendly Posse."

That thought set Father thinking hard about priorities. He was a half-hour away from blasting through to Wong. There were ten imperiled men below and one woman among the redwoods, perhaps in trouble, but then perhaps not.

"I can't get away for another hour," he barked in frustration at Snowden.

"Then I'll go alone. Catch up with me when you can."

"You don't know how many men are there. The Posse's probably set an ambush. They're not interested in Harriet. They're using her for bait, to lure us away from the mine. Do you have a weapon?"

"You bet. A Winchester. It's old but I'm mighty good with it."

"Harriet's got a Dragoon and plenty of ammunition. Let's hope it gets dark before the Posse moves against her. She's a clever woman who will know how to hide until daybreak."

"Let's hope there's some compassion in these men."

"You're a man of God, Malachi. Pray for it. I've seen decency in the cruelest of men."

"And I've seen cruelty in the best of them," the minister snapped back.

Sappers working in front of Theo and Snowden inched out of the conduit where they were working. "The charge is ready," Hendrik Schloesser declared a minute later in the self-assured voice of one who performed such tasks routinely. "I say, clear everybody off level three. Better yet, we'd better clear 'em out of the whole goddamn mine. There'll be so much dust nobody will be able to breathe anyway. And if the vent caves in, there won't be anything worth seeing. You can say good-bye to your Chinamen right now."

"I'm going after Harriet," Snowden announced.

The press of events made it impossible for my father to respond. One inclination was to join the churchman, but first he had to wait for the blast results. If it failed, he'd need Malachi at the mine to pay and dismiss the army of workmen so hastily assembled. If it worked, he must supervise the final push to reach Wong and his men.

My father ushered those around him from the face of the new cut in the direction of the main shaft, away from the blast area. Many were seasoned miners who didn't have to be warned about remaining in a dangerous place. From there, they were happy to make their way to the surface.

At the jerrybuilt mine adit, Dad hobbled into the fading light of the evening. A crowd of men, almost the entire rescue team, had gathered in anticipation. He noticed that though these men cared not a whit about Chinamen, they had begun to show signs of bonding with those trapped below. Deep in a dark mine, men couldn't distinguish the shape of a man's eyes or the color of his skin. They shared a common conviction that God had designed men to live on the crust of the earth, not below it. Those who descended below the earth's skin defied nature and survived in the depths not by right but by divine sufferance.

Snowden grabbed Father's shoulder, blocking his passage. "Can't wait any longer. If you need to stay here, then let me go to Dr. Horn."

Dad's body was numb. His bones felt like rubber and his flesh burned with fatigue. "When those charges blow, this operation's nothing but history, my good reverend. One way or the other, somebody's got to stay and pay off the men. They won't wait patiently for me to return before they ransack the place. If they don't get paid, they'll hunt us down and string us up on the first tree. You're absolutely essential here, Malachi. I need you. You understand that? I need you badly. A man of God must talk with Wong. Somebody's got to tell him about Mei Yok. That I refuse to do."

"We're waitin' for your order, Gallager," Schloesser called from beside the adit.

My father's eyes flashed over Snowden for an instant, then back to the German before he snapped, "Then blow it, man. Fire it up. Give us either the Promised Land or the apocalypse."

Three minutes later, a blast reverberated outside the mine. Level one filled immediately with an orange-brown dust that hung suspended in swirling air currents. With a cloth over his nose and mouth, my father was the first to reenter and head for the top cross-cut, followed by muckers who carried torches fed from cans of oil. At each elevation the dust was thicker and slower to clear. Men coughed and hacked. Dirt absorbed the natural lubrication of the eyes and caused painful burning. Excited voices echoed through the vertical shafts. The torches flickered; several guttered out for lack of oxygen.

Father approached the vent leading from level three to level four on legs that felt surprisingly strong. In the best-case scenario, gangue material and loose rock torn by explosives would be scattered on the floor; in the worst, the vent's air passage would be blocked by tons of rock from above.

Smoldering dust cast the scene in a macabre glow. What he saw exceeded his worst expectations. Huge piles of rock completely obliterated the vent. Dad threw his hands up to his forehead, closed his eyes to screen them from this horror, and, for a brief moment, he wondered if it were practical to put his miners and muckers to work against this now-impenetrable wall between them and the miners imprisoned below.

"Tell us where you want to start, Mr. Gallager," a sub-foreman asked from behind.

Dad turned on him. "Looks useless to me."

"Then listen carefully, sir," the foreman shot back. "If my ears don't deceive me I hear a faint tapping behind that rubble. The Chinks are digging at the other side. I'd be a cursed soul in hell if I didn't try moving this rock to help."

"I must be too tired," my father gasped, "but if you hear something, man, then go for it. Let your muckers start from the point nearest the tapping."

They brought seven exhausted, dirty, dehydrated, and sick Chinamen to the surface two hours later. Wong stayed behind to help remove a lad with two broken legs and another with violent convulsions. Three men had perished and were buried by their countrymen in a makeshift cairn on level four.

Last to climb out of the hole was their leader. In open air outside the mine, someone threw a blanket over him to protect against a chilling wind.

My father placed his arm over the Chinaman's shoulder and hugged him close. He was about to tell him about Mei Yok, but held back, preferring to leave this to Reverend Snowden. Instead he announced, "You're a father, partner. They tell me your son's a healthy baby. Any idea what you're going to name him?"

Wong was slurping a cup of water. He lifted his lips from the rim of the cup and smiled a broad and consuming smile. His teeth were covered with grime, but there was animation in his eyes. "Freeman," as though he had already given much thought to the subject. "I was indentured when I came to America. But my son was born under different circumstances. He must always know he's a free man. Call him Freeman, Freeman Wong, that is, if his mother agrees."

"Mei Yok's in the redwood forest. Harriet is with her." Dad said, giving it to him straight and without embellishment, the only way he felt comfortable talking.

Wong's eyes fell to the ground and for a long while he seemed to fold into his own thoughts. His eyes rose to look at my father. "Where? When?" he asked.

"When trouble started here, she must have fled to the redwoods. That's the only place I could think she might be. I was busy here, so Harriet and Lee Shi-tong went searching for her. According to Lee Shi-tong, Harriet delivered your son, but Lee said that when he brought your son here, Mei Yok was in a bad way."

Wong fell back into his thoughts, which my father respected. "I understand," he finally said.

"Now you and your men must wash. Drink, eat, and rest. I want all of you to visit the nurse in the mine cabin. She'll treat everybody until I bring the doctor back."

"Ready to go, Theo?" Malachi Snowden interrupted.

"Got that Winchester you claim to shoot so well?"

"I do. A repeater with plenty of shells."

"Very good, then fetch Lee Shi-tong here and give him your rifle, Malachi. I must have someone here that I can trust. You're our paymaster now. I'm going to have to wire Charley Crocker for more cash to pay all the bonuses we promised. Reporters will probably show up in a day or so. Wong's men need medical attention. See that Mabel Dickerson gets whatever she wants. I'm counting on you to manage things here for me."

To Wong, he said, "Let's pray for Mei Yok. I know how much you love her."

He nodded agreement and bowed slightly. "I brought her to this country sight unseen. Despite your warnings, Theo, she is good for me. I want to see my boy. Then I'm going with you to the redwood trees."

"You're not fit," my father complained.

"Look who's talking! By the looks of you, you're not in much better condition than I am."

"Then you'll have to postpone seeing little Freeman until we get back. We have to get moving right away."

With the rising sun, Lee Shi-tong led Dad and Wong to the site where Freeman was born. There, they were met with a terrifying sight. Eight spent .36 caliber shells were strewn on the ground beside a shallow grave where Mei Yok's body had been hastily buried in conifer dross. Scattered about were scalpels, saws, needles, sinew, dressings, and drugs from Harriet's medical bag. Dad inspected for signs of blood and found none. The spent cartridges proved that the Posse was up to no good. Harriet had obviously put up a fight, but her aim could not have been very good in the dark. Like a pack of wolves on the hunt, men could move through the dark forest with relative impunity, probing from different directions to test how well defended she was and slowly using up her ammunition.

While my father imagined what had happened, Lee Shi-tong circled behind the redwood that served as a headstone for Mei Yok's grave, providing Wong with privacy to grieve for his dead wife. Having been prepared in advance for what he ultimately found, Wong bore Mei Yok's death with resignation. When he was buried in the mine, he was certain he would never again see her or the baby she was carrying. He dropped to his knees beside the grave and recited words in Cantonese, careful not to tarry long, for while his soul mate was dead, there was still a chance that Theo's friend was still alive. It was Lee Shi-tong who found the tin cup he had once tried to fill with water. Farther away Wong discovered broken branches, the beginning of a path made by several people dragging something heavy. Perhaps Harriet.

Father stuffed his pockets with the abandoned medical instruments and drugs then followed this trail. His eyes detected a spot of coagulated blood on a yew branch. And there were others nearby, but spaced at considerable distance.

Lee Shi-tong followed the trail like an Indian scout, his head down, his eyes devouring the path for clues. The trail led over a creek into a neighboring stand of relatively young redwoods. On the far bank, Wong was climbing to higher ground when a voice beckoned him. "Over here. Over here. I'm beside the stout sequoia with the fire scar."

He rushed forward, inspired by Harriet's voice, however weak. She was lying on her back with her legs propped up in a V-shape against the redwood trunk. Her hair was covered with conifer thistles; her clothes, splattered with mud. A petticoat was bunched into a blood-soaked bandage between her legs. Bloody abrasions discolored her cheek and neck.

Dad dashed over and fell to his knees beside her. "She's been shot!" he declared as Wong and Lee Shi-tong arrived.

Her hazel eyes rose to meet his. She was too weak to turn her head and waited until he knelt into view before correcting him, "Shot with semen, not bullets."

"They raped you?" Dad planted his hand on her forehead and leaned far over so he could feel her breath on his cheeks.

"Six of them, at least. One at a time. They hurt me bad. I've been bleeding for hours and have lost a lot of blood. I've tried to stop the flow by lifting my legs."

"I'll get 'em for you, Harriet. I promise. I know how to hunt down the men who did this. Goddamn animals like them always boast. The minute one mentions a word in a saloon, I'll know. I'll bring 'em to you and if you want to shoot their balls off, that's fine with me."

"First things first, Theo. I won't enjoy shooting them if I can't stop this hemorrhaging. Wounds like this generally don't stop on their own. They've got to be sewn up. There was a medical bag where they surrounded me. If they haven't taken it, there should be needles and suture material inside." Her signature dimples signaled a faint smile. "Otherwise, notify my family in Boston, won't you, Theo?"

Wong and Lee Shi-tong stepped back, averting their eyes. Wong said, "Thanks, Dr. Horn, for helping Mei Yok."

"Too late to save her. Is your son all right?"

"They say my boy's fine, thanks to you. But I haven't laid eyes on him yet. You're the problem now?"

"Find my medical bag."

"I've got most of what fell out there in my pockets," Dad said. "I had a hunch we might need it."

"Good, because I'm going to need your help, Theo. They ripped my insides pretty bad. I can't work on myself between my legs. And I haven't got the strength even if I could. I need your hands and your eyes. You've got to suture up the wounds."

"You want me to sew you up?"

"Why not?"

"I'm an engineer not a doctor. I've never done anything like this. Besides, it's improper."

"I worked on your genitals, Theo. Now it's time for you to work on mine."

"This isn't the same thing."

"I'm no different from half the human beings on this planet."

"I wouldn't know where to start."

"I'll talk you through it, step by step. Wong, you and Lee Shi-tong, get some water. Boil it if you can. Then find anything that reflects like a mirror. I'll be able to see what's happening and guide Theo."

To my father, she said, "This isn't difficult. I know you can sew your clothing, so you can stitch flesh. Have Lee Shi-tong boil the instruments. You must get your hands clean, real clean. Use salt from your saddlebags if there's nothing more pungent. You'll have to help me into position. Use my petticoat for a sheet. There was a vial of morphine in my medical bag. I'm going to need it."

My father's brain went into overload. He would rather have faced a gang of snarling, hungry wolves than do this. Or enter a dangerous mine and light a fuse. Or swim out into the bay and rescue a bunch of hapless Chinese workers. For sheer terror, nothing compared to what was being asked of him now. He found his hands shaking and blood rushing to his head. For an instant he thought he might faint.

Harriet urged him not to delay. The loss of blood enervated her strength and increased the danger that she would go into shock. Lee

Shi-tong returned from his horse with a flat machete blade to use as a mirror, but its steel siding produced too little reflection to be useful. Boiled water was easier to provide. Harriet conditioned herself for extreme pain by sniffing from the vial of morphine. Dad fussed over a flat place to arrange her blood-soaked petticoat for bedding. When he lifted her onto it, her pelvis was completely exposed. Lee Shi-tong and Wong discreetly turned away.

During the final preparations, Harriet noticed the two Chinese standing off to the side. "You'll have to look sooner or later. I'm no different from a Chinese woman. Don't just stand there. Theo's going to need help. Wash your hands in hot water. Stay close." She adjusted her legs, grimacing with pain.

My father inhaled a long breath and held it, dropped his head to his breast, then slowly lifted his eyes to focus on her pelvis where coagulated blood stuck to her dark pubic hair. Fresh blood continued to ooze slowly from the wounds.

Her voice was weak and raspy. "Describe to me exactly what you see. How many tears on the labia?"

Father ran his eyes on both sides of the orifice, counting three rips.

"What about the fleshy hood over the clitoris, at the very top?"

"I don't see any tearing."

"That's good. Tell Wong to kneel beside you. Take the cleanest cloth you have and soak it in the boiled water. Then clean off the wounds, one small area at a time. Don't worry about hurting me."

Wong ripped a portion of the cotton petticoat and plunged it into water he had boiled in an all-purpose pot that accompanied every saddle kit.

"Now thread the suture through the eye of the needle and dip the point into the water. Hold it there until you're ready to sew."

Dad's powerful fingers, better accustomed to seizing an ax handle or a hammer, were unsteady. He relaxed himself by taking deep breaths. When his nerves steadied, his fingers began to respond. His uneasiness with working in the private region of a dignified woman waned as he trained his eyes upon the needle and suture. Beside him, the Chinamen also seemed to overcome their discomfort and slipped into supportive roles.

"When you're ready, let's first sew the tear on my left side," Harriet said calmly as though she were a doctor instructing a medical student.

"You'll bind the tissue from the inner leg out along the large lip. The needle's curved, so it will come out on the side opposite the tear, then pull tight, both sides should knit together. Just pretend you're sewing clothes, Theo. Neat, small stitches. I may wince, but don't worry about that. You didn't die when I worked on you at the Seafarer's Hospital, and I'm not going to die when you stick a needle into me."

For my father, the first stitch was the most difficult. It hurt him to see her grimace with pain. After inserting the needle on the opposite side of the labia, he was pleased to find the torn skin bind together. As the two lips bonded, less blood oozed from the wound. Her pain seemed diminished with each new stitch. That made it easier to concentrate on suturing. Each insertion was more confidently located. The complete closure of the first tear produced a sense of elation among the operating team. Not only could it be done, but together they had done it.

Harriet was conscious enough to cut short the celebration. There was more work to be done, particularly on another tear farther forward. Because this smaller rip provided less room to insert the needle, Dad was forced to enter surface muscle in order to tie it together. That one, Harriet told them, was likely to leave a lasting scar. The third and last gash at the rear was the longest, but for physiological reasons that Harriet didn't understand, it bled less. Experience gave my father more confidence. He was surprised that the largest rupture took the least time to suture.

When it was over, Harriet held onto Dad's hand. She was conscious, but still writhing in pain. She had taken all the morphine my father had found at the rape scene. The excruciating pain between her legs was something she had no alternative but to suffer.

"Ride back to the mine," my father ordered Lee Shi-tong. "Get a wagon. This woman can't travel by horse. And bring along some bedding to make her comfortable. We'll take her directly to the clinic in Copperopolis. I want a real doctor looking at this. A doctor must take out these stitches and redo it properly. And take Reverend Snowden's Winchester. If anybody tries to stop you, shoot first. You may not get a second chance."

It was nearing noon when Harriet first stirred. She opened her eyes and tried to move but pain forced her to reconsider.

Dad said in a low whisper near her ear, "Lee Shi-tong should be back soon with a wagon. I'm taking you to the clinic in Copperopolis. A physician visits there every other day."

"Thanks, Theo," she said. "I never had such a good medical student. Is Wong still around?"

"I'm here," he answered, bending over to speak in a hushed voice.

"I'm sorry about Mei Yok. If only I had arrived earlier. I buried her where she lay."

A slight smile emerged on Wong's cheeks, a smile Harriet did not see. "That's the right tree, the one she chose on our honeymoon. Before we leave, I'll make repairs on the grave. In a few days I'll come back to make it permanent."

"I counted eight cartridges at her grave," my father said. "You know who the men were?"

"It was dark. I couldn't see much. They were strangers. One was called Jake. The other, Louis. They came at me from all sides."

"Whose blood did I see on the trail here?"

"I shot one in the buttocks. Before they raped me, they insisted I give him medical attention. The bullet went clean through his rump, so there was nothing to do but stop the bleeding and bandage him. Would you believe it, for my help he joined his friends and raped me? I think he was number five, but it was so awful I didn't pay attention."

"You must be bitter as hell."

"You bet I am. If I could shoot the bastards I'd make sure their wounds got infected. One part of me wants to hurt them real bad. But that isn't likely to happen, so I'm not going to torture myself with thoughts of revenge. Rape is horrible, Theo, but it isn't the end of the world. I could milk this terror for all its worth among women in this state. I could petition Sacramento to punish the bastards who rape women. But while I was praying for someone like you to come and help me, I made a pledge to God. If I survived, I wouldn't let this ruin my life. To become a perennial victim and feel sorry for myself would only compound the tragedy. I promised God I wouldn't do that, and I won't."

Dad leaned over her face and brushed away hair that had fallen into her eyes. He then planted a kiss on her cheek. "You're quite a woman, Harriet. You don't have to lift a finger against the Posse. I'll get them for you. And that's a promise. The only way I won't catch them is if they leave the state, and I doubt they will."

She remained silent for a long time before speaking very slowly. "Thanks, Theo, but I wouldn't want you shooting innocent men. It was dark. I can't identify a single one. Wong's okay. His child is all right. You're here. It's time to count our blessings."

"What if you get pregnant?"

"It's the wrong time of the month," she said. "This is my business, remember, and I know my cycle. I can't get pregnant for at least ten more days."

After two days in the hospital at Copperopolis, Father installed little Freeman Wong and Harriet in a convalescent home where they employed a wet nurse for the newborn. Harriet agreed with Dad and Wong that the less the public learned about the attack on the mine and the subsequent rape the better. How naive they were.

Though my father pleaded with Sam Clemens not to write about the tragedy, he penned four articles for the *Territorial Enterpriser* that in syndication circulated up and down the state as well as in Chicago and on the Eastern Seaboard. A battalion of aggressive reporters descended on the mine, looking for follow-up stories. Mark Twain's final column, Rape in the Towering Trees, titillated the nation's prurient interests. Curious readers from coast to coast demanded to know details of how a female surgeon from San Francisco was so brutally abused and what law enforcement officers planned to do about it. Anybody familiar with the way things worked in the gold country knew that the sheriff would make a preliminary inquiry then prolong an investigation until the public lost interest. The sheriff wasn't about to challenge local citizens who had placed the badge on his chest.

Harriet played the role of a suffering victim poorly. Compassion from feminist groups meant little to her. The self-righteous chivalry of men even less. What she wanted was punishment for the rapists, but that, she was realistic enough to understand, was out of reach.

With Wong's permission, she moved little Freeman and his wet nurse into a Stockton sanitarium to hide them until some new injustice would grab the public's attention.

Meanwhile Malachi Snowden helped Wong and my father settle their debts. During the wild hours of rescue, no one had paid much attention to the vast inventory of food, equipment, and services rented or purchased, on the spot and with little or no price controls. The bills for these necessities far exceeded Dad's ability to pay from Charles Crocker's eight thousand-dollar advance. Snowden's last function in camp was to account for everything in a ledger book and have Dad execute promissory notes for all unpaid debts.

After conducting memorial ceremonies for Mei Yok and the three Chinese miners buried in the mine, Reverend Snowden recited an emotional good-bye to the Heckendom. An hour later, he set out to rejoin his wife and family in Mokelumne Hill. The following day the remainder of Wong's original mining crew left for the Sacramento Valley in hopes of finding work on the river levees.

Within a few short hours, there were no men left in the once-bustling camp. Mine machinery lay dormant, inviting rust and decay. A single gray squirrel, delighting in his unexpected solitude, explored what so many humans had left behind. Wong and my father fell into a silent, gloomy mood. Neither had the strength nor the inclination to tend to numerous chores. They lolled away daylight hours bathing in water heated by wood stoves. Neither mentioned the uncertain future. They retired shortly after sundown and slept until sunrise. There was plenty of uneaten food left from the stocks hastily purchased by Snowden. Dad and Wong consumed gargantuan quantities of venison and bread. They agreed that as soon as they felt strong enough, they would visit Harriet and Freeman. Their only happy conversation was talk of Freeman Wong.

Three days later they traveled by wagon to Stockton. Wong was tickled to hold Freeman in his arms and rub his nose against the baby's cheek. The child's bright eyes and buoyant smile restored his father's spirits. Harriet confirmed that the infant had an easygoing nature, a surprising gift considering his touch-and-go fight for life at birth.

"He looks like his mother," Wong said. "How sad that she never saw him."

My father noted the Chinaman's syntax and thought he now spoke English better than most mountain men, certainly better than most miners. He left him to play with his child and stepped close to the wicker chair where Harriet was resting and said, "Sorry about all the newspaper coverage."

"So am I, Theo," she replied. "People who write stories in the papers haven't the foggiest idea about what really happened in the redwood forest. They write fiction, not fact. But I guess that really doesn't matter, now does it?"

My father then said, "Several feminist groups in San Francisco have anointed you their hero."

"It doesn't suit me. If the truth be known, I'm no heroine. I didn't do anything besides deliver little Freeman and get myself raped."

Dad's hand rested on her shoulder. "I'm worried about your health."

She looked up and planted her hand atop his. "Women's bottoms heal pretty fast, probably because they must be ready for childbirth. And you, Theo, any pains in your groin?"

"To tell the truth, I was so tired I became almost numb to everything below my waist."

"Any plumbing problems?"

"I'm getting better."

Harriet adjusted her position so that she had a full view of his face. "I don't know if I thanked you for saving my life. I probably wouldn't have survived if you hadn't come along. I couldn't stop the bleeding myself."

He squeezed tenderly. "I could say the same about you at Seafarer's Hospital."

She rose from the chair and planted her hands on both Dad's upper arms. Dimples in her cheeks deepened as she let a slow, inviting grin spread across her lips, revealing her broad, well-proportioned teeth. "A few days ago I used a mirror to observe your sutures. You weren't bad for an amateur. The doctor who examined me was impressed."

"I don't know what to say, Harriet. Truth is I can't believe I did it. When I try to conjure up what happened, my mind goes blank. Blank! I can't recall a damn thing. It's almost as if I wasn't there."

After lunch, Freeman's wet nurse came to fetch the child. Harriet, Wong, and my father sat in a French garden to watch the feeding. Wong gleamed with pride and hovered over the suckling baby. Harriet and my father remained on a garden bench some distance away, absorbing the warm afternoon sun and speaking only intermittently.

Dad eventually said, "From here, I'm taking Wong back to the redwood forest. He wants to work on Mei Yok's grave. He keeps talking about a pledge they made to each other. It was something religious I don't understand. He's got definite ideas about where the grave should be placed." He paused as though uncertain whether or not to ask a question. "Do you feel well enough to come with us?"

She shook her head. No.

"Sorry, I shouldn't have asked. If I were you, I would never want to return."

"I have recurring nightmares. Tall men stand over me like those giant trees. I'm trying to purge that image from my memory, but it keeps returning."

He took her hand in his and held it on her lap, rubbing tenderly the coarse skin along the knuckles. "Sorry, Harriet. You must be furious. I promised you, I'll get those bastards and bring them to you on their knees. One by one."

She placed her free hand on top of his, massaging the protruding veins below his wrist. "Vengeance isn't the answer, Theo. It will only embitter me. I must walk away from this and blot it out of my mind. I'm prepared to let God do the punishing."

"You're the strongest woman I've ever known."

"Not strong really. Perhaps I'm just practical. When I think about getting gang raped, I can't escape several facts. First, I could have bled to death in the forest, but thanks to you, I didn't." She paused to let Dad absorb her indebtedness then lowered her voice, hesitating over the choice of words. "The second fact is that not only didn't I lose my life in the forest, I didn't lose my virginity either. I was never a sleep-around girl, mind you, but I want you to know I've never been the virginal type. Long ago I decided not to marry, so why pretend to be chaste and turn away good lovers?"

A prolonged silence hung between them until it was eventually broken by Harriet. "I debated whether I should tell you that. Maybe you'll think less of me; well, that's up to you. I don't want secrets between us, Theo. And while we're on the subject, there's one last fact I have to mention. I didn't lose any vital organs. All I lost was my pride, and pride is within my power to restore. I'm absolutely determined to do just that. In a few weeks, I'm returning to San Francisco. I want to get back to my practice. I intend to put this matter out of my mind by doing what I do best."

Father wanted to say something, but words stuck in his throat and he could not manage a single coherent phrase.

She knew he was struggling and made it easier by asking, "And how about you? What are you and Wong going to do now?"

"Well," he said, happy to switch to a subject less fraught with emotion. "We haven't got many alternatives. Damage from the blasts is extensive. Wong's crew has left. And we've spent all Crocker's money. My lumber business is not only broke, but deep in debt. Wong thinks he's discovered a vein on level four, but I'm not going down to get it. If he wants to try, he's on his own. I've told him a hundred times, it doesn't make any difference whether he strikes a vein or not because white men in these parts won't let a Chinaman get rich."

"Does he understand that?"

"He didn't before. Maybe he does now."

When the baby fell asleep, Wong found Harriet on the sanitarium terrace and gazed out with her toward the Sacramento River in the distance. Dad was dozing in a garden chair nearby.

Wong said to her, "If you had not come, Freeman would have died. I appreciate what you did for Mei Yok. And what you've done for Freeman and me."

"Wong," she said after a moment's reflection, "I've been thinking about what will happen when I'm strong enough to leave here. If you want, I'll take Freeman to San Francisco. He and the wet nurse can stay at my home until you come for him. You can live with us too if you want. There's plenty of room. I'm sure we can find a job for you in the city."

He looked surprised. "You'd do that for me, Dr. Horn?"

"I never thought much about having an infant around, but I'm finding it more appealing than I imagined. Freeman has aroused in me the maternal instincts I didn't want to acknowledge. You can stay as long as you want."

"You're very generous."

"I'm no saint. I have my motives."

He looked puzzled.

With her finger she pointed to my father dozing in the wicker chair. "That's my motive, Wong. That man over there. I'm fond of you and your son. But above all, I'm a practical woman. As long as you stay with me, he'll come to visit. Otherwise, other ladies will distract him. Take care of him for me, will you? He has a knack for getting into trouble while watching out for others. Somebody's got to look after him."

"Nobody tames a wild horse like Theo. Not even you, Dr. Horn."

At that moment, Dad woke up, embarrassed at having dozed off. He stood up and approached them.

"We were just talking about you," Wong said.

"I get the willies when people talk about me."

"Well, don't," Harriet interjected. "We agreed that sometimes you're a grumpy pain-in-the-ass. Most of the time you're just a lovable sonavabitch."

The redwood forest provided a solemn setting as Wong and my father approached Mei Yok's grave. Over the long years the giant sequoia had been silent witnesses to much history. The death of a Chinese mother and the gang rape of a woman were not the last of what they would see. A crisp autumn breeze hissed through the higher branches with a crackling sound. Wong and my father marched toward the shallow mound of nestles and conifer cones Harriet had piled above Mei Yok's body. There were signs that a predator, perhaps a badger, a marmot, or a silver wolf, had nosed into the nestles looking for food. The creature had evidently smelled death and turned to other prey.

Wong knelt beside the grave while Dad hung back. The Chinaman was not surprised that his wife had fled here. It was as if it were ordained between them. When Wong spoke from his knees, my father understood more. "This is not the right tree. Mei Yok chose that one over there for her grave. And mine, the large one facing it. We wanted the branches to touch. She must have become confused in the dark. Is it right for me to move her, Theo?" He thought about that for some time. "How important is it that she be buried in a particular tree?"

"She once chose it herself."

"Her body's decayed, Wong. If you insist, we can move it, but it won't be pleasant. We can construct a more substantial grave here."

Wong stood up and pivoted around on the balls of his feet to survey the site. He stepped away for a better angle and eventually called to my father. "That one there. See how its branches touch with this one. If Mei Yok stays here, then I'll take that one. It's not as large as my original choice, but tall enough." He pointed with his arm. "You see, Theo. I want to rest under the roots of that one."

Dad was confused until Wong explained. "If I die, bring Freeman here. Help him to bury me in the roots of this tree. Show him where his mother is buried. Ask him to come here from time to time to light incense for both of us, but don't insist. Make it a request only. He shouldn't come if he doesn't want to."

"Sure, pal."

My father threw an arm around Wong's shoulder and gave him a brotherly hug. "But I suspect you'll grow old with Freeman. Bring him here yourself."

"Let's make Mei Yok's grave stronger."

"There's enough timber on the ground to build a mausoleum. It'll last long enough for the ground to absorb her bones."

"Then she'll be lifted through the trunk into the branches," Wong added.

After they had built a substantial housing over the new grave, packed the niches with mud and stones from the creek, my father and Wong led their mules through the woods on foot.

"Thanks, Theo," Wong said. "I mean, for saving my boy. I don't know how you knew to send Harriet here."

"I read your faces when I first met Mei Yok. I asked if you had come directly from Frisco, and you told me you wanted her to see these trees. I remembered them from the first time we came to test nitroglycerin. With Crocker and that terrible Scotsman, MacGreggor. You told Crocker and me how old these monsters are. We didn't believe you."

"But I was right, wasn't I?"

Dad pouted. "Old yes. But not quite as old as you thought."

That remark touched off a vociferous argument.

CHAPTER FOURTEEN

Tamalpais

The mining camp was deserted when my father and Wong returned to shut down the property and mull over the future, acknowledging that without money starting again would be futile, despite the vein discovered on level four. Dad recognized a sea change in Wong's mood. Days trapped inside the mine coupled with the loss of his wife had not only sapped his physical strength, but drained the perennial optimism from him. Complacency now dulled the sparkle in his eyes and a monotone softened the crisp certitude in his voice. From this withdrawal, Father concluded that his partner had finally accepted the limitations on what a Chinaman might hope to achieve in a white man's country.

They drew humor from an observation that Charley Crocker believed the Heckendom to be a *borasca* mine, despite Wong's instincts about the presence of gold deep within. If they could convince a buyer that a profitable vein existed below tons of rubble, they might satisfy at least a portion of their debts. If not, then the mine would remain little more than what it was when they had taken possession of it a year before. Much time and sweat had been lost. Far from bringing prosperity and happiness, Crocker's gift to them had become a source of death and impoverishment.

Together they worked in silence, performing symbolic death rites by destroying the mine's entrance with a series of blasts to prevent unauthorized scavengers from entering. Next they boarded up the old head-frame and burned down what was left of the already crumbling adit, turning the old Heckendom into a ghost.

When the hour to leave finally arrived, dark thunderclouds overhead threatened to drench them, but, responding to what they felt to be heavenly pity, refrained from actually raining. They stood gloomily outside the cabin and surveyed their camp for the last time. Neither spoke about their shattered dream. Dad climbed onto a wagon loaded with personal belongings and took the reins, waiting for the Chinaman to join him. Wong's eyes absorbed visual memories, as though certain he would never see this place again.

"I still want you as a partner in the lumber business," my father reminded Wong as they turned in the direction of the track leading toward what was left of the once-thriving mining town of Arnold. "Fifty-fifty. We'll build a house in Eureka or Arcadia and you can raise little Freeman there. We're certain to make more money than in this place."

Wong said nothing, and my father let him mull over his own thoughts. They had passed the mine track and were on the road when Wong spoke again. "Mr. Crocker made us partners at the Heckendom. The partnership you're offering is different. Theo, I must be realistic about who I am. Nothing more than a coolie laborer. I'm flattered by your offer. White men don't take Chinamen for partners."

"I can't think of a better man than you, friend. And there are plenty of white men I wouldn't partner with, even if they gave me sixty percent interest. You're the only one I want."

"I can't, Theo. I'm going to accept Dr. Horn's offer to stay with her awhile in Frisco. I must find a way to bring up Freeman. We have some money left, you know."

Dad pivoted in the seat and glanced over in surprise. Adversity had obviously affected Wong's mind. Not only were they flat broke, but they had piles of debt that might never get paid off, even with the best of intentions.

"Remember, I told you that I hit a vein on level four. Five ounces per ton, I reckoned. What we took to the surface, we milled. I sold the dust in San Andreas. It amounts to twelve thousand six hundred dollars and it's all deposited at the Wells Fargo Express. I thought it wise not to put the account in my own name, so I placed it under yours. Half belongs to you; half to me."

My father's eyes grew large and his cheeks flushed. "Jesus, Wong! You're goddamn amazing! What more reason for me to want you as a partner? That money could build a lot of timber roads, pay a lot of salaries. That's a helluva start!"

"Maybe for you, but not for me. I won't cut down those old trees. I just can't. Redwoods in Humboldt are cousins of the giant sequoias here. Mei Yok's spirit now rests in one of them. If I cut a relative, her tree will be angry with her spirit. I can't cut redwoods in Humboldt or anywhere else. You're stronger than I am, Theo. You do it, but not me. I have over six thousand dollars to invest. People in Chinatown may think I'm nothing but a mountain man now, but I'll show them. I can learn to be a city man. I like business. Mr. Crocker has told me he would help. Besides, the change will be good. Certainly for Freeman."

Father decided not to argue. In time Wong might reconsider. If nothing else, a few days in the noise and squalor of the city were bound to change his opinion about urban life.

After Harriet recuperated, she returned to San Francisco with young Freeman and, a few weeks later, Wong accepted her invitation to stay in her home on Laguna Street. Dad also returned there to complete his recovery. The first opportunity he had to steal away from her hospitality, he met with Crocker who, like Stanford and Hopkins, had moved from Sacramento to San Francisco to reap some of the financial rewards now that the United States was joined from coast to coast by his railroad. Dad found his former employer in his new, extremely opulent office on Third Street in San Francisco, near Townsend. Crocker had a busy schedule but had made time to see my father.

There was not much that happened in California that the old railroad magnate didn't hear about, and events at the Heckendom were no exception. He appeared unimpressed with the rescue operation Dad and the Reverend Snowden had mounted. Because he had spent the entire down payment for timber roads in Humboldt County on rescuing the Chinese from the Heckendom, Dad was uneasy about bringing up the subject. Crocker possessed the sharp instincts of hunting carnivore and just sat silently at his desk, cleaning his fingernails with a silver pick and depositing the residue on a sheet of white paper before him.

My father had no alternative but to introduce the unpleasant question of the spent down payment. "There wasn't time to consult you about money for this operation," Dad said while sitting in a chair opposite Crocker's enormous mahogany desk, strewn with piles of account papers. Stale cigar smoke hung thick in the air.

Without lifting his eyes, Crocker replied, "So, my eight thousand's gone and, no doubt, you've come for more."

"I came to tell you how I spent the money. It's gone and I don't expect you to replace your investment. You still have twelve percent of the partnership in the Humboldt County Timber Company. You don't have to add a single penny more. When I start making money, you'll receive the first distribution. The fact is Wong removed some gold out of the old Heckendom before it was sabotaged. My share is six thousand, three hundred. I intend to put all those funds to work on roads. I'll begin modestly and build the business slowly. You have every right to be annoyed with me."

Crocker rose from his seat and angled from behind the desk, then planted his heavy rump on the top, directly in front of my father. "When I heard what you did, Theo, I was hot as a branding iron. I trusted you. I didn't attach strings to my money and I was convinced that you blew it. It was a good thing you weren't here to receive a tongue-lashing. But over the past month I must have gotten soft. The more I thought about it, the more I began to think that you made the right decision. It took money to free Wong and his compatriots. No one mounts an operation like the one you did on promises alone. Nothing but cold cash would have produced the manpower you needed on short notice. I don't want you to repeat what I'm gonna say cause if you do I'm gonna swear Theo Gallager's a malicious liar. But the truth is, Theo, I'm delighted you spent the money on Wong. In a way, everything you see here goes back to that incorrigible Chinaman. The Central Pacific. This office. My home. All the investments I've made since then. And yes, of course, the mountains of things Mary's purchased to clutter up her life. You know better than I that we would never have gotten out of the Sierra without Wong and his countrymen and their indefatigable energy. During the winter of '68 we were worse than insolvent, borrowing from Peter to pay Paul. I'm not saying the track would never have been completed, but certainly not by me, Leland, Mark, and Collis. Old Charley here was broker than a hobo on the rails. Another month stuck in the mountains and my venerable partners would have turned on me like lions in a Roman arena."

Crocker threw an unexpected hand in Dad's direction. "You did a good job at the Heckendom. I wouldn't have been as noble as you. Or as able. You're gonna need some more cash to add to your six thousand. I'll have my secretary advance whatever you want. Remember: Don't be stingy. You can't run a successful business without spending money. And lots of it. I intend to make a call on Wong and Dr. Horn as soon as I can. I want to take a gift to Wong's kid. What's his name?"

"Freeman."

"That's an odd name for a Chinaman."

My father joined Crocker on his feet as they stepped toward the door, arms wrapped around each other. Dad said, "Wong arrived in California indentured. His son was born a free man. You might have forgotten, Mr. Crocker, but you were the one who paid off his servitude pledge after Cape Horn."

"Did I now? I'm forgetting details like that these days. But I must say how much I like the idea anyway."

Dad gave an affectionate tug on Crocker's soft midsection. "Don't tell me you're losing your memory. You've got an elephant's memory for numbers."

He nodded his head. "Yes, sir. Numbers have always been easy for me."

"Wong hasn't forgotten what you did for him, and never will. Gratitude comes naturally to him."

At the door Crocker restrained my father for a final question. "Doctor Horn. Fine woman, Theo. Very fine woman. You got any intentions? I mean, the settlingdown kind?"

Dad blushed, dropped his chin, and pouted. "It's complicated. She's better than a fine woman, Mr. Crocker. Better than you know. But she's also fiercely independent. I don't think the thought of marriage crossed her mind. But if it did, she'd be interested in having a family."

"You'd make a mighty fine father."

His eyes dropped before rising to meet Crocker's. "You've forgotten what happened to me on the bay. I'm only half a man these days. With the organs I have left, there's no way I can become a father."

Crocker planted an uncomfortable double pat on the top of the shoulder. A long pause elapsed in which he just grunted, unable to make a fitting response. "Well now, well, after you've been in Humboldt, come back and report to me. If additional capital will make a difference, don't be shy. It's my business too, remember. Never saw an undercapitalized business succeed, that is, with one exception—the Central Pacific."

The Kalamath River

From February to April, Father surveyed a grid for timber roads to the Kalamath River where logs could be floated downstream and milled. During those months he made a preliminary selection of old-growth redwoods for cutting and labored over details pertaining to the complex operation of moving timber over difficult terrain. Even after the trees had been milled, transporting finished lumber to market on coastal scows was a formidable task. The business could fail at any of its numerous choke points and Dad was determined not to let that happen.

In mid-April at Easter, his lumbermen left the forest for a fortnight to rekindle connections with what families they had. Dad took the opportunity to visit with the only family he knew on the West Coast-- Wong, Freeman, and Harriet.

Since Chinese guests, regardless of their social or economic status, were seldom invited to the homes of white people in the city, Harriet hosted Easter dinner in her house, careful not to invite friends so that Wong and little Freeman could sit at the table and enjoy the feast as social equals. She was radiant in a forest-green taffeta dress that offset the flame-colored red of her hair, with a bone brooch necklace that dropped into a generous cleavage. She placed Freeman's crib beside the table so he could be present while they ate. At dinner they politely avoided talking about the Heckendom, studded as it was with so many bitter memories.

"I love having a baby in the house," Harriet confided to my father after Wong had taken his son upstairs to put him to sleep. "But I fear Wong will take him from here soon. As far as I'm concerned, they can stay as long as they want. But this is no life for them. When the door's closed and I don't have visitors, Wong is free to do whatever he wants. But in public he insists on playing the game and acting as if he were a servant or cook. I believe for my sake. I've told him not to fear the rumors. They never bothered me in the past and they won't get to me now. He won't say so to my face, but I know he detests the charade, and I don't blame him one iota. Diego tells me he's been looking for a home in Chinatown because he wants Freeman to know other Chinese children. And he wants him to speak Cantonese. There's talk of eventually sending Freeman to China for some additional schooling."

Dad interrupted, "Funny, I never thought of you in a domestic role. When I think of you, Harriet, it's at the hospital. In a white medical smock. With patients flocking around. Is your practice back to normal?"

"More or less. But it's even more unpleasant than in the past. Word spread how I was gang raped in the mountains. My male counterparts have trouble thinking of me as a victim. They want to believe that somehow I enticed the rapists to do their dirty business, which only confirms what they already suspected—that I'm a woman of loose morals. They treat me as spoiled fruit. In the past, their wives never invited me to their homes but were at least cordial when we were introduced at social affairs. Since the rape, they will barely speak with me. I tried inviting them for tea, but they made excuses. I'm not sure when this will change, if ever."

"Sounds terrible. That's why I hate city life, Harriet. This town is full of phonies and hypocrites. I'd love to explain to those bastards what you really did in the forest."

"Thanks, but I don't think they're interested in the truth."

The couple strolled into the sitting room where gifts were stacked on a side table. "Mostly for Freeman," she said, locking my father's arm close to her side as if she feared he would suddenly disappear. Diego placed a silver tray with coffee on a low table. She bent over and poured, her bone medallion dangling from her long, thin neck.

My father eased back into the cushioned sofa and studied her. "Has the horror begun to fade? I must say I really expected you to break down, but I don't think you ever have."

She smiled. "Thanks for asking. The truth is that I still have nightmares. When I relax and let my mind go, terrible images creep in. That's why I try to keep busy. I can still hear the breathing of those men on top of me, smell the tobacco on their breath and feel their sweaty bodies. There's still residual soreness between my legs, though when it hurts, I'm reminded of the best mountain surgeon a girl could wish for. I hate those men who did it to me, Theo. You're the only one in the world I can tell how much I really hate them."

He moved from the sofa to take a seat beside her, where he whispered. "So what do you do with all this hate?"

The hardness in her features faded and the blush of an emerging smile punctuated the dimples in her cheeks. "You want to know the truth, Theo? The real truth? The no bullshit truth?"

Of course. That's why I asked."

The smile broadened and she cocked her head in a girlish manner. "When hate burns inside and I feel ready to explode, I conjure a mental image of *you*. I'm not sure why, but when you're in my thoughts the anger subsides. How can I hate men when there are gentle people like you? I've never seen you vengeful. You've shown me that there are better ways to live on this planet than with hatred. It's your noblest virtue, you know."

He blanched. After a few long seconds, he said, "Harriet, I'm always speechless around you."

"Happy Easter," Wong declared, poking his nose through a crack in the door to warn of his entry.

"And a very happy holiday to you too, Wong," Harriet said, recovering quickly. She stood up, stretching her long arms in Wong's direction to guide him to the sofa for coffee, which he had begun to enjoy more than tea.

For the holiday, they exchanged gifts. Dad had brought Harriet a large, flowering redwood burr that could sit on her coffee table and flower throughout the year. She had a sheepskin parka made especially for him. Wong received a business suit and a pair of city shoes. For my father, Wong had purchased in Chinatown an ivory statue of Hotai, the laughing god whose fat belly Chinese folks were accustomed to rubbing for good luck. And for Harriet, he bought a dashing Chinese turquoise gown studded with sequins. A pile of toys awaited little Freeman in the morning. They drank brandy, laughed and sang mountain songs until well after midnight.

There was never an Easter as joyous as the one in 1871. There were other good times and also some bad times. But never was the bonding among these three so complete and their happiness in each other's company so fulfilling.

Easter day, Wong remained at home tending to his son while the nurse took the day off. Harriet rose at the crack of dawn, packed a picnic lunch, and stuffed a canvas bag with camping gear. Wong was already dressed and boiling water in the kitchen for coffee.

In the guest room, Harriet leaned far over Father's shoulder and woke him with a kiss on the cheek. "It's a special day together, Theo," she whispered. "An outing, to my favorite place. We'll walk and ride and if we want we'll come back after sundown. If not, we'll return tomorrow.

Let's let Wong run things here. He's the most capable father I've seen in all my years of delivering babies."

Dad's head was still spinning from the evening's brandy. He was curious about her plan for the day, yet enjoyed the thought of being alone with her. After breakfast with Wong, a buggy transported them to Meiggs Wharf at the foot of Powell Street. An hour later they were aboard a paddle-wheel ferry headed past Alcatraz Island to the Village of Sausalito, known for its herring fishery. A crisp spring breeze blew whitecaps over the water and dusted them with a salty spray. Sheltered from the wind on the leeward deck, they basked in the warm April sun that reflected off the vessel's white paint. Large gray and white gulls swooped down to ride air currents above the stern and snatching in midair table scraps that passengers tossed overboard.

Harriet, now dressed in riding pants, had arranged to rent a pair of saddle horses for the day and, after tying her camp bag on one horse and the picnic lunch on the other, led them along a trail to the valley mill. They rode westward, on a logging trail through coastal chaparral and manzanita. A thick, smoke-like morning fog clung close to the mountains and burned off as the sun rose in the midmorning sky. A salty scent from the Pacific Ocean filtered through scrub pines that gradually replaced low shrubbery. The lumber track they followed led into a thicket of extremely tall, slim coastal redwoods, reaching some 160 feet into the air and screening out the sky overhead.

Harriet and my father rode in silence through grove after grove of these giants, cousins to the sequoia of Calaveras County. She led on her filly, while he kept his eyes on her shoulders, watching them bob to the horse's gait. He could make out the curved lines of her bottom rising and falling in the saddle as the horse ascended the steep incline along the expansive base of Mount Tamalpais, whose silhouette the aboriginal Indians believed looked like a sleeping maiden. The trail led along a clear stream where they stopped to let the horses drink. Dad cupped his hands under the running water and fed Harriet from his palms.

Four turkey vultures circled overhead in a warm updraft off the mountainside. From the valley, the trail ascended more precipitously. On the less protected, windswept escarpment, the redwoods thinned. Wild wheat grew as high as the underbellies of the horses. As they rode further, they found themselves above the tree line, where the open expanse provided a panoramic view of San Francisco Bay to the south.

And to the west, through clouds of fast-moving fog, the blue-green mat of the Pacific. They dismounted and led their horses on foot, climbing a rocky incline toward the peak of Tamalpais. The sun had begun to poke through broken clouds and tease them with warmth.

They tethered their animals in a sheltered stand of miniature oak and, with their camp bag and lunch, strolled still higher through a green meadow. Songbirds hidden in the grass welcomed them with a chirping symphony.

From the summit they viewed San Francisco and the tiny villages of Marin and, as far as the eye could see in the opposite direction, the Pacific Ocean.

"Look, Theo!" Harriet spun on her heels like a young girl and pointed north. On the horizon, a snowcapped peak jutted into the sky. "Mount Shasta. At least a hundred miles away!"

They sat on a flat rock near the summit, facing the northwest and gazed out along the California coast. Their shoulders and arms touched firmly as though supporting each other's weight. The position satisfied both and neither made any adjustment.

"I need your advice on something." Harriet tilted her head to the side and looked at my father from a close angle. "I'm thinking of helping Wong get started in the import business. I've got family stock in Atlantic Northern Industries that I could sell. It's clear that I don't need the money for myself. My medical practice now provides me with a very comfortable living. I think I owe this to Wong and Freeman, though I can't tell you exactly why. He's your partner and I wouldn't want to do anything to offend you."

Dad canted his powerful jaw sharply. "Once again you take me by surprise."

"Atlantic Northern is dead money," she said, continuing with an earlier thought. "Not that it doesn't produce income, which it does. But I've been on the coast so long now that it seems remote and dormant. I'd rather use my investment to help people here in California. Better yet, people I know and respect, like you, Theo. If you wanted, I could put the proceeds from the stock into your timber business. Into roads up north. Or divide it, fifty-fifty, between you and Wong. I've thought hard about that too."

"Why take on scraggy, irascible partners like Charley Crocker and me? That's a fate I wouldn't wish on anybody."

"The money's there. Plenty of it. But I don't want business to get between you and me. We've fought enough, Theo. But if the money went to Wong, that would be different, wouldn't it? I don't know much about business myself. Wong's been talking to Mr. Crocker and nobody knows how to make money better than he does. I'm thinking about matching whatever funds Crocker invests. Of course, I'd require that he apprentice with Mr. Crocker first. I don't expect you to give me an answer now. I'm asking that you think about it a while."

After a lunch of ham sandwiches, boiled eggs, and Napa red wine, my father lay on his back and looked at the clouds moving eastward overhead. Harriet put the plates and leftover food back into the picnic basket, then, for a long while, sat beside him, unabashedly staring at his features.

Her lips were close to his and the hazel-green of her eyes contrasted against the blue above. As he began to pull himself up, she eased back to provide room. They settled, almost together, touching.

"Theo. I want to ask you a favor. A big, big, big favor. Perhaps the biggest a woman could ever ask of a man. Perhaps far more than I should."

He was feeling the warmth of her presence and reached out to take both her hands in his. The inclination to satisfy almost any of her wishes was strong. All his powers were at her disposal.

Words seemed to come to her and but failed to find expression. She eventually said, "Since Freeman's been living in my home, something's happened inside me, Theo. I told you, I'm frightened that Wong will take him away. One part of me wants Wong to stay with the baby. The other part of me knows it's a mistake. He must make a life for his own family. The baby's taught me that I have just about everything I've ever wanted—a lovely home, a good profession, family money. Many friends. A professional reputation, perhaps somewhat tarnished since the rape, but still a reputation for good medicine. I have everything, absolutely everything except what I now want more than I ever imagined. I want a child of my own. I need something bigger than all these foolish things I've surrounded myself with. Freeman's taught me what it is. It's children that make our struggles worthwhile. Can you understand this, Theo?"

He planted a gentle kiss on her cheek. It was natural and easy and, for an instant, he felt that she might pull back. But she didn't. "You deserve a child, Harriet. You'll be a fine mother."

Her eyes caught his and captured them. "I guess I didn't make myself as clear as I should have. I don't want just *anybody's* child. I want *your* child, Theo."

He remained stone silent. Words refused to come.

"When I close my eyes and visualize the father of my child, it's you. I've done it over and over and over again. And each time, I see you. No one but you, Theo."

"Children are for married people, Harriet," his voice cracked with emotion.

"A mere convention. I never played by the rules of society; you know that. People already talk about me. Let them talk some more. I don't give a damn."

"Even if I could, which I can't, it would be wrong. Fathering a child out of wedlock wouldn't be fair to the kid. Or to you."

"We could make accommodations for that."

"No sense arguing, Harriet. You know as well as I, I can't be a father. Not with you and not with any other woman." He released a wry laugh. "I haven't got the equipment. You know that." She reached up and took his head in her hands, pulling his face close, her lips almost touching his. "Listen to me, Theo Gallager. Listen to me. This is Doctor Horn speaking. I told you before and I'm repeating it now. I removed your right testicle. But your left testis is perfectly good. One of Theodore Gallager's is worth a dozen of other men's. A man like you doesn't need both. One's enough. Trust me, Theo. Trust me, please." "Don't kid yourself. Even if I wanted to, it isn't there. Face the brutal, cold facts. I haven't had an ejaculation since then. I can't, Harriet. You can't run from facts. They always get you in the end. I just can't manage it."

"Not with other women, Theo. But I'm different. Do it with me, Theo. I know you can. Maybe not on the first try, but we'll make the kind of love that will draw it from your loins. I know every gland between your legs. I know your insides better than you know them yourself. And you've seen mine. We're both damaged. I'm broken no less than you are. There's an intimacy between us no other couple can duplicate. And I, for one, don't want another man to try. I know we can do it together."

He sighed. "I've wanted to make love with you from the day we met aboard the steamship *Japan*. You must know that. But I've kept my hands off so you could find a real husband. Not a wanderer and vagabond like me. You need someone stable, to give you the family life you deserve."

"You're the *only* one I want, Theo. No one else." She bent forward and placed her lips on his. He leaned toward her, taking her in his powerful arms.

When they broke their embrace, he said, "I won't consider it, Harriet, unless you marry me. In the immortal words of our mutual friend, Wong Po-ching, *No marry, no kiddy.* That's the deal, lady. Take it or leave it."

"California's a wild state. We don't need old conventions here."

"We may not, but any kid we produce will. Years ago, I could have fathered innumerable children if I chose to. But I never wanted that. There's something old-fashioned in me. Wild stallions and mares both come into pasture when they get old."

He kissed her again on the cheek. "If you'll have me, we'll try to make a child together. And I'll make one further concession. If we don't succeed you don't have to go through with the wedding. We get hitched only if there's a kid. That's my pledge."

Harriet rose to her feet and stepped away from him, then climbed onto a rocky outcrop where the view of San Francisco was unobstructed. From his position, he watched her arms move first from her hips to her front, then clasp behind her back. She eventually left the rock ledge and walked to a second outcrop, from where she rotated in a slow circle to regard the panorama, her gaze slipping over him as though he were not there. The horizontal movement slowly evolved into a vertical nod of affirmation. From the distance, she let her eyes fall on him and her cheeks soften into a wide smile.

Her arms were outstretched as she closed the distance and knelt down before him. "You drive a hard, hard bargain, Mr. Theodore Gallager. Long ago, I abandoned thoughts of myself as a married woman. Matrimony made no sense for me. Motherhood was unthinkable. But in my plans I never envisioned someone like you. Once in each lifetime an angel comes close enough to touch. Only a fool would not grab such an angel and hold on for as long as she could. So now you know, Mr. Theodore Gallager, that this lady's in love with you and governed by her instincts not her mind. You've destroyed my resolve to remain single and independent. I formally declare my acceptance of your marriage proposal."

She paused, tilting her head sideways like a schoolgirl ready to startle with a wild idea. "But with one condition on *my* part."

"A horse trader, I see," Theo's lips pursed. "So what's your condition?"

"That I keep my family name, Horn. And my professional name, Dr. Horn."

"I'll meet you halfway. How about a hyphenated name? *Gallager-Horn* sounds kinda neat to me. It's got a smart rhythm to it, don't you think?"

"Not as smart as *Horn-Gallager*," she said, stretching her chin toward his ear and with her teeth nibbled at his lobe. Her lips rested for an instant on the outside of his ear, where she whispered over the gusting wind, "We'll be Horn-Gallagers then. And what's more, I'll extract from you the most wonderful child a husband and wife could ever hope for." She rose abruptly and stepped toward the camp bag, fumbling with ropes that secured it. When it was open, she withdrew a thin cloth for the ground and a horse blanket for warmth.

He rose and marched over to her, grasping her in an all-enveloping hug, his lips against the freckled skin of her neck. "Mrs. Horn-Gallager, you're not thinking of doing it here, are you?"

"It's my time of the month, Theo. If I'm ever going to be fertile, it's now. I can feel it in my pelvis. Women know the exact moment when they're ready. Look around, Theo. We're touching the heavens here. What better place? And what better day than Easter Sunday?"

The sun was now high in the sky. They spread the cloth in a hollow where granite outcroppings stopped the wind. The blanket shielded them against cold. There was no shame in being naked before heaven. None in seeing the curvature of bone and skin that formed two sexes, each with different architecture designed to fit together briefly for the most divine act humans can perform. And there was no embarrassment in looking, touching, and kissing.

"I feel you against my cervix," she moaned between heavy breathing.

His gasps for air were also short. "You envelop me. Warm and tight."

"You belong here, Theo. Only you."

He closed his eyes against the strong sunlight, directing the powers of love through his torso into the loins. His member was inexorably firm, slipping now along the lubricated pathway of her body. Harriet's breathing shortened into quick pants. Her head fell back and her mouth opened wide. A primal cry rose from her throat and escaped into the afternoon air. Suddenly he felt her contract around him.

"Now, Love, fill me," she whispered.

He pressed hard, narrowing his concentration on the dark, unexplored origin of his sperm. The sensation lifted him along a rising sexual plateau, higher and higher, but still far from the peak. Over and over he pressed. Harriet meant more to him than anything in life, even more than he once wanted to bash through the granite at Cape Horn. But the gap between desire and achievement seemed unbridgeable. In earlier days, he could get whatever he put his mind to. By focusing his strength success always came. But this was different. Here he was defying nature, not amending it.

"I can't do it. I just can't. It won't come," he exclaimed.

"It comes to *your* Harriet, Theo. No more *I's*, just *we's*. And *we* can. Together."

He looked toward the sky and for an instant saw fog roll overhead then let his eyes fall on the face of the woman who would be his wife, if only one testicle would fire.

"Yes, Theo. It's there for both of us to touch."

"How I want it, but it isn't there."

"I know you can. I know we can." Harriet spoke from deep in her throat. Her eyes fixed on his chin and seemed to find a strength she knew existed inside.

A large red-tailed hawk swooped down along the canyon siding and snatched a field mouse in its talons, suddenly pumping hard with its wings to gain altitude. The flapping sound echoed in my father's ears. How this creature knew where to find what it needed to stay alive was a mystery of nature. As the raptor rose in an updraft of warm air reflecting off the mountain, my father felt the fiery source of life erupt from his groin and surge through ducts at the base of his member. Heat produced an incendiary gush of pressure.

An instant later, the miraculous fluid of new life surged from one human into another, ending its long journey in the uterine cavity of the woman my father adored.

I, Corinne Horn-Gallager, was conceived at that moment on the peak of Mount Tamalpais and some nine months later was born in San Francisco on 3 January 1872. Most folks remember and celebrate their birthdays, and they know little or nothing about the biological binding responsible for their presence upon this planet. There can be no greater mystery than how we are absolutely nothing, not an ember nor seed nor thought, until our mothers and fathers find each other. And when they do we enter the world.

To know from where you come is to know who you are.

For me, the most solemn date in my life is not my birthday, but the Easter Sunday when I was conceived.

CHAPTER FIFTEEN

A FINAL NOTE FROM CORINNE HORN-GALLAGER
April 1956

Many soldiers returned from the battlefields of the First World War wounded, bitter, and broken. Not so with my son, Henry Theodore Craine, who came home with a metal plate grafted into his hip, but with a heart tenderized by the suffering he had seen. After exploiting his youth and damaging his health, the Army discharged him. While convalescing, he entered Yale University as an undergraduate and later stayed in New Haven to study law.

When Henry was a boy I would take him across the country to visit the spirits of the Wongs and Gallagers in the redwood forest of Calaveras County. My husband accompanied us once, but the majesty of these giant sequoias failed to impress him sufficiently for a second trip. In subsequent years when Henry and I journeyed west, he preferred to visit museums in New York.

Henry's injured hip caused him much pain, but did not deter him from walking in the mountains with the aid of a sturdy stick. He learned to climb over granite rock to alpine lakes and snowcapped peaks with the agility of a mountain goat. I knew then that one day he would leave the East Coast to answer the siren call of the West.

It happened sooner than I thought. After three years of apprenticing in a Philadelphia law firm, he joined a new practice in San Francisco.

When I made my biannual pilgrimages to California, we would rendezvous in San Francisco and then travel together to Calaveras County. It became clear that, like his grandparents, Henry had become emotionally attached to these redwoods. But each year they seemed more vulnerable to the saw blade. Lumber mills had sprung up in almost every valley, and new roads brought mammoth logging trucks to the county. Since he devoted much of his free time to conservation efforts, it came as no surprise when he left his law firm to open a small practice specializing in environmental law.

During my visit to California in 1954, Henry gave me a wonderful gift. We drove from San Francisco up Route 26 to the old gold town of West Point, then over the Blue Mountain Road to the site of my father and Uncle Wong's gold mine west of Buck Mountain. At eighty-one, I limped more than Henry and had difficulty moving about. But together we hobbled over the hills to the mineshaft. Time had erased all but the weathered head-frame sculpting the entrance. I retold stories of his grandfather's and Uncle Wong's futile search for a quartz vein. Such tales had been told many times, yet Henry never seemed to tire of them.

We arrived by car at the redwood grove by two p.m. The number of vehicles parked on the shoulder of Highway 4 alarmed me. In previous years only hiking enthusiasts knew the location of our beloved sequoias, but now it seemed that everybody knew our secret. Henry helped me onto the road. The two of us tottered forward until I paused to read a large wooden sign guarding the entrance to a path mulched with pine dross.

"I can't believe this!" I exclaimed as I stood in wonderment. The signpost read:

A GIFT FOR THE AGES FROM THOSE WHO LOVE THESE REDWOODS
BIG TREES CALIFORNIA STATE PARK

Following other visitors, we walked along a path bordered by ponderosa and sugar pines, incense cedars and black oaks. Slowly small redwoods took their places in this woodland garden. We eventually emerged into an opening between groves of much larger sequoias and stood there among hundreds of visitors.

At the base of a massive redwood named *Uncle Tom's Cabin*, Governor Paul Kylemeyer dedicated four thousand acres of virgin forest to the perpetual care of the citizens of his state. The name *Big Trees State Park* was made official. The governor failed to mention who originally coined this name, though I suspected even California historians didn't know about Uncle Wong. I wept as the governor thanked, on behalf of all Californians, my son and his friends, who had tirelessly raised the funds to purchase these lands from the heirs of the Pickering Lumber Company and then, God bless them all, deeded their new property to the state park system.

You can't imagine my relief to know that the Gallagers and Wongs would now rest in perpetual peace, their souls ever mingling in the branches of these eternal redwoods. During the dedication nothing was said about who was buried in Big Trees. When I later inquired about the oversight, Henry told me that our family graves remained a secret, even to those who had donated funds for the land.

He was right to say nothing. The last thing the Park Service needed was for hundreds of well-meaning people to bury their loved ones amid these sequoias. God had never designed the roots of a tree to accommodate graves. Clearly only a few could be granted this burial privilege.

The following year, my health began to fail and I made only one more journey to the beloved forest. After I became too lame for travel, I realized that my eyes might never again gaze upon the giant redwoods. It was a major adjustment, made somewhat easier by the assurance that I had still one final pilgrimage to make. I had every confidence that, like the previous morticians in our family, Henry understood the meaning of reunion.

One summer he brought my grandchildren to visit me in Connecticut, traveling by train over the track their great-grandfather had built. Along the route, they made three overnight stops. In Utah they visited the historic Promontory Summit, where the Central and Union Pacific Railroads met and hammered down the renowned golden spike. That night they slept in a hotel twenty-three miles to the east, in a town that, eighty-three years before, had sprung up along the tracks to service the new railroad.

Henry spent the next day searching old records in the town's two churches. My parents always claimed that they were lawfully married, but given their lifelong struggle against social convention, few in San Francisco believed it. For certain, they were not married when I was conceived. With help from a retired Methodist minister, Henry discovered something I never thought existed. In June 1871, when my mother was six months pregnant with me, my father took her by rail as far as Ogden to show her the track he had built for the Central Pacific. They must have stopped overnight to recall the momentous event that occurred at

Promontory Summit two years before. My son found in church records an entry stating that on June 2 of that year the Reverend Thaddeus T. Cornwall, minister of the First Methodist Church, bound together into holy matrimony Harriet Horn and Theodore Gallager.

Henry left the best surprise for last. When I asked in what town this First Methodist Church was located, he shared his discovery with an omniscient smile. "Why it was in Corinne, Utah," he replied.

End

Author's Note on Memory and Imagination

Every story has a beginning before the beginning. *Destiny's Children* began when I was six years old and my parents rented a small cottage at Lake Tahoe for our summer holiday. When my grandfather died suddenly of heart failure, my mother and father packed me up early one morning to dash back to San Francisco for various death rites in our home town.

We were driving on the Donner Summit over a two-lane highway that snaked through the Sierra Nevada Mountains, thick with large trucks on their transcontinental passage. On this morning a blizzard blanketed the road with fresh snow, completely snarling all traffic in both directions. Such summer storms occur infrequently, but when they do they become legendary in the minds of the local people. My father stopped the family Mercury behind a long train of vehicles buried in impassible snow. We were literally perched on the summit with a panoramic view across Donner Lake.

I can remember staring beyond this glacial lake to precipitous mountains on the other side where wooden sheds of the Southern Pacific Railroad, the successor to the Central Pacific, protected the track from avalanches that might easily tumble a passing train two thousand feet into the gorge below. As a child I couldn't imagine anyone climbing the steep granite wall, certainly no one hauling the equipment to build a roadway. I asked my mother, "Mommy, who built those tracks?"

"Chinese people did," she replied.

I couldn't get this out of my mind. The notion of men coming all the way from China to build an impossible railroad in an impossible place was impossible for me to imagine. The vision just stuck in my childhood memory, leaving many unanswered questions. During the many years that elapsed after that, I yearned to know someone who participated in this gargantuan feat.

A half-century later, once *Destiny's Children* was written, I finally did.

Roger E. Herst

3790931

Made in the USA